Praise for *Girl with Skirt of Stars*:

A stunning mystery debut by a gifted story-teller! Girl with Skirt of Stars is a head-long plunge into a mystery intertwined with the mysteries of Navajo culture and rendered in language as gorgeous as the Southwestern landscape. Look for Jennifer Kitchell on the bestseller lists!

—Margaret Coel, author of *The Silent Spirit*

Page after page, this is breathtaking writing! Readers who loved Tony Hillerman should rejoice—Jennifer Kitchell follows in his tradition of suspense steeped in cultural issues. Kitchell deserves a spot atop the bestseller lists.

—Christine DeSmet, author of *Spirit Lake*

Girl with Skirt of Stars is a gripping debut novel with an intriguing cast of characters. While deftly interweaving Navajo culture and mysticism into a compelling murder mystery, Kitchell tackles the serious issues of water rights in the Southwest and of the wide canyon between Navajo and white world views and justice. Fast-paced, the novel is compelling until the reader has turned to the very last page.

— Annamarie Beckel, author of *All Gone Widdun*

GIRL WITH SKIRT OF STARS

Jennifer Kitchell

ISBN# 978-1-932636-56-7 Softcover

Library of Congress Control Number: 2009925858

Cover Design: Antelope Design

PRONGHORN PRESS

www.pronghornpress.org

"Character, like a photograph, develops in darkness."
– Yousuf Karsh

"We remember so little that what we do remember takes on an extraordinary weight."
– Nicole Krauss

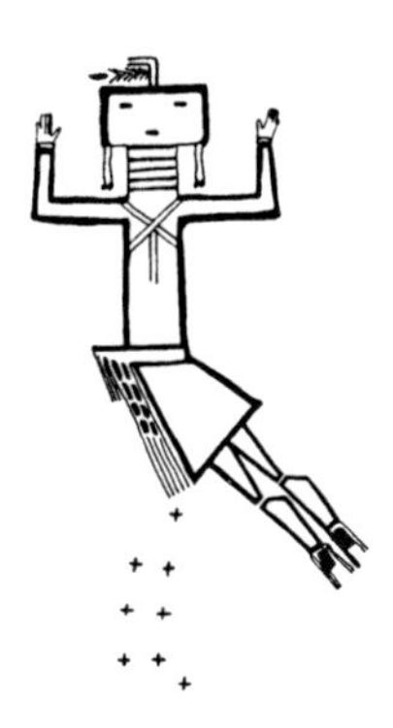

With low tongue and open mouth, the man began soft as a jazzman to pull off the seduction. He faced west. Anyone who believes dawn breaks in the east has never waited for light in the desert.

He imagined them moving to him, to where he lay perfectly hidden, as dawn played its trick, the rising sun conspiring with the open curve of horizon. True first light came racing toward him from the west.

Ghaaji already, the Back-to-Back month. Like all who are taught first as children, Lilli Chischilly, with her advanced degrees and abnormal fluency, still emotionally recognized two seasons to the year, not four. *Shi*: summer—say it out loud and you can feel the female softness. *Hai*: winter—say it out loud and you can feel the male energy. But in October the two meet, face-to-face. *Shi* stops. So does *Hai*. They look at each other, sometimes for days, until *Shi* turns around and shows her back to him, then walks away. He watches her disappear until he, too, turns and walks on. The Back-to-Back month, October, the month that separates what was from what will become.

The man licked the back of his hand to wet it and pulled the slippery skin tight between his lips, and then began to blow, first the whines and whimpers, then the panting squeals, and then the scream of something dying.

Before the light came, he'd spritzed himself with piss, commercial quality, to up the ante, because they were sexual and territorial. It was all part of the con.

She'd better hustle, get herself on the road. Not every day one refuses a big-time politician, least of all in Window Rock, Arizona.

In bare feet, Lilli stood beside her empty bed brushing out her hair with her head hung between her knees. She straightened up and swept the long shank of black hair off her neck into the twist of the *tsiiyéél*. Her hands felt clumsy. Nerves. She undid her hair completely, felt the blood rush to her head as she let it fall again, swung her head up and made a twist that held.

The searchlight-turquoise earrings she'd worn yesterday lay handy on the dresser top. She slid them through the fleshy holes in the lobes of her ears and then had a different idea, sliding her fingers into the open dresser drawer to find her favorite pair, their stone more green and mottled. But her fingers pulled out instead the old loose snapshot she'd never framed.

Memory has such compressive power.

Two skinny kids on a horse without a saddle, smiling with their teeth. *Alkéé naa'aashii,* Two-in-One, the Following-After-Pair. She could feel the rhythm of the gallop shifting beneath her, the warmth of the breathing barrel of horse between her legs. She and Jerome—they'd spent the totality of their lives together, until one day he was gone.

She stared at the photo as if it had answers. How do you ever replace someone like that? She'd lived with the same answer for years. You can't.

And now she heard he was back "home," alone. She wondered why, she wondered for how long, and most cruelly she wondered why he hadn't even bothered to find her. She turned the photo face down in the drawer and pulled out the earrings, feeling the weight of the stones as she pushed the cold silver wire through her ear.

There they were, abnormally curious, the three of them skylining toward him. Now was the critical moment. He blew, double tonguing the final bleats of distress.

He needed two, but not just any two because one had to be male and one had to be female and they had to be a sister-brother pair. To up the odds, he sighted the heavy caliber automatic with a decent scope that was flat-shooting and dropped all three.

He pulled the last one, so beautiful and still, and laid it next to the other two males, silver belly side up, and opened its legs. A female. Perfect.

A string of electric power poles emerged in apparition. The early light caught their connecting wires that flashed in parallel ropes of silver. He took out his knife, spat on both sides of the blade, and made careful incision.

Her long skirt lay folded on top of her dresser. Lilli picked it up, intending to step in, but set it back down. In pride of place beside it stood two framed photographs. She picked up the one of her father and her, just the two of them, together. He'd died by the time she was nine. In this photo she looked fearless, her parka-covered arms sticking out. She sat on an old tire and her father sat behind her with his legs wrapped around her, and they were sliding down a hill extraordinarily white with snow. The photo must be the reason that moment forever stood so bright in her mind. She'd never really remembered it.

She glanced at the other framed photo—a wedding basket and four hands, the smaller two hers, the long-fingered hands Jake's. They'd had a traditional wedding, at night, and the disposable camera with its built-in flash had overexposed the image.

She finished slipping into her skirt and looked around the empty house. Jake was gone for at least a week or two over at *Tsai Skizzi*, with his uncle who was down with a broken leg and needing so much help. The light of first dawn had nearly arrived. She snatched up the keys and a pile of files from the kitchen table near the door, stuffed the files into her briefcase, then went out to her car.

When he opened the door he saw the man wedged on the floor between the front and back seats struggle, even though his feet were tied together and his arms pulled behind his back.

The penis with its testicles and the vulva and vagina of the sibling pair were still warm as he stuffed them into the man's mouth. He'd made the incisions big enough to be more than choking size because he didn't want the man to try to swallow. He slipped a short stick between the man's teeth to push the pieces deeper, far enough to fill the back of the man's mouth and block the windpipe. Then he stretched the duct tape across the mouth and pressed the adhesive tight.

He pinched the man's nose, collapsing the thick nostrils against themselves. The unmolested extra male he buried. But he had plans for the sister and brother. He put the sibling pair in the flatbed, blinded for a moment by the full brilliance of dawn reflecting off the chrome bumper.

He could have dumped the man anywhere with his mouth full. Even this far off road he'd be found by the eyes of the vultures and condors who relentlessly scanned for roadkill and garbage. Because that's what the man was: garbage. But he wanted the man's death to tell a special kind of story.

Sunlit from behind at low angle, the Dodge glimmered in a sheath of early light.

Lilli opened the driver's door and skidded the briefcase to the passenger seat as she slid herself in. She turned the key, picking up yesterday's Lotaburger wrapper from the floor, heard the old motor try to catch, and smelled the fumes from the exhaust as it failed. Then she let go of the key. On the hood of the Dodge lay two strangely still animals with their bellies turned up and their legs splayed apart.

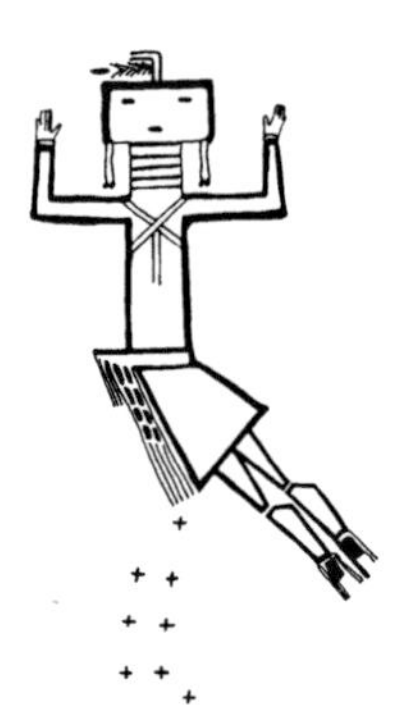

Dead, yes, and mutilated, and hand-delivered to her.

Lilli Chischilly felt thick-headed as she drove knowingly, recklessly, too fast from where her home sat alone atop a dry wash without any neighbors. The contrail of a jet plane unraveled over her head into a skyline of foam white as suds. Someone had gone to disturbing trouble to catch her attention.

And make her late. She stepped through the door lettered Historic Preservation Department. She wanted to enter her private office, keep the lights off, and think.

She hadn't factored in Etta. The woman hopped up from her desk guarding Lilli's office door to stop her.

Etta, whose office wardrobe favored oversized sweatpants, looked improbably overdressed this morning. Lee's campaign stop, of course.

"Where'd you get lost?"

"Car trouble," Lilli said.

Yet wasn't that the truth? Even after hiding the stiffened and mutilated bodies out of sight under some rocks, her mind was still stuck on the initial image. A macabre still life.

"Bitsoi called, looking for you," Etta said. "Hated to tell him you was late."

"I'll call him."

"Nope, no need. Bitsoi left the message with me." Etta was enjoying the moment.

"And you're going to share that message?"

Jake liked to call Lilli The Gatekeeper, the way she used her fancy words and her natural-born stubbornness. Mule-headed, he might say, too. Maybe she deserved Etta.

"Been a change of plans," Etta said. "Bitsoi says the man's delayed."

"Lee?"

"Who else?"

Lilli heard herself exhale. "For how long?" So now they were both over-dressed.

"Forty-eight hour hold-up."

"But he is still coming?"

"Day after tomorrow's the new timetable."

So she had a reprieve—more like another forty-eight hours to suffer over the decision she'd made this morning to refuse Lee and his colossal ego.

"Oh, something else while you was late," Etta said. "Man calls himself Jerome Bah going to be in the office—maybe another twenty minutes."

"Jerome Bah? Here?"

"Told me you two grew up together. No Lee, so?"

"Here, in my office? In twenty minutes?" Lilli's mind felt fuzzy.

"Man said he was already in Window Rock."

She had imagined their reunion so many times. In her mind, their first sight of one another always took place close to home, definitely outdoors, certainly not with a desk between them, and definitely not with Etta on the other side of a thin door.

She entered her office and set her briefcase down on her desk. She touched the back of her hair, tugged at her skirt. Then she shut the door. She sat down and started trying to make neat, rearranging the mess of papers that were off-limits to Etta.

The put-down, the saying "running on Navajo time" was a cultural jab misinterpreted by the white *bilagáana* who surrounded them to mean "whenever." But "Navajo time" was something different. It meant starting with an intention, and then having to change course when something unexpected happened.

She straightened her earrings, adjusting their weight, but her mind was years away. No, absolutely not. She wasn't going to let this happen. She hated the idea that his first image of her would be as a woman trapped inside an office. No, this was crazy as a soup sandwich.

She re-opened her door to Etta's desk.

Etta looked up. "You okay?"

"Tell Jerome Bah to find me outside, up in the Window."

"You don't look dressed for rock climbing."

"Etta..."

The mind lays down memory like ruts. Some are so deep you return to them again and again and wonder if you'll ever get out.

Waiting for Jerome Bah to materialize, Lilli drew her knees up under her skirt and leaned her back against the cold rock. At this height, the buildings of stacked sandstone below her blended into the land. The unusual landmark, carved by wind and water, had once been called *Tse'gha'hoodzáni*, but that was too difficult for the *bilagaana* to say. Now it was officially called "Window Rock."

She heard someone climbing up from below. Was the past really coming back to her, in the flesh? A man's head appeared. She didn't move. She said nothing. Then the man stood before her, awkwardly, with most of his weight on one leg.

"*Yá'át'ééh*, Lilli."

She had waited eighteen years for this to happen.

It's foolish to believe memory is static, or reliable, like some archive in the storeroom of your mind. Of course he was all grown up now. But she couldn't keep herself from staring. Somewhere inside this man she'd never seen before was the boy. She just couldn't find him yet.

She quickly stood up and held out her hand, startled now by the odd difference in their heights.

"Never imagined you taller than me." Hadn't they once been exactly the same size?

And the man *was* taller—by maybe seven inches—and thin and, well, nothing about him looked complicated or urban. Jeans, a belt, a long-sleeved shirt.

The very last glimpse she'd had of Jerome, he was sitting alone in the back of his family's pickup, loaded for life in L.A. The truck was missing its tailgate, but Jerome was gutsy that way—sitting on the edge of a bouncing flatbed, letting his legs dangle out.

"Tall, huh? Yeah, and I'm remembering you—you know—skinnier."

"What are you saying?" She realized she was smiling. Was this really Jerome who had moved away and broken her heart?

His face had been softer once, and now his jaw was squared off. But when the man got close enough to take her hand, she could see the same scar interrupting his eyebrow, all her fault.

"Oh, nothing."

Yes, he smiled with the same grin. But not with the same eyes. Something was very wrong about his eyes.

"Like that you kept your hair long, Lilli. You look good."

The Following-After-Pair. They'd grown up more than a hundred miles north of Window Rock, near Red Rock and Cove, just east of the dark spruce-covered Lukachukai Mountains.

She had so many questions. "Where you been staying?"

"My aunt Marvina's old house. You remember that place?"

"Sure." Marvina's old place wasn't impossibly distant. It had been empty for years. "How long you been back?" It was another way of asking the most important question: *why haven't you come looking for me?*

"A couple a weeks. Been flying around, lots of primitive takeoffs and landings. Man, in fact, just offered me the job."

"What, here?"

" 'Official tribal pilot,' says Bitsoi. Hauling him and whoever else is important enough to avoid ground travel on slow roads."

"What? Wait. You became a pilot?"

"Didn't think I was smart enough? Hey, who are you to talk? Heard you went and became a lawyer." He rolled his eyes like they'd lost their compass.

"A job with Bitsoi? So you're coming home?" What had happened to his life in Los Angeles, she wondered.

"Signed something looked legal enough to me. Not

official on the payroll though till the next cycle. Which makes me a free man and I'm here with an invitation. Come on, Lilli, let's the two of us go up."

"Up? Up where?"

"For a fly. Want to show you some amazing sights."

"You're really a pilot?"

"What? And you became a chicken? Don't worry. FAA licensed and all."

"But I have commitments..."

"Not what I hear from Etta. She tells me your day's wide open. Can't hardly refuse then, can you?"

She knew she was stalling. "You haven't told me much about yourself. Or Los Angeles."

"Grew up, says it all, doesn't it? Looks like we both did. Asking around, I heard you got married."

True, eventually she had said yes.

"How about you?" she asked.

"Military, pilot's license, went to trade school in photography, got married. Built a photo studio in the house. I was up in the sky when..."

His voice seemed far, far away. Then it seemed he'd forgotten her.

Finally she said, "When what, Jerome?"

"When the house felt the blast before the fire—gas leak from a water heater in the basement." He fumbled in his back pocket for his wallet.

"Here's all that survived—this was in my pocket when..."

He handed her a professional photo in black and white.

She studied the image, a *bilagáana* woman, lightly freckled, like a half-child herself, holding a baby, sleeping in her arms. She couldn't see either of their eyes. The baby's eyes were closed, the woman's looking down.

"Oh, Jerome."

All that survived was this photo? She reached out to take his hands. He pulled back. She watched him put the photo away without looking at it.

"You must have kids," he said. "How many?"

"No," she said, thinking how she almost had. "Hasn't happened." A stillborn is given no name, only The One Who Had Not Uttered A Sound. Jake had put the baby in the ground.

"Come on, Lilli. You have a free day, I have a free day. Let's get out of here."

Why was she refusing him? Maybe for just a few hours she could put a crease in time, fold time in such a way the two of them touched again.

Or maybe this was a big mistake.

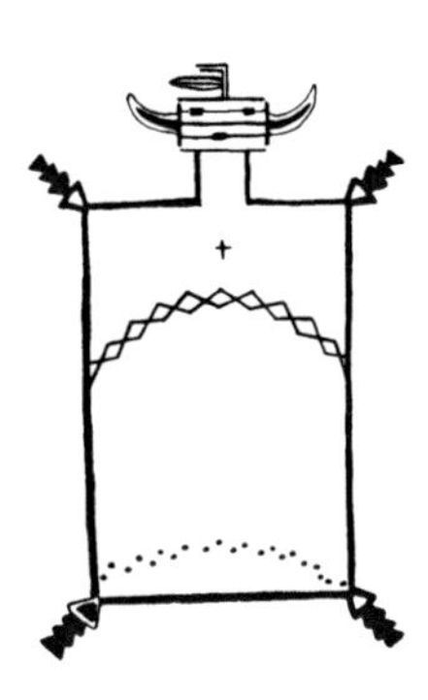

Given the extra forty-eight hours to worry about all the campaign hoopla that was poised to descend on Window Rock, Lilli hoped Bitsoi wouldn't panic and call a special meeting and find her missing. Because they were definitely leaving Window Rock behind.

She tried to stay relaxed and logical. But Jerome seemed odd to her, off in some strange way. She watched him as he watched the highway and the morning traffic. She wanted to ask, *What brought you back?* And she wanted to hear him say, *You did.*

"Where are we headed?" she asked instead. Apparently not the modest airport in Window Rock.

Jerome didn't seem to have heard her. She let it go. Well, Ganado was close and had an airport, but no, now they were traveling in the wrong direction. Good, because Ganado wasn't much—a dirt runway with soft sand that ran to gullies when it rained and you had to watch out for livestock. Probably they were headed to a real airport.

She studied what she could see of his profile. The longer the absence between them had grown, the more she'd longed for this day. And yet the more she'd been afraid of it. She'd always known it would be a different Jerome who came back.

Just like she always knew she still loved the boy, never had stopped loving the boy. But maybe that boy was gone forever now, lost to time and who knew what else. His adult life had been shattered in Los Angeles. Maybe he'd drawn himself down a deep hole that was dark and full of guilt for being the only one of his new family who survived.

She cleared her throat, a little too dramatically, then raised her voice to bring him back from wherever he'd drifted off to.

"So, what airport are you planning on?"

"Huh? Oh, don't usually use an airport. Generally prefer a substitute."

"There's a substitute?" For an airport? Why had she made so many assumptions?

"Not that particular on runways. Something flat's all I need. Give me three hundred good feet."

She watched the passing electric poles, regular as a heartbeat, thinking how when they were kids, she had been at least as daring as Jerome. Maybe not anymore. Every flight she'd ever taken—mainly to Washington, D.C.—had made expedient and necessary use of a runway. Where was he chartering the plane? Or did he now have permission to use Bitsoi's?

This might be turning into a very bad idea. She tried settling herself on the sun-warmed vinyl of the passenger seat. She needed to get to know Jerome again, slowly.

"Nice truck. So what's in the trailer we're towing?"

Jerome took the sharp turn north onto old Highway 666. "The airplane."

"What do you mean the airplane? Our airplane?"

"The very one."

"You're not serious?" Lilli craned her neck for a better inspection of the trailer through the rear window.

"I trailered it all the way here from L.A."

"Just how small is this so-called airplane?"

She'd assumed, without giving it any real thought, that they were going to charter a plane for a short flight or, knowing Jerome, maybe unofficially joyride in Bitsoi's official plane, and look around the airspace over Window Rock, take a glide over the Defiance Plateau.

"Hey, this is a special invitation. My own personal airplane. FAA-certified, just homebuilt. OK, maybe more like an ultralight."

"Ultralight? Like a kite?"

"Not at all, you'll see. It's got two perfectly fine wings. And an engine."

"Imagine that." Her tone betrayed her confusion.

"It's designed to fold so I can tow it, see. Save the flying for the best part."

She realized she should have asked Jerome a lot more questions before agreeing to this.

"How high does this...thing..." She tried to keep the anxiety from showing itself so plainly to him. "How does it get off the ground?"

"Three thousand feet's possible, but I like hovering a lot closer. More like bird height."

Jerome pulled into a convenience store, the trailer tracking smoothly behind the pickup.

"Let's gas up. Need some fuel for our flight."

Convenience stores seemed to be taking over the earth.

"They sell aviation fuel at convenience stores these days?"

"AV gas? Doubt it. Fortunately, my plane prefers regular unleaded, just like that sorry Dodge of yours. Want to help fill the jugs?"

Lilli slid down to the asphalt from the height of the cab and felt the tension cramping through the backs of her legs. As she held the fuel hose, the fumes from the urgent swill of gasoline made her turn her head away. She topped off the first jug with foam the color of root beer, and handed it off to Jerome who sealed it and provided the next jug. She carried the last container to the door of the trailer where she got her first glimpse of a wing and a strut.

"I don't know, Jerome."

"Don't look so worried. It doesn't resemble a real plane till I get it out of the trailer and all unfolded."

An origami airplane.

Back in the pickup, the October light that felt so crisp outside now seemed heavier, almost milky. Jerome hadn't turned over the ignition yet. She took advantage of the moment and leaned over to lightly touch the ragged star on his temple, just above his right eye.

"See you still have your scar."

"And you and I both know how I got it."

"Grew nice with you."

"Like a cattle brand."

She remembered how they used to pretend it wasn't from skin punctured open when she climbed on the branch with him and the branch let go, that instead it was where they shot the magic in. Just the two of them that day. When they were kids, it was just the two of them hours at a time, day after day, inhabiting each other's world fully.

He started up and they were back on the road, heading generally north. He wasn't the same anymore and yet he was. She realized how effortlessly she found comfort in just being with him, like this, as if the smell of him was comfortable. But was it really *him*?

Jerome started asking her questions: her family, the old school and the kids near their age, of some of the neighbors. She had a harder time asking questions about him and L.A.

So it wasn't going to be the Crownpoint airport either. She wondered exactly where, or what, he would decide to call a runway. But by the way he took a couple of back roads as a shortcut and they accelerated past Becenti Chapter House she sensed he knew his way around.

"So—you're a lawyer. Etta, back in your office, made sure I understood that. But what do you, you know, actually do?"

"Work with the HPD, the Historic Preservation Department. Repatriation, protection, lots of legal wrangling with the *bilagáana*."

"You never wanted to take that lawyering off the reservation, make some money?"

Like move to L.A.?

"No, never did." The opposite really, she thought. Protect her people against the lawyers money can buy. She understood the punchline to, "When does a person need a lawyer? As soon as the other person has a lawyer."

"What about you, Jerome? What kind of photography do you do?"

"Whatever pays. Freelance pieces, headshots for the aspiring resumé in L.A., ad work. My specialty, though, involves this little plane."

Leaving L.A. behind, coming back, would be an enormous change. She wondered if he could really do it.

"Tell me more about the specialty."

"I hate manufactured landscapes. Prefer looking down on natural land, the more isolated and undisturbed the better. Sometimes I catch people, too, in that crease between the earth and the sky."

"Wouldn't people be awfully hard to see?"

"Not if you don't go too high." He gestured toward the dash. "Open the glove compartment."

She followed his instruction.

"I've had my plane up plenty these past few weeks, experiencing the land I knew as a kid, but knew only from the ground. See that cellophane envelope?"

"This one?" She pulled it out.

"Go on. Take a peek inside."

She set the envelope in her lap and gently slid out several enlarged images, all obviously taken from the sky.

She let out a breath, a little too loudly. "Wow, I had no idea—these are really beautiful, Jerome."

More than beautiful. Her gaze traced the sinuous curve of light and shadow playing against each other along an entrenched arroyo. The next photo showed a circular mound, something mudded, the roof, she realized, of a hogan. In the next several photos, she saw the same figure. A little girl, running.

"You do see people. What's she doing?"

"Running, then standing on her head. I developed a whole series. *The Upside-Down-Girl.*"

"Do you know her?"

"I could only watch from the sky."

Lilli let her mind go back to the photo she kept framed on top her dresser, of herself sledding in the snow. A photograph fixes the moment. She wondered how you would remember your own life, if a different series of photos had been taken and saved.

"These are amazing, Jerome, the way they look down on everything, so widely yet so close." Startling, abstract, intriguing. Like nothing she'd ever seen before.

"You must have some amazing equipment," she said.

"Ah, credit the equipment. I thought Lance Armstrong said, 'It's not the bike, stupid.' "

She laughed. "You're right."

She slipped the envelope of photographs back into the glovebox. They soon left the numbered highway behind and headed down a dirt road that finally took a long dip, and then Jerome jockeyed the trailer into a position that suited him and she got out of the truck.

Odd, how now she couldn't really define what kind of man she had imagined he'd become. Probably because she'd never let that happen. Kept him in her heart intact, the image of the boy instead. But he was clearly different from the boy.

The top of El Huerfano to the northeast was visible, the most prominent landmark she could recognize. "El Huerfano" stuck on maps, a name applied by the Spanish who saw how isolated the mesa was and called it "The Orphan." But it was *Dzil ná'oodilii* in her language, *The Mountain-Around-Which-Moving-Was-Done*.

She wondered what it would look like from above, in a slow flying machine. In the Creation Story, Changing Woman bathed her newborn twins, Monster Slayer and Born-for-Water, in a rock basin on top of the mesa.

Lilli followed Jerome around to the trailer. Was she really going to go up in the air with him? She could always beg off, say she'd watch from the ground.

"Just how many miles are in your flight log?"

"You don't think I'm authentic?" He gave her a long look. "Thousands, Lilli."

Jerome opened the back doors of the trailer and hauled out a ramp, then unchocked the wheels and rolled out a flimsy looking contraption with folded wings.

"Where's the rest of it?"

"Relax, you'll see. This all works."

He disappeared into the trailer, then re-emerged with two matching jumpsuits. "Here, put this on. Plane lacks a few things, like enclosure."

"Maybe I'll just watch you."

"Get suited up. You can't refuse me now." He held the suit out for her.

She hesitated a moment and then took hold of it.

"Where should I change?" It must be the same Jerome. He could still make her do crazy stunts.

"You weren't so modest when we were young."

"Yeah, well..." She looked around. No cover in sight. Lilli positioned herself in a crouch behind the open door of his truck and did her best.

She materialized, swimming in an oversized zip-up suit that made her feel like she was ready for a dogsled in the Arctic.

"As any lawyer would ask under the circumstances," she said, "where's the release slip?"

"What do you mean?"

"Legal document where I absolve you of liability and sign my life away."

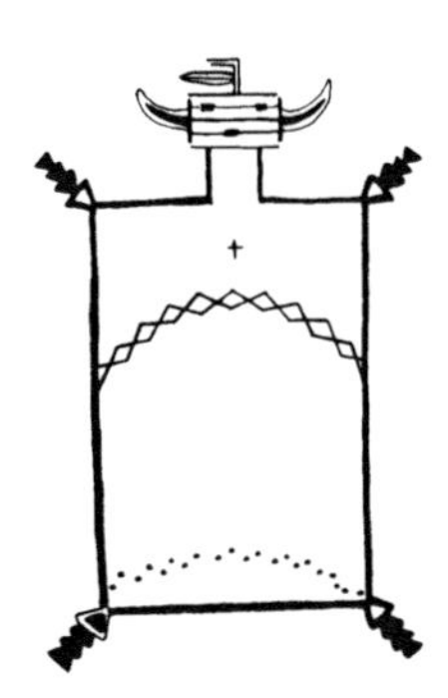

Plane? More like two flying chairs.

Lilli sat nearly immobile, strapped in with a safety harness, helmeted, and warm in the padded flight suit with all four cuffs rolled up. The word "airplane" seemed quite a stretch. There simply was nothing like a cockpit.

"Here, hold these." Jerome still had both his feet on the ground. "And I mean hold on to them." He held out a camera and large lens. "They can't survive a drop from the sky."

Like she could? Lilli took the equipment from him, but she abhorred losing yet another degree of freedom: her two hands.

He seemed so preoccupied, pulling and prodding and checking on things, something about tightening the fuel line. As she impotently watched, she couldn't help thinking how in the odd logic—not of the brain, but of the heart—Jerome was to blame, wasn't he? If he'd been home, somehow the explosion would never have happened.

She watched him buckle the chinstrap of his helmet and finally join her in the seat to her left. In some sort of futile safety check, she pulled on the black harness holding her to her seat. The engine caught.

This really was going to happen.

They started to roll over the dirt road and she felt herself bouncing. She imagined she felt the tail lift off but no, a big bounce on the fat tires. They were back on the ground and then suddenly she knew they were airborne, a change in state from earthbound to buoyant.

There went another degree of freedom.

The smell of the earth was a surprise. Lilli took a deep breath. They sailed ahead of their own exhaust. The wings banked and she grabbed the metal bar.

"The FAA lets you fly like this?"

"Come on, you'll be fine. Go ahead, open your eyes." Jerome patted her padded knee.

She felt so vulnerable. If she leaned out, just the slightest, she had a clear sightline beyond her shoes with nothing at all between her and the ground. All she could think of was a perfect combination for falling out of the sky—slow speed, low altitude, a pilot preoccupied with a camera lens.

Like cold spun glass, the air streamed across her bare face. The only thing actually keeping her legs from dangling beneath her with the pull of the earth was a heel pan.

"Feels like I'm dangling from the talons of a bird."

The sensation was magnified because she couldn't see any engine. That all sat behind them, apparently to not obstruct the camera view, to give his cameras the full eye. Even the dials and gauges sat behind him. Jerome's knees, she noticed, were in charge of the controls, which allowed his hands to be free.

"Hand me the equipment," he said. "Steady."

She tightened her calf muscles to keep her feet firmly on the heel pan. Her legs felt queer. She passed him the camera, and then the lens. How did that saying go about there being old pilots and bold pilots, but no old bold pilots? Knowing Jerome, he probably thought he could be the first anomaly.

Still climbing. She hoped he had a sixth sense about fuel. But her worries faded. The unobstructed view was spectacular. Did Jerome remember the stories of the earlier worlds, how light changed with each creation from the First World, in blackness, to the blue light that filled the Second World, to the yellow Third World and the Fourth all full of white light until emergence into this world, where light changes by the moment. *The Glittering World.* The landscape below them curved like ribs.

As the horizon opened even wider, she thought that in his own way Jerome must have been "coming home" these past few weeks, first revisiting the landscape. Then her. Tomorrow, maybe some people they used to know.

She looked out to the wide encircling horizon and wondered if he'd watched the Pollen Pair from the air, the way they lay facing each other, the Male One's head at Chuska Peak, his neck Narbona Pass, his legs stretched along the Carrizo Mountains, the Female One's body across from him along Black Mesa, her feet coming to rest at Balakai.

"No! Jerome..." Did he think they could fly this contraption inside a cloud? They were so close she could see the wisp of the edges of vapor swirling, burning off like smoke. She suddenly swallowed wet air, all the way to her lungs, a gulp of cloud river.

"Jerome, I don't like this. You're on visual."

"Relax. Just like to grab images of the boundaries, how light dissolves into suspension. We're not going inside."

Where exactly were they?

Jerome seemed intent on the horizon. Like a slow dream, a peculiar landscape beneath them resolved itself.

The Hoodoos.

Of course. As if they swooped over another planet. She'd never seen so much detail, unveiled. The Hoodoos of the Bisti were roadless, a wilderness, remote and isolated. She'd only experienced them from the little you could see from the road.

But in this light, the glowing tapestry of balanced rock lay exposed, the sandstone streaked as complexly as folded dough. He flew even closer, and the warm light illuminated the individual stacks, each rock pillar becoming its own strangely weird candle, with a tall shaft and a balancing rock caught on top. Such a silent place, so wild and inaccessible. A primitive world, stark and raw.

Jerome slowed their speed, dropping them in even lower in a slow glide.

A man seemed to be watching them approach. He lay splayed on his back, on the flats between two twisted Hoodoos. As Jerome throttled down with his knee, taking them even closer, her mind filled with an odd thought. The man looked to her exactly as if he had fallen from the sky.

"Jerome—do you see that man? Down there."

"Looks dead."

Jerome lifted his camera to his eye.

The next morning Lilli was driving too fast, ignoring her throbbing tires. She began to obsess over the obvious: with the mutilation, she couldn't know if the coyotes were both male, or both female, or one male and one female. Why was she so sure that was important?

Because she was Navajo. Everything for a Navajo is in some important way male or female.

Before she let her mind run too far amuck, she'd better find Charley Pete. She forced her mind to slow down and think. Even more disturbing than the fact that they had been draped over the hood of her Dodge was the careful, almost surgical, mutilation of the two bodies. And then that someone deliberately, and so knowingly, had hand delivered the "message"—whatever it was—in the middle of the night. Specifically to her. Someone was trying to threaten her, bully her. Was that it? Or was it meant to be some sort of accusation? They'd put the mutilated coyotes in full view, impossible for her to ignore.

Maybe the grisly message was purely secular business. She hoped she could still catch Charley. She swerved into the parking lot of the tribal offices, slipped into her usual parking space, slammed the door, and took off on a fast trot toward his truck.

She could see Charley, still loading the truck, and Selwyn, too. She scuffled through a drift of cottonwood leaves, leathery and flat, most the size of pockets. She should slow down, make a little chit-chat, but she couldn't stop herself. She planted her feet a little wider than necessary and faced both men.

"*Yá'át'ééh*. You guys got a minute?"

Selwyn Keeswood shaded his eyes. "Lilli Chischilly?" In his faded T-shirt, Selwyn had the softly arched spine of the young, with his jeans low on his hips. "What'd we go and do?"

Charley Pete, a Master Trapper and twice again as old as Selwyn, leaned his stiff weight against the flatbed. "We in trouble again with you legal types?"

Charley had one of those slow-moving mouths that look hinged with a strong spring. He was chief of the hook-and-bullet boys. Not that they weren't trained in wildlife ecology, but the label referred to their budget receiving funding from the wallets of people who bought hooks and bullets, a tax levied on the sale of arms and ammo, rods and lines and lures.

"Admit to nothing, Charley," she said. "Always a good opening legal strategy."

She shouldn't seem so rushed. They'd smell her fear. She decided to stall by asking the obvious. "What are you guys up to?"

The two were stacking sections of PVC pipe, the kind

that's used in construction to carry water behind walls. The pipe all seemed to be about a yard long though, which didn't make much sense for plumbing. Didgeridoos, she wondered? She'd once been walking across the plaza in Santa Fe when she'd heard the unmistakable sound of the Australian aborigines' instrument. She'd followed the sound until she found its source, a kid blowing through a sawed-off PVC pipe. But as she leaned over the bed of their truck, she saw that each pipe had a trap-door.

"Trapping owls today," Charley said. "The burrowing kind."

Lilli knew the bird, a short-bodied thing that seemed to walk on stilts.

"You think they'll just give themselves up, saunter into these pipes?"

"We're a tad smarter. Stuff their exit burrow, see, so it don't give them another way out. You sound mighty interested. Want to come along and watch?"

"Ah, not today. But thank you. No, I have a, well, a question for you." Her voice didn't sound natural at all, not to her own ears. She tried at least to keep her voice slow.

"Yeah? Go on."

"Sanctioned, or otherwise..." She tried not to be obvious about the way she was controlling her intake breath. "Been any contests, you know, those coyote calling contests?" Maybe she was way off the mark.

"Not enough work, huh, to keep you busy in your own office?" Selwyn, Charley's assistant, grinned at her.

Were her two mutilated bodies part of some strange contest? "I need some details," she said.

"Woman's serious, Selwyn. Can't you read her face? These are male fantasy games, Lilli. Sure you want to get involved? Right up there with killing homosexuals for sport."

Selwyn feigned hitting his forehead with the flat of his hand. "You mean they don't kill them for meat?"

"Ignore him, Lilli. What kind of details you looking for?"

Charley's upper lip sported a sparse mustache, a dead give-away his ancestors included someone with Spanish blood since no natural Navajo ever needed a shave.

"How a contest is arranged, how it's scored," she said, trying to flesh out a fuller answer. "And what happens to the carcasses?" She hoped she'd slipped that last part in a little more naturally.

"Coyote calling—it's a luring game, Lilli, that's the front half. Then it's a killing spree."

She thought of those unnaturally still legs. Their noses had been toward the windshield. The arrangement of laying them on their backs had seemed deliberate, and odd. She didn't trust her memory to measure how long she'd sat with her hands holding the steering wheel, doing nothing as the long fur, creamy white on their upturned bellies, ruffled in the small breeze. Finally, she'd gotten out of the car and walked around to the front of the Dodge. She'd made herself stand still and look. How had she crossed someone so cruel as to arrange this mutilated offering on the hood of her car?

Then she'd had to lift the pair off, one at a time, and find them a secure burial under a cache of stacked stone.

Charley cleared his throat and spit, bringing her back to the moment.

"One very curious animal, coyote is, kind of like you, Lilli. A feather will attract him, see, even a ticking clock. But best of all is the talent involved. Go on, Selwyn, explain the talent to the woman."

"Sure, the Magical Lip Squeal. Mouth-blown."

"Selwyn here, he's too modest," Charley said. "He can swirl that long tongue of his around real good."

"Little practice and you can make your mew, your caterwaul, your sob," Selwyn said. "Sounds like something hid behind a rock, or in the grass, in distress, see. Coyote comes to you, all curious."

"My personal opinion, some contestants more into amusing themselves."

"Charley's got a point, besides it has its drawbacks—blowing mouth calls—the way it ties up your hands. When coyote does come close, there you are playing riffs with both hands and your shooter in your lap."

"Which makes the electronic boxes so popular," Charley said.

"Sure, keeps the hands free, plus don't take any more talent than buying batteries. You buy your pre-programmed calls: Little Baby Cottontail In Distress, Little Fawn Separated From Its Mother. Set the speaker down, finger your firearm. Kill Slim Trotter as he vectors past you."

In the Creation stories, Coyote is one of the Holy Ones. An animal in the secular realm, yes, but one of the Holy Ones, too, in the sacred realm. Logical and always persistent, Coyote among the Holy People made the hard calls in their earlier worlds of creation. When Coyote was asked in exchange for his counsel, "What would you like?" He answered, "I want to be in everything."

And so he is.

"But what makes it a contest?" Lilli said.

"Goal of coyote calling contests is head-on simple: a dead coyote. Lure 'em and kill 'em, that's the game, Lilli. Widespread sport, if you don't mind the term. Make it an attractive contest? Sure, single entry, team entries. Entrance fee. Official start time. Cash prizes. Highest body count, there's a winner, and biggest one bagged."

"Just to show their sense of humor, prizes, too, like for

the ugliest. And let's not forget the perfume game neither."

"Right. Teams of contestants are doused in coyote sex glands. Pure coyote glands. Can buy the stinkin' stuff by the pint. More of that fantasy game, see, under the design you'll get a coyote in closer if you're reeking of his conspecific's anal gland."

Now things were getting a whole lot closer to the mark of the mutilation. But how was she going to ask the next question without arousing their suspicion?

"There'd be a market." She took a shallow breath. "For 'parts'? Is that what you're saying?"

"Hey, Coyote In a Bottle. Sells real well."

"Can you give me more detail? You said glands?"

An explanation was forming in her head. Maybe this was nothing as cruel and creepy as it had seemed just a little while ago. Maybe she could off-load this problem onto Charley and relieve her mind at the same time.

"Gee, Lilli, didn't know you was so interested."

"Be nice, Selwyn. Coyote glands include the reproductive glands, and the anal glands. You can tell by the carcass, way they dissect the animal. Take out the vent tube, maybe an inch of the anal tube around the—excuse me—bung hole."

"Sometimes they take the urinary tract, too."

"Sure. Get lucky, like Selwyn says, skin an animal with a full bladder. All scent-for-sale."

"Well, what about that cache of coyotes your department found? That one last spring?" she asked.

The grisly news made it out of Charley and Selwyn's office to the front page of the newspaper. Lilli, sitting with her lawyer credentials in the HPD hadn't been involved. But now she wondered what more had happened. And who'd been found guilty.

"Ever charge anyone?" she said.

"Went bust. All we ever found was the carcasses. Forty dumped in Salahkai Wash, presumably after the prize money was divvied up."

Well, her two coyotes weren't dumped, nor hidden, but used instead to draw attention. Her attention.

"What made you so certain, you know, from the carcasses?" How should she say this? "I mean, how did you know there'd been a coyote calling contest?"

"Pretty obvious. Each coyote had its mouth taped shut."

"Stimulated even our curiosity," Selwyn said.

"We opened all the snouts," Charley said. "Found ourselves a plastic ball inside each, laying on the tongue."

"Numbered plastic balls. Part of a keeping-track system, you know, to tie each coyote to its shooter."

"Way to keep score."

No, that wasn't at all the same. Her two coyotes had had their mouths hanging open.

Charley took his hands out of his pockets. "So, Lilli, this is great and all, swapping stories, and we're on the payroll in or out of the parking lot. But those owls are waiting on us."

"Sure. Hey, thanks for the information." They were going to find her next request particularly curious. "I'd be real appreciative—you hear of any more coyote killings, you let me know?"

"Let you know? You do have a lot of time on your hands," Selwyn said.

"Come on, Selwyn. Sure thing, we'll let you know."

Lilli felt the vibrations from their truck rolling past her. She closed her eyes to shut off stimuli. Was it a business transaction, two coyotes, mutilated for their glands? She didn't believe that at all, did she? No, she was definitely the intended target but the message was still too cryptic for her to read.

Well, whoever was trying to disturb her had succeeded.

With her eyes still closed, words were coming back to her. A song. She remembered the ceremonial words from Coyote Way:

With Darkness Girl, he ran.

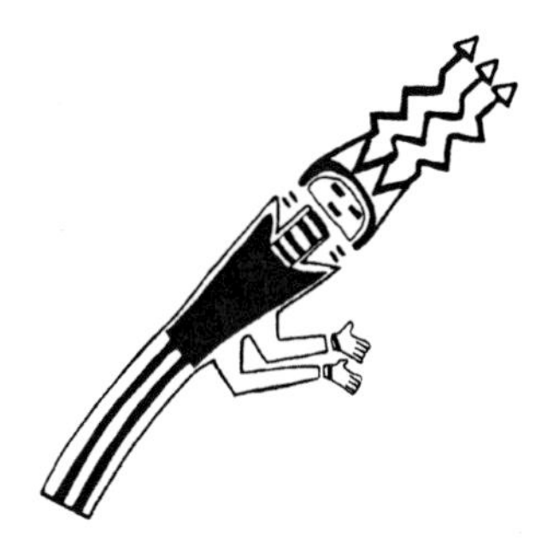

Annie Henio stood beside her squad car. Her extra long legs were familiar. Annie had such long legs she looked good even in the thick brown pants of the police uniform. Lilli greeted her by taking Annie's hand, holding it softly, then following her in through the doors of the medical facility.

"Good to see you," Annie said. "How you been?"

Was Annie the decoy, to make it all seem normal? Witnesses were always interviewed, Lilli reasoned. But they weren't normally interviewed in the presence of the Medical Investigator. Something strange was about to happen.

"Fine, *shidoni,*" Lilli said to her old friend. "Been too long."

Trying to keep up with Annie's long stride through the med school corridors, she remembered how Annie's legs had always earned her the aisle seat for added comfort on the bus rides for the 3A circuit of girls basketball pairings in high school. The two of them bouncing together on a shared seat between away games to Ganado, Many Farms, Monument Valley, facing the Lady Hornets, the Lady Mustangs.

Legally, the Hoodoos placed the scene of death in the jurisdiction of New Mexico, and New Mexico had a medical examiner system. Which meant any suspicions about the cause of death would necessarily lead the police to the medical investigator, who would begin his questioning at the precise location of death before authorizing removal of the body. She knew that. And, like any lawyer, knew, too, that cavalierly picking the body up, removing it from where it lay in the Hoodoos, would have been bad protocol.

Still, everything had seemed so strange, especially Jerome—more interested in photographing the man than in the mystery of the man. She'd argued with him, her mind's emotional center triggered by the man's helpless splay and the way his face turned up toward them. She'd insisted they land. Jerome had strongly disagreed, pointing out how the Hoodoos had a complicated texture that didn't lend itself to finding a smooth piece of runway. And then there was the obvious.

"If I airlift the body out, Lilli, where does that put you?"

Instead, Jerome had set the plane back down exactly where they had lifted off, on the temporary runway next to his truck and trailer. She had immediately called the body's location in to the police.

Now, hopefully, the explanation would turn out to be simple in its conclusion: death from making a stupid mistake in the desert, heading off-road into the wilderness without enough water. But she knew better than to be caught complacent or off-guard. Homicide required the Office of the Medical Investigator. Suspicion of violence, too, required the OMI. Not death from running out of water.

"So, I was surprised, Lilli, when I heard you were involved. Something about a joy ride, you and Jerome Bah?"

Annie seemed natural enough. Just chatter between old friends.

"Something like that."

But obviously someone higher up than Annie wanted information from her. Or a reaction.

"So?" Lilli said. Best to ask questions if you don't want to be answering any. "What did your guys find on the ground?"

"Found us a dead Navajo," Annie said. "Almost looks like he dropped from the sky."

Lilli's mind was slow at first. She hadn't calculated the odds. But the police apparently had. Dropped from the sky?

"Have another question," Annie said.

"Sure."

"Which of the two of you decided to fly up over the Hoodoos?"

"Jerome invited me to take a ride." Lilli hoped her hesitation hadn't been noticeable. "But it was my idea to fly over the Hoodoos."

Now what do you call that, besides a bald-faced lie?

She followed Annie through the marked door.

Jennifer Kitchell

Duane Fatt had his future planned. He'd hardly spread the newspaper open and there was Lee again, staring up at him off the front page above the fold with his half-salute, half-goal-slammer gesture and always the smile, the beam of a man who knew he was one of the Chosen Ones. But did it really matter? Because Lee was never going to become anyone's president.

The waitress poured a refill of the coffee. The newspaper was full of how the politics was getting more and more lopsided with victory pretty clear from telephone polls. The senator from Utah, Mr. Lee, was going to win.

They should have interviewed him, Duane thought. If someone stopped him on the street, conducted an interview of his thoughts on the election, he might have said, "Well, a lot can change."

Duane looked through the plate glass window of the truck stop to the noonday traffic on the interstate, then to the horizon. He liked being back in desert country, close as he'd felt physically to Mama in a long, long time.

Nursing his coffee with one hand, tracking the newsprint with the other, he tried not to think how things hadn't gone well the last time he saw Mama. He wouldn't make that mistake again. This time it would be different because he was going to please her. She should have received his letter by now. *Watch the news.* That was all the letter'd said.

The prison psychiatrist had always wanted him to talk about Mama, but he knew better. That was all between him and her. There was love there, always had been. It wasn't perfect love, Duane knew that. But he would never believe it wasn't love.

Maybe Mama hadn't come to visit, never wrote neither, but the prison system had transferred him around like a ballplayer with a sprung arm, so she'd just probably lost track of where he was. One thing he knew for sure, he wasn't going to tell Mama nothing yet about his plans. Bragging wasn't his style.

"Duane Fatt." The psychiatrist had always said his name as if it was some question. Ever since he was a kid, his name had been a joke. If he had a lottery ticket for every time he heard, "Hey, Fatt, how come you so skinny?" Mama'd always said to pay no mind, besides it was a medical condition, nearly, the way he wiggled, even sitting in a chair, just always kept some part of himself moving.

Of course it bothered him how Mama and his brother shared their same name and he was stuck alone with Fatt.

"Was your daddy's name, Duane," Mama had tried. "Hell, guess I just took a shine to having his name on something."

The waitress wiped the counter in front of him with a tired sponge, didn't bother with eye contact as she set the saucer down centered with a doughnut, the kind that finger-dented when you touched its maple icing. Krispy Creme could make out in these desert towns, catering to a people living poor off jobs that made them overeat instead of putting money in the bank. A primitive kind of logic. Only now it worked in reverse: rolls of human flab were a sure sign you weren't one of the Chosen People.

Fatt took a bite of doughnut and felt the sugar dissolve. Yes, get yourself a plan and a lot can change.

Being a woman, Mama used to close the door and cry as her way of answering a humiliation. But he'd always preferred to strike back, inflict the pain. Point was, this would mean a real lot to Mama and he'd like to show her how he'd been listening. How growing up, he'd heard her. She'd always carried that hate, down deep and heavy, how way back her kin knowed they wasn't natural born to the family that took them in. Thing was, now he was going to do something about it.

In prison it had all been a quiet burn, you didn't decide nothing. But he'd made himself a plan and now all he had to do was act, carry the plan out to its natural conclusion. He had himself a future. Something Mama was going to like a whole lot.

He'd considered a slew of options. Going after Lee in broad daylight, in crowds where Lee was trying to squeeze as many hands as he could grab. Or in the middle of the night, finding Lee in a hotel room. The way Duane followed the campaign, reading the paper, watching the tube, he felt like some nervous stock market trader keeping an eye on the numbers to make the right move. Timing, all about timing, and nerve.

He put his head down closer to the page so he could

study the photo of the man. Hell, Lee was a true born-and-bred Westerner. "Fit," the reporters liked to say. Could still jog and mountain bike with the heart and legs that had carried him ten years ago. Couldn't contrast better with his opponent. Night after night on the motel TV Lee's opponent came across as a wimp with thinning hair and an Eastern city-boy accent that was all up in the nose.

But had Lee ever faced a desert rat? A desert rat with good aim could take out the whole party.

Because Duane was going to kill Lee. The fuck. He was going to massacre the sitting duck.

"Annie, excellent, there you are. Ah, and Ms. Chischilly, a pleasure."

Lilli turned toward the deep voweled voice. The air in the over-chilled room hung with the metallic smell of blood. The medical investigator, a licensed physician whose patients always presented dead.

"This is a first, isn't it, Ms. Chischilly, you in my laboratory? I remember the two of us in court together, am I right? And a cross-examination from you."

"It is, Dr. Trybek," Lilli said. "And thank you for having me."

"Oh, I'm a natural show-off."

And formidable. Be careful, she reminded herself. Among lawyers, Trybek was whispered about. Lilli remembered her days with the Attorney General's office in Albuquerque, and a senior lawyer warning her about ever taking Trybek for granted. "Man loves to give a deserved spanking."

"Well, my dear, you've picked a dandy. Seven thousand death rulings to my career and counting, but none ever like this."

None like this? She felt herself stiffen. She'd come, curious to find out more about the man in the Hoodoos. Now she wanted to get through this without having to answer too many questions. She noticed Annie, too, seemed to be acting curiously stiff.

"Ms. Chischilly—may I call you Lilli?"

Trybek held a piece of chalk he'd been using to write on the blackboard behind him. She couldn't help but notice how the chalk was smeared yellow and red from the fluids of things he must explore.

"Of course."

The man removed his rubber gloves.

"Elected against an autopsy."

That seemed odd. Autopsy was a surgical procedure. Trybek would have held the man's heart in his hand, weighed it, removed the skull cap to get at the brain, maybe squeezed urine out of the bladder for a drug test. Why not all the evidence that would allow him to paint a detailed picture of what precisely had gone wrong? The cause of death, as distinct from the mechanism of death, as distinct from the manner of death.

"Shall I start then, Lilli?" Trybek wore paper booties and they made a soft sliding sound as he moved about.

"Please."

"Yes, well then, let me present Mr. Bilgehe."

From a row of identical stainless steel drawers, Trybek slid out a body draped with a white sheet. Would Trybek be kind to her and keep the sheet over the body?

"The vitals? One of your people. According to his driver's license, sixty-one years old. Cursory exam? In good health, except for his bad knees. Arthritic swelling. We need a cause of death determination now, don't we?"

Trybek pulled back the white draping from the man's face and upper torso. "To quote the poet: 'The unclothed body is autobiography.'

"Focus, Lilli, if you will, on just the mouth. What do you notice?"

Did Trybek really mean for her to respond? There were obvious traces of adhesive. He didn't wait for her answer.

"On close inspection," Trybek said, "it was standard duct tape. A sixty-one year old male, then, who has experienced death from suffocation."

But why would Trybek consider that extraordinary, after seven thousand bodies needing explanation?

"And so..." He stopped himself.

She'd seen him exhale with his portentous, "And so..." just that way in the courtroom. He had something like a punch line coming.

"A classic case, my dear. Our Mr. Bilgehe bit the bag." Trybek looked at her so expectantly.

"I'm sorry. I'm not understanding."

"Bit the bag? As in scrotum, Ms. Chischilly. Care to see more?" From behind a cabinet door, Trybek retrieved a glass jar and held it at eye level. "Take a peek. I retrieved the contents from inside Mr. Bilgehe's cheek cavities."

Lilli peered into the specimen jar.

"He had balls in his throat, Ms. Chischilly, blocking the windpipe."

"Balls?"

"Testicles, shall we say, and the intervening penis."

He offered her the jar. "Coyote testicles."

Her fingers tightened around the cold glass and its contents that swirled slowly in a liquid shimmery with preservative.

"Perhaps you'll notice more with better light." Trybek took the jar from her and raised it toward the overhead fluorescent. "There were also, inside Mr. Bilgehe's mouth, the vaginal lips and etcetera of a coyote female."

"What?" She really needed to sound surprised.

"And so—unless our Mr. Bilgehe was dining on the nether parts of coyote and just happened to choke in the process—being out there all alone in the Hoodoos with no one to offer the Heimlich maneuver—"

She sensed Annie watching her.

"One blue man, Ms. Chischilly. Cyanotic. His blood was deoxygenated. Accidental? A choking? No." Trybek coughed lightly. "Decidedly not accidental."

She noticed he'd dropped the familiarity of calling her Lilli, just as he would on the witness stand.

"The testicles were shoved to the back of his throat, with intent to asphyxiate. The petechiae—excuse me, the evident hemorrhage in the lining of the eyeballs—supports my conclusion: suffocation."

The official cause of death, then, coyote genitalia? And the mechanism of death: choking of the airways? Manner of death: homicide?

"As I've explained to the police, placing those genital parts in the back of the mouth? The act was punitive."

Punitive, yes. But what about symbolic?

So this had officially turned into a full-blown murder investigation. She looked again at his jar full of evidence. She needed to know.

"Does Mr. Bilgehe..." Why couldn't she just keep quiet? She absolutely did not have to speak. "Does he show signs of being moved?"

"Oh, a perceptive question, Ms. Chischilly. Apparent location of death, the Hoodoos of the Bisti. But the actual location? *Bisti* means 'badlands' in Navajo, is that right?"

"*Bisti*?" She looked over at Annie. "Yes."

Bisti Badlands, that's what the *bilagáana* called the place. But *Bisti* meant badlands in Navajo, too, so she always heard a stutter, the same concept in two languages, the "Badlands-Badlands."

"And Hoodoos? Another Navajo term?"

"Geologic term, I think," she said. "For something unnatural, weird." At least in aspect.

"Well, the answer to your perceptive question is, yes, the sediment in the tread of Mr. Bilgehe's shoes and the sediment of the Hoodoos quite obviously do not make a match. But I'll leave that to Annie and the police."

He cleared his throat noisily. "What I will attest to is this: the cyanotic coloring, the eye membrane hemorrhaging? Mr. Bilgehe was alive when the coyote parts were inserted. These show active attempts on the part of Mr. Bilgehe to breathe, attempts that failed."

He placed the evidence jar on the table.

"So, Ms. Chischilly? You're a specialist, am I right, in Navajo culture? I think we have a message here, don't you?"

She shouldn't admit to that but what else could she say? "Yes. Apparently so."

Yes, there was a message written in this man's death, and it included the hood of her Dodge. Something logical to the murderer. Something obviously about *Ma'ii*, the Coyote. She thought of how *Ma'ii* can represent the power of uncontrollable sex. And there was more she was definitely not revealing, not to Annie, not to Trybek. Maybe Trybek had the coyote parts that played into the murder. But she had the two coyotes that had been mutilated. The murderer had something symbolic to tell her.

"The question is..." Trybek looked playful but she knew better. "Can one decode this intriguing message? Care to take a stab at it?"

She looked over at Annie who was studying the floor.

"No, I really can't make any sense of it," she said. "Not at all. Can you, Annie?"

"Uh...no."

"But you'll think about it, Lilli?"

"Certainly," she answered Trybek.

"And if an idea forms?" he said.

"I will let you know."

She was involved before she ever saw the dead man. She was part of the crime or at least its cover-up, because she was going to leave the coyotes buried, until she figured out why. And what kind of serious trouble would that turn out to be?

Another perfectly abnormal day. She'd never met the man, not in person.

Lilli Chischilly peered outside to see if she could see him. All she could see was too much traffic. Presidential front-runner Lee, the center of so much anticipation, still remained at large or well hidden.

When Lee finally made a live appearance, she expected a mega-watt charmer. She knew the quip, "Politics is Hollywood except for the ugly faces." Well, this time politics had itself a Hollywood face.

Someone's foot accidentally found hers and she winced from the unexpected pressure. The Navajo Nation Inn hummed with strangers. Her forty-eight hour reprieve was definitely over. She'd never seen so many agitated people sporting so many versions of urban shoe.

The festooned campaign bus added to the spectacle.

Twenty minutes ago, its doors had opened to disgorge the rumpled press corps who'd squeezed past her into the cramped banquet facility with its tables and chairs pushed into compliance. She checked the time. Nine official minutes to go.

Lilli scanned the faces of the campaign press imagining their odd codependency, traveling with the candidate like competing dance partners who jostled for extra intimacy, and then tattled. Hadn't they reported how presidential contender Bush, the recovered adolescent, drank near-beers with the press corps at the back of the plane? An act of camaraderie this election's candidate would never mimic.

Lee, a practicing Mormon, probably wouldn't even swallow caffeine. At least on film he seemed the very image of clean living, a Westerner who not only jogged faster than the campaign press but took to mountain bikes and dirt.

She remembered images of Nixon's sallow eyes, how the then-president had played true to form, trusting nearly no one, using the Navajo reservation as a forsaken place so remote no one would discover his secret rendezvous. Nixon and his shadowy friend, Bebe Rebozo, were always rumored to have had trysts at an isolated old trading post.

Well, this was a lot more public. She'd never seen so much Washington, D.C., on the reservation. The campaign bus straddled the limited parking asphalt, forcing an overflow of vans and sedans and pickups to trail along the narrow shoulders of Route 12 like flotsam after a storm.

She still had her own plan in place. She would refuse him. She didn't like Lee. She certainly didn't trust the man. No way she was going to help his campaign agenda. Still, there must be some very special reason the campaign was temporarily camped out in Window Rock.

Well, let's get it over with.

Another abnormality was having Bitsoi at her elbow.

Shouldn't the president of the Navajo Nation have more pressing business? Surely he had a chair waiting for him beneath the patriotically spangled banner.

"You ready for this?" Bitsoi cupped his hand to his mouth and leaned close to her ear to be heard above the babble.

Boom mikes stalked the air above their heads. Cameras, cued for confected photo-ops, swiveled their round eyes toward the cobbled-together stage.

"Quite the circus," Lilli said.

"You'll be fine." Bitsoi steered her through the crowd to two chairs in the front row. "Let's sit here."

She felt foolish so close to the stage but obliged Bitsoi and spread her long skirt across the tops of her legs, then finger-tucked stragglers that'd fallen out of her hair knot. Yes, she could handle witnessing a staged press conference. But the decibel level surrounding them made it too loud to bother trying to say much. Talk would have to wait.

She watched equipment-freighted experts work among the ropes of electrical lines attached to an array of microphones that would carry the voice of the candidate to the chairs reserved for official press corps and then to the crush of campaign staffers, lobbyists, local reporters, and the merely curious.

To be seated so close to the swinging kitchen doors with an empty stomach was punishing. The kitchen grill in overproduction added its smoky droplets of fat to the air. The juxtaposition of Washington bureau dress shirts and polished shoes and the smell of mutton made Lilli think of her last meal in D.C.

She'd been uncomfortable. They'd put her up in some overly marbled hotel where you couldn't hear yourself think for the din of the waterfall in the lobby. And then, just when she'd slid into her room and out of her shoes and was trying unsuccessfully to convince herself she hadn't made a complete fool of herself speaking into a microphone before the Congress of the United States, someone had knocked at her door. She'd peeked through the little round bullet hole but didn't recognize the man so, with a kind of false logic, she had opened the door.

"Room service."

Surely the wrong room. "I didn't order anything."

"No, ma'am, it was sent up to you." He handed her a card. The lobbyist.

A few minutes later she was down the elevator and into the night street to where, from her taxi, she'd seen the dark figures protected from the cold by nothing more than a doorframe. She'd opened her coat and taken out the food wrapped up in the hotel's towel. The eyes that looked back at her weren't completely part of this world, but fingers reached out and took the food. She'd kept hold of the towel.

"The thing is, Lilli..."

"What?" She couldn't hear clearly.

Bitsoi's breath funneled into her ear. "You impressed them in Washington." He smiled at her.

She certainly didn't think so. The next evening had been especially painful. Her official Washington host, the lobbyist, took her to his favorite restaurant and pressed the lamb on her. His favorite dish, he explained, and told her how the lamb is marinated a certain perfect way in that little part of Italy his ancestors came from.

All she'd been able to think of was how she had carried the lambs with their pink tongues and curly fleece the way his children probably carried their dolls. And how she could still lay down so completely motionless on the ground that the lambs would come nibble on her, just to see why she'd stopped moving. How could she explain to that man that Navajo always ate the tired, old sheep, never the lamb?

A striped shirt with a loosened tie who couldn't possibly be Lee stood at the podium.

"Lee's running late."

Groans from the first several rows.

"I know, I know, you all have press deadlines, especially for the east coast. So I'm going to get us started."

The man was remarkably energetic, nothing like the star they awaited, but he worked the crowd like the warm-up vocalist for a rock concert.

She'd read the polls on Lee. Victory was nearly his. From what the analysts were saying, winning California and its electoral votes was the linchpin to the remainder of the campaign. And Lee surely knew what Californians wanted: an ironclad guarantee. More power, *cheap* power, and lots more water.

She could almost read the PR copy, with photos of Lee surrounded by his pretty wife and his twin sons.

A man who gets his hands dirty, studying complex issues for himself.

A man who leads with action.

Did they intend the irony by stopping briefly in Window Rock? Because on the reservation the statistics were heavy toward the crush of poverty, unemployment, and lack of both enough electricity and running water.

But this warm-up staffer was good. He had the room laughing with him. Only the more she listened, the more she saw him as a professional shapeshifter, like the one who throws pebbles on the roof of your hogan at night, and when you run outside, all you ever see are the fleeing shadows of a four-legged animal.

People all around her started to stand. Lee leapt onto stage. The shapeshifter grabbed Lee's hand and lifted both their arms high. Adrenaline seemed to energize the crowd.

Lee stood centered, perfectly still, in pitch-perfect pose.

She must have closed her ears for a moment. She must have been letting just her eyes study him as he prowled the stage from left to right and back to center, his arms always in motion, because somehow she'd missed his words of greeting and political-speak until she heard him say, "It is our Manifest Destiny to work Nature..." His voice in the over-filled room was surprisingly fluid. It rose in volume with no apparent exertion.

After the press conference, Lee was supposed to make his way to her office for an in-person request. Certainly Etta was expecting him, the way she had the place so gussied up. Etta would want the door open. Lilli'd close the door. Lee would spend a minute gushing something obtuse about the Native American vote, and then he'd make his pitch. How they wanted her to help deliver that vote.

"In this great country of ours, the greatest on earth, with all its great minds and resources, we, together—yes, together—can tame Nature to meet our needs."

The press scribbled on their note pads, trying to keep up. The red lights of the cameras on both sides of the stage glowed.

"With bold technology, we can outsmart Nature, get her to give up more of her great wealth..." He paused. He made eye contact all over the room.

"And today, here, in Window Rock, Arizona, capital of the historic Navajo Nation, I want to emphasize my announced decision to get up-close and personal with a big, big issue: fresh clean bountiful water, and electric power. Starting Monday, I will take time out of my busy campaign schedule..."

Because he was so far ahead in the polls?

"To experience the greatest, the mightiest, the most significant of our river systems—the Colorado."

What kind of PR stunt was this? Is that what was happening? California's energy and water needs, like those of Vegas and Phoenix, rode on the backs of the Hopi and the Navajo.

"But don't you worry, I'll be in touch all along the way. I won't leave the campaign press stranded. Technology will allow me to converse with you all, even from a mile deep in the Grand Canyon."

Where did this come from? His campaign strategy handlers must have run this scheme through marketing gurus and test subjects and knew they had a winner.

"And I will not forget our Native people. I plan to pay homage to the people who still live their daily lives connected to the river. I plan to develop a deep understanding of our partnership.

"I want to see all there is to see, and so I've invited someone to accompany me, someone who will be a marvelous addition to the trip, someone schooled in the culture of these diverse groups of people we are all so proud of, and I'd like to call that person to the podium, now."

Everyone in the room hushed.

"Lil-li Chis-chil-ly." He extended his hand in her direction.

She turned to stare at Bitsoi. He was beaming like a proud parent.

"Will you please come up and join me? Let's give a round of applause to Lilli Chischilly, a full-blooded Navajo and member of the Navajo Nation Historic Preservation Department. Lilli, what do you say? Let's roll!"

She'd been captured by the enemy. It was all very public. She must look quite the fool. Out of nowhere music started to pump, *Rolling, rolling, rolling on the river...*

Was this ambush someone's idea of a joke?

She didn't even know how to swim.

Duane Fatt rested his shoulder blades against the wall at the back of the banquet room. Easy picking, fingering out the assigned Secret Service agents. The way they watched everyone except Lee. The Navajo woman blinking into the camera flashes looked surprised. As if Lee and his handlers just politely asked her to grab her ankles.

Duane liked being this close to Lee, finally sizing up the man in person. Ever since he was a little boy, Mama had ranted about how the Lees were their natural enemy. So much TV and radio and newspaper coverage with its Lee-this, Lee-that must be driving her nuts.

In prison there'd been time for trying on various scenarios of killing Lee. But Mama wouldn't be proud unless he killed Lee and his wife and his children, all in one fell swoop. Only that could balance the debt.

Well, start the clock ticking.

Mama should have received his letter by now. *Watch the news.* That's what the letter'd said. He sure hoped she hadn't moved. No, she'd be there. When it was all over, he'd get himself to her and she'd be proud, would want to hear every detail from the plan to the finale.

He scanned the applauding crowd. Nobody was paying him any mind.

He leaned away from the wall and pulled his wallet from his back pocket, flipped it open to the plastic-protected photo of just the two of them. A young mother with long hair and a small boy with hair spilling into his eyes smiled at each other. After all these wasted years, he'd go directly to see Mama smile at him again. Not one of her pinched-up smiles but the one that was soft, like when he was small.

Yes, there was love there, always had been.

GIRL WITH SKIRT OF STARS

Bitsoi sat behind his executive desk with his large eyebrows and too tightly fitted shirts. Lilli knew she should sit down herself. She was too mad to even try.

"Where did you get such a dumb idea?"

"Gee, Lilli, I'm surprised you're surprised. You really were surprised?"

"That I'm going to provide escort service for Lee, for what? A week?"

"Five nights, six days."

"And you thought a public blindside was the way to go with this?"

"I thought this was all arranged."

"No, most definitely it was not 'all arranged.' " She felt maneuvered, tricked, even bullied.

"Gee, Lilli, I'm sorry. Those people in Washington, that Dougan fellow up on the stage—I understood they'd got your okay on it. Told me they just wanted my approval."

She wanted to condemn Bitsoi for his complicity but he appeared half-sheepish, half-puzzled, almost as if he was telling the truth. Of course Lee didn't stay to talk to her in person. He was behind schedule, due in a string of big city appearances. He'd pulled out of Window Rock in a hurry.

"Now it's too late," Bitsoi said.

To refuse? No, it wasn't.

"Just what did you go and tell them?"

Bitsoi let out a grunt of air. "That I'd be proud to send you along on such an important trip."

"Whatever were you thinking?"

"They told me they needed someone who spoke good English, you know, college words. A kind of cultural interpreter. Couldn't help but give my blessing."

What was the real reason? Someone they could use to their advantage, she was sure of that. Bitsoi had better not be leading her on. There better not be a deal in the making. She wouldn't put it past the misguided ambitions of some of the Navajo Council, even Bitsoi. If Lee could get the Navajo Nation to broker—what had he called it, a "deep partnership?"—no, the man was dangerous.

"I'm not remotely one of theirs," she said. "I don't even plan on voting for this man."

"That's personal business. You don't have to tell them that."

No, Bitsoi or not, she was not going to let this happen.

"Listen," she said. "You have to come up with a different proposal, someone else. What's wrong with them taking an expert from the National Park Service?"

"Very specific, how they want a Navajo who can represent the Navajo Nation. They don't want any connection to a federal employee."

Here she'd been worrying about Lee and his staffers scheduled to meet with her following the press conference. And she'd been anticipating his request for help garnering the Indian vote, trying to decide how she was going to refuse him, face-to-face, in such tight quarters. But to accompany Lee on the Colorado River? Like what, a modern-day Sacajawea?

"Listen, Lilli, this man's going to win the election. Eight years? We need a friend, not an enemy, in Washington. You, of all people, understand me."

"You actually think we'll get some good out of this?"

"To put you with Lee, for that amount of seclusion? Could never buy that much ear time."

She'd more likely make a complete fool of herself.

"And he very specifically requested you, Lilli."

"He asked for me?" How could that possibly be?

"By name. Mentioned no one else. I told you, you did something there in Washington. Made a big impression."

So that's what had gotten Lee's attention, her going to D.C. as an expert witness?

Bitsoi had sent her on that mission, but the idea to frame the argument was her own, a legal ploy, to use the federal Native American Graves Protection and Repatriation Act to include water. She'd testified before Congress on why water is a cultural resource of critical dimension to the survival of the Navajo people, and NAGPRA a federal law that could be enforced through the courts. But she never imagined it would land her in this predicament.

At least Bitsoi had the courtesy to give her time to think.

She walked over to his bank of windows. He stayed quiet. Unlike her single window with its view of the parking lot, his faced out on the skyline of red rock perforated with the nearly perfect eye where she'd sat and waited for Jerome.

Other than whoever made the delivery, only Lilli knew

about the coyotes on the hood of the Dodge. She'd become someone's target. Chosen, though, by who? Someone who obviously didn't want to make the delivery in person, in daylight, and confront her with whatever was driving him to that kind of insanity.

Was the point to scare her, or to make her obsess? Because that's what she was doing, going over and over what had happened, trying to keep her memories completely accurate. She remembered how Jerome had seemed oddly detached when they'd spotted the man lying on his back in the Hoodoos.

And now she'd gone and provided him with an alibi, telling the police it was all her idea to fly up over the Hoodoos. She was like a mother duck feigning a broken wing, trying to lead the police away. But from what?

Trybek had been very specific: a homicide. Punishment would need to be meted out, a criminal act defined. She couldn't let things just happen, as if gravity were in control. The police and Trybek could be playing dumb, too. Already she felt like an accomplice. She wasn't a defense lawyer. Did Jerome understand that?

Settle down, Lilli. So it was his idea to fly up over the Hoodoos. That wasn't evidence of *mens rea,* didn't prove criminal intent.

Somewhere deep in her brain, trying to lodge itself closer to the surface of her consciousness, was a question she was trying to squelch. Could Jerome know more than he said? Maybe six days and five nights as far away from the reservation as she could get was a good idea. On one condition.

She'd made up her mind.

She pressed her lips between her fingers as if to keep them closed. Then she turned away from the window to face Bitsoi.

"I'll go with Lee if..." She straightened her shoulders. "On one condition."

"What's that?"

She wanted out of this command performance with Lee, out of this debacle. But maybe she could broker her own deal.

"I don't go alone."

"But you won't be alone, Lilli. Lee's bringing his family, and that Dougan fellow, and..."

"No." Sometimes words surprised the brain as if the mind wasn't responsible, hadn't sent the very words to the tongue. "You're going to have to talk Lee into taking two Navajo."

"Two? What are you talking about?"

"Jerome Bah. Said you hired him, a licensed pilot..." Either Jerome needed her help or he was part of the plot Bitsoi had made behind her back with Lee. The words spilled from her mouth. "Said he starts in a few weeks on the next payroll."

"So?"

"If I go, Jerome Bah goes."

Bitsoi's eyes widened. "But what if there's no room for him?"

"You got me into this. You figure it out."

Jennifer Kitchell

Duane Fatt liked the smell of the woman's skin in the flowered dress. In the disguise of the crowd, he pressed himself close to her as they flowed behind their appointed guide, leading them all on the last tour for the day at Glen Canyon Dam. He could afford an hour of pretending to be normal.

As her scented hair passed in front of his face, he sniffed a little too eagerly. He caught his mistake and put his hand over his mouth to pretend he'd coughed.

He was no good cold sober, not with women. Sometimes if he got the fourth drink back before the fifth began to narcotize his tongue, he could play with words women like to hear, talk a woman into getting into his car before she realized she'd made a big mistake.

As the guide led on, Duane dutifully scanned the canyon gorge of the Colorado River plugged with this gargantuan spew of concrete. What the hell? He leaned out over the edge of the dam trying to quench his dizziness, reveling in the full-vomit effect of looking down seven hundred solid feet of bowed cement.

"Sir! Bring yourself in from the edge, sir! Now!"

Without making eye contact with the man in the uniform, Duane stepped back from the edge. That was a slip-up. *Never, ever, draw attention.*

"All right, then," the guide said. "The keystone arch is the trick, that's the engineering principle that makes this work. It transfers all that pressure of holding back the river to these tight canyon walls."

Duane tried to make like he belonged and to pay better attention. He had an unfortunate dislike, though, of men—or women—for that matter, in uniforms. *And you know what, Duane, you better rein it in so you don't get singled out again, maybe culled from the tour herd.*

"Any questions so far?"

"How much concrete is in this thing anyway?" The woman asking seemed half of a man-woman team in matching Harley-Davidson shirts with advertising down their sleeves.

"Sure, let me put that figure in some perspective. Crews worked to pour concrete twenty-four hours a day, seven days a week, and never let up for—would you believe?—four whole years."

"You hear that, hon?" The woman stretched her arms around her man's waist.

"Go on, son, give him your question," said a long-necked man in a sleeveless T-shirt as he pushed his teenager out ahead of him.

The boy unsettled his shoulders. "What are all those, like, black dots all over the rocks?"

"Good eyes, son. Those are the black heads of bolts.

Everyone find them?"

Duane eyed his group. Of course he saw them. Ever since he could remember he'd had what Mama'd called an eye for noticing.

"Well, let me explain what you don't see," the guide said. "Each one is seventy-five feet long, that's right—like a mesh of steel needles, knitting these cliffs together. Another trick of the trade, to hold back the force of all this water."

Pushing for a cave-in? What about sabotage, Duane wondered. Don't suppose that's part of the guided prattle.

The Monkey Wrench gang old Ed Abbey made famous had planned on acting like suicide terrorists, loading up houseboats with explosives and driving them toward the dam. But, of course, since 9/11 and the attack on the Twin Towers, there were guards and cameras and special boat barriers at water level.

Duane had thought long and hard about making the killing of Lee seem like part of a horrific accident. Why not the newspaper headline:

FEDERAL DAM SABOTAGED
KILLS NEXT PRESIDENT

But, no, that'd miss some of the whole point of the killings because, hell, he planned to take direct credit.

The guide mustered his group forward. "True story: we almost lost the dam once to Mother Nature. Happened the year way too much snow fell in the Rocky Mountains."

A shrill cry from a hawk on the hunt caused Duane to look up.

"Just too much water coming at us. Engineers here responded with a full-bore release, spillways as wide as they go, water jets on maximum high. The emergency plan was in full operation."

"What happened?"

"It was real obvious we were in for big, big trouble when the water shooting out downstream suddenly turned bright red."

"Red?" The father upstaged his son. "You mean the rock was giving way?"

"Exactly. These red cliffs—this is all Navajo Sandstone." The guide flagged his arm. "Sandstone's friable, made up of grains, and it was experiencing way too much pressure to hold. The cliffs actually started to dissolve."

"Wow, what would have happened?"

Duane looked around him. Did these people have no imagination?

The guide threw his arms up over his head. "Whoosh! Boatmen like to say, 'If this dam gives way it'll be a twenty second ride to Los Angeles'."

The once-mighty, now castrated. That was the real story.

Duane took one last look downstream beyond the concrete plug and focused his eyes to the very bottom where the Colorado River, stripped of all freedom and forced to submit to the greater glory of electricity, bubbled up in boils of frustration.

Money talks. Isn't that what Mama used to always say? The river works, the river pays.

"Sir? Keep up with us, sir."

Me? Shit.

Duane crossed over to catch up with his group, all now peering at the sullen water upstream from the concrete thumb. Far as the eye could see, nothing but silenced water, waiting its turn at the dam. The river had gone from wild and free to a captured stiff.

"If you all will now follow me down into the dam itself.

This way, everyone."

Duane was thinking ahead already about the elevator descent into the bowels of the dam and how he'd maneuver himself close to the sweet-smelling woman in the flower dress, maybe press against her thigh in the elevator shaft.

"Oh, let's stop here just a moment." The guide turned to anchor his troupe.

"Technically, what you're seeing upstream from the dam is the Colorado River, but we call it Lake Powell. A dam-created lake."

Didn't look so much like a lake, Duane thought. Looked artificial, this bathtub-lake with a white ring of scum around it.

"Seems to go on and on, doesn't it, hon? How big is it?"

"Let me ask you a question," the guide said. "Which would you guess is longer, the coastline from Canada to Mexico or the shoreline of Lake Powell?"

"Lake Powell? Really? Hear that, hon?"

Interesting how some people were always the talkers and some people were never the talkers. Mama was definitely the talker in his relations.

"Yes, ma'am, just to fill Lake Powell took the Colorado River seventeen years."

Duane scanned the freaky flatwater spreading its skinny fingers across the desert. He loved the desert. Clean, that's what the desert was. Clean and forthcoming. Said one thing and meant it.

"Time to load the elevator."

Duane hung back until the scented woman stepped in front of him and then he made his move, quick, let out a little laugh when people said to move back and make more room. He pressed his thigh against the thin flowers of her dress and enjoyed the ride, all five hundred twenty-eight feet of vertical drop.

From deep inside the concrete, they exited the elevator and poured into a cavernous room lit eerily in hospital green fluorescence. The entire cavern was as uncluttered as a movie set for something sci-fi. His flock, following the guide, formed a tight circle around a yellow yolk-looking thing, perfectly round, with a gleaming red head like a perky robot.

The high-pitched hum was starting to drive him crazy. Duane half-heard the guide explain penstocks and turbines. He'd read somewhere in the exhibit room how inside there were miles and miles of tunnels that let inspectors do their job of close-inspecting the bowels. An entry point for sabotage, open to the right man, but he wasn't that man. No way they'd be hiring felons.

"Eight tunnels channel the river into this very room where every minute of every day..." The guide's drone deepened. "One-point-three million gallons flush through each penstock to flow against the blades of these reaction turbines.

"The river's push turns the shafts that connect to the rotating generators. Acre-feet of water in, kilowatts of electricity out."

"Out here in the desert? Seems too empty for all this." The woman in the flowered dress surprised him with her soft sweet voice. "Where does so much electricity go?"

"Power goes west," the guide said. "A five-state grid."

Follows the money, lady, Duane wanted to say.

"My son was wondering, sir, if the river never stops flowing, how do you store the electricity?"

"We can't, son, trying to hold electricity's about as easy as holding an ice cream cone on a hot day. All of our electricity rides out of here on transmission lines."

Duane had a question. *What if you sabotaged the electrical output? How long could you gum up the operation?* But not really the payback he was after.

The way Mama'd always explained their family history, his people had been tricked into laying down their arms and walking out to "safety," women and children first, men following.

He really did like his newest plan better. Smacked of more appropriate vengeance.

How did that saying go? *An eye for an eye and pretty soon we're all blind.*

Yeah, he liked that.

Pretty soon, Lee, we're all blind. Soon as the brain goes dead.

Lilli Chischilly drove north in too much of a hurry, toward Jerome, toward Roof Butte, over a shortcut through volcanically pierced land: *Tsézhiin'íí'áhi*, Black Rocks Protruding Up. She tried to divert the unquiet in her mind by concentrating on her driving and pushed on the sticky accelerator, forcing a side-slip over dirt rutted as corduroy.

She was never sure how to run these washboard roads. High speed kissed the tops of the ridges, avoiding the troughs, but put the tires out of touch with the track and her steering deteriorated. Low speed hugged the contours, vibrating her teeth. She could ride the ripples only so long. There had to be a better way, something between bobble and bounce. She was looking for that indefinable zone of control.

She tried loosening her grip on the steering but the memory of Jerome's odd detachment sat fat and unsettled in her mind. She remembered especially the combination of dark and cold in his voice. When she'd spotted Bilgehe from the air, he'd registered no surprise, just banked the plane and raised his camera to frame the image. As if the body somehow embellished the landscape.

Now, as if her mind was driven by the axle, she kept rolling the question around in her head, trying to second guess what had been done with the body. The law was explicit. You could embalm, bury, or refrigerate, so long as you made your decision within twenty-four hours of death. She imagined Bilgehe, unsettled in police limbo, inside a refrigerated stainless steel drawer in the MI's lab.

Well, there it was, Jerome's aunt's old place. She hadn't been here in years. Didn't look like much of anyone had been here in a very long time.

But Jerome's truck and trailer gave him away. She got out of the Dodge and walked toward the old house. The warmth of the sun overhead flooded down the middle of her back.

She didn't dare play her hand too early. She needed to act smart. When it came to court, to exercising *bilagáana* words of the law, she could be persuasive, but she wasn't at all certain about selling her plan to Jerome.

She stepped up onto a stoop improvised from an overturned crate.

Only the deepest cracks in the closed door in front of her face still held any trace of blue paint. She shifted her weight. How long should she wait? Perhaps she should knock, L.A.-style. Before she could firmly decide, the door opened. She must be insane. How did she imagine talking Jerome into coming with her and this next President-of-the-United-States?

"Lilli, hi. Heard your car. Guess I lost track of time. I'm not ready."

She'd always loved the way Jerome's smile revealed teeth so flush with alignment. What was wrong with her? He seemed in high spirits. Why was her mind adamant that something was queer and very wrong with him?

"Still working on something—come on in."

Lilli stepped inside. The adult Jerome in an adult home.

It felt odd to be all alone with him in such an empty house. As if they'd stepped into their future.

She was there to take him off to a Shoe Game and get him to mix with people, at least that was her excuse for coming by to pick him up. Tonight the Shoe Game would attract scads of people from miles around and she'd told him she'd re-introduce him to folks he once knew, help ease him back, try to jump-start his return home.

"Follow me," he said. "Almost have something ready."

She followed him down a narrow hallway toward the increasingly acrid smell of ammonia, and then into a tight bathroom. He closed the door behind them, pulling across the door frame some sort of jerrybuilt drape. He flipped off the light and immediately the room was bathed in an eerie red.

"Nothing fancy. Shower bottom works as an adequate enough wet lab."

In the darkness the faint red light made his face look strangely flat. She knelt beside him, the hard wooden floor pressing into her shins. The shower floor was full of stoppered bottles and trays.

"Want you to have a souvenir." He slipped a sheet of shiny paper out of a box and into a tray of liquid.

When was she going to make her move, broach the subject, convince Jerome to give up five nights and six days and come with her and Lee?

"Series of chemical baths."

With a pair of tongs, he slid the exposed paper through

a series of flat trays as she watched an image create itself.

What was wrong with Jerome?

The unmistakably eerie shapes of the Hoodoos appeared, and then the distinctly familiar shape of a man on his back. She tried to imagine Jerome's intentions. No way he could believe she'd want a souvenir like this. No, whatever this was about, it was being driven by something in Jerome's mind.

Jerome rose from his knees and clipped the wet image to a line stretched between the walls. She pushed herself up. She hadn't said anything in response to his "souvenir" and she noticed how he hadn't said a word, either.

He clicked off the safety light and opened the door.

"I've more to show you."

Maybe, like her, this Bilgehe had been a passenger in Jerome's plane, but slipped out of the safety harness. Jerome might have tried to catch him and failed. *Poor try, Lilli.* Might explain how Bilgehe got into the Hoodoos, as if dropped from the sky. Not how he got his mouth full.

She followed him into a bedroom with a hastily thrown blanket spread across a bed. On its empty surface, Jerome laid out a sequence of black-and-white enlargements.

"A series," he said.

Meaning, she supposed, they were ordered according to some fashion, maybe a place or a timeline? The first image captured a swell in the surface of a landscape familiar to her, the way it was dotted with a sea of sagebrush. The geometry of the image was crisp, almost hypnotic. From the sky you could clearly see how each plant controlled the water, because each bush was rimmed in a perfect circle of bare sand.

In the second enlargement, Jerome had caught the odd overhead image of a small girl in the act of running. Then, in the next image, the girl was beyond the middle of the frame and in an unbroken chain, trailing behind her, lay her footprints in the sand. Lilli moved closer to the bed. She tended to look at things not straight on but with her neck turned slightly, to the left. It was years into being an adult before she ever figured out why. Her eyes had two different focal lengths, so when she cocked her head to the left she moved her left eye back, placing her right eye a twist closer.

She looked up at him, standing over her.

"You showed me a photo of this girl, didn't you? That day we drove out with your plane—what did you call her?"

"What?"

"You had a special name."

"The Upside-Down-Girl?"

"That was it—yes." His Upside-Down Girl.

He placed several more images on the bed, the girl turning to look behind her. The girl doing a headstand with her legs in the air.

"One more, of the White House."

She thought he meant D.C. She expected to see the fence in the foreground of the two-story residence of the President of the United States. Instead he'd taken her north of Window Rock, closer to Chinle, down deep into Canyon de Chelly where, incandescent in reflected light, lay the ancient ruin. He'd meant their White House, *Kin níí'na'igaih*, the House of the Horizontal White, gleaming from a black cleft in an enormous sheeting of cliff, the place where the Navajos had first seen the dance of alternating male and female.

What could this possibly mean? Jerome was silent for so long Lilli gave up looking at the image and tried looking at him instead. He was a deeply wounded man, she understood that, but what was going on?

"This is part of the same series?" she said, finally.

"You're a professional, a mouth-piece who uses words." He didn't make eye contact.

She held silent.

"I use wordless images," he finally said.

Brilliantly executed, she wanted to say, but something about the tightness in his voice made her keep quiet.

He said nothing more.

"Try me—try me with words, Jerome. What's going on?"

"OK. You tell me the hard truth." His face looked harsh, or shameful, or cruel, or maybe it was just a momentary thing. "Tell me: do you think I'm still Navajo?"

"What? Of course you're still Navajo. What are you talking about?" She needed to stay as calm as the empty bed between them.

"I don't feel right. I came home but I feel, I don't know, strange—*Ana'í*."

"Alien? You're not an Alien, Jerome."

Did he really believe he wasn't Navajo any longer, that L.A. had washed it out of him? She tried to think of something to say. Not *Ana'í*.

"How about we agree you're *Anahjí'*?"

"What?"

A single word, almost as succinct as your wordless images, she thought.

"*Anahjí*? In one word it means someone-who-is-among-us-again but separated-by-a-barrier."

How could it be otherwise? Jerome living in L.A., never coming home until now? The barrier of separation had grown thick.

"Describing you, Jerome, I'd say it means 'Navajo Interrupted'."

"Navajo Interrupted, huh? Unlike you, right? You're still here. You're Navajo Uninterrupted—unbroken, whole?"

Maybe she shouldn't have given him the word, maybe she shouldn't have answered him at all, or maybe she needed to soften her words, but she watched the way he held his face rigid, and she let the comparison stand.

"Well, Ms. Navajo Uninterrupted, let's see how clued-up a Navajo you really are. You figure it out."

He turned his back on her and gathered his photographs, removing them from the bed.

Figure out what, Jerome? Why can't you go ahead and use words? But she clearly heard him hiss one short Navajo word. "*Nila*." He had to know she'd heard him.

It's up to you. That was *nila*, the Navajo imperative.

He abruptly turned back around and faced her. His eyes were cold.

"Give up on me, Lilli. It's your safest bet."

Safest bet? Come on, Jerome, she wanted to say: it's me and you. We don't do safe bets. But she held her tongue. People have their dark sides. She tried to read his eyes. Was it shame that made Jerome so dangerous to himself?

"No, you know what?" Jerome's voice suddenly seemed animated. "I want you to come with me. Yeah, I need you to come with me. Let's go find that girl."

"Who? The Upside-Down Girl?"

"Definitely."

"We're going back up in your plane?"

"No, we can take the Dodge. Just a detour on the way to this Shoe Game of yours."

At least he hadn't changed his mind about tonight. But when was she going to ask what she'd come here to ask? Before he got too carried away on a goose chase after some little girl he'd seen only from the sky, she'd better make a stab at it.

"Jerome? I need...I need to ask you...well, have you been watching the presidential campaign?"

"That mess that came to Window Rock?"

"How this presidential contender Lee says he's going to run the Colorado River?"

"Publicity stunt, yeah, all over the news."

"I want..." *Come on, don't hesitate.* "I want the two of us to go with him."

"Go with what, this Lee? You nuts?"

Maybe she was trying to be alone with Jerome. Maybe that's all that was happening. She wanted to be alone with him.

"Maybe, but I'm also serious."

"Seriously nuts—oh yeah, I know that look." Jerome's eyes narrowed. "I don't believe it. You're actually going with this clown?"

"Come with me."

"Didn't realize you'd become so influential, played such high stake games."

"Me? I'm not."

"You're not what?"

"Come on, Jerome. Think of the light, think of the light on your film. You'll never get an opportunity like this, chance of a lifetime to be so alone."

"Alone? That man travels in a throng."

"Not this trip, there'll be no one else in the canyon. Security risk. The whole place will be closed down for him."

"I don't get it, Lilli. This some part of your job?"

She thought about Bitsoi's blindside. "Apparently."

"You're insane. And you want me to make the same mistake?"

Jerome turned from her and stared out the small bedroom window that framed a struggling piñon. Beside it, she could see the Dodge.

"From the bottom up, Jerome. The opposite of being airborne. The most spectacular canyon on earth. Imagine the light."

He turned from the window and smiled one of his goofy smiles. "It's a crazy idea. I mean, on the scale of extreme ideas, this is one of your best."

This Jerome she recognized.

"But don't you think you're hallucinating?"

"Just come with me."

"No way this Lee is going to give me a ticket. No way you're that persuasive."

"Wanna bet?"

"Are you a legend in your own mind? Not even the important Lilli Chischilly could sell that politician on giving me a seat."

No, he was right, she couldn't. That was entirely Bitsoi's problem. "Bitsoi will just have to tell this man we Navajo travel only in pairs."

Jennifer Kitchell

In his eighteenth-story hotel room window, Duane Fatt stood naked, surveying the Las Vegas strip below. Night bright as day. From his vantage point he could make out neatly lettered advice painted on the side of a brick building: "Life hurts. Jesus cares."

He entered the tiled bathroom, turned on the water and swirled the showerhead to full bore. He waited for the glass door of the stall to blank over with steam and then stepped in under the spray, planning to stay until the hotel ran out of hot water or his skin went raw.

He had money, and he had guns. Had as many and as good guns as money could buy, ever since he was old enough to understand they were nothing to skimp on. Money flowed to some types and they wasted it, but he had discipline there, and had a different sort of ideas. Didn't trust anyone else either, not to be in the know while they waited for him to get out. No, the money and the guns, just as he left them. Undisturbed.

Too dark tonight to go see the site that mattered so much to Mama. Which meant tomorrow morning—which meant he had the whole night to himself. Fully waterlogged, he toweled off, wiped the steam from the mirror and combed out his hair. Familiar jeans hung on the hook behind the bathroom door. He zipped and buckled his belt, and then he adjusted the alignment of his wallet.

He removed it and took another peek at the photo. He swore time slowed down whenever he examined her face. There was one thing Mama always said was due her and he'd give it to her.

He could still become a good son.

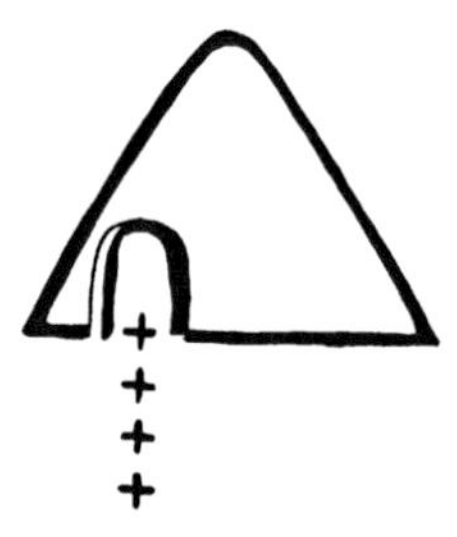

"Think we've missed it?" Even for the reservation, this was a bare pocket of land. The shocks of the Dodge took each bump and amplified them. In a defensive move, Lilli juked the wheels around the next major rut.

"Not yet," Jerome said.

Of course, he had no name. By way of evidence, he held only the photos in his lap. According to his sky coordinates, his Upside-Down-Girl lived off the western flank of the isolated spur growing larger on the horizon.

They passed a double-wide trailer house on a metal skirting. Passed a fading Pentecostal church sign. The cloud-free October sky filled the horizon with its thick blue. As she slowed for the sharp turn, Lilli saw another sign of *Hai* in the hides of the four horses standing close to the road, their coarsening winter coats giving their flanks a roughened look, the way teenagers spike smooth hair with gel.

She needed to bring Jerome forward from a sweet spot.

"Remember all that riding the two of us did in the back end of your dad's pickup? That one missing its tailgate?"

"Recall some heavy bouncing. Me having to grab onto you."

"No padding in a flatbed." The wind lifted her hair, blew bits of desert across the windshield. "Couple of kids with skinny butts."

"One of us seems to have rounded out," he said.

"Hey!"

Haze from the dust lined the road ahead of them, backlighting the strips of rabbitbrush that followed the ditch. In the low-angled light of late afternoon, its flowering tips glowed.

"Look at that. *Nizhóní,*" she said. Beautiful.

"Like you." He said the last two words so softly she might have imagined them.

"So, what do you need to get from this Upside-Down-Girl?" She figured Jerome needed a legal release, part of the business end of being a photographer.

"I want someone who speaks for the girl to, you know, give me their permission. Can you put together Navajo words that say that?"

"That function legally as a release statement? Sure."

Translation, though, was a funny game. She sometimes found it impossible to keep herself out of the way. Like when in the capacity of the HPD she took a deposition for a court proceeding, and the deponent had next to no English. She had trouble not helping the witness out, second-guessing what part of their answers to translate and what parts, given the twists of logic of *bilagáana* law, to let drop.

Not that it'd impress Jerome any, but she was licensed.

A bona fide Certified Interpreter between Navajo and English within the federal court system. You were expected to make exact translation of what was said, not to clean the words up, or dumb them down. But in her opinion those rules made a faulty assumption—that the two systems spoke the same "language" at a deeper level.

When she asked a question of a traditional Navajo speaker, she understood why he might begin his answer talking about an earlier world, and jet and abalone, and Air-Mist People and Five-Fingered People. Answers can stem from a set of beliefs as much as from a set of sensory observations.

"Hey, I think that's it. The turnoff." Jerome raised himself from the seat.

The rounded shape of a female hogan appeared maybe a half-mile away. Past the curve, an abandoned car with a shattered windshield sat on its rims. Any evidence of tires long gone.

"This must be it. Yeah, I'm sure. Pull over."

No secret they were here. In such flat land, their approach must have been quite visible.

She stopped the Dodge and turned off the engine. No people in sight, but there was evidence of habitation, a low mud oven, a stack of firewood, a galvanized wash basin. Jerome remembered to stay in the car. His fingers beat out a rhythm against the dashboard. They would need to wait until someone came out, because no polite Navajo approached another's doorway, unexpected.

"I've never done this before," Jerome said.

"What's that?"

"Deliberately photographed someone from the air."

Did he mean someone alive? Because what about Bilgehe, on his back in the Hoodoos?

"In L.A., sure I photographed people, all the time.

Studio shots. Those people knew they were getting their picture taken."

Was Jerome admitting that his swooping from above, so close to the ground with a camera in his hand, was a lot like snooping?

She suddenly sat up. A woman had appeared in the doorway of the hogan with a little girl, maybe six or seven years old, who now shadowed behind her as the woman approached them. Lilli slid out of her car door almost simultaneously with Jerome, the two of them on opposite sides of the Dodge.

"*Yá'át'ééh,*" he said.

The woman said nothing.

Lilli watched the woman, so plump in the face, stand perfectly still except for her fingers that smoothed the girl's hair that was parted off to one side and tied behind her ears. Both the woman and the girl wore flat tennis shoes, the woman's beneath a free-flowing skirt of purple flowers, the little girl's shoes the washed pink of a lamb's tongue. The child tucked her head against the woman's thick leg.

Jerome remembered his manners. He named the clan he was born to, *To'azoli,* Light-Water People. Following tradition, he named next the clan he was born for, *Dziltl'ahnii,* Near the Mountain People. Among these quiet people Jerome's voice seemed unnaturally loud.

Lilli caught herself watching him. Could he remake himself? He'd come back to the reservation, back to her. But what other act would it take?

"My name is Jerome Bah. This here is Lilli Chischilly."

Her turn. "I am Towering House clan," Lilli said. "Born for Bitter Water."

The woman squinted into the sun. "We are born to *Dilzhé'é.*"

Bird-Voice People.

"I saw you coming," the woman said. "Thought you was my sister coming to get us. I'm Melanie Naha. This is Asan, my niece."

Jerome started to explain he was a photographer and Lilli could see how the woman's face looked suspicious. Asan held a wad of white string between her small fingers. Maybe she could help the woman relax by playing with the girl. Lilli crouched down in front of her.

"What are you making?"

Asan bunched her shoulders up to her ears and tucked her head into the cavity as if to hide, but her fingers never stopped. She extended the string, moving it in and out of loops until a perfect shape lay stretched between her two small hands. *Hastiin Sik'ai'í*, Man With Legs Ajar.

Lilli used to love to create order from an apparent mess, making string figures that started from nothing but a limp tangle. Even now in the top drawer of her office desk she kept string. She got relief, moving her fingers in the preprogrammed ways she'd learned as a child, felt the small stirring of pleasure when she did it right and the figure appeared.

"Lilli? Help me out." Jerome's voice seemed at ease.

"Of course." She smiled at the little girl to excuse herself, and stood up and walked over to the Dodge.

Things seemed to be going well. Standing next to Melanie, Jerome held out the envelope holding his photos. "We can use this big hood as our table."

He was properly not inviting himself inside the hogan.

"Asan, go get you a clean shirt," the woman said. "You want to go to the Shoe Game."

"The Shoe Game, at Benally's?" Lilli asked. "Near Tsaile?" Not that far away. There would be easily a hundred people there tonight.

The woman nodded.

Lilli hadn't seen any sign of a serviceable vehicle. "We're going, too. You and Asan? Do you need a ride?"

"No, my sister and her kids, they coming to pick us up."

"Here." Jerome placed an enlargement in Melanie Naha's hands. She held the photo of her hogan, the way Jerome had caught it from the sky. The roof looked like a lid. Melanie seemed puzzled. Her eyes narrowed. She seemed to be asking, why he was showing her this picture?

"Let me see if I can help." Lilli pointed to the butte behind the hogan, and then she touched the shaded curve in the corner of the photo, and repeated herself. The woman turned around, then restudied the image.

"How did you do this?" the woman asked.

"From a sort of special airplane."

The woman turned again to the butte, then back to the hogan, then her eyes seemed to go inward. "What the bird sees."

"*Aoo'*." Exactly.

Jerome laid out four more photos that showed the hogan getting farther and farther away until it was out of the frame entirely. Then he pulled out another set of photos and placed them next in a new series on the hood of the Dodge. These were the images he'd just shown Lilli, at his aunt's place, of the girl, running. He laid down next what seemed to be his favorite, the image of the girl—his Upside-Down-Girl, Asan—standing on her head with her legs in the air.

The woman looked up at him, startled.

"You can speak for the girl? I need to ask for your permission," Jerome said.

Lilli watched his face. Something in the intensity of his eyes told her he knew he was making trouble.

"What?" The woman was clearly upset.

"I came to ask you—for your release," Jerome said.

"Get out of here. Who are you?" The woman spit out some words in Navajo and disappeared inside, behind a closed door.

"What'd she say?"

Lilli studied Jerome's face. She understood exactly the words Melanie Naha just spit out. But to Jerome she said, "I couldn't understand her."

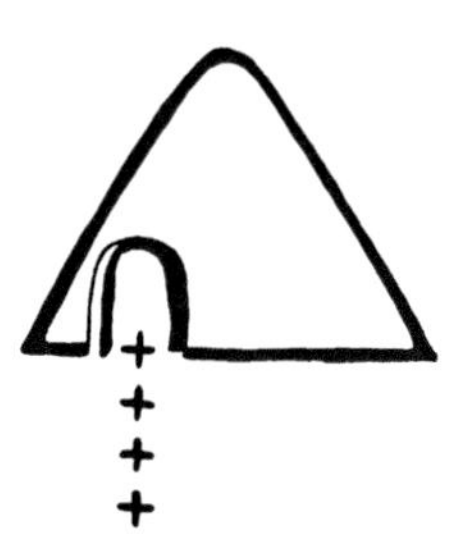

Based on the sprawl of vehicles spread around the Benally's, the Shoe Game had attracted a crowd.

"Maybe now you're old enough, Jerome, you'll stay awake," Lilli said. "Get the jokes we missed out on when we were kids."

As soon as the door opened, she felt the heat from the fire. "Can get a whole lot bawdy."

"That a promise?"

Jerome followed her in.

There had to be eighty, a hundred, people there tonight. There was pent-up demand. October launched the winter season when the prohibition against playing the game lifted. But admit it, she thought, you're worried about how he's going to behave.

"Hey, Lilli! So, who's your friend?" Pete Toadlena's

flattened moon face contrasted with Jerome's raised cheekbones and long straight nose.

"Come on, Pete. Look a little harder."

"I'm looking."

A barrel stove in the middle of the dirt floor had the place stoked dangerously hot, but the edges of the hogan were cold as night. *Hooghan*. The simpler spelling of "hogan" had slipped into English, probably because there was no true paraphrase, not in a single word. "Home," most non-Navajos would say, but *hooghan* was much more than home. *Hooghan* was about harmony, about the whole of everything Navajo.

"You don't recognize Jerome? It's Jerome Bah."

"Jerome? Jerome Bah, like when we were kids?"

This could be a huge mistake. She wanted tonight to work, for Jerome to feel comfortable with these people, to feel he was back home.

"Hey, it is! Hey, Jerome, where you been, man?" Pete Toadlena extended his hand and Jerome took it and held it.

"Been in Pueblo de Nuestra Señora, La Reina de Los Angeles de Porciuncula."

Jerome released the hand.

"Enormously precise about location now, isn't he?"

"Just like a good Navajo, Pete. Think he told you he's been living in L.A.," she said.

Nobody except Lilli had to know how all he had left of his L.A. wife and child was tucked away in his billfold.

She nudged him. "Come on, Jerome, don't be such a smartass." But she felt relieved. It was the old Jerome again. They were going to have a good time, she decided, and stay late.

"Gone so long, huh? Better put Jerome, yeah, definitely on the other team," Pete said. "Man probably forgot how to play."

"No way I forgot, not how to play the Shoe Game."

Lilli'd had the same concern and on the ride over she'd provided a refresher course, how One-Walking-Giant taught the People to play the game that decided whether the world would be a World of Lightness or Darkness. In that first game, Owl was the original cheater. Coyote, too, kept switching sides, trying to end up on whichever side won.

"Let me give you some advice, man." Pete held out his half-empty mug. "Better tank up on caffeine."

Oh, oh, trouble. She smelled the liquor first, just before she felt the harsh hand on her waist. The man—whoever he was—reeking of booze, shoved her aside, lurching unsteadily toward the hot stove. "Out of my way, *sha'áád*."

He'd slurred the insult, but it was clearly directed at her. Jerome's arm came up to stay him.

"Watch it, man."

But no one would tell a drunk to leave. The argument would go: he came, he watched the Shoe Game, maybe he was thinking of the Holy People. Maybe he needed to come.

She remembered the night Jerome's father came home drunk and refused to get out of his truck. He kept gunning the engine, louder and louder, until Jerome finally went outside to get his father to turn the engine off and come inside. Instead, Jerome's father went after him like live target practice, the engine all revved up, twisting his pickup in tighter and tighter circles, trying to run Jerome over. She wondered how moving the family to L.A. could have made things better.

Something smelled good. Lilli turned to look over her shoulder. Elreda Cly, wide as a mother-in-law, smiled back.

"So it's Jerome Bah, come home a man, huh? Well, don't you go and say you don't remember me."

With her head kerchief knotted tight beneath her chin, Elreda offered out a plate of roasted *achee*.

"Bet you craved this. Don't sell this in L.A."

"Sheep string?" Jerome lifted a chunk off Elreda's plate. "Definitely. Always crave *achee*."

Lilli took a piece of the offered origami intestine and chewed, savoring the crunch. To make *achee* was a commitment. You pushed the full intestine of the butchered sheep between your fingers and squeezed out whatever the sheep had eaten, and then you rinsed the snaking intestine until the long tubing was a pale pink rope, all squeaky clean and hollow. It took practice. You started the coil around your finger, rolled it nice and tight, slipping it off in a twist to make the final curl.

Elreda's husband came over to join them, an old man with skinny legs and too few teeth. He draped his arm over Jerome's shoulder.

"All grown up, huh? Look at you. Remember how your grandmother called the two of you?"

He pointed with his lips to include Lilli. "She called you both 'Two–in–One.' *Alkéé naa'aashii.*"

"That's right," Jerome said. "*Alkéé naa'aashii.*"

Lilli smiled. When she was a kid she'd thought it meant simply Two-in-One, that's all. Like twins. Now that she was older she knew more. She knew the word had a sacred twist. The Two-Who-Followed-One-Another.

When the Shoe Game finally started, Pete came over to rib Jerome, how he'd deliberately chosen the other team, the Side of the Day People.

"No cheating, hear?"

"What are you saying about my players?" Elreda kept the two of them with her and the People Who Travel at Night.

"Just trying to throw your concentration off," Pete said.

"What concentration?" Jerome was enjoying himself. "Game of blind chance."

Lilli hid behind the hanging blanket with Jerome and Elreda and the rest of their team, so the other team couldn't see what shoe they hid the ball in before they buried all four shoes, under a mound of dirt on the floor of the hogan.

The outcome was never transparent, not until the game was nearly over. With its stone ball and one hundred and two yucca leaves to keep score, the Shoe Game would drift back and forth for hours, probably ending in a tie, reinforcing the Navajo balance between opposites.

Something familiar caught Lilli's eye. She hadn't noticed Melanie Naha and Asan come in, but there they were. The little girl looked clean and neat, with a new shirt on. She still held her string. Lilli realized she hadn't thought through how Jerome might behave. Keep your distance, she wanted to warn him.

She gave Melanie and Jerome's Upside-Down-Girl wide berth. But she found herself turning her head, tracking the little girl, even while she pretended to be paying attention to the game.

Jerome left to relieve himself, outside. As the Shoe Game played on, Asan sat alone on the floor, playing with her string. Now she seemed to be looking hard for someone. Where had Melanie gone? Asan stood up without the string. Lilli saw it laying on the dirt floor. Asan started to sway.

"Ha!" Asan gave out a short cry and stiffened.

She looked peculiar. Her eyes were open, Lilli realized, but they didn't seem focused. Asan started smacking her lips and then the little girl's eyes rolled up into the top of her head and she looked toward Lilli with two open eyes, white as marbles.

What was going on?

Asan started to spasm in jerky shakes with her head snapped back, and then her arms and legs flexed out of control as if she were seizing. From the corner of her eye Lilli saw Jerome, talking to Melanie. They seemed to be arguing. They hadn't yet noticed Asan. Lilli lurched for the girl as she fell toward the stove, a fecal smell spreading thick along the floor. The girl started tearing at her clothes. No, Lilli wrapped herself around the girl, ignoring the stench, trying to shield her from the fire, and the stares.

"Iich'ahi'."

She heard the muttered word, the accusation, distinctly. She didn't turn around to see who'd said that. Moth Crazy, Moth Madness, that was *Iich'ahi'*.

The little girl was trembling.

Lilli heard the word whispered again.

Iich'ahi'.

Literally, the One-That-Goes-Into-The-Fire. She lifted the child's small weight. The girl's eyes stared vacantly up at the ceiling. Where had her mind disappeared?

Lilli started to push people aside.

Melanie Naha came toward her. Lilli started to hand the girl off. Now what? Why that look? She tried to read the woman's face. There was shame there, definitely. She saw hatred, too, fierce in the eyes and directed at her.

What had Jerome said? No, what had Jerome gone and *done*?

The shoulder of Tsaile Butte rose in the dark, blanketed in black ponderosa. A few hours ago Lilli had lifted the receiver saying, "Yes?"

The voice that responded sounded ancient. A man's voice. He knew English because his first few words to her were in English, but then he slipped into Navajo and stayed there. He told her where to find him. The voice seemed to know exactly who she was.

Now she opened her car door and stood in the silence. The bowl of night sky mimicked the reflecting surface color of the lake. Lilli's pupils widened slowly in the indigo velvet. Another car that had been hidden in the darkness emerged. Should she walk toward it? No, she'd stay close to the Dodge. She held her keys cupped in the palm of her hand.

She didn't have to stay, that's what she kept repeating

to herself. She'd hear him out. She could say no to whatever this was all about.

"So, Lilli Chischilly. Come closer."

Even at this distance, the voice could only be his.

"Find out who I am. Come closer."

A man rose up from squatting near the ground. "Come, find out. Do you know me? I think you do."

She stood still and didn't move away from the Dodge.

"No? Then I will come closer to you."

The man who approached her was rail skinny. A yellow flame suddenly appeared between his face and hers. He must have struck a long wooden match, the kind you use to light fires deep in the belly of a barrel stove.

And now everything about this made absolutely no sense.

"So. You do see who I am."

His eyes had the hoods of old age.

"Yes," she said.

He nodded toward her car. "You are alone with me?"

The call of a night bird bounced across the black water. An owl was out hunting.

"Yes."

But why would this man be here?

"So. Do you know of *Nááhwíílbiihí*, the Great Gambler?"

"*Aoo*," she said, staying in Navajo with him. Of course she did.

"Some say the Great Gambler is He-Who-Always-Wins, but that is wrong. The Great Gambler is He-Who-Wins-You."

His voice seemed so much stronger than the bony shoulders that held up his head, as if on a stalk.

"Tell me the truth. Does that nosy Bitsoi know you are here?"

Why would he be asking about Bitsoi? When you were

sick—in the head, in the body—your family made arrangements with the *Haatalí* for a curing ceremonial. Not the other way around. Never the other way around. The *Haatalí* did not come looking for you. Yet here he was. She should use his name.

"No, *Hosteen* Ahboah." She'd inserted the *Hosteen* to show respect.

"How about that man at the center of so much fuss? The television-man who wants to be president, this Lee?"

"No."

What was going on? Why would the oldest *Haatalí* of the Navajo people insist on meeting with her at all? And why here?

"The other *Haatalí*..." He closed his mouth. He seemed to be weighing something. "They told me no, not to tell you. I have been warned not to trust you. So, I have decided to act alone."

What did he mean by that? Why would the *Haatalí* even be talking about her? You had to experience the *Haatalí* in the healing ceremonials before you could ever understand the word. Most *bilagáana* called them "Singers," an impoverished translation. "Singer" in English described a crooner, someone in the choir, someone on a stage. Other *bilagáana* called them "Medicine Men."

"If I had your fancy kind of words I would talk to this television-man, this Mr. Lee myself. But he would see only the messenger, an old man with few teeth, talking bad English. Maybe a fool. Maybe a fake."

She'd made one very faulty assumption. This wasn't going to be about the coyotes, or Bilgehe's murder.

"So I have decided to risk trusting you. You are with the Historic Preservation Department?"

"The HPD? Yes."

"Perfect." He chuckled thinly from high in his throat.

"I have something needing preservation."

Ahboah beckoned her to follow as he walked toward the nose of the Dodge. He turned around in front of the Dodge and faced her.

"Take off your clothes."

"What?" Was this an old man's idea of a joke?

"Take off your shoes. Take off your shirt. Take off your long skirt."

Lilli didn't move.

"I am an old man."

Maybe he was old, maybe he was crazy. Maybe he wasn't really alone. She fingered the keys in her pocket.

Ahboah stood still, as if to waste no energy. "He's going to destroy it."

"What?"

"Lee. He's going to destroy it. You are going with him. Yes, I hear you are going with this Lee. And I want you to guide Lee to it."

Did this old man not understand? What difference would it make, that she had English words and legal words? Lee was no listener, he was a man with a golden mouth.

"I don't understand."

"No, not yet. Shh, no more talking." Ahboah's hooded eyes locked on hers.

He reached out his spiny hand and touched the top of her head and then the middle of her forehead.

"Take off your clothes."

She hesitated.

He nodded. He was a patient man.

She stepped out of her shoes.

He nodded again.

She fumbled with the top button of her blouse. He closed his eyes and she let her eyes dart behind him, trying to see farther into the darkness. She had trouble with the last button. Then the blouse fluttered open. She slid it off her bare shoulders and shivered in the night breeze.

He nodded again. His eyes were open. The waistband sat above her hips on a hoop of elastic. No buttons to manipulate, no zipper. She pressed a palm against each hip and grabbed a bunch of cloth. She didn't want to remove her skirt. It made no sense.

She pulled and the skirt stretched over her hips and then lay puddled around her stockinged feet. She lifted the skirt to her chest and he held out his arms. He took the skirt from her and placed it on the fallen blouse. He nodded again. She balanced on one foot and slid off a sock, then the other foot and the second sock. The ground beneath her bare feet felt hard and cold.

"Come. Now lie, belly down."

She realized the keys were in the pocket of her skirt. She started to lower herself into a squat, bending her knees.

"No, not in the dirt. Here." He patted the Dodge. "Get up on the hood of your car. Nice big hood you have here."

She slid face down over the hood. The metal under her belly radiated warmth from the engine heat.

"All the way. Get your belly to the middle."

Lilli scooted forward and felt her legs extend out behind her. She felt vulnerable. And ridiculous. And afraid. What if a headlight suddenly turned on and she wasn't alone with an old man? But he was already singing.

She felt his stiff hands first stroke the backs of her bare thighs, the cup of her knees, down the backs of her calves. The sharp point of his finger drew lines across the soles of her bare feet.

In the darkness, he pulled her legs apart, bending her knees, pushing her ankles together, then holding her feet and moving them up and down, over and over again, the voice calling out to Frog, calling to Child-Born-for-Water.

His piercing ancient voice carried in the darkness, calling out, too, to Water Woman, to Blue Female Slender Reed, to Turtle Man, to Toad Man, creating a nest of prayer. As if he was spinning her a cocoon of protection out of song, *Hosteen* Ahboah walked around the car hood, singing into the night out over the black water, pushing her elbows, then her wrists together, and again, and again. She felt herself balanced on her belly, moving like a water bug.

"Now. Follow me." Ahboah waited while she slid off the hood of the Dodge. Why couldn't she get dressed? She wrapped her arms around herself to try to stay warm. At the shoreline of the black night water, he stopped and nodded.

"Walk in beyond your knees."

"No." She looked at the water.

"Don't worry so much."

"I'm not going into the lake." She was going to grab her clothes, forget the shoes, get back to the car. But he started to sing, a different song. Why couldn't she bolt? The keys were on the shore, with the pile of her clothes. He was an old man. He wouldn't be able to stop her.

"Enter the water, now. I will come with you." He took her hand between his dry scaly fingers.

She stepped into the still black liquid that parted beneath her. She felt ooze between her toes. She had never, ever, been inside deep water. She knew rain that came rarely. She knew desert sweat baths where the heat of hot rocks drew water out of the skin. She knew going dirty.

"Deeper," he said. "Still, deeper. Now give me your other hand and lie down on the water, just like on the hood of the car. You are *Ch'al* and the Frog swims."

The water felt her weight. She was too heavy for it. She

didn't feel at all like Frog. She was going under. She felt panicky. He slid his hands under her belly and lifted her buoyant weight.

If she still had her skirt on, it would be floating around her head.

At least she had her clothes back. Ahboah was nimble in the dark, like an old goat. The trail down seemed lost. Lilli followed the descending back of his white shirt that night-glowed in the dark.

"Here we are."

Here? She sensed the way the night sky had disappeared, that something sat over their heads.

"Let me warm you, first. Here, hold the flashlight for me, until the fire catches."

In the restricted pool of light, she watched his fingers tender a pile of dry leaves until the tinder caught. He fed the fire, banking a tripod of small logs over the eager flames. As the fire grew, the surrounding wall of rock became visible.

"Do you know where you are? Watch, above."

She felt shaky, even next to the fire.

As the firelight swelled, a ceiling materialized, a rock roof held in place by painted crosses, hundreds of them, each a four-pointed star. She'd heard of such places, but never been under one before.

Star ceilings. An ancient protection. When the First World was dark, Black God made stars from bits of glittering mica to hold up the roof of the sky. In special places, her People painted four-pointed stars to hold up the roofs of rock.

Ahboah stirred the fire with a stick, sending a flush of sparks into the air.

"You do not need to know the meaning of what you will

show Lee. Maybe when you see it, you will understand it, maybe you will not. That will depend on who you really are."

She felt drawn into the fire as she listened to the changed tone of his rock-amplified voice.

"I will tell you enough. What I will tell you...this is why you will go down the river. I will tell you especially how to find it, when you are leading this Lee."

He used their language so there would be no mistakes of translation. The Grand Canyon was *Tsélché'ékooh.* She knew the truth of the first of what he told her, how when Carson came with his guns and soldiers, after the massacres and the scorched earth march, nearly all were captured and taken as prisoners to the concentration camp at Bosque Redondo. But not every single living Navajo. A few had managed to hide.

"Hardly any, but those few fled west, hiding out in the deeper canyons," Ahboah said. "They were sick with starvation, despair. They knew they didn't have much time."

Nothing would have been written down, not on paper, not in their language. Theirs was an oral culture, carried in the minds and the mouths of the People.

"Two *Haatalí,* too, escaped Carson. I know this. You are not supposed to know this," he said. "They hid something three times. But then came the earthen dam, the one the *bilagáana* call Navajo Dam on the San Juan River, that made Navajo Lake, that drowned what they'd hidden."

To name the drowning of the sacred lands of the Dinétah "Navajo Dam" and "Navajo Lake" had always made her think of the Germans naming Auschwitz something like "Jew Park."

"Then came the concrete, the one the *bilagáana* call Glen Canyon Dam, that made Lake Powell, that drowned the second hiding place."

Ahboah poked at the dying logs but already the fire was too low for her to see clearly into his eyes.

"There is one last place, still safe, deep down inside the Grand Canyon. The one hidden the best. This Lee..." Ahboah seemed to cackle. "They are a little afraid of you, you know. A Navajo lawyer lady who has already spoken in Washington."

Oh, she positively doubted that.

"But you need protection."

That she didn't doubt. She tried to imagine herself riding a wild river, coursing deeper and deeper into a canyon they said cut more than a mile into the earth. She imagined herself each night trying to fall asleep with a life jacket around her neck.

In the dark under the protective star ceiling, Ahboah began to sing them both into another world. In his hand, he held mirage stone powder to make her invisible. She knew somewhere in the singing he would rub it into the bottoms of her feet, then into her legs and her arms, into her chest and her back, into her face and the tops of her eyelids.

Lilli understood she would be taking her clothes off again.

Jennifer Kitchell

The place was empty and Duane Fatt liked it that way, being up here on Dan Sill Hill all alone, south of Enterprise, just a two hour zip up the interstate out of Vegas. This was as close as he'd felt physically to Mama in a long, long time. He'd heard Mama tell the story about this exact place on Dan Sill Hill so many times he must've thought she'd made it up. A bedtime story for two little boys with big ears.

He opened the bottle of beer still cold from the convenience store and tossed the twist-off cap to the brush, scaring up a scrub jay that got noisy before it circled and flew off down toward Magotsu Creek.

"You boys know your seed won't never be right," she used to say to him and his brother, even though it wasn't clear to him for years what "seed" meant.

"Just like my seed ain't never been right. Not till

someone revenges them people that wronged us."

Mama always believed she came from the seed of one of the children the Mormons had spared, one of the infants or little ones too young to talk, spared the death those wicked people'd bestowed on all the others.

"Sure," Mama said, "them little ones didn't have the words to witness, but they seen. Didn't nobody think of that, how those poor baby eyes had to see their mamas and daddies and family all killed?"

Then when he got older, Mama took to bringing him and his brother here on pilgrimages to the hill where you could see how it all happened, all spread out below you. The killing landscape.

"Memory picnics," Mama used to call them. She'd point out exactly where her people had come into the valley of the Magotsu, camped there, fallen under siege, made a big mistake surrendering to a lie, then marched with their so-called "new saviors" to their own blood bath.

Well, Mama must be going practically crazy since for months the headlines everywhere on the newsstands, the TV, were all "Senator Lee" this and "Presidential Front-Runner Lee" that.

The senator and his family—since the blood bath—yes, they'd done real well. In fact, yesterday Duane watched Lee being interviewed on the TV, watched as he traced his lineage proudly back to a unique spot on the map, Lee's Ferry, named in honor of John D. Lee. But John D. Lee had been the brains behind the blood bath. What kind of a country has heroes like that?

'Course nobody except a few stragglers ever made it off the tourist circuit up here to Dan Sill Hill overlooking Mountain Meadows, to connect this John D. Lee of Lee's Ferry fame with the massacre that had changed the fortunes of Mama's family forever. 'Cause Mama's family had never made it to their promised land.

Duane squatted down on the heels of his boots. He preferred to act, no matter the cost. Point was, now he'd like to show Mama how he'd been paying attention.

Mama would always point out the details of geography first, how behind Magotsu Creek, beyond the soft rounded mountains, began the southern edge of the Escalante Desert, the direction from where her people had come, heading west. The odyssey of her people interrupted by a massacre the Mormons called their "Blood Atonement."

The airplanes into the Twin Towers in New York City didn't invent nothing new, except for the equipment.

Duane straightened up to walk and felt his left knee tighten. Along the path leading to the back side of Dan Sill Hill, a bronze sign with white lettering reflected in the noon heat. He stopped to see what all the scratch marks were about and favored the knee. Someone had obviously used the point of a knife to edit, and now scratches crossed out some words nearly completely but underlined others. Duane read beneath the scratches, half-aloud to himself and the chattering scrub jay.

"This Iron County Militia consisted of Latter-day Saints (Mormons)" – now it was heavy vandalism with lots of scratch marks trying to obliterate the next words – *"acting on orders from their local religious leaders."*

By contrast, the next few lines were underlined for emphasis: *"Complex animosities and political issues intertwined with religious belief motivated the Mormons, but the exact causes and circumstances fostering the sad events that ensued over the next five days at Mountain Meadows"* – the rest of the sentence was underlined, too – *"still defy any clear or simple explanation."*

He could hear the wind talking to him. He could hear voices. Duane stopped reading for a minute until the sounds quieted down in his head.

He started to read again: *"Then late Friday afternoon, September 11th..."*

Had it really been September eleventh? 9/11? So it was.

"The emigrants were persuaded to give up their weapons and leave their corralled wagons in exchange for a promise of safe passage."

Just like Mama said, every time she told him the story.

"Under heavy guard, they made their way out of the encirclement. When they were all out of the corral and some of them more than a mile up the valley, they were suddenly and without warning attacked by their supposed benefactors... At least 120 souls died in what became known as the Mountain Meadows Massacre... Seventeen children under the age of seven survived."

Well, that must have been Mama's kin.

Duane tipped his head back to let the beer fill his throat till the overflow started to dribble out of the corners of his mouth, then he swallowed hard. Standing up here on the hill, the land spreading out beneath him looked soft and inviting, the encircled valley, its creek of fresh water running through. Not much traffic. Tourists, heading between Vegas and Zion National Park or Salt Lake City, kept to Interstate-15 and rarely came this way.

Duane moved toward two silver pipes, hollow and open, set up like those binoculars at the ocean where you drop a quarter in and try to spot the sleeping seals. He squatted his tall frame down to a more average height and peered through the short pipe on the left. The cement held the pipe in place, in order to center the eye on where Mama's people had made their camp, the place where they'd fought under siege for days and days until they fell finally for Mr. John D. Lee's trick.

Then Duane stretched himself up and went over to the second sighting pipe. He bent low enough to line up his dominant eye. He let it rest where the pipe aimed, on the precise spot where Mama's people had taken the cruel surprise. Just like looking through to a bloody bullseye.

He took the last swig of beer, swished it around, felt the foam go down. Such a quiet place. He could hear that scrub jay still belting its heart out.

Duane went around next to the monument of names. He sucked on his finger to get it real wet and then traced the wetness over some of the lettering chiseled into the flecked granite. Helped bring out the names. Pleasant and Amilda, Eliza, Solomon. Now there was a name: America Jane. There were way too many names, and each name showed the age of the person killed, too. Just look at all those children.

Duane swung the beer bottle over his head to give it a little punch and sent it out sailing over the scrub oak. Not much of a picnic, Mama. But he wasn't ready to leave, not quite yet, wanted to refresh all the details, get the picture sharp and raw in his head.

See, he had a new opportunity. He was going to erect something even more prominent in the public eye than this forsaken spot, something that would sear into the memory of people's minds for a very long time. Make the books, too. You murder someone—a husband, a wife, a stranger—it didn't matter, it might only make the local news. But you murder this hot-shot presidential contender Lee—and his wife, and his children, and anyone else fool enough to be with him on the river—and you make all the news.

Mama would be sure to hear.

One more night before Lee put in at Lee's Ferry on the Colorado River, with all the news media in tow. Having trouble finding sleep in the motel bed, Duane sat up and opened the pages of his copy of Carleton's honest-to-God official Report recorded by Congress of the massacre of Mama's people. He knew the story by heart but it was always good to read the details again, just to sharpen the edge. The part he liked best was how the Mormons took time out from the killing to go on up to Hamblin's house, have something to eat. The people they were killing weren't going anywhere.

He loved the signature line: *J.H. Carleton, Brevet Major, U.S. Army, Captain, First Dragoons.*

Duane traced with his finger down to the part in Carleton's report about the wagons. As he read he could almost make them out in his mind, below him in the soft valley he'd visited that afternoon.

> *Dr. Brewer, US Army... says the train consisted of, say, forty wagons... about forty heads of families; many women, some unmarried, and many children... They were well dressed; were quiet, orderly, genteel; had fine stock; had three carriages along... this was one of the finest trains that had been seen to cross the plains...*
>
> *The emigrants had nearly nine hundred head of fine cattle, many horses and mules, and one stallion valued at two thousand dollars. That they had a great deal of ready money besides. All this the Mormons at Salt Lake City saw as the train came on...*
>
> *Here, opportunely, was a rich train of emigrants – American Gentiles – that is, the most obnoxious kind of Gentiles...*
>
> *The train of emigrants proceeding southward from Fillmore toward the Mountain Meadows are next seen...by a Mr. Jacob Hamblin,*

a leading Mormon, who... lives in the summer time, at the Mountain Meadows. I here give what he said, and which I wrote down,sentence by sentence, as he related it...

"I asked them how many men they had... They said they had between forty and fifty." 'That would do to tie to,' I told them... that the Mountain Meadows was the best place to recruit their animals before they entered upon the desert."

Duane moved on with his reading to the part that talked about how when the killing was going on, some of the men took rest breaks, pitched a little horseshoe quoits. You know, between the murdering.

There was time enough for some to go up to Hamblin's house for refreshments. No danger of the emigrants getting away. It was all safe in that quarter. "There is time enough for us to have a 'quiet' game of quoits. The other boys will take care of matters down there."

And then there was the first trick, that didn't go far enough, the painting themselves up to look like Indians, rather than Mormons.

Jackson says they were sixty Mormons led by Bishop John D. Lee... That they were all painted and disguised as Indians... That this painting and disguising was done at a spring in a cañon about a mile north east of the spring where the emigrants were encamped... The Mormons say the emigrants fought "like lions."

Good on Mama's people.

...and that they saw they could not whip them by any fair fighting. After some days fighting, the Mormons had a council among themselves to arrange a plan to destroy the emigrants. They concluded finally, that they could send some few down and pretend to be friends and try and get the emigrants to surrender.

Duane leaned back against the headboard of the motel bed. Would he have fallen for such a cheap trick?

John D. Lee and three or four others, head men... had their paint washed off, and dressing in their usual dress, took their wagons and drove down towards the emigrant's corral... The emigrants sent out a little girl towards them. She was dressed in white. Had a white handkerchief in her hand which she waved in token of peace...

They talked with the emigrants an hour, or an hour and a half, and told them that the Indians were hostile, and that if they gave up their arms, it would show that they did not want to fight; and if they, the emigrants would do this, they would pilot them back to the settlements... Finally the emigrants agreed to these terms, and delivered up their arms to the Mormons with whom they had counselled. The women and children then started back towards Hamblin's house, the men following... Higby, who had been one of those who had inveigled the emigrants from their defenses, himself gave the signal to fire, when a volley was poured in from each side, and the butchery commenced and was continued until it was consummated.

This was one of Duane's favorite places in the report, where it talked about what a kind soul Mrs. Hamblin was.

> *Mrs. Hamblin is a simple minded person of about forty-five and evidently looks with the eyes of her husband at everything. She may really have been taught by the Mormons to believe it is no great sin to kill Gentiles and enjoy their property. Of the shooting of the emigrants, which she had herself heard, and knew at the time what was going on, she seemed to speak without a shudder, or any very great feeling; but when she told of the seventeen orphan children who were brought by such a crowd to her own house of one small room there in the darkness of night, two of the children cruelly mangled and the most of them with their parents blood still wet upon their clothes, and all of them shrieking with terror and grief and anguish her own mother heart was touched. She at least deserves kind consideration for her care and nourishment of the three sisters; and for all she did for the little girl, "about one year old who had been shot through one of her arms, below the elbow, by a large ball, breaking both bones and cutting the arm half off."*

He liked, too, to read about the wolves.

> *The scene of the massacre... was horrible to look upon. Women's hair in detached locks and in masses, hung to the sage bushes and was strewn over the ground... Parts of little children's dresses and of female costume dangled from the shrubbery or lay scattered about.*

There were doubtless atrocious episodes connected with the massacre of the women which will never be known. Mr. Rodgers, the Deputy Marshal, told me that Bishop John D. Lee is said to have taken a beautiful young lady away to a secluded spot. There she implored him for more than life. She too was found dead. Her throat had been cut from ear to ear.

Tender mercies were not taken.

Some of the women had their underclothes left... My own opinion is that the remains were not buried at all until after they had been dismembered by the wolves and the flesh stripped from the bones; and then only such bones were buried as lay scattered along nearest the road.

The wolves had dug open the heaps, dragged out the bodies, and were then tearing the flesh from them. I counted nineteen wolves....

The property was brought to Cedar City and sold at Public Auction... The clothing stripped from the corpses, bloody and with bits of flesh in it, shredded by the bullets from the persons of the poor creatures who wore it, was placed in the cellar of the Tything office...

And Duane liked to read next about what the Major did about it.

I gathered many of the disjointed bones... I buried in a grave...around and above this grave I caused to be built... a rude monument... surmounted by a cross hewn from red cedar wood... On the

> *transverse side of the cross, facing towards the north, is an inscription carved deeply in the wood: Vengeance is mine! I will repay, saith the Lord.*

And then he read again the way the Captain ended his report of the whole butchering affair to Congress: *Signed, James Henry Carleton, Brevet Major, USA, Captain to the First Dragoons.*

No, vengeance is *mine,* said Duane Fatt. *I* will repay.

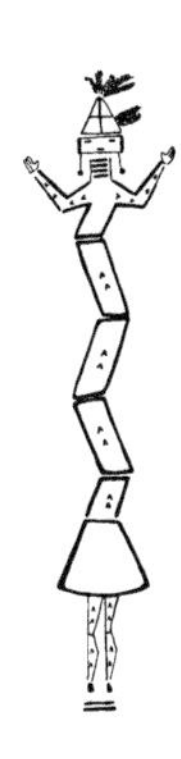

What seemed impossible was about to begin. But first Lee's hustlers and handlers apparently had something subtle, like Julius Caesar's ride into Rome in mind, his star-studded campaign bus the imperial chariot, because Lilli had received her directive. Launch on the river at noon. That was the official timetable. But a photo session here first, at the dam, and then they would all, excepting Jerome, ride together in the campaign chariot to Lee's Ferry where the media waited for Lee in a swarming knot.

Lilli pressed her arms in tight to her belly to smother her jitters, trying not to think about how she was going to travel for days on an artery of water, and to corral her loose shirt from becoming a kite in the updraft induced by the concrete waterfall that was Glen Canyon Dam.

To settle her nerves she looked out from the height of

the dam's observation deck to the fixed horizon, toward the familiar shape of *Naatsis'áán,* Head of Earth, rising fully rounded as a woman's breast. John Wesley Powell, the first *bilagáana* down the Colorado River, restamped their landscape, titling their sacred mountain after a deserter from his own expedition. Mercifully, his tag never stuck. On *bilagáana* maps this hemispherical peak still appeared as Navajo Mountain.

Downwind, uniquely visible even to the orbital cameras in outer space, a piece of the modern world revealed itself. Another misnomer. Rising vertically in the wilderness from three parallel emission towers was the ever-present white spume of steam and sulfur dioxide of the Navajo Generating Station, "Navajo" in name only. The power station was run by and for the Los Angeles Department of Water and Power, Tucson Electric, the Phoenix Project, and Nevada Power. Whenever the high sky was motionless, the spume of exhaust rose in a dazzling white plume, taking on the trajectory of a narrow-necked mushroom cloud.

She watched the campaign bus execute a wide swing into the dam's parking arena. Can't keep dawdling. Time to commit to one plan or another.

Relax, she told herself, they're going to issue you a life jacket. No, she had a better idea. There was still time to sneak off, grab Jerome, and flee.

Trying to make her way to the door of Lee's bus, Lilli circumnavigated its aluminum shell and felt the heat of the engine running. Even in park, the Lee presidential chariot painted in curving stripes of red and white all speckled with blue stars gave the illusion of motion.

As she passed, a conversation high above her head carried out a window of the bus.

"What's holding up my speech?"

Lilli glanced up above her head at the row of lozenge-like windows perforating the bus. She certainly knew who that was. Lee's voice dripped thick, a liquid baritone, designed to address a crowd. Just like a *bilagáana,* she thought, to run the air-conditioning full bore and then keep the windows open.

She found the only door, shut tight and without a handle.

"Where's that woman?"

"The Indian?"

The other voice was much higher pitched and traveled in the nose.

"Yeah, the Indian," Lee said. "The little Navajo lady."

"She has a name: Lilli Chischilly. You be nice."

"She can't come alone? How the hell did we end up with two Navajos?"

Lee pronounced the plural "ho": two Nava-*ho*. A native speaker would say "hose," she thought, two Nava-*hose*.

"Quid pro quo. We wanted her, she wanted him."

"Let's hope he's not a boyfriend."

"You said you'd be nice."

"I especially don't want a loose cannon along with a full clip of film."

"Won't happen. He's agreed to our rules. No photos of you, no photos of the family—hell, no photos of me."

So, they'd had their own conversation with Jerome. Well, in a very short time, she'd know. Because she couldn't stop worrying about whether Jerome would really be there, waiting for her at Lee's Ferry. All she knew for sure about Jerome was that he'd received a bona fide press credential, something to get him past the roadblock.

"All right, fill me in a little deeper," Lee said. "This Indian woman?"

"Lilli Chischilly. She has a name—try to remember to use it."

"She came recommended by our people?"

"Absolutely. She's the one we want. She's fluent in both cultures, and she's photogenic."

"Knows how to work a deal, though, right?" Lee said.

"Use your charm. You've got six days with the woman."

Lilli smiled. Six days or sixty, did Lee really think he could "handle" her?

"Are we paying her?"

"Think we should? Listen, I could offer her a retainer."

"No," Lee said. "Better if we're not paying her. You know, back in Window Rock she didn't seem so pleased when I tried to hold up her arm with mine."

"Needs a little persuasion, that's all."

"So what else do you know about her?"

"Like your women short? She's that. No criminal record, nothing beyond a couple speeding tickets. Hell, how do I know what she's like? She's a woman."

"Maybe she can help handle the twins because my wife can't. But she's a lawyer, right?" Lee said.

"Trained as a lawyer, done work with the Prosecuting Attorney's office in Albuquerque. But it's all tribal stuff."

"So she's not really a lawyer?"

"Not corporate, nothing like that. But she can be articulate as hell. Even testifying in D.C., smack in the face of Congress she didn't fluster."

"So she'll make good sound bites?"

Sound bites? Where would they have gotten the idea she was even remotely on their side?

"Should be effective. Only the Indians could try to force a lawsuit, trump us in the courts. Listen, you're going to be real sensitive, understand?"

"Of course." Lee sounded bored.

"I'm serious. We may want to appoint her to something official, you know, once we're in office. Take her with us to D.C."

Bitsoi had pretended dumb, was that it? This sounded way too informed. Just exactly how involved, Lilli wondered, was Bitsoi?

"Come on, Dougan, what's holding up that speech?"

"It's coming. Listen, you read the speech, you take a couple of questions. Keep it simple: twenty-first century is all about water and energy. Who has it, who needs it, who sells it, who keeps it. You're putting yourself where your mouth is."

"I'm putting my oar in."

"Precisely. I like that, use that: yes, putting your oar in, running the hardest working river in the nation. And a full media throng waiting. What do you bet we get headlines: 'Lee Departs Lee's Ferry'? Name solidifies you to place."

"You're the campaign strategist," Lee said. "All right, I'm relaxed about the election."

"So sure of its outcome you can spend special time with your family, concentrating on the water and energy needs of our great nation, and the big plan you will reveal."

The business of mythologizing, she thought.

"You know, you're right. Where is that woman?"

The other man's voice.

"I'm going to step outside, see if this Chischilly woman's lost."

The closed door of the bus opened and a man stuck his head out.

"Ms. Chischilly, terrific, right on time. I'm Dougan. We haven't officially met, have we?"

She recognized him now. He was the warm-up man from the stage in Window Rock before Lee had appeared. He came down the steps of the bus and laid an air-conditioned arm around her shoulders.

"Hey, Berdell? Lilli Chischilly of the Navajo Nation is here."

Trussed up, wasn't she, for this command photo op, a piece of campaign staging of solidarity with the dam.

"Listen, Ms. Chischilly..." Dougan squeezed her arm with a little pressure. "Before things get too crazy, let me say, welcome aboard. Am I pronouncing you right?"

But Dougan wasn't listening. Lee emerged through the open door. Where Dougan's eyes were too small for his head and darted incessantly, Lee had eyes that locked.

"Ah—Ms. Chischilly? Such a pleasure."

The splendid mouth.

She'd promised herself one thing. If she stepped foot in that boat, the least she could do was refuse to be anyone's fool.

"Great, let's execute the plan," Dougan said.

A man draped in camera gear followed behind him. "How about, first, the two of them—Lee and Ms. Chischilly—with the campaign bus?"

"Now, some photos with the dam, yes, a little wider apart," Dougan instructed. "Let's get the dam, just behind Lee's shoulder."

Lee was The Show, no surprise there. But how in a few choreographed minutes had she so thoroughly become a prop?

Duane Fatt hung his head out over the river, let the blood rush, felt dizzy. Funny how light changed everything. Upriver, the water rushed toward him all smoky green in the pinched canyon but straight down, under the bridge, foam like whisker stubble collected in an eddy. Something about the shadows turned the river metallic and he watched scabs boil up.

"Once the highest steel-arch bridge in the world" proclaimed the sign. And now obsolete. The original Navajo Bridge pretty obviously hadn't supported traffic heavier than pedestrians in a long, long time. The new bridge took that weight, channeling Route 89A traffic between Bitter Springs and Vermilion Cliffs, but Duane walked out on the old spandrel bridge, his two feet straddling the double no-passing lines, keeping the faded yellow stripes between his legs, out to the hump in the middle.

According to the sign, the big bolt holding the halves together was five hundred feet above the Colorado River. He inched up his pants and knelt on the pebbles crevassed with cracks. The riot of color, pebble bits of orange and mustard with tiny stringers of pink, interrupted his concentration with so much detail. But then he stuck his head through the fretwork of crisscross railing with its openings just big enough to squeeze through. This close it was real evident how the railing silver wasn't real, it was paint the color of duct tape.

Damn, he needed to pee. He unzipped his fly. He was about to let loose through the railing when he had a better idea. He jogged across the empty bridge, back to the monument that really pissed him off, reading fast past the incised lettering in granite that proclaimed to the whole damn world:

This Monument Erected
To The Founder
JOHN DOYLE LEE

He sprayed urine in sweeps across the chiseled words:

WHO, WITH SUPERHUMAN EFFORT
AND IN THE FACE OF ALMOST
UNSURMOUNTABLE OBSTACLES,
MAINTAINED THIS FERRY
WHICH MADE POSSIBLE THE
COLONIZATION OF ARIZONA.

– – – – –

FRONTIERSMAN, TRAIL BLAZER,
BUILDER, A MAN OF GREAT
FAITH, SOUND JUDGMENT, AND
INDOMITABLE COURAGE.

Like hell. You suppose in corners of Germany there are stone monuments erected to Hitler? And now every single American who went this way would read the damn lie and not know better than to believe it. Tourists, too—little mamasan and papasan from Japan. Nothing but a chiseled lie.

He zipped his fly. Time to find a nice little hidey-hole for the day of the launch.

He scrambled down the slope to a ledge in the footings under the bridge. Perfectly invisible.

Waiting wasn't his strong suit. Duane chewed the skin on the inside of his cheek until he raised an ugly swelling, then let his tongue play with the welt. Checked his watch again. He'd slid into the hidey-hole in the dark, hours before the raft should glide into view. From his back pocket he pulled out his thumbed copy of John D. Lee's *Last Confession*.

He got so damned irritated thinking how they'd all let that bastard Lee stay a free man, for twenty whole years after the Mountain Meadows Massacre. Lots of people knew exactly where he was living, free as he pleased—hell, even John Wesley Powell visited Lee.

Duane had certain phrases of Lee's *Last Confession* nearly put to memory. But why be shy? He was all alone with the wind. And ever since those 9/11 events with the terrorists flying their airplanes into the Twin Towers of New York on a mission from God, he'd loved reading out loud the way Lee had put such a religious spin on his motives.

Duane cleared his throat and began to speak: "Last Confession and Statement of John D. Lee written at his dictation." Then he chose those words he'd underlined in black ballpoint pen and threw them out for the wind to carry:

I did not act alone; I had many to assist me at the Mountain Meadows. I firmly believe that the most of those who took part considered it a religious duty to unquestioningly obey the orders which they had received.

Believing that those with me acted from a sense of religious duty on that occasion, I have faithfully kept the secret of their guilt, and remained silent and true to the oath of secrecy which we took on the bloody field, for many long and bitter years.

The substance of the orders were that the emigrants should be decoyed from their strong-hold, and all exterminated, so that no one would be left to tell the tale, and then the authorities could say it was done by the Indians.

Clever idea, that one.

Higbee then said to me, 'Brother Lee, I am ordered by Church President Haight to inform you that you shall receive a crown of Celestial glory for your faithfulness, and your eternal joy shall be complete.

Our leaders speak with inspired tongues, and their orders come from the God of Heaven.

The sliding scream of a hawk on the hunt interrupted him. Duane looked up to search the clean sky. The red-tailed hawk hovered above him and let out a *keeer-keeer* before it soared off toward the Vermilion Cliffs. He checked upstream. Nothing yet but river coming toward him. He played with the muscles at the top of his spine and then settled back to wait.

And just who the fuck sent John D. Lee on assignment to run the ferry? Why no other than Brigham Young, Leader of the Latter-day Saints up in Salt Lake City, who wanted his Mormons to be able to cross the Colorado River and expand themselves farther into Arizona. So good old Lee, free as that hawk, started ferrying people across this piece of isolation, the only river crossing for more than three hundred miles, and just whose boat did he get to use? One of John Wesley Powell's—Powell himself gone back to Washington, D.C. So don't ever think this Lee wasn't a man free with important connections.

And the man had even more wives than those Islamic suicide terrorists get promised. Only seventeen virgins, right, for each one of them?

Duane could feel the impatience rising up his nervous system but he knew he'd come real early and had to stay put. In prison the psychiatrist liked to mouth his opinions into the little recording device he'd held up to his lips as if Duane weren't even in the room. "Lack of impulse control." Or did the psychiatrist think those words were too technical for him to understand? Duane jammed his hands deep into his pockets. He had plenty of goddamn impulse control. He had a plan and the plan was smoothly under way.

He'd trust no one. Depend on no one. Leave no witnesses behind, just like the Mountain Meadows Massacre. Then he'd make it back to Mama because, otherwise, how would she know it was him? He didn't plan on getting caught.

He was no publicity hound, not like this Lee running for president. Not like those religious terrorists neither, whose audience is God. His audience was personal, a piece of business between a grown man and his mama.

Shit, he wanted to call her, hear her voice again, but he wanted even more to surprise her. No, he wanted to tell her. Insurance, just in case something went wrong. Maybe he *should* tell her. She'd keep the secret. Maybe he should make one little phone call, say something real brief and hang up, maybe, "Mama? It's me, Duane. Watch the newspapers. Just a couple more days."

But what if she had a big mouth and got to itching to tell, told someone who would never tell, and that somebody promised until they got to bursting, and the itch got so big it had to be scratched? That's how people got themselves caught. Not that the cops are so smart as that the perps are so dumb. They start a chain that keeps on growing.

He felt stiff, sitting so long in his hidey-hole. He cracked his knuckles, one joint at a time, then stretched his jaw open, rode it up and down to his chest. He closed his eyes. For months now he'd let play in his head, clear as a vision, the details of the Mountain Meadows Massacre. How some of the prettiest women had been hauled off to the bushes by those churchmen for a little rough sex before their throats were slit, and then how their clothes were removed once all the killing was done. How those holy men had taken away everything of any value, even the shoes, how they pretended they'd buried the dead, but really they hadn't bothered, had just left them for the wolves to come eat.

And then Lee lived—unpunished—for twenty more whole and free years.

Not at all Duane's experience. Hell, he was just goofing off. They'd had to send that woman guard into his cell, and he'd bit her, even though the bitch had on enough riot gear to choke a horse. And then it had been a coffin with air they called isolation and him naked under video cameras, and way too much time alone to think.

But like Mama said, Lee had tricked a hundred twenty of her people, men and women and children, into slaughter at close range and for his trouble got all sorts of assistance to live free, even entertain visitors. Some punishment, that.

Shame, Duane thought, he didn't have himself a set-up so he could pull off that kind of in-your-face, beg-for-mercy killing. No, he needed the killings all to happen fast, way before those Secret Service agents knew even where to fire. He'd have to explode heads as fast as he could.

According to the newspaper, now, even a Navajo along for the ride. Nice piece of luck. Completed things, the way old John D. Lee and his men painted themselves up to look like Indians. Just another clever lie, costuming and painting up to lay the blame on the wrong shoulders.

Lee and his family: the wife and two kids. I mean, he understood this Lee wasn't the same Lee who stopped his Mama's family on their flight to wealth, that this blond wife wasn't the same seventeenth wife of Lee's who'd sheltered him all those years. It was the symbolism that mattered. Mama would understand that.

Because didn't this Lee, like a show-off, take public pride in his heritage? Look at how he's staged things so he'll be photographed for eternity launching himself from Lee's Ferry, never once mentioning how ferryman Lee celebrated in monuments and on maps and as the Mile Zero of the whole fucking Grand Canyon was a cruel trickster, a liar, a woman-raper and a baby-killer who hid behind the robes of the Church. Did it all for the Higher Glory.

Well, then, suffer the little children to come unto me.

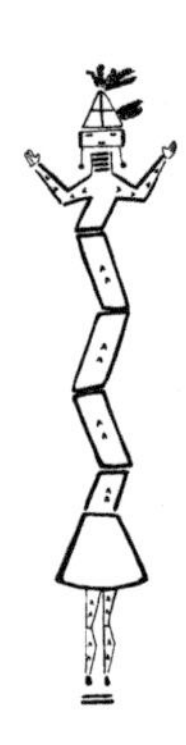

Lilli stepped off the campaign bus onto a sand beach alive with people on a mission and all in a hurry.

"Stand back, ma'am. Need to load through here."

What kind of vessel had she imagined?

A rubberized raft of pontoons, enormous and inflated like oversized sausages with snouts, sat aground on its nose. The busy ones jumped up onto its platform and jumped off, waded through water and secured supplies with ropes. The small golden-haired woman trying to shepherd twin boys must be Lee's wife.

Someone shoved an orange contraption Lilli's way. "Find me again if you can't get this cinched. And make sure it's tight."

The thing was puffed with stuffing. She'd never traveled before on water, never held a life jacket.

Her right arm slipped in easily enough but she struggled to pull the life jacket around and behind her and thread her arm through and as she twisted she felt someone behind her lift the jacket into position. Instinctively, she turned around.

"Jerome?" Lilli felt the drain of her own deep exhale. This was really going to happen. "You're here."

"Doesn't mean I don't think you're crazy," he said.

Just her and Jerome. Well, and nine other strangers. In a boat.

She wished there was some privacy, but she could see now there wouldn't be, not during the day. No, they'd be crowded together. She'd have to wait until tonight to get him alone enough to really talk.

"Loading—come on, you two. Follow me."

Apparently all introductions were to wait.

But she couldn't help thinking that the two oddly silent men already in the raft must be Secret Service and armed.

And then nearly on schedule, the raft launched and all was in motion. The river moved beneath her like a thick muscle, emphatically alive.

She had the two of them, Jerome and her, locked away in a crucible, a J-rig, about to careen down into the bowels of the earth protected by a couple of Secret Service agents who—should anything go wrong—would push them out of the way in a stampede to defend the presumed next First Family.

Lilli's neck chafed against the life jacket's bloated collar. Her hips, her shoulders, the bottoms of her feet shifted weight about as if she rode a rubber sheet whose corners obeyed the jerks of four warring demons. She leaned back awkwardly from the waist and flinched as Lee's backcast whizzed out over her head.

The ready press corps obviously came first, with a

planned photo op of Lee hooking a trout, all within camera range. The man was something to watch, a natural athlete, so comfortable in his skin. And determined. Lee would probably risk wrestling a snake if one dropped in the boat and the cameras were rolling.

Conspicuously absent a life jacket, Lee stood with his left foot up on the bow of the raft and snapped the rod, executing a sinuous backcast that changed direction as he whipped the line out ahead, placing the lure on a patch of dark water.

Trying to avoid eye contact, Lilli studied the body language of the nine strangers in the raft, and the singular Jerome. They were about to enter an alien world where the river was the sole trajectory, the artery. And Lee's Ferry was the official jump-off, the put-in, the genesis: Mile Zero.

Lee's Ferry, with the apostrophe before the *S*. Clearly the ferry that once belonged to Lee. But interesting how history can rewrite itself. She'd noticed how the spelling sometimes became Lees' Ferry, an odd typographical switch as if there were lots of Lees that once ran the ferry, not the one John D. Lee with his seventeenth wife. And even newer sign-makers were dropping the apostrophe altogether. Lee's Ferry was morphing into the neutered Lees Ferry.

The J-rig took a sharp spin. She couldn't tell if the sudden nausea she experienced was from her panicked mind or her uneasy stomach. She'd never been so literally to the liquid edge of the reservation.

What was peculiar about Navajo boundaries was how their edges ran straight only where there was no water. The northwestern rim of the reservation presented itself with scalloped edges and meanders, even goosenecks, on a high resolution map. Because where the boundary ran alongside flowing water, the politicians had been quite careful to keep the water on their side, apart from the Navajo.

Lilli moved her gaze off Lee and tried peering into the future, downstream, but she could see only as far as the next bend. You'd never guess from offshore at Lee's Ferry that you were about to enter one of the great wonders of Earth, a canyon where water sliced through rock-hard time as sharply as a knife carving tallow.

She tried to envisage beyond that bend, to where they'd finally be out of sight of the press. What then? Lilli imagined a line of authority that naturally divided two worlds, the upstream world they were leaving and the world below, a raw, unpeopled wilderness. When push came to shove, then what?

Surely the boatman working the raft from the stern had every right to believe he was in charge, the way a captain is in command. But she'd seen enough of Lee and his ego to know he'd never believe he wasn't the one in full control. Lee gave orders as naturally as another man might breathe, and he was, after all, The Show.

Along shore, the crowd of press-credentialed elbows and arms jockeyed for a better angle to grab their photos and video clips. Dougan was trying to cheerlead, ever mindful of the long lenses.

"What's going on—come on, bring me in closer." Lee's voice, nearly under his breath, carried a hiss. "I need a tighter angle."

"For chrissake." Dougan directed his voice clearly to the boatman. "He wants the shore, toward the press."

As Lee's chief handler, Dougan probably pictured Lee more like the ball than the quarterback. In the huddle Lilli imagined it was Dougan who clearly called the plays. But he'd know enough to pander to the man's ego.

"Come on," Lee hissed a little louder. "Position me."

Would Lee, so publicly, fail? He strained against the wind. Maybe there wasn't going to be a trout, after all. Lilli tried to imagine being under water. Because in an expert's hand, the trout sees only the shadow. The line with the hook is hidden.

A pair of dusky blue herons with serpentine necks circled uneasily overhead, then settled in a cottonwood tree. Something along the shore suddenly looked familiar. A small figure stepped out of the thick tamarisk. How do you suppose the old Singer managed to get past the roadblock?

Lilli watched as *Hosteen* Ahboah threw pollen from the pouch around his neck, flinging it up in a golden arc. To the Secret Service agents, it must look like an old man just waved. Ahboah was doubtless singing, too, but she couldn't hear him over the noise of the river.

Still no trout. Dougan pressed closer to the boatman, trying not to make a scene in front of the live cameras.

"Lee's losing advantage. Can't you see? Change your position."

But the boatman didn't comply. He pitched the power of the rig deftly against the river's pull, his full focus on the water. Already Lilli knew she was in the middle of one big pissing contest.

"Lord alive, he's done it!" Dougan moved back to make room as Lee leaned over and came up with a glimmering trout.

The man stepped up onto the floats and held his prize, a shimmering muscle quivering with life. Then Lee rotated with the fish held high, giving the cameras their due. A perfect execution. All according to plan.

Now they could leave the cameras. In a few minutes they'd round the downstream bend and enter the Upper Gorge of the Colorado River. It wasn't too late. She could use signals with Jerome. They could jump. *Are you crazy*, her other voice shrilled. The water's moving like a locomotive. You'll be swept apart.

Or she could give Jerome the signal, and he'd nod, and she'd jump, and he wouldn't, and from the water she'd see Jerome waving at her from the raft as it disappeared.

The boatman—"Mitch"was as much as she'd heard so far—stood facing them, a wedge-shaped man with wide shoulders and tight hips, but it was his wiring that impressed her. Lilli sensed the man was as alert with potential as the gap between spark plugs.

"All right, we're out of camera range now. Time for a reality check."

He pushed the bill of his cap to the back of his head and squinted into the sun. "You ride with me there's two rules. Hard and fast, no exceptions."

"Rule Number One? Life jacket stays on. Period." He looked directly at Lee. "Never want to see anyone in my boat, again and that includes you," he said pointing at Lee, "without their personal flotation device. PFD's job is to keep your body afloat."

Even a dead body, Lilli realized. So it's not necessarily a "life" jacket. It's a "float" jacket: even a dead body would bob up again wearing its float jacket if it didn't get snagged under water.

"Understood," Lee said. "Boys, pay attention."

Lilli's knees involuntarily started to open and close as if she were trying to remember how to swim. She couldn't swim. Maybe the reason she couldn't breathe, either, was because her life jacket was so tightly buckled across her chest.

The raft had no real seats, nothing like a movie theater, or even the planks of a rowboat. Lilli followed what the others did—all except Mitch—and sat on the edge of the pontoon sausages with her feet toward the center, riding directly on the tubes.

"Rule Number Two? Participate in your own survival."

Lilli looked at the faces of the nine strangers who would populate her entire world for the next six days. What, specifically, did he mean by that?

"Two hundred twenty-six miles of water ahead of us and a hundred sixty-six rapids. We flip through a rapid—not something I plan to let happen, you understand—but if it does flip, I can't get to all of you at the same time. So you participate in your own survival, hear? You keep your feet pointed downstream, you keep your head up. You make like a log."

Lilli pulled on her jacket's bottom belt to cinch it even tighter. She had no qualms, really, about Mitch's expertise, or his safety record. Dougan would have made sure this particular boatman was the best, with only superbly competent runs under his belt. After all, Lee was on board, and so was his family. But Lilli knew what she saw. Everything in Navajo has gender and she had no doubt, watching Mitch maneuver, that for him the river was personal.

She tried to put herself in his place. She imagined he

experienced the river as a wild, powerful woman who ran from him, again and again, a woman he could never get enough of.

"Now we're through with the rules," Mitch said. "I want to introduce Suzanne. She's my Swamper."

Suzanne, young and lithe and sun-bronzed, dipped her head in a mock bow.

"Your backup?" Lee drank from a wide-mouthed water bottle.

"No, like I said, she's the Swamper."

"We swamp, she bails?"

Lilli noticed how Suzanne didn't answer for herself. She cued first—always—on Mitch.

She certainly was beautiful, one of those long-legged women who don't wear much clothing. Not outdoors anyway. She was dressed in special shorts and a scoop-necked shirt for adventure sports, and it was hard not to continually watch her when she moved, the way she economized, didn't hesitate before she leapt, didn't waste time bending her knees but leaned over with her knees locked, her small rounded bottom beneath the lavender shorts stretched tight by the effort.

Lee's wife, maybe a decade or two older than Suzanne, was pretty as a sandpuff blossom in her blouse and matching shorts. Lilli looked down at her own legs covered to the ankles in a cheap pair of nylon pants. Nothing at all from the clothing designers for wilderness travel. She had on an old hat to keep the sun off her head and a pair of sunglasses linked behind her neck with a stout rubber band attached to her collar with a safety pin. She didn't remotely look like she'd ever done this before.

"Swamper grabs anchor on shore, and she does the grunt work in camp, the cooking, and the dishes."

"I'll take real good care of you."

So Suzanne was the hostess who probably knew how to

soothe even the really difficult customer. Like Mitch, she'd have been handpicked for the assignment.

"So, Suzanne, you've already met Mr. Lee," Mitch said. "Reason we got the whole river to ourselves. And Mrs. Lee."

"Oh, let's drop the formality," Mrs. Lee said. "Just everyone—please—call me Brianna."

So, Mitch and Suzanne ran the operation. Lee was The Show, Dougan was the strategist. Lee and the First Family were the asset, and the two Secret Service agents would do everything in their power to protect that asset: in rank order, Lee first, then the First Family. She and Jerome were the token Natives.

"And these are my sons," Lee said.

"The Lee boys," Mitch said. "Twins, huh? Now let's see if I got this straight. You're twelve minutes older?"

"Yep, I'm older."

"So that makes you the little brother by a body length?"

On shore, Lilli had watched how the wife and the boys were mostly ignored by Lee. Lee had the skills of a great flatterer, could make you feel you were the most important person in his life for one focused moment, between the interruptions. But that didn't work so well for intimacy. His sons probably knew they weren't the most important people in their father's world. A lesson his wife must have learned a long time ago.

"Boys? How about you give these people your names?" Lee said.

The older boy jumped from his sitting position. "Me? I'm Kent." He was quick as if his idle was set high. "My little brother, he's Kevin. Rhymes with 'heaven.' "

And Kent rhymes with what, she wondered, *bent*?

The two boys weren't identical, not in height, or bulk, although their two faces resembled each other if you imagined a fast version and a slow version. Or maybe it was just that their hair was blonde, like their mother's, and cut alike.

"Moving on, Suzanne, this is Mr. Dougan," Mitch said.

"Let's skip the 'mister' part. Been called Dougan since I was a kid."

Mitch turned toward her. "And Lilli Chischilly, is it?"

"Yes. Hello," she said, turning to make eye contact. She thought of making some more formal statement, maybe welcoming them to the watery edge of the Navajo reservation, but decided against it. She wasn't sure how deeply she and Jerome were to be included. Lee's wife and the two boys would be treated as, well, children. Mitch and Suzanne were logistics. She and Jerome were so clearly the outsiders.

"I've met your friend here, getting all his camera gear stowed away. This is Jerome Bah, everyone," Mitch said. "You two work for the Navajo Nation?"

"Yes, that's right," she said. Well, nearly so. Bitsoi had apparently hired Jerome even though he wasn't on the tribal payroll yet.

The last two members in the raft remained silent.

"Care to introduce yourselves?" Mitch had nodded to the two men who were anything but invisible. They didn't seem to speak either.

Dougan jumped in. "This is Mr. Koonce. And Mr. Heaney, and they're employees of the U.S. Department of the Treasury."

What was wrong with just saying it straight out, Lilli wondered, that these two were Special Agents?

"First names will be fine. I'm Frank." The squatter of the two Special Agents nodded in the direction of his equal. "This is Boyd."

"Excuse my lack of civics, you know, but is this

customary?" Mitch pitched the question out in the open. "To guard someone just running for President? I mean, we haven't had the election yet."

Dougan took the bait, answered for Frank and Boyd who might be quick with their hands but seemed to prefer to open their mouths last.

"Since an assassination during a presidential campaign, yeah, it's the law," Dougan said. "Since Bobby Kennedy got shot. Now, six months out ahead of a presidential election, government assigns protective coverage to the leading nominees—presidential, vice-presidential, and their spouses."

So already Lee belonged to the United States, an asset to be protected at all costs as far as Frank and Boyd's directive went. Just like Mitch and Suzanne, she imagined these two agents were also handpicked. Though the assignment must seem like a piece of cake to them, a dream shift, what with no crowds, no traffic, nothing to worry about.

She tried to imagine being them, two men trained to see everything through an enemy's eyes. To worry about the vulnerability of bottlenecks and choke points. They'd have training in firearms, of course, and physical fitness—pretty obvious from the way they carried themselves. And counter-sniper tactics, emergency medicine, communications, probably even experts in cold water survival. And lots of simulation time with various scenarios of, what had she heard it called? Attack on Principal?

Well, fortunately that would be a moot talent on this trip. Lilli tilted her head up to receive the afternoon sun. She knew some about protective training because the Bureau of Indian Affairs agents and the Indian Police Academy were brought up to speed at a satellite branch of FLETC, the Federal Law Enforcement Training Center, located in Artesia, New Mexico, just south of Roswell. She remembered being told that at FLETC in a single year of federal firearms training, fifteen million rounds of ammo were fired. Probably trained the Shadow Wolves, too, the Native American special unit made up of tribal Indians who patrolled the southwest borderlands.

After the election, maybe Frank and Boyd would get assigned to the rooftop of the White House, or the Presidential helicopter or limousine. But the art of protection would remain the same. Think like an attacker, because it's the attacker who chooses the time and the place and the method of attack.

She tried to more thoroughly imagine their job. They'd pledged allegiance to a code of ethics that included self-sacrifice. In an instant without any hesitation they'd dedicate their own lives to one simple directive: protect the First Man at all cost. If possible, keep the First Family intact.

Lilli hadn't signed on for self-sacrifice with Jerome. Yet as she looked around the group, she realized she shared an odd kinship with those two men. She was trying to be Jerome's protector. And he'd given her a challenge, "You're Navajo, Uninterrupted. You figure it out." Her mind went back to the man on a table with wheels in the Medical Examiner's vault. And to the same man on his back in the Hoodoos.

"Well, Frank, and Boyd," Mitch said. "We have ourselves a problem. What's with the armed holsters under your life jackets?"

Mitch pointed to a stash of metal boxes. "How's about you lock those weapons up in these watertight canisters?"

No answer. And no movement.

"What the...? Someone from our headquarters must have cleared this with you already," Dougan said. "Title 18, Section 3056, United States Code says the Secret Service can carry firearms."

Lilli guessed Frank and Boyd were probably armed in the ways of the twenty-first century that had nothing to do with holsters.

"There's that difference between 'can' and 'may'," Mitch said. "My experience is when things go wrong they go wrong in a big hurry. Recommend you keep your powder dry."

"That concern went out with the last century." Dougan moved toward a position Lilli would have said was way too close to Mitch.

"Listen, man," Mitch said. "There's no one—literally, no one—on the river or in the canyon with us. Your guys even swept the air space clean, so it's all off-limits while we make this run."

"Even so. These men have their job to do."

"Looking out for Number One. Yeah, I get that. But I don't put one person's safety above another's, see."

"Listen now." Lee stood up.

Maybe he'd had enough of people talking around him as if he were deaf.

"Boyd, is it?" His voice resonated just above the pitch of the moving river. "And Frank?"

Did he really not know the names of the men assigned to die for him? But then he'd be used to Secret Service agents at a distance, scouring faces in a crowd, riding on ahead. This experience would be new, she realized. Secret Service as people, literally in the same boat.

"Yes, sir," Frank answered.

"I hear Mitch, his recommendation," Lee said. "Don't you think your equipment will be best served if it doesn't wash overboard or get soaking wet? Go ahead, put it in safe-keeping."

"Yes, sir. With all respect, sir, you all can discuss the merits. Won't change for me and Boyd. We stay armed."

So the pissing contest was well under way and had just added a couple of new players.

Lilli leaned her head back as the final piece of manmade landmark she'd recognize passed over their heads. High above her, the arched span of silver glinted with reflected light and then Navajo Bridge, with its dedicated monument to John D. Lee, receded until it, too, vanished behind the river's twist.

Give security time to clear out, Duane thought. Stay put. He remembered backward how with the silencer screwed in, he'd aligned the familiar optics, focusing his concentration and adjusting for heat mirage and wind. Reminded him, too, of the hours he used to spend, even as a kid, target practicing in the desert on Grade A eggs, pilfered out of Mama's refrigerator. He'd almost never missed a scramble on the first shot.

Damn he was weak. He hadn't heard her voice, except in dreams, for years. He'd laid on his back in the dark, night before last, and gone and dialed the old phone number. It was all he could do to keep breathing, so slow, the way you almost stop your heartbeat before you pull the trigger, because she actually answered. He so gently smothered the phone against the receiver and killed the connection. Too soon for talk.

He had difficulty, anyways, imagining her in the

present, realized he liked remembering when she was a whole lot younger and before he'd started to get into any kind a serious trouble.

Think about something else, Duane, think about the target. He fingered the smooth bullet down deep in his pocket, a tough choice because one decision kind of contradicted the other. In speculation the spinner with the full metal jacket would enter neat and blow out the exit wound. The tumbler would release instead on impact and blow out maximum tissue at the entrance site. But he'd felt himself leaning toward a design that would enter and roam around. The high velocity should enter smooth, then burst out. Even better, the expanders with the semi-jacket in the middle would feel the tissue and amplify, ripping up the brain.

Images of Jackie Kennedy's pink suit and Jack's head, with the face intact, the entrance wound to the back of the skull, flooded his memory. He planned to be positioned high, too, same way Oswald had positioned himself in Dallas, shooting down. He thought it'd be more impressive if Lee's family saw Lee's head explode from the inside out.

He thought about his little target test, how he went out into the desert for a tricky shooting gallery, a stinking shooting gallery once he opened the trunk and pulled out the first cardboard box, starting to sag, full of overripe melons the produce manager had set by the dumpster, including a couple of long-neck squashes and a sack full of bruised pears. What a reek! He remembered trying not to give in and breathe, how he held his breath as he lugged the three boxes out to a rocky ledge. How he had to turn his head to grab a lungful of air. Then he aligned them all, readying himself to start with the cabbages and move in ascending order of difficulty to smaller and smaller targets and harder shots.

A tease of rain had hung in the distance, one of those

desert drops where the air absorbs the rain before it ever has a chance of finding ground. Duane had opened the first box of ammo, feeling thirsty. He'd picked up a smooth piece of stone and popped it into his mouth to suck on, an old desert survival trick—at least that's what he'd used to do as a kid to settle down a thirst.

Nothing like being in the desert, though, during a soaking rain. When he was a kid, you could catch so many frogs after a summer monsoon, all come out of their hiding. He'd pull apart cheap strings of red firecrackers and stuff their gullets, then watch them go hop, hop, hop—blam! You wouldn't think people could be almost as easy. He'd sort through people, find those looking for signs of kindness. You could almost smell how some people were going to believe him when they shouldn't. Trust was such a bad idea.

Duane had set the ammo box on the ground. The roots of a creosote bush lay in a necklace of litter. A piece of captured sunlight glowing emerald green flashed up at him from within the severed neck of a liquor bottle. Down the knotted rope of fence posts, a crow flapped, curiously tame. Duane moved closer to it and the bird turned out to be a shredded garbage bag caught on barbed wire, its black plastic lifting in the wind.

He loaded the ammo, raised the gun to his dominant eye and found his first target. He squeezed the trigger slowly, felt the recoil, squeezed again and considered the silent explosions, one after another, in ascending order of marksmanship. Then he walked up to the rock ledge to examine the damage but couldn't find much in the way of result. The vegetable pulp was gone or spread too fine. Seemed like bone might behave way different from melon rind. He had himself a new idea.

He put a handful of expanders in his pocket and took off on foot. God, he loved the desert. Nothing emptier, nothing cleaner. Never had to explain himself.

Perfect.

Duane had stretched out prone on his stomach and centered the optics. The explosion of the Hereford's head had been so soundless it surprised even him. Duane jogged the distance to judge the new results. The cow's neck was a stringy stump without a head. But he'd looked around and finally found himself a piece of ear, with a bit of nose.

GIRL WITH SKIRT OF STARS

Mile Zero at Lee's Ferry was ten river miles behind them already and they were alone with each other. A wilderness with no easy way out. Lilli could try and pretend she needed to vomit from motion sickness but she knew anxiety was more likely the cause. Her breathing was much too shallow. She tried to get her lungs involved. The path ahead of least resistance lay through water.

In her sightline sat the nearly rigid Secret Service agents. Maybe it was their behavior, hyper-vigilant and trying to be invisible at the same time, or maybe it was the way they were so obviously armed, that made her wonder if Lee, this close to becoming the next president of the United States, had explicit enemies.

She kept her toes tucked under the safety line. She wanted to reach out and touch Jerome's hand. What was he thinking? Born Navajo—that put you on the tribal roll—and Jerome, in his veins, was full-blooded. But that wasn't the same as *being* Navajo. Being Navajo was a state of mind.

Her calf muscles ached from permanent tension, the way she'd seen beginners take to a horse the wrong way. As a kid she'd learned how to stay on bareback by pressing her legs against the horse's warm ribs, and sometimes Jerome wrapping his arms around her. But the raft's motion beneath her was peculiarly weird. She sensed the surging spirit of the river but couldn't find its gait.

Mitch let it be known he liked to quote John Wesley Powell, whose words he read aloud:

We are now ready to start on our way down the Great Unknown.

She watched the ever-fleeing shoreline. A quick shadow of a coyote emerged and held still. Or had she imagined it?

"Hey, Mitch, I read there was one deeper canyon in the world," Lee said. "Someplace in the Andes."

The boatman engineered a sweeping path through the reflective surface of the traveling water, causing it to change color.

"Nope. We've entered the deepest canyon in the world."

"No, really, I think it was called Colca Canyon."

"Fact's a fact. There may be places in the Andes or the Himalayas where there's more difference in elevation between river level and a mountain peak, but that glory goes to the mountain, rising up."

Suddenly Mitch maneuvered her side of the raft to almost touch the cliff. What was he doing, trying to ram the rock face?

"Here all the glory goes to the river," Mitch said. "There's no other place on earth with such spectacular incision."

"Really?"

"Good eyes, now," Mitch said. "Scan the cliff just above water level. Catch that lettering?"

First she saw the *F* and *M* etched in the buff-colored rock face, and then very plainly the word *Brown*.

"*F. M. Brown*. You all see it? Here's the exact spot Frank M. Brown flipped his boat and drowned."

Lilli watched the bad omen as it receded from her.

"Four days later," Mitch said, "Another two men in Brown's expedition drowned, including the fellow who scratched Brown's initials."

Mitch swung the raft back out into the middle channel.

"See, F.M. Brown thought he'd outsmart the river, shave a little money off the budget. Refused to outfit his expedition with jackets. Just want to underline my iron-clad Rule #1: Your PFD is always on and buckled tight."

Lilli fingered the four buckles in succession from the waist up, wondering exactly how a vest stuffed with synthetic fluff could keep her right side up and finding air.

"Little orientation next."

Since Lee's Ferry, Mitch had done his job standing with his legs spread open while the rest of them sat.

"Navajo reservation to our left, isn't that so, Lilli? All alongside us for some sixty more miles. We're also in what good old John Wesley Powell named 'Marble Canyon.' What do you suppose was in his head?"

"How's that?" Lee said.

"Sure isn't marble. Go figure. All the spectacular polish on these cliff walls reminded Powell of those slippery marble floors in government buildings, back in Washington."

Even in wilderness, Lilli thought, bureaucracy surrounds. She didn't see marble, she saw velvet skirts hanging in folds, the way some of the polished layers of rock curved and creased.

"Sheen we're seeing," Mitch said. "It's all river work, all water polish."

Lilli could have spoken up and added how the Navajo had their own name for this part of the canyon, that they called the gorge *Na'ní'á Hatsoh*. But she'd decided to stay quiet until somebody cared enough to ask for anything Navajo. Being Lee's assigned cultural interpreter was the least of her worries.

"OK, boys, little tributary coming up has the name of Soap Creek," Mitch said. "How come 'Soap' in so much wilderness?"

"How should I know?" Kent said.

"Me neither," Kevin echoed.

"Named by Jacob Hamblin," Mitch said.

"Now wasn't he one of John D. Lee's good friends?" Lee asked.

"That's right, that Hamblin," Mitch said.

The two of them together at Mountain Meadows, Lilli wanted to add. Wasn't it Hamblin whose wife took the babies, the few survivors the Mormons didn't kill, the ones they thought weren't worth the trouble, being too small to talk? Hamblin had his name on features on the reservation, like at The Gap in the Echo Cliffs where Hamblin's Ridge ran high.

"So down this tributary creek Hamblin shoots himself a badger," Mitch said. "Cooks it overnight in a pot and while he's sleeping all that grease from the skinned badger boils over and mixes with the alkaline waters of this little creek. Next morning Hamblin has himself suds everywhere, a whole new recipe for soap."

Even as Lilli smiled with Mitch, she was thinking how someone among her People must have noticed when you cut open the slick root of the yucca, *tsá'ászi'ts'óóz*, you raise a creamy lather. She was still smiling as, against her will, her mind turned to the memory of the alkaline taste of yucca suds on her tongue the morning they lifted her head and made her drink to deliver the afterbirth of the One she and Jake had buried. The stillborn. The One Who Did Not Utter A Sound.

"OK, boys, time to get serious. Or maybe the boys are a little young for physics," Mitch said.

"No, go ahead. A little physics will be fine," Lee said.

"*Hot Na Na* is the name of the next wash, boys," Mitch said. "Your tongue, right, Lilli? Care to help us out?"

"With physics?" Not her strong suit either.

"How about a word translation?"

She looked over at Jerome, watching her, but decided not to put him on the spot. "Sure, in Navajo? *Hot Na Na*, means a narrow tight space."

"And that, see," Mitch said, "that's the secret to cause and effect. Can you feel it? Pay attention to how the river is shifting beneath us."

She sensed the quickening, the speeding up.

"*Hot Na Na*: the canyon narrows, forcing an increase in speed," Mitch said. "Here's the simple physics of it all—carrying power of the river increases with speed to the sixth power, boys, now that's by a factor of a million."

The Swamper interrupted to remind them all to drink plenty of water, and Lilli realized she'd have to let go of the safety line with one hand to unclamp the carabineer that clamped her water within reach. She tightened her toes further under the safety line.

"OK, boys, little more physics. What causes a rapids?" Mitch said.

No volunteers.

"Nice example is heading our way," Mitch said. "Rock gets in the way of the river, that just riles her up. River has a mind of her own."

Yes, Lilli thought to herself, to Mitch the river was most definitely a woman.

"Serious now, want you all to get yourselves good and ready for this rapid coming our way. House Rock Rapid. Rock big-as-a-house. Can you hear it announcing itself?" Mitch's voice carried just above the growing roar.

"How big is this thing?" Lilli realized she'd just blurted her fear out of her mouth.

"Rapids are rated like earthquakes, from 1 to 10. House Rock can go as high as 9."

"Jesus alive, a 9 already!" Lee said. "Bring it on!"

"You all hear me good, now. House Rock Rapid is a definite Two-Hander," Mitch said. "You hold on seriously to something solid."

Lilli felt Jerome wrap his arm around her waist. Wasn't he supposed to hold onto something solid, two-handed, participate in his own survival?

"Don't look so scared," Jerome said in her ear. "Remember what they say. 'The worst thing about death must be the first night.' "

Lilli could see no warning of what was about to happen, nothing but a calm surface of deception. The curiously smooth tongue of dark water flecked with odd stringers of foam rolled toward them, a siren's tongue beckoning them into the hidden maw of the beast of House Rock Rapid. She tried to read Mitch's posture. He looked intent, absorbed, his whole body on full alert. His private affair with the river-woman was about to intensify.

She doubted he even remembered they were with him.

Yet something in the way Mitch kept his weight more heavily on one foot reminded her of a tightrope walker, or a Hopi Ya-Ya magician, testing the wire with the leading foot, getting ready to let go. Except Mitch would have them all out on the high wire with him when he let go. And never the same high wire, she thought. No, every run, every rapid, every season, the river would be different.

She realized she was reading Mitch rather than watching the river. She sensed by his eerie concentration that he was still using his brain. His shoulders shifted. His head held still. He looked to her like a man actively calculating a plan. He seemed to be distilling cues coming fast and toward him, knowing better than to fight the river, readying to become one with her passion.

The roar from the rapid invaded Lilli's brain. She gagged and back-swallowed. In a split second Mitch would have to commit, and then it would all become animal instinct, no more brain, because there'd be no time to think.

She felt the river quicken and pick up speed. She'd never experienced adrenaline like this, so sound-driven. And then for one long moment her senses focused through the river's eyes. She saw the past, what had happened to it, how the freak storm surged out of the side canyon and dropped its load of rocks bigger than houses. She saw the river furious to clear its path, struggling to smooth its belly, two elemental forces locked in battle.

"Grab on!" Mitch shouted.

Some primitive part of her brain took over. She clutched the safety rope with both hands and shoved her feet in fully under the rope on the floor of the raft. And then her mind locked.

Angle, position, momentum? Lilli felt the raft turn, and then from beneath her she felt the raft tremble and lift. It started to pull rather than submit, as if even at this last moment it could escape. But then it turned sharply toward the silver tongue of moving water and made the full commitment. She felt the plunge and the rip. Shockingly cold water smashed in her face, dumped in her lap, stunned her lungs awake. She heard so much thunder it was as if she heard nothing. Even time vanished.

They were no longer a raft full of people, they were hurtling like an enormous beast in the jaws of another enormous beast. For one long moment she saw individual droplets of water thrown up out of the churning trough but then chaos was everywhere, everything happening so fast her eyes were nearly useless. Except what she saw was hopeless—giant rocks in their way, chutes and lateral waves swamping in from the sides. What had seemed frantic and churning now, so close up, was remarkably steep with drop-offs and rolls that came out of nowhere. A wall of rock sped toward them. No, they sped toward the wall of cliff. The raft banked in a wrenching shudder. The river spit them through. She heard screams.

"What a ride!"

"Yowza!"

Lilli was soaking wet. She looked around her. Lee and Dougan and the boys were all chattering in the aftermath like thrilled survivors. She vomited over the side. So much for any vestige of dignity.

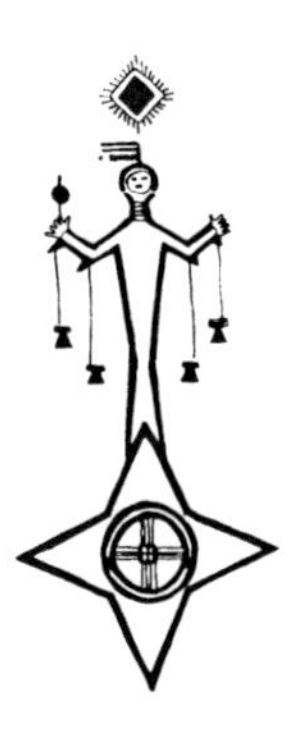

Maybe it was being half-hypnotized by the pulsing fire that brought out the storyteller in Mitch. He seemed to feel the need to entertain them tonight, their first night on the river, to hold them captive, yet Lilli was so anxious to leave. Surely it was nearly time for bed. She sat on the sandbar, upwind of the campfire, her impatient brain waiting for everyone to head off to their tents so she could finally be alone with Jerome. Tonight would be their first night together as adults. She planned on keeping things soft and quiet between them tonight, warned herself not to get headstrong with any of the hard questions yet, just try to strengthen the bond between them she knew was still there.

The Swamper had seemed confused as she separated gear and handed one tent to Lilli, another to Jerome.

"Two tents? Oh? Sorry—of course." Lilli had stopped

herself from explaining but couldn't stop herself from thinking how Jerome had left too young for them to act on the sexual urgency that might have followed.

"So, boys, you heard about the One-Armed Man, right?" Mitch stirred the coals, sending sparks up into the night air.

Kent and Kevin flanked their mother, who balanced between them on a canvas sling of a stool with three legs. Lilli sat on the bare sand of the sandbar, her knees bent, holding a little of the weight of Jerome's knee against her own. She knew the answer to Mitch's question but kept quiet, remembering back to a grey afternoon.

The Man With One Arm.

"John Wesley Powell. Big hero of mine." Mitch poked at the fire, making the coals pop, and pitched a branch of dry piñon on top. She inhaled the familiar scent of vaporized resin.

She and Jake had driven west past Coconino Rim and stood in the strong wind where a lonely memorial to John Wesley Powell rested atop a cemented stone cairn. Cast in bronze, the face of the *bilagáana* explorer stared out across the miles of canyon below, flanked by the names of those who risked the journey with him into The Great Unknown. The list was surprisingly short. Only six names. An edited list, she realized. The man didn't credit deserters. Missing was the name of the man who quit early, before the real test ever began. Missing, too, were the names of the three who deserted him in the canyon, much later. The three who were never found.

"Man didn't even know if there was going to be an exit," Mitch said.

"People told Powell there was none, no exit, told him he was making a fatal mistake, that the river dove underground somewhere deep in the canyon. But the man defied them all, and he did it with only one arm."

"Wow, so—like on a dare?" Kevin said.

"More like necessity, Kevin," Mitch said. "The man fought under Grant in the Civil War, lost an arm to the Battle of Shiloh."

"Yeah, Kevin, like on a dare." Kent rolled his eyes at his younger twin.

"Didn't stop him," Mitch said. "Powell ran it all, with his right arm amputated."

"Brave man," Lee said.

She knew a fair amount herself about Powell. For good reason. She'd studied water law, and Western water law always started with the man called Powell.

"Down here, in the canyon, Powell pretended to the protocol of war," Mitch said. "Kept himself apart, even at every meal, he never ate with his men."

One of those mechanisms, Lilli thought, of underlining who was in charge. The Secret Service agents seemed, also, to be pretending to the protocol of war.

She stared at the pulse of the dying fire and then at the two agents as they drifted, without a word, completely out of sight. They never settled themselves with the group, not even around the fire, sustaining instead—just as they'd done through dinner—an inarticulate physical distance well beyond the fringe. And all through dinner she'd found herself sneaking glances at them. It fascinated her that despite their wooden faces these two were trained to read morbid intention in a split second.

Their two tents sat pitched as sentinels, one on either side of the Lee family compound.

"Well, boys, Brianna, it's getting late," Lee said. "Time we make our way back to the tents. Thanks, Mitch, for the fire and the stories."

Dougan stood up, too, and followed. He'd snuggled

his tent a discrete distance from Lee, in slightly more rocky real estate.

"Yes. Night, all." Jerome abruptly stood and brushed sand from his pants. Lilli started to get to her feet, too.

"Lilli?" Mitch rose up. "Can I trust you with the fire? Need someone to stay behind and make sure it's out."

She wanted to refuse, to follow Jerome. "Sure." She sat back down.

"Thanks. First night out, Suzanne's been busier than sin. Good night then."

Lilli listened to Mitch's voice find Suzanne, and then their two voices fade out of range. They were headed back down to the water.

"Boatmen's rules," Mitch explained. "Suzanne and me, we sleep on the raft. Never trust the river."

Lilli took up the fire stick and stirred the ashes, causing them to cackle. Darkness amplified the sound of the river. An illusion, but it didn't make the sensory trick any less real.

She tried not to react to Jerome's abrupt departure. Her mind started to wander back to before Jerome had called her office in Window Rock. Only two people knew about the coyotes on the hood of the Dodge, she and the person who put them there. She kept seeing the two coyotes in her mind as animals someone mutilated and then hand-delivered to her. Why was she visualizing them so literally? Sometimes, like Mitch, Coyote was the one who told the stories. A Messenger.

She instinctively turned her head toward the restless voice of the river. The details, then the shape, then even the presence of the raft disappeared into the blackness of the night.

So far, so good. Plenty of nervous energy and it all under control. His car stashed off trail and invisible from the air with its camouflage of brush, and plenty of cash in case he gave up on his own wheels taking him back to Mama. Lee and the rest of them would be on the river by day, on the sandbars by night. Already tonight they'd be asleep. All Duane had to do was keep under rock cover like the desert rat he was, moving in the dark shadows to get in position ahead of them, and wait. Time was on his side. They would come to him. But he had prerequisites as to where, and the Zone of Silence was the one perfect spot. He would be there, ahead of them, ready and waiting.

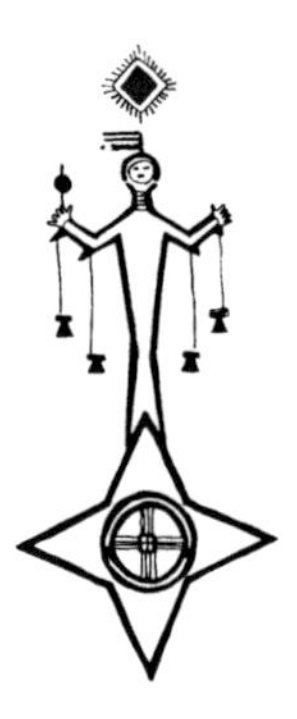

Suffocating in the artificial closeness of the tent's sloping walls, Lilli lay wide awake, horizontal and alone. She fidgeted with the sleeping pad and repositioned herself. Every time tonight's firelight caught the side of Jerome's face, and especially his eyes, she'd been startled by the image of the boy he'd once been. That boy was trying to go home. She was sure of it. And she knew, absolutely, that she was home to the boy. But what about the man he'd become? He hadn't been waiting for her. Their first night together and he'd excused himself, in public, and disappeared.

She sat up in the dark and groped in the creases of the tent floor until she found her shoes, crawled out, and noiselessly made her way to where his tent lay staked. The doorway was closed and her fingers confirmed more. The tent was zippered shut. Running a finger along the cold spine of the zipper, she called out to him in Navajo, awkwardly, trying not to let her voice carry to the other tents.

Nothing, no answer. *Give it up*. She could hear her own advice, she just couldn't abide by it.

She unzipped the flap of the doorway enough to push her head in. No sound of his breathing. She flicked on her flashlight. Even his bed was gone. She quickly turned off the light. He could be anywhere.

She crawled back to her tent and took her shoes off and stuffed her legs deep down into the strangely narrow sleeping bag, hoping the warmth would dissolve her resolve to fight, because her mind was in revolt against any idea of sleep. She tried another line of logic with herself. Jerome had spoken to her in his language where photographic images replaced words. She was the illiterate one.

Maybe he was waiting for her to catch on, or catch up. She thought back to his aunt's place, and then the bed he'd quickly smoothed, and the blown-up images he'd laid across the bed. He'd given her a challenge. "You figure it out," he'd said. "Let's see how traditional a Navajo you really are."

She must have finally dozed off because she felt disoriented when she heard a sound, close to her head, like the noise of mechanical fingers. She sat up. The tent zipper teeth were separating.

"You're actually sleeping inside this contraption?" The whispered words came unmistakably from Jerome.

"What's happened to you, Lilli? Lost all sense of adventure? Come on, I got us way better seats for the night show." Jerome grabbed at the edge of her sleeping pad. "Give me this thing."

She slid out of the sleeping bag and backed out of her tent on her knees. In the distance, a glowing light—maybe a cigarette—hovered and then moved slowly around the perimeter of the camp.

"Secret Service?" she whispered.

"Suppose they ever sleep?" Jerome whispered back.

She followed him up an incline.

"Here we are." He spread her sleeping pad next to his. "Lie down and settle your head upslope. See? Way better show."

He lay down beside her, the two of them on their backs, looking up at the night sky.

"Never seen the night like this," she said softly. Above them, the sky had been scissor-cut, and a long river of stars flowed over their heads. She realized that, at night, only what the river had cut into the rock was revealed as sky, hiding the rest behind stone.

"Ooh! " She sat up suddenly. "What was that?" She'd felt the weight of a pebble, and then another, bounce across her stomach.

Jerome found the culprit in the beam of his penlight. "Probably a Secret Service toad. Not everyone sleeps at night."

She imagined capturing the tiny toad with its soft white throat, cupping it between her hands, feeling its long digging toes. One of the Night-Movers. When the rains came, the night would be full of their mating calls.

Jerome switched off his abbreviated beam of light. She breathed in the smells of night, the Night-Bloomers, bypassing the thinking part of her brain.

"This is nice." So much sweeter than being inside the tent, alone.

Maybe some of what she smelled was memory, but she sensed stalks of yucca nearby, with its white flowers lustrous even in the dark, signaling with scent to their long-tongued partner moths who would come to them at night, rubbing their moth chins against the male pollen of the flower, then rubbing against the receptive tip of the female. Carrying on with life.

Jerome rolled over alongside her and propped his head up. "Remind you of all those nights, just the two of us, lying on the ground together? No fancy pads or sleeping bags."

She felt his warm breath on her face. "Yes, looking up at the Sky People." She'd slipped into Navajo without intention but it seemed right. "At the House Made of Darkness."

She lifted her arm to point to a constellation. "See it? *Hastiin Sik'ai'í*? Old Man With Legs Ajar." She wondered if she should have kept quiet, if he was now thinking, too, of the man lying face up in the Hoodoos.

"Remember how we liked your uncle to show us his gazing powder?" Jerome said. "We'd watch him dip his finger in the powder, then pull the stuff across his eyelids."

"Hmm." Her uncle was what they called a Stargazer, a diagnostician. The recipe called for grinding together the lenses of the eyes of five of the night birds. Would it help her diagnose Jerome if she could pull gazing powder across her eyelids?

She turned to face him more directly. "When will you tell me more about you, about what you've been doing?"

"Díí tł'éé' da'iilwosh doo," he whispered in Navajo, brushing his fingertips across the lids of her eyes. "It doesn't help to see it coming."

She wasn't going to give up so easily. "We really need to talk, Jerome."

"Shh. Not yet. Sit up. Let me sit behind you."

He got up on his knees and slid around behind her as she sat up. She felt his hands massage her shoulder blades and her neck and the shaft of her spine at the back of her neck. She remembered her *Kinaaldá*, after Jerome had left the reservation, how the hands of the women, her mother and grandmothers and aunts, molded her, changing her from the girl she had been before the bleeding started, to the woman she needed to become. Something stronger.

"I'm not a good Navajo," he whispered in her ear. His voice was so still and the words so slow.

She wanted to turn and face him and hold him. But she stayed facing forward. "Why do you say that?"

He said nothing.

"You have a good beginning, Jerome, a good core."

"I stopped being Navajo a long time ago."

Trust me, she wanted to say, you didn't.

"You know..." Slowly she turned around to face him. "Two days ago, at my office, I had two men come knocking at my office door."

"Mormons?"

"Neither with a black book in their hands. The Federal Bureau of Irresistibility." What was she planning on saying next? How they were abnormally curious about Jerome and his plane and their flight path.

"Have they questioned you, too?"

"No," he said.

Probably just evidence of a lousy joke her mind was playing on her, putting things together that didn't go together. Of course, Jerome didn't kill the man.

Morning, Day Two.

Lilli lay on her back with her eyes open. This was a new intimacy, the crowding together of tents full of strangers. She felt disoriented in such a strange landscape. She lifted herself up on one elbow to confirm what she already sensed. Jerome was no longer sleeping at her side. Where do you suppose he'd disappeared to?

She had to pee so badly she felt pain. Sleep was definitely over. Still, she didn't budge. She blew into her cupped fingers to try to warm them. No, she'd move as soon as she could see her way to the water.

Another of the boatman's firm rules: pee only in the river's wet zone. Park Service rules too: No stinking up the canyon. Use the natural flush.

Night was nearly over. From all the starry broth that lit

up last night's sky only two stars blinked back at her. She slid deeper into the sleeping bag to gather warmth, remembering how conversation between the two of them had stalled out.

He'd gone mute, pretending to sleep even though his breathing so clearly exposed the sham.

A faint brightening began and she sat up. She glimpsed a wing, and then another, and imagined the swarm of bats still night-feeding above her, catching moths, loopily using their tail membrane as the capture tool. They'd fade away with true dawn.

Still, not a human sound. No one moved about camp. But the palest of light spilled into a corner of the sky-eye between rock, and then the distant tip of a cliff caught the first glazing of colored light, and blushed red. Up on the surface of earth, a crack of light pries open the night horizon like a lid and dawn rises, but down here, she realized, dawn must fall. Dawn would slowly work its way down rock until it found the river.

As she waited for more light, the surface of the water began to mutate from black to glossy green. She couldn't stand the pain of waiting any longer. She slid out of the sleeping bag, straightened her clothes, and picked her way toward the water. The sharp air carried the slight scent of tamarisk.

"Whoo - oosh!"

Lilli wheeled around to face the sudden sound.

"Hey, sorry, didn't mean to startle you. I just lit the gas."

The Swamper, bending over her portable kitchen, became visible.

"Give me twenty more minutes and we'll have some hot coffee."

"Thanks."

"First night's always the strangest. Hope you slept OK.

Apologize, too, for Mitch's idea of bedtime stories."

"Sure." The one Lilli immediately remembered from the campfire was how a man named Hansbrough, on the second-ever exploration of the canyon, had drowned near where they were camped, but his head was never found—not for another twenty-seven years, showing up miles and miles downstream.

But she was going to have to make it to the river's wet zone. "I've really got to, you know—pee."

"Good timing. No one's about yet."

Lilli headed upstream. Such a beautiful way to experience Dawn Boy and Dawn Girl, letting them find you at the bottom of a canyon this deep. She took off her PDF to give herself some maneuverablity with getting her shirt up and her pants down and walked out as instructed onto the wet zone at the river's edge. What a peaceful place. She looked upriver along water illuminated as if it were a golden path. It took her a moment to realize the glow was a reflection of dawn-lit rimrock riding the surface of the dark moving water.

Easy for the men. They could send a warm arc well beyond the wet zone, aim for the river itself. She didn't know exactly how this was going to work, what with needing to be modest. But her shirt was long.

She pulled against the elastic of her waistband, sliding just enough of her pants off to give her a bare backside facing out to the other shore. She couldn't feel the baby yet, only the morning sickness. When the baby grew enough to begin to move inside her, her People would say that was because the Holy People had sent a small Wind. The child's In-Standing Wind, that was a different wind, one that wouldn't enter until months after birth, at the baby's first laugh.

She forced herself to concentrate on squatting down and trying to relax.

It happened fast. She felt her feet slip out. She felt the sudden shock of frigid water. Then the water moved her away from shore. She knew she should be struggling. The river felt fluid but rough and powerful at the same time. She tried to kick out with her legs but the water was in a hurry and it held her legs together.

She realized she was being dragged under, she was sinking. Ahboah had tried to teach her of water in a dark lake but what did he know of rivers? *Tééhooltsódi,* the Water Monster, firmly held her. She felt dreamy, overpowered, drugged. She was going to die. She was now completely under water. She knew she shouldn't open her mouth but her brain was screaming at her to take a gulp. Another part of her brain screamed *No! That's the wrong way out!* She couldn't help herself. She gulped for air and felt the pain of water rush her lungs. The water would fill her, and be heavier than air, and she and the baby would travel underwater for miles and miles, and never be seen again.

So this was drowning, so nearly dreamlike, as if she was both moving in a world without air and watching herself drown.

Lilli felt her one self moving away from her other self. She was trying hard to hold on, to not give up. She must be slipping out of her mind.

She felt something grab at her, claw at her, almost human the way it pulled her body against it like a hug. She tried to scream, *No, Jerome!* They'd both drown. She felt his heart pounding against hers.

She'd pull him down. She tried again to scream, *Let go of me, Jerome! Save yourself!* Why wouldn't he let go? She tried to kick away from his grip.

Her brain sent a frantic stream of messages to her lungs to take another gulp of air. *One more!* But it was a trick, there was no air, and now they were both going to drown.

She felt a sudden jerk, like a surprise stop. Something slid up under her back. Jerome let go of her. She felt herself buckle in half. A mouth pressed hard and insistent against her mouth or maybe she was dreaming. No, this was too fierce—what was Jerome doing?

"Get out of my way!"

The voice seemed to come from so far away. She wished she could talk. She wished she could be heard. Her lungs seemed collapsed. Where was Jerome?

"I know what I'm doing, we have a near wet-drowning."

"The hell you say, it's a damn dry-drown. Get off her!"

The voices sounded as if they were coming through water. She knew she should open her eyes and try to explain but she didn't seem to have control anymore.

"Heimlich jump-starts the breathing..."

Lilli felt a crush hoist her up and squeeze her, sharp, from behind.

"We don't allow the Heimlich."

"We do the hug."

"Wastes time, can make it even worse. We go straight to mouth-to-mouth."

"No. Mouth-to-mouth's futile if the airway's full of water. Need to compress the lungs..."

She felt a finger jam inside her mouth.

"Makes it worse, dangerous, you compress the stomach..."

"I'm telling you, her larynx spasmed—closed her airways."

"Laryngospasm? Can hold your breath for only so long."

"Bought her time."

"Glottis relaxes, asphyxia follows—she's damn lucky."

"Stupid."

Lilli gasped for air.

"That, too."

Something squeezed her belly. She was going to vomit.

"Looks like she was in and out so fast her lungs stayed oxygenated."

"Man! You really flew!"

She recognized a voice. That was Mitch's voice, but it sounded disembodied, as if her ears were full of water.

"How the hell did you get to her that fast? Adrenaline wings?"

She tried to turn herself toward where the other voice was located, toward Jerome, to better hear him.

"She went the wrong way."

Boyd's face moved in front of hers. She closed her eyes again.

"Huh?" That was Mitch's voice.

"Women downstream, to pee? Those were your directions: men upstream. She went upstream, she went the wrong way."

"She came to you?"

"Watched her hang herself out over the water. Waited to give her a sense of privacy. Damn lucky mistake. Slipped in, she floated toward me."

Mitch lifted her chin and cushioned her head between his two hands as if he was trying to read her future. She tried to concentrate on what he wanted from her.

"Throw a cadaver in the river, you know, you'll never find any water in the lungs. Cadavers don't breathe."

Where was Jerome? She wanted to say something but she still couldn't find her voice.

Mitch lowered her head back to the ground. She seemed to be lying on sand.

"Lilli? Can you hear me? Sitting you all the way up now, slowly. Here we go."

She felt Mitch's big hands cup her shoulders and then he lifted her from the ground and kept pulling until he held the weight of her chest doubled over her legs. The Swamper materialized in front of her. She folded Lilli's fingers around a cup.

"Hot coffee. Take it, Lilli."

"You lace that with a mountain of sugar?" Mitch said.

"Sure did." Suzanne stepped away from Mitch.

Where was Jerome?

"You drain that cup, Lilli, you hear, cause we're not going anywhere, not until your insides are brought back to a human body heat." Mitch's voice cracked. "What in the hell did you not understand about wearing your life jacket? Jesus, the stupidity!"

Her eyes were beginning to take in the small crowd that had gathered around her, the way onlookers gape at a crash scene.

"This goes for all of you, hear?" Mitch said.

"Wet zone is slippery. You damn well pee with your life jacket on."

Her throat burned with muscle spasms. She tried to sip the hot coffee gingerly, as if through a straw.

"Jerome?" She tried to say his name and wondered if anyone heard her.

"I'm here." He knelt in front of her, with his camera around his neck. "Gee, Lilli—what did I go and miss?" He pressed his hand against her cheek.

She closed her eyes. It was Boyd's heartbeat that had pounded against hers, wasn't it? She'd felt the raw desperate strength and imagined Jerome, fighting for her. But it hadn't been Jerome at all.

Lilli sat on a flat rock with her back to the river. She felt completely stupid. She was certainly more tanked up with coffee than she'd ever been in her life. She avoided looking at anyone. In her paranoia she imagined Lee impatient that she was throwing them all off schedule. She decided to make a move to speed up the process, or at least give the impression she was trying. She removed the blanket wrapped around her shoulders. Her hair was still wet, but she really was beginning to feel warm again.

She'd been told in explicit language to do nothing but sit still and warm up. Jerome would pack their tents and gear, and she would build body heat. Once the heat reached her brain, she was sure she'd be even better able to feel the full spectacle of her stupidity.

She always found herself in moments of crisis to be thinking fast in Navajo. But in their language, control went to the greater intelligence. In their syntax, water could never drown a person because a human had the greater intelligence and should be smart enough to keep out of the way. Speaking with the structure of Navajo words, she'd never say *the river drowned her.* The proper syntax would be *she let herself be drowned by the river.* She had free will. She knew, too, all about life jackets.

"Come on, Dougan, let's loosen up that old arm of yours." Lee juggled a softball between his bare hands.

"Catch? Uh, I'm not much of a ballplayer."

Lilli watched Kevin try to hide his disappointment at not being included by walking away.

Lee took off on a short run across the sandbar and lobbed the ball to Dougan in a high perfect arc.

How precious time like this in the canyon must be to the boy, to have his dad to himself away from the campaign. But not away from Dougan. Too bad, she thought, remembering her own father. A father and a child are bonded forever. Even death can't end that bond. Memory won't let it.

She watched the two grown men play catch, and imagined Lee aging, growing more and more upholstered in flesh. But now, as he shagged a low ball, then lobbed a high return, he had such a natural grace, he looked almost like a teenager.

She heard the *quork* call of a solitary raven and scanned the cliffs until she found the bird, keenly watching them. The raven was a master of word play. *Quork* was a favorite call but sometimes it was *kek-kek-kek*. She watched as the black bird selected a lower perch, closer to them. And then there was the gong sound of the raven, and the grunt, and the rasp, and the girgle. In winter, she loved to watch a raven shovel snow, all the while dressed like a skinny Navajo in shiny black pants, its belly feathers covering up those naked legs.

And what about the eyes? The raven can play mind games. Blue-eyed babies grow into dark-eyed adults with a solid white membrane they can pull over their eyes like a shutter. Fast as a window shade they can make an eye that's alive become a dead-looking eye.

Lilli decided to drain the last of her coffee, hoping they wouldn't force another refill on her. She ran her fingers through her hair, still a little wet, spreading the long strands down her back.

"Hey, you stupid crow! Ugh, Dad! It barfed berries all over my backpack!" Kent, the older twin, held up the evidence. "Nasty!"

"Drag it through the sand, son," Lee said from a distance.

The boy seemed loath to even touch the backpack,

maneuvered it instead between two sticks to avoid the mound of sticky red berries.

His brother came over to inspect the regurgitated pile.

"Hey! My sunglasses are gone!" Kent kicked sand at his brother.

Kevin turned his back to make a shield. "Didn't touch your sunglasses!"

"Then where are they?"

The thief let out another *quork*.

"Boys? What is the problem?" Lee carried the ball toward his sons.

Lilli stood up, a little shaky on her feet.

"I think I see them. Up there. Is that them?" she said.

"Where?"

"The ledge—there, up above us. Shiny things attract these birds."

"That stupid crow! Dad, it stole my sunglasses!"

"It's a raven," Lilli said.

"Like I care." Kent dropped to his knees, picked up a stone and hurled it at the bird.

More evidence of her stupidity? Now why had she gone and said that?

"Kent, go on." Lee held the softball momentarily in both hands over his head. "See if Mother's got another pair of sunglasses." Then Lee lobbed the ball, hard. Dougan shook the sting out of his catching hand.

"So, a raven and a crow?" Dougan said. "Not just two words for the same thing?"

She tried to concentrate and speak up. "Completely different birds," she said. *The bird that thought like a human.*

"How so?" Lee caught the pitch.

"Raven's maybe four times heavier. With a pointed wing, curved bill. Croaks instead of caws." She'd said enough, decided not to explain how in a bunch of ravens, the dominant male plays more tricks, uses feather erection to make himself look even bigger.

Like the problem with these two twin boys, Lilli thought. To make a clear hierarchy, only one twin could be dominant. But there was no natural age ladder between them, only one measured in twelve minutes. And Kent and Kevin weren't genetic twins either, not the same blueprint with two heads of consciousness. They were siblings who seemed to uncomfortably covet the same nest space.

Lee took a careful grip on the softball, cocking his wrist. "Hey, son, want to play?"

Without enough warning, Lee released the pitch toward his gentler, slower son. Kevin went forward, miscalculated the distance and the ball thudded at his feet.

"How about you, son?" Lee feinted a false pitch toward the other boy.

"Nah." Kent turned his back.

So far, Lilli had seen Kent show enthusiasm only when he straddled the front pontoon through the big rapids with the Swamper hooting alongside him. In fact, the one thing she'd noticed both boys shared on this trip so far was a keen interest in the Swamper.

As she watched Kevin throw the dropped ball back to his father, Lilli started to think about evidence. The raven had made a clean theft, but then had fallen prey to display, showing off the sunglasses, so out of reach on the ledge. She'd done the opposite with the evidence, had buried the two coyotes. She hadn't thought to worry, though, about what other forensic evidence the police might already have.

She'd seen the murdered Navajo in the medical investigator's lab. But what other forensic evidence did the murderer leave behind? Her mind started to race.

"Lilli? Feeling normal? Your color's looking better." Mitch stood in front of her with his hand on the top of her head.

"Yes, I'm much better, thanks," she said.

"You sure? Look me in the eyes." He seemed to be giving her a test with his built-in crap detector.

She gave him a level stare. "I'm fine."

"All right, everyone, load up, let's get underway," Mitch said. "Doubt I need to remind you all about wearing your PFDs."

Once moving downstream in the sunlit canyon, Lilli tried to avoid looking at the river directly and focused instead on the canyon walls. She was fine, except for a little cramping low in her groin. She suddenly needed to reassure herself. Her right hand instinctively touched her left wrist, seemed troubled, felt around under her sleeve. No, she must be encircling the wrong wrist. She clearly remembered fingering it as she walked out to the wet zone. She reversed the search but the bracelet of hammered silver and turquoise Ahboah had placed on her for protection was gone.

Duane Fatt leaned his backpack into a boulder of conglomerate rock that was all mixed up like pudding, and temporarily lifted the weight off his hips. He felt hollow-hungry, like Mama used to say. But it wasn't time yet to eat. Work the plan, that's what he kept repeating to himself. Just wait the craving out. Didn't carry much natural fat on his frame, was all. Closing his eyes made him remember how back in grade school some lady with a swinging wattle under her chin would come into his classroom every single morning and make a beeline, set a little box of milk down on his desk just cause he was naturally too skinny.

Better get going. A dry wind picked up dust and blew it across his face. He must have inhaled too deep the way he started to choke. He slid his tongue across his teeth, gathering up the grit, and started thinking about the desert outside

Mama's house, how she told him a Hollywood movie was shot right there, south of Mountain Meadow, pretending to be the great desert of China, and how John Wayne in a skinny rope-licorice kind of mustache pretended he could ride camels, just like Genghis Khan.

The shade felt sweet. He slid out from under the pack and forced himself into deep breathing. Just need a couple minutes rest.

Voices? Duane came immediately to attention.

Jesus F. Christ, he'd been so careful, traveling like a dark shadow, and now this. He had company hiking toward him, no use pretending he didn't.

Odd they hadn't hid from him.

Well, too late now to pretend. They'd all seen each other. Duane stepped out so they'd have to stop. Wouldn't do to show surprise.

No, better keep his voice friendly, better keep his voice calm, authoritative, too.

"You two a little far from home, aren't you?" he said.

Just how long do you suppose they'd been watching him while he sat there with his stupid eyes closed?

Neither one answered.

"You boys Navajo?" *Or hard of hearing?*

Seemed to him the two men held unnaturally still, and now they was looking at each other as if figuring out which one was going to open his mouth and say something.

"No, sir." The older one who'd said nothing nodded at the younger one as if signaling to keep on talking.

"We're Hopi."

"Hopi, huh?" Their hair was black and slippery, same as Navajo. "Kind of far from home, aren't you?"

Again with the no answers.

"This whole canyon's closed to hikers." Duane made a

show of clearing his throat. "You knew that now, didn't you?"

"No, sir."

No, it wasn't natural the way these two men had so little to say.

"No, sir?" Duane kept his voice louder than usual. "You didn't know that? You watch TV? We got the next president of the United States of America down in this canyon. Wants his privacy. You understand?"

"Yes, sir."

He liked the way the talking one was answering him with respect. It was the gear, wasn't it?

They probably thought he was on some government payroll. *Hell, Duane, they won't tell anyone they saw you. They don't have a clue about who you are. But you don't know that.* And now it was starting to bug him the way the older man was holding on so tight to an old sack.

"Why don't you boys show me just what it is you got in that there sack."

The one doing none of the talking didn't like this request, did he? Seemed to stiffen up.

"You heard me," Duane said.

"Nothing, sir." The younger face look perturbed.

"Nothing? Now, boys, looks more like something. Open up the bag. Open that thing."

What difference does it make, man? You're just stalling.

The older one handed the sack to the younger one who removed the leather thong. Duane took the sack from him and peered in, and then he rolled the edges of the sack over to get a closer look at a white substance nestled in the bottom.

"What the...? You guys running drugs?"

"No, sir."

Don't fuck with me, he wanted to say, but he could see he still held their respect.

"How about I make sure, maybe take a taste?" He didn't wait for their permission, just poked his finger down, then put it in his mouth and sucked.

"That there's nothing but salt."

"Yes, sir."

"Yes, sir?"

"For ceremony. It's Hopi salt."

Duane didn't think he should show ignorance by asking straight-out the wheres and whys, way down here, of finding "Hopi salt."

"How far you boys been walking?"

"Down to where the Little Colorado meets the big river."

He needed to think. They'd have a truck, wouldn't they? Parked as close to the end of any dirt track as possible. Probably turned off at Cedar Ridge, past Tooth Rock, across that maze of dirt roads.

Now what if they go and report him? What if they just mention seeing him, to somebody?

"Anyone else coming on up behind you? Anyone else moving salt?"

"No, sir."

He'd spend a little extra time, doctor things up.

"Someone waiting for you back at your vehicle?"

"No, sir."

Too bad they had to go and surprise him.

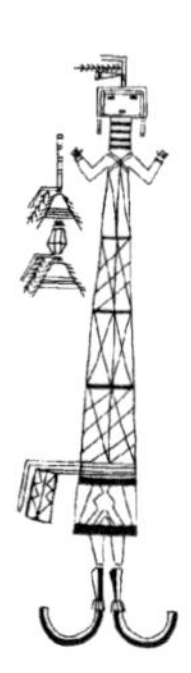

Mitch wanted her in the raft, by his side, insisted on it. What Lilli wanted most was for the rest of today to be uneventful. The cliffs—Mitch chanted out the strata names, starting at the top with a, "Kai-bab, To-ro-weap, Co-co-ni-no, Her-mit, Su-pai"—the cliffs that had seemed high when they pushed off at Lee's Ferry were now impossibly high. Already he had let them know they were three thousand feet deep into the earth, and cutting.

She sat beside him, feeling the river breathe beneath her. Two pilots, yet so different a medium. Riding in Jerome's little airplane, you knew you were pulling off a mechanical stunt. If the engine conked, you'd drop. But the river embraced, made you feel she would take you—or your bracelet—with her, no matter what.

She tried to imagine Mitch off the river, a man for whom

there would never be enough. As soon as this run was made and his chapped lips began to heal, Lilli saw his mind turning back on itself. She was sure he would replay all his moves with her, his river, remembering especially where he'd made a mistake or, miraculously, where he'd sliced the rapid nearly perfectly, but then, inevitably, he would feel the suspicion. He would begin to imagine that the river—his river—was changing, and he would feel his hips start to ache for her.

It wouldn't matter that he was gone too much, that his wife or girlfriend was lonely and wrapped herself around him at night. He would achingly doubt that the river was still his. Cooped up inside four walls, looking out windows, he would barely survive. He'd need another run. No matter how old he gets, she thought, for Mitch, it will always be the same. He will find peace only in those moments of pure chaos when he is up against her, his river, and she is spectacularly wild.

"Your color's better," Mitch said. "How are the nerves? Still a little shaky?"

"I think I'm back to normal," she said.

"Good to hear. So let's see how your tongue's working. What do you think of this entrenchment?"

An evocative English word.

"Thought 'entrenchment' described the opposition," she said. "A political term."

"Could be," Mitch said. "But now you're experiencing an entrenched river. A trapped river."

"Why trapped?"

"Water as a scalpel. Colorado Plateau rises with geologic time, river responds by cutting down into the rock, incises itself, looking for a way out. Instead, just gets itself in deeper. No escape."

Down-cutting. Language you could apply, she thought, to a river or a presidential campaign.

She liked how comfortable Mitch seemed on the river. Like in so much else she experienced, her eyes tried to be the main portal to her mind, to dominate the sensory feel of riding deeper and deeper into the canyon, but there were six human ways of experiencing the river, and she'd felt them all.

Sight. The *bilagáana* named what they saw: the color red, Color-rado, a river of blue water that turned adobe red when it rained. But the Indians who lived down inside the canyon, the Havasupai, used a different experiential sense and named the river for its sound. *Hakatai,* that was their word, the Large Roar.

And then, she thought, there were the other ways: with her tongue catching the flavor of the water spray, the smell of that spray, like mist, that lifted the scents of the river corridor up off the shore and into the air, and then there was her skin. Already her skin had felt river-pleasure and river-pain. And then her mind, the sixth sense, always in motion, weaving intuition and memory and connection.

"Hey, Dad?"

"Yes, Kevin?"

"This man Lee and Lee's Ferry? Are we really related?"

Lilli realized she'd closed her eyes and now opened them to the sound of Kevin's voice.

"Absolutely, son," Lee said. "Makes you proud, doesn't it, to be a part of history."

"Why no apostrophe, dear," his wife said. "You know, I see it on signs as L-E-E-S Ferry?"

"Government decision, I imagine. Harpers Ferry, Lees Ferry. Doesn't change the facts. We're definitely related."

Interesting numerology, Lilli thought, how everything on the river was referenced to Lee's Ferry. Like highways. She'd been a licensed driver for years before she ever realized the web of interstate highways had a numerology, a system. All the even numbers, like Interstate-40 that grazed the Navajo Chapter House at Lupton, headed east-west across the country, whereas all the odd numbers like Interstate-17, that pointed to the home north of Flagstaff of White Corn Boy and Yellow Corn Girl, ran as north-south arteries. But in the Grand Canyon, Lee's Ferry was the linchpin.

The top dog.

Numero Uno.

Every feature along the river had its official position zeroed in at Lee's Ferry. The man's name lodged itself in the back of your brain.

Lilli stood along the river's edge, per Mitch's orders, with the tail end of a line wound thickly through a series of knots. Something special was about to happen.

"Hiking to Paradise," that was all the enticement so far out of Mitch's mouth.

A funny word, "paradise." For some of these people maybe paradise was The Kingdom Come, something that happened after death. Or maybe, for Lee, it was the expected Day After Election.

"What do you mean, without you?" Dougan fumbled with trying to hang a chartreuse water bottle from his daypack.

She could tell Mitch enjoyed squaring up against that city boy. But if it were actually true, it didn't sit well with her either, because she wasn't keen to enter the canyon on foot, leaving Mitch behind.

"I'm staying put," Mitch said.

"You're not coming with us?" Dougan worked on tying an odd-looking handkerchief over the pale skin at the back of his neck.

"Your hearing is fine."

Those two—Dougan and Mitch—would probably never appreciate one another, Lilli thought. Mitch was one of those people who think for themselves and go do. Not Dougan. He was one of those who orders others to go do.

"Yeah, well, let me interject some legalese," Dougan said back. "That idea sounds negligent."

"Negligent? What, you don't trust a woman? Or is it something specific about a particular woman?"

"I'm not taking that bait. No, Suzanne's great. I just think you need to lead us," Dougan said.

"Not a possibility. Never leave the raft: one of my firmest rules."

"Come on, Lilli, help me bolster my argument," Dougan said.

"You men don't need a referee," she replied.

"Not even Lilli could change my mind," Mitch said. "Concrete rule: I stay with the boat, even at night. Sleep on it, remember?"

"Tie on an extra safety line."

"No way. Tide's coming."

"Don't bullshit me," Dougan said. "Even a Brooklyn kid knows tides pull on oceans."

"Didn't say it was natural. But once those engineers did their dirty work, I got Bureau of Reclamation tides coming at me from all that sucking."

"From what?"

"Daily sucking. All that Vegas and California and Phoenix demand for electricity. Tide satisfies demand."

"What? I don't believe you," Dougan said.

"Electricity doesn't keep. Get it? They need more kilowatts, they let more water through the dam. And that creates a tide."

"So plan for this tidal pulse. Make the calculation about

the height or something, and tie up the raft."

"Nope, could get surprised by a spike in demand and we all come back and find the boat hung up. No, I'm staying put."

Mitch made his way toward Lilli. He seemed to be able to take Dougan only in small doses. He transferred the rope from her hands to his, and then rested his elbows on top her shoulders.

"You are one short Navajo, Lilli Chischilly."

She could admit that. Height wasn't everything. Still, she wouldn't want to admit to the ridiculous sense of relief she felt knowing they were going to turn their back on the river, even take off their personal flotation devices and hike on solid ground to whatever Mitch kept calling paradise.

"Lost sight of the man. Where do you suppose he's gone, where's H.A.?"

She knew who Mitch meant. She'd heard him use "Hardened Artery" talking with the Swamper, and now it seemed the codename had shortened to H.A.

"He's over there." She nodded toward Lee. "Helping himself to more water."

Lee was filling his camel pack, one of those water bladders you carry on your back with plastic tubing that snakes over your shoulder and feeds your mouth. She carried a bladderless affair, the old-fashioned canteen once so plentiful at surplus stores.

"All right everyone, listen up. Going to get this show on the road," Mitch said. "Lilli here, she's our official Cultural Interpreter. You have questions, you ask her. We white people have legal access, some would say ownership, of the Grand Canyon. Indians have pride of place."

Not as effective a tender.

"She knows the way?" Lee said.

"For that, you all follow Suzanne."

"Then point me to paradise." Lee flashed a grin.

In a few minutes they were all strung out with Suzanne in the lead and Kent, the older boy, immediately behind her, nearly as tall as she was. Lilli noticed how the Swamper's bare legs were coated in a layer of sunscreen that held flecks of sand, giving her legs a downy silhouette soft as antler velvet.

The Swamper. Lilli liked hearing an English word fill an unusual slot. But she and Jerome had already given the Swamper a Navajo nickname. Tingling Maiden, the one Coyote named *Ch'ikééh na'azílí*. Kent seemed especially to have adopted the Tingling Maiden. His brother Kevin had fallen in behind, close to his mother. Lee paired up with Dougan. The Secret Service agents were a natural pair. As she was, with Jerome.

Lee took the water tube out of his mouth. "So, Lilli, start as our interpreter. Mitch said we'd be hiking through Wata-ho...whatever. Is that a Navajo word?"

"*Watahomigi*? No." Lilli looked at Jerome. "That's Havasupai."

"Have a-what?" Lee stopped in front of her.

"The Havasupai people." Who, not a what, she wanted to say. A tribe, she decided not to say.

"Tell us more."

"They still actually live in the Grand Canyon, in a side canyon called Havasu. Their language was only oral, until maybe twenty or thirty years ago." Kept all to themselves.

"That would require some major isolation," Lee said. "So, is their language some close cousin?"

"To Navajo? No. Two completely different linguistic families."

"Boys?" Lee raised his voice to catch the attention of his sons. "Navajo language, boys, nothing like it." He leaned on his tapered metal hiking pole. "We used them as Codetalkers."

"Dad, we saw the movie. Nicholas Cage, the Marines."

"Kill the Codetalker! Protect the code at all costs!" Kent pantomimed the quick kill of his brother with an imaginary knife.

"Hey!"

"Son, take it easy."

"Like in the movie, Dad. Can't let the enemy find a live one, torture the code out."

Kevin had such slower firing synapses. She was beginning to get a feel for the close quarters with his older twin, how Kent seemed a little off, a little too aggressive.

As the trail steepened and they all found themselves working harder to climb, Lilli fell in place behind Jerome and let her mind wander as she set her feet dutifully to follow the placement of his, letting her mind loose.

Coyote was present at the Beginning. It was Coyote who placed male genitalia on the sky side and female genitalia on the earth side. But she was quite sure something more was being told in the man's murder, some message she hoped the medical investigator continued to fail to decipher. There had to be a reason the killer forced the man in the Hoodoos' mouth full. The longer she hiked, the more certain she became. The gesture was an enactment of something specifically Navajo.

"Son!" Lee cupped his hands to carry the shout. "Kent!"

The boy was far above the group and seemed to have gone deaf, too. He spread up and down over the slickrock like lubricant.

"What are you holding on with, son?"

"My feet!" Kent went higher, completely off trail.

"Careful now! Come on down with the rest of us."

But Jerome took the opportunity to ride up the slickrock

too, loaded with camera gear, readying, she supposed, for when paradise might materialize.

Lilli read the evidence, wondering if the others had even noticed the curved notches cut into the rock, protruding from the cliff like thick lower lips. Come the monsoons, the slickrock would send red waterfalls through these chutes, changing the best laid plans.

She'd been hiking for nearly an hour, with increasing fatigue and increasing pleasure. The trail followed a corridor almost too beautiful to describe. It wasn't just that the rocks surrounding them were thinly layered, but that even the layers were layered, and even those layers were layered again until the burnished rock beds became so slender and curved she felt she was entering something organic.

Suzanne stopped. She held up a hand, gathering them toward her.

"Get ready. We're almost there. Can't see it yet. Just another couple of bends in the trail."

As they moved forward, a special world revealed itself.

All the thinly peeled layers focused into a central slit in the canyon wall. A trickle of water, the remains of the creative force, ran down the slit like a golden rope. And then Suzanne led them around the final curve. The rock cliffs opened up and Lilli felt she'd stepped inside a reflecting sphere. A silent pool of water was mirror. And every surface curved.

She thought of Mitch back at the boat. Paradise has so many meanings. Bliss, rapture, cloud nine. If he'd asked her for a Navajo word for paradise she'd have said there was no specific synonym. The answer though to what Mitch found here seemed obvious: Paradise was something female. The hike was like a long walk up a woman's legs.

"Go ahead, Lilli, interpret for us what you see." Lee crouched on a wide rock ledge.

She needed to launch into another answer quickly. She forged ahead, wondering exactly where she was going.

"I see the Trinity of Water. Water Present, Water Past, Water Future." And then she embarked on an explanation of monsoonal weather and the lipped notches in solid rock and the fossilized paths desert water followed over slickrock, imagining for them the waterfalls running red with dissolved canyon. And how this reflecting pool they now stepped into was ephemeral and would disappear soon, drying up to curls of mud under which life would hide, waiting for the earth to turn. Waiting for water.

Jerome stood above her, above the reflecting pool, behind his tripod, preferring the camera lens to his own natural eyes and film to his own lockbox of memory. If only she could as easily see the Jerome Present and the Jerome Future, the way her own memory held tight to the Jerome Past.

Mitch definitely liked the verbal set-up, egging on, leading a person farther down a path once that person initiated something. Tickled him, in some odd way. But as Lilli sat next to Mitch in the stern, she began to worry about his current motive and her involvement. He had her positioned squarely and deliberately between himself and Kent. Maybe he realized she'd come to share his conclusion, that she didn't like the boy much either. Or maybe Mitch would try to use her to tease the boy, lure him out into more dangerous territory.

She was going to have to watch herself.

The river ahead of them seemed to change color continually. Its spray briefly enveloped her as they pierced through a series of riffles. *Time is a river.* Isn't that what she heard *bilagáana* say? She thought it a poor metaphor. Unlike time, this river had a mission.

"Hey, Mitch? See that big cave?" Kent abruptly nudged her aside, squeezing between her and Mitch.

"Yeah?"

She found it easily, a nearly circular black hole perforating the cliff of red limestone, so accessible from the river's edge.

"Hey, Mitch, come on, you're going past! No, stop!"

She could understand Kent's craving to climb into its black mysterious mouth.

"You ain't seen nothing yet," Mitch said. "Cave of all caves coming up, and we're gonna stop."

"Yay!"

Hosteen Ahboah hadn't mentioned anything to her about other caves in the canyon, or about caves along the river.

"Mitch, does this cave above us have a name?" she asked.

"Stanton's Cave. Same Stanton, second-ever expedition twenty years after Powell—expedition that didn't believe in wasting money on life jackets. You recall?"

"I remember." The initials F. M. Brown inscribed where he drowned.

"After three of Stanton's crew got themselves drowned and with one of the survivors crying like a baby, Stanton stashed their gear in this cave. The expedition came to a complete stop. Stanton didn't try to run the river past this cave, not with the survivors."

"Chickened out? Squawk, squawk!" Kent said. "But how'd they get out of here?"

"Decided to trust their feet for the retreat."

"Cool, come on, Mitch. I can talk my dad into it. Let's go explore it!"

"Cave's closed," Mitch said. "Place today is full of bats, one giant maternity colony teeming with pregnant Townsend bats, all come to roost."

"Way cool! Come on, Mitch, let's go see 'em!" Kent bounced on the collective air-bladder seat beneath them.

"Off-limits, Kent. You don't hear so good. See, there are rules against bothering these bats."

"Hey, Kent?" Kevin had decided to join them, too. "You see that big cave up above?"

"Yeah, but that's nothing, right, Mitch?" Kent said. "Really big cave coming up. And we're stopping."

"Here, Kevin." Mitch offered Kevin a seat on his other side. "Right you are, we'll be stopping. Say, boys, this next piece of river is mighty interesting." Mitch winked at Lilli. "Ever hear of a hermaphrodite?"

"A queer?" Kent rattled the seat by taking to his knees. "Fag, homo, queen?"

"No, not a queer. Something that can mate with itself," Mitch said.

Even Lilli hadn't heard that definition, quite, of a hermaphrodite.

"I'm asking you a serious question, boys. Ever hear of a creature with both parts, you know, male and female?"

"On the same body? Hah, sure—like Kevin."

What was Mitch up to?

"On the same body, yes. A creature that can self-fertilize," Mitch said.

"Fertilize? I don't get it," Kevin said.

"How about, say, be both the Mom and the Dad," Mitch answered.

"Of the same baby?"

"Yeah, weirdo, of the same baby." Kent balanced on his knees.

"The Grand Canyon has a true hermaphrodite."

"Where?"

"See that water spout?" Mitch said.

Lilli turned, too, for a better look at where Mitch was pointing.

Clear water popped out of the red cliff as if through hoses and then fell in freefall, kicking up a mist, a cloud of spray that caught and twisted the light. Then the spray hit a turnout in the cliff and it transformed back from mist into running water, bouncing in riffles of waterfalls down the layered red rock.

"There's the place, the unique home in all the Grand Canyon of the amber snail. I kid you not, a real hermaphrodite. Pretty neat adaptation in a river this wild. One little snail gets separated from the rest, no mates."

"Yeah! Can still have sex!"

Kent's idle was set way too high again.

"With itself?" Kevin asked.

"Yeah, Kevin, have sex with yourself!"

"Can reproduce," Mitch said. "Even without a mate."

"You got something you're not showing me, Kevin?"

"Shut up, Kent!"

In the Navajo Creation Story, *Nádleeh*, the One That Is Both Ways, appeared in the Fourth World. Traditional older Navajo held the man-woman of the hermaphrodite in esteem. They would never make fun of it being both ways. But, these days, younger Navajo grew up steeped in *bilagáana* culture where she knew making fun was rampant.

In general, their tradition saw femaleness in everything that was male, and maleness in everything that was female. But she was beginning to see that these twins, both boys, were not the same in that trait either. One was so much more full of maleness than the other.

Mitch stood up. "Can you all hear me?"

On this quiet stretch of river, the others had chosen the

front of the raft, with the cool updrafts created by the nose of the raft separating the air gliding just above the water.

"Eyes open now," Mitch said. "Like Babylon, we're about to pass the incomparable Hanging Gardens of Vasey."

The cliffscape that appeared, as if from a dream, was startling. A piece of pristine tropics came cascading out of the red rock cliff, glowing green as a hallucination.

"Weren't for the poison ivy, we'd take a closer peek," Mitch said. "Vasey's Hanging Garden is full of maidenhair ferns and cardinal monkey flowers and watercress and orchids—and something else, right, boys?"

"So Mitch is teaching you something. Excellent, boys," Lee said. "What else?"

"Uh—a snail, Dad."

"I see, well, who was Vasey?"

Mitch angled the raft to hold their position a little longer. "A man who never set foot in the Grand Canyon. Getting his name on it was a gift."

"A gift? What do you mean?" Lee asked.

"Powell. He named it after a friend back home, thinking how Vasey would have loved this tiny gem. Powell, himself, didn't even take time to stop."

"How come?"

"My opinion? The man had survival on his mind."

A fraction of a mile downstream Mitch beached the raft. The cave opening had perfect beach access, and Mitch drove the raft up to let them embark under the overhang. The word "cave" hardly seemed appropriate. Lilli tried on some other English words, fixing on "amphitheatre" for the way the rock opened up like a giant eye.

She wondered what it would be like to be here alone, or with people adult enough to hold their silence. As she entered the void, moving away from the light toward the deep black interior, Kent hurled a yodel, and caught a bounce. The boy was quick with his mouth, and just as quick with his movements. A dangerous combination, she thought. Narcissism and inexperience.

She heard some of the others questioning Mitch for the statistics.

"Great acoustics. What's this monstrosity called?"

"Redwall Cavern."

"Who found it?"

"Powell, of course. He told the world he'd found a natural theater with room for fifty thousand concert-goers."

"You think that's right?"

"One could argue. But the number that could fit inside this place is huge."

Lilli made her way to the cheap seats at the back, where the wall of the cavern sloped to meet a floor of sand. She sat down to take proper notice of the way the amphitheatre's opening created a single Cyclops, an eye that framed the canyon from river to distant rim.

The soft coolness of the sand floor against her nylon-shrouded legs felt good. And then Lilli noticed what she was sitting in, and among. Hieroglyphics. The sand beneath her recorded the furtive comings and goings of theater attendees with tiny feet. Mice.

Lee and the others seemed less interested in exploring and stood along the open edge of the cavern. From her distance, the backlighting made them into matchstick-sized silhouettes. Jerome, too, had disappeared with his cameras.

Mitch found her in the near-dark. "Thought you'd like this place. The Inner Gorge of Marble Canyon's finest piece of solution."

Knowing Mitch, she knew he'd stopped to take a look at Stanton's cave at least once, off-limits or not.

"What about that higher inaccessible cave?"

"Stanton's cave? So you sensed I've crawled up and peeked?"

"Kind of guessed you might have."

"Yeah, well, it was a most special cave, once. Ransacked in the 1970s when some archaeologists pulled out a cache of perfect split-twig figurines of a spirit-animal. Carbon-dating said they were made by someone four thousand years ago."

So, a ceremonial cave. She wondered if *Hosteen* Ahboah knew of that cave.

Kent raced toward them in the dark, flinging the beam from his flashlight from one side to the other.

"Hey, Mitch, where are you?"

"So much for any peaceful contemplation," Mitch whispered. "Yo, Kent, over here."

"Come look! There's a queer bunch of flowers."

"And that would be interesting because?"

"They're blooming in the dark!"

"Come on, Lilli, alley oop." Mitch helped her to her feet. "Time we get back on the river, anyway."

She and Mitch followed Kent. The plant was in full bloom, glowing white as if a tiny flashlight hid in each trumpet-shaped flower.

"What do you think, Lilli?" Mitch said.

She knew why it was open. It was looking for its pollinator, a long-tongued moth, that would come to it only in the dark.

"Plant is fooled into thinking it's night," she said.

Kent's enthusiasm had attracted his brother and Jerome to the night-blooming plant.

"What kind of plant does that?"

"Oh, has lots of names, this one," Mitch said.

Of course he knew it. He'd just been egging her on.

"Datura. Jimson weed," Mitch continued "Want to warn you, Kent, it's hallucinogenic."

As if danger weren't an invitation.

Mitch looked back into the cavern one more time.

"Okay, no stragglers. Let's get back on the river. We've miles to go before we sleep."

She followed Lee and his wife on board. With an audience, like the press at Lee's Ferry, the couple had been masterful at evoking gestures that gave the impression of great caring between them, and pride. But the audience on the raft lacked the clout of crowd they'd grown used to, and Lilli noticed how the stage business between them was fading.

The river, too, would be unkind. The woman's golden hair, cut nearly as short as her boys, was looking flatter and stale. She might soften, Lilli thought, and relax into being so out of the limelight. Or she might go brittle and vacant. Lilli decided she'd have to make more of an effort to talk with her, the two of them among so many men. What she wasn't sure of was if her gesture would be welcomed.

Here comes trouble. Dougan and Lee probably weren't going to bully her yet. But she expected they'd isolate her—no witnesses—and then play tag-team. Lilli stood up uneasily on the moving floor of the raft. Like a whistle, a lone peregrine falcon split the tapered air between the canyon walls in a sudden dive to kill.

"About to find land. Grab on," Mitch called out.

Lilli sat down hard on the raft's inflated bladder. The Swamper adroitly jumped to shore and the raft shuddered against this change in plans.

"Hold on, everyone. Let her tie us up," Mitch said.

The Swamper wrapped the line around a thick trunk, forcing the raft to hold its snout upstream.

"OK, Dougan," Mitch said. "This is obviously it."

Thirty-nine river miles already from Lee's Ferry, past

Shinumo and Tatahatso, and they'd found the obvious man-made cavity. Its litter gave it away. Now Lee and Dougan, and apparently she, would pretend to examine the test tunnel of the infamous Marble Canyon dam site with its one projected leg on the Navajo reservation. Was the man really serious about placing another dam in the canyon?

Within minutes, the Swamper spread a slick oilcloth on the ground to act as picnic central. So piercingly lithe, Lilli thought as she noticed how the men, and especially the twin boys, watched. Suzanne had a natural sensuality, sexual and athletic at the same time, the way she bent from the waist, perfectly logical, efficient even, except it lifted her bottom up in the air as if her *nitl'aa'* were her head.

"So, Mitch, come clean. River runners like yourself," Dougan said. "You'll vote with us, right? You prefer having the dams."

"Go back to warm beer and soda pop?" Even in the shade of his brim, Mitch held his eyes in a permanent squint.

The man had a collection of caps. This one's stitchery proclaimed above its beak *River Runners Are Meanderthals.*

"What red-blooded American would vote for that?"

She didn't get what Mitch meant until he held up the mesh bag of aluminum cans. Of course. No more warm soda pop. The dam refrigerated the river, by letting it out only at the dam's frigid bottom. And every mile, Mitch took advantage, towing their mesh bag full of aluminum cans behind them, in water shockingly cold. But pretty soon they'd be guessing which aluminum can held what beverage because the labels were fading to oblivion as the river's sediment load gave the traveling cargo a scour.

"Temporary fix, though," Mitch said. "Dam won't last."

"Course it will."

"Two hundred years. So say the experts."

To a politician, she thought, two hundred years was expediently forever.

"What will finally end it?" she asked. Besides sabotage or political will.

"It'll shit itself in, if you'll excuse my English. All the glory of Marble Canyon will be nothing but a mudflat."

"Come on, everyone, help yourself." Suzanne held a stack of plates.

Lilli stood at the end of the line, in front of Mitch. Thanks to the miracle of dry ice, they were eating well.

Back in Window Rock, what had Bitsoi tried to tell her?

Lee likes you can think bilagáana *law, same as him. He don't want some old Navajo prattling on and on. He wants to cut to the chase.*

Be careful, she thought.

In the center of the picnic spread was a plate heaped with Guerilla cookies, a secret recipe so far, but two obvious ingredients were the whiskers of coconut and the pointed seeds of sunflowers. Lilli found herself, however, becoming even more addicted to Nutella, a concoction the Swamper said was born of necessity with World War II rationing, a buttery cream of hazelnuts and chocolate with quadruple the carbohydrate punch of peanut butter. At home, she ate piñon nuts gathered from the dirt when they fell this time of year—some years boom, some years bust. She ate them whole, never bothering to grind them except with her back teeth.

Mitch touched her on the shoulder. "You know, there's this side canyon behind us. Always wondered, never asked. Shinumo? One of your words?"

"Hopi, I think." To get to the Colorado River the Hopi had to cross the Navajo reservation, a traverse they made repeatedly to their *sipapu*, to pay respect, to gather salt. "Some people say it refers to an ancestral tribe."

She was about to sit down next to Jerome. Nothing was going well so far, neither her preparing for Lee and Dougan, nor her gaining access to the inner workings of Jerome's mind. She might as well admit there was little chance of being intimate with Jerome. That would have to wait until tonight, their second night. And now Dougan caught her eye and motioned her to come up the talus slope and join him where he stood with his weight on his downslope leg. Above him lay the gaping tunnel entrance, cluttered with machinery parts.

She joined him, leaving Jerome behind, and then Lee joined the two of them, brushing crumbs from his face.

"You know what I'm thinking, Dougan? You relax here, enjoy your food. I want Lilli to myself."

"No, I'll come..."

"Sorry. Change of plans."

She watched both men's eyes closely. If Dougan was the quarterback who really called the plays, and Lee was more like the ball, was this about to be the con, the feint, that old high school ploy, the pump fake?

But Lee had already turned upslope and gained ground. She scrambled behind as he scaled the talus to the obvious hole.

"So this is where it once almost happened..." Lee waited for her to catch up. "This is the dam our government almost built?"

In legal choreography, it was always tricky not to give away too much too soon. "Yes, this is the test site," she said.

And the site had passed the test. All the equipment of the team of government surveyors had been floated in—not on water, but on a sky cable, four thousand feet long.

"Made a goodly mess," Lee said. "Just look at the size of this tailings pile."

The spoil heap. According to the experts, the site was

"perfect" for a second dam downstream of the Glen Canyon dam, even if it would have its one flank firmly anchored on Navajo land.

Lee entered the man-made opening and she followed him into the stale air, adding the beam of her flashlight to his. Steel tracks and more abandoned machinery sat inside. She felt cold. In the low illumination she estimated the drift tunnel went back fifty feet or more into solid rock. Deeper holes punctured both sides of the river, test bores that ran for hundreds of feet, gauging the strength of the rock.

Was it too obvious to say out loud what kept running through her mind like a loop? How everything so far—slender Marble Canyon with its incised halls of polished stone, the hidden pool and onion-rock Mitch called paradise, Vasey's oasis, Redwall Cavern with its perfect acoustics, its seating for thousands—would all be drowned by a dam?

"Seen enough? Think I have. Let's find ourselves some air." Lee led them out to the mouth of the tunnel and fresh air.

Lilli looked down at the relentless river whose voice had been muted inside the hole.

Just the two of them, off the record, no witnesses. Was that why Dougan was missing?

"All right, sit down, no one's going anywhere without us," Lee said.

She found a level rock. Lee sat opposite her and smiled. In his pre-Senate days he had been a decent trial lawyer, she knew that much about him. And trial lawyers were compulsive planners who didn't like surprises, didn't like being outmaneuvered. Well, neither did she.

"You know what they say, Lilli. The twenty-first century is all about energy and all about water."

And the exploiter wants to be ahead of the curve, she thought.

Lee didn't fear Congress. What he feared were the courts. Meaning the Indians. Meaning the Navajo. Meaning, she supposed, a Navajo lawyer.

"What California wants—and I absolutely plan to deliver..." Not even a hint of a smile remained, not on his mouth, not in his eyes. "Is legal guarantee. Legal guarantee of water."

She felt a surge of adrenaline, an urgent sense to move. Legal guarantee, meaning what? Lee wins the election. And then Lee plays God? That was the plan, wasn't it? He captures water. He generates power.

Legal guarantee meant that even if there was an unfortunate change in the weather or the climate or the snowpack, California would get its water. No matter if there was enough, no matter if there was none for the others. No matter what.

"So, just the two of us, Lilli. I'm showing you my cards. What have you got?"

Why can't an ancient culture be left alive? They'd already suffered Bosque Redondo, the Long Walk home, the Bureau of Indian Affairs, the missionaries, the English language, the removal of their children to boarding schools for years at a stretch, the television invasion. But maybe the power brokers in Washington had found the final solution. Take away the water.

Lee must have thought she was too slow in answering him, that she was uncooperative.

"Fine, let's start with 'Use it or lose it.' You Navajo haven't used it. Means you lost it."

The power phrase, his opening gambit—"use it or lose it." True, a legal argument could be made that by not using more of what the courts called "wet water," the Navajo had lost claim. But a counter argument could be made, too.

"Doesn't mean we've lost claim," she said. "This is a federal issue, not states rights." Which turned the tables on Lee. "Federal treaties precede the states entering into independent water pacts."

Which put the Indians on top. An obviously untenable position for Lee.

She watched his face.

"Your reservation runs a total of how many miles along the Colorado River?"

Where was he headed now?

"Seventy-eight miles," she said. "But the boundary is not 'along' the river. We own to the middle of the river."

No, she doubted she could ever be on Lee's team.

"To the middle? You're trying to say that for seventy-eight miles you own half the Colorado River? Oh, I most definitely disagree."

"The Navajo's western boundary was set aside by Executive Order." Nothing the states had a finger in. "That Executive Order clearly states that the boundary of the reservation is the center line of the Colorado River."

"Oh, that's rich, the center line? Well, maybe it did, big mistake. But that mistake's been corrected. Trumped by the Grand Canyon Enlargement Act."

"No, they tried trumping it. But according to federal law that Act is clearly invalid," she said. "It was subject to Navajo consent. And..." Legally, as Lee so plainly knew. "We never consented."

To be pushed from the center line of the Colorado River to a distance off into the desert, with no river access at all?

"Easy sidestep. The legal question of boundary is real different from the legal question of water rights."

Water *rights*? Now there was a euphemism. At last tally, the average person in Phoenix gobbled up, what with dishwashers and washing machines and lawns and fountains and pools, some three hundred gallons of water per person per day. She was a true desert dweller, couldn't even imagine that quantity of gluttony.

"Yes, but we have mainstream rights to the river," she said. "Reserved for us upon creation of the reservation." He knew the precedent, she was sure of it. "The Winters Doctrine."

"Nope. Your so-called mainstream water, Lilli. It was never quantified."

The man had a point. In Winters, the amount of water reserved for the tribes was not specifically quantified making the matter inchoate—a lovely English word but loaded to the ears of the law—meaning unclear, tentative, not definitive.

She had a clear counter. "U.S. Supreme Court, Arizona vs. California. Defined quantified by intent."

"Intent? You mean PIA?"

So the man did pay attention.

"Yes, PIA. Practically Irrigable Acreage. To the extent Navajo land is irrigable we have rights to that quantified amount of Colorado River water."

"We'll see, won't we? Give me a year in Washington."

Did he actually think he had a clear shot?

"PIA is no longer the exhaustive test. Try on 'habitable acreage'," she said. "Supreme Court more recently declared the tribes entitled to all the water necessary to make the reservation habitable."

What did Lee think? That an educated Navajo like herself, with two college degrees, was an oxymoron? Once educated, she couldn't possibly retain Navajo values?

"Listen, Lilli, let me be candid. California wants a legal guarantee of water and I plan to deliver."

The Navajo needed so little water. They were used to having to haul water by hand and by pickup truck. But only the very young saw issues as simple. She was too old for that. Water and energy were tortuous problems, complicated by the clout of money and the need for votes.

"I'd like you to hear me out. I told Dougan to stay put below with the rest of them because I want to make sure you understand me, Lilli. When I move to Washington, Dougan's expecting his reward. A Cabinet appointment. Interior. That's my plan."

Dougan? Whoever headed the Department of Interior in the Lee administration would have their fingers on all the important buttons, of course, the perfect position for overseeing construction of a new dam.

"He could make life miserable for your people," Lee said.

"Is that a threat?"

"An inducement."

The two Secret Service agents relocated along the periphery of camp. They didn't socialize, she noticed, except with each other. They were paramilitary, she supposed, and always on duty. How much longer before Dougan and Lee called it a night?

Jerome sat next to her, around the fire, messing with a stick in the sand at their feet. Funny, the mystery of love. How each of us who once loved holds the other one inside us.

Above the canyon rim where her husband Jake lay tonight in their bed, the moon behaved so differently, first clearing the horizon and then bathing the terrain in white light. But already the river had Lilli down deep, nearly a mile below the rim, and the moon itself hadn't showed, only its probe as it frisked the black cliffs.

She felt Jerome's knee brush against hers.

When they were children, they'd trusted each other

completely. But so far, she hadn't liked the behavior of the man, the way Jerome had just showed up on the reservation, never once called from L.A., never told her in advance about the possibility of the job with Bitsoi.

At least the obligatory circle around Mitch's campfire was getting smaller. The two boys had drifted off first, disappearing right after dinner.

A small wind carried the smell of released resins across the dying fire toward her. In a little while everyone would go to sleep, and she and Jerome would again—their second night—be wrapped in the darkness. Together. She was afraid she'd squander this time they had, removed from the rest of the real world, isolated from Jake, and whatever else they'd find waiting for them at the journey's end.

Like a dog to an itchy welt, her mind came back to the same obsessive worry. Did Jerome get the drift—how Bilgehe's body, splayed out in the inaccessible Hoodoos, looked as if it had fallen from the sky? In a *bilagáana* courtroom, using *bilagáana* law, circumstantial evidence could convict, especially with murder.

Maybe she was too focused, maybe she was the one who couldn't see the obvious. The man lay dead in the Hoodoos, true enough, but the killing took place someplace other than the Hoodoos. Wasn't that the MI's conclusion? Which meant that a dead man was transported into the Hoodoos. But why? There were other ways of hiding a body. The answer that kept leaping to the front of her brain was always the same. To make an image, to compose a message. She came full circle back to Jerome.

The fire crackled in the darkness. She tried to organize her fears.

Mitch interrupted her thoughts. "You agree, Lilli? Lee thinks I'm trying to bait him."

"How's that?" She hadn't been paying attention.

"Which he is," Lee said. "Denial, Mitch, it's not a pretty thing."

"I'm not denying anything. All I'm saying is John D. Lee was in hiding. He hid out at Lee's Ferry."

"Hid? What does Mitch mean by that?" Dougan said. "Hid from who?"

"No one," Lee said. "John D. Lee served his people well. Ferried hundreds across the Colorado River, safely."

Hundreds came, like tamarisk, Lilli thought, with its long tap root and insatiable thirst.

"It *is* sweet, you know," Mitch said, "to hear you make a saint out of a boatman."

Mitch stood at the edge of the fire, his thumb in the journal. "Was hoping the boys would be here but it's getting on. Think I'll share a little more from John Wesley Powell before we call it a night."

"Sure, go ahead, I'd like that," Lee said. "The boys are probably with their mother. Go on, give us a short read."

"We've followed the exact route of his exploration," Mitch said, "but it helps to hear the man's own words:

> *You cannot see the Grand Canyon in one view, as if it were a changeless spectacle from which a curtain might be lifted, but to see it you have to toil... through its labyrinths.*

"Amen to that," Lee said.

"*The Great Unknown.*" Mitch sat the journal on his lap with his finger marking place. "Rumor had it—and Powell had no way to know different—that there was no way out of the canyon by water."

"No exit?"

Mitch reopened the journal. "Indians told him the river dove underground, that he'd be stuck." He continued to read:

> *It is a region more difficult to traverse than the Alps or the Himalayas, but if strength and courage are sufficient to the task, by a year's toil a concept of sublimity can be obtained never again to be equaled on the hither side of Paradise.*

"Nice ending to the night, Mitch," Lee said.

There's that word "paradise" again, Lilli thought.

For Jerome today, paradise was probably the capture on film of the play of rock-reflected light on water. Yet there was no way a camera lens could ever capture all that her senses—her ears, her breath, her skin—had experienced today. Jerome was probably high, too, from the sheer physical thrill, that out-of-body sensation of flying through rapids.

She stared into the fire, restless to be left alone with him. The part of the flame that was blue she found hypnotic, the way it would appear, dance, and disappear. She was starting to feel tired. Maybe she could pull him away from the fire.

She gathered up her empty cup.

All the while listening to Mitch, she'd noticed how Jerome messed around drawing lines in the sand. As she stood up, she saw the lines from a higher angle. The sand around his feet was incised with swastika.

"Eee-iiii!"

Lilli turned toward the night and its scream. It was the boy, no, one of the boys—she couldn't be sure which one—and he was nearly naked. He was running toward them, not to stop, more as if he would trample the fire. And he was jammed into a siren of a scream.

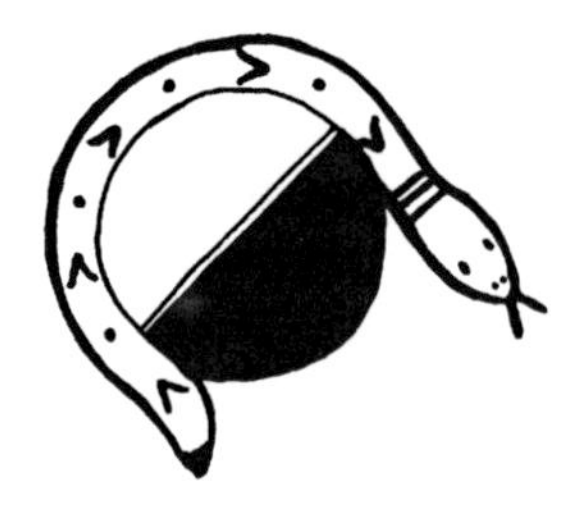

Maybe the two boys were just having fun, the way the one chased after the other so fiercely. Lilli watched as Kevin, in the lead, streaked through camp ahead of his brother, who was fully clothed but for some reason Kevin was nearly naked with just the boy-tight whiteness of his underpants glowing oddly in the darkening night. Then the scream like terror came again and she knew it was no game.

A snake, a scorpion, a fall? But the scream was too full of on-going terror. Worse, she sensed the boy wasn't running toward them for help, he was running away from something. What?

He changed his course—he'd changed his mind. She couldn't understand what was happening, but she ran toward him instinctively, just as a Secret Service agent materialized out of the darkness and brought the boy down, toppling him in a tackle and nearly knocking Lilli off her feet.

The boy kicked at her but she threw herself on top his flailing legs. He seemed even more alarmed now that they held him, his face distorted with horror and panic. His bare skin felt so hot, so flushed.

"Get off me!"

Frank held his shoulders pinned under him and pressed the side of his head to Kevin's chest. "His heart rate's enormous, it's galloping!"

The other agent carried the twin in an arm lock. Frank wheeled his head up to confront Kent.

"Your brother's heart is thumping out of his chest. How long have you been chasing him?"

"He went crazy on me. I was trying to catch him, to stop him."

Beneath her, Kevin was trying to throw her off as if he had the energy to run back into the night.

"I can't see!" The boy struggled wildly and spit but she knew better than to let go.

"What the...? He's lost his eyes."

The whites of Kevin's eyes had disappeared, like a raven in reverse, she thought, the eyes she saw were round and strangely black.

"His pupils are so dilated, something extreme..."

Blown? She didn't want to say it out loud. The boy was in some sort of overdrive.

"Let me get a rate..." Frank kept the side of his head pressed to the boy's chest. "Way too fast! I'm getting more than 140 beats per minute!"

If he got loose he'd bolt for sure. Where? Into the night? Into the river?

"Damn it! His heart's still climbing!"

"They're coming for me!" The boy's eyes, fully dilated,

were seeing something.

"Feel behind his head..."

Everyone seemed to be talking at once but Lilli willed herself to hear only Frank. "Maybe he hit his head."

"Nothing's wet." Frank rolled the boy's head between his hands. "No sign of bleeding."

"Allergic reaction—anaphylaxis? Think! Did your brother get bit by something? A snake?"

"No!"

Didn't make sense, she thought, not a snake bite. No, the symptoms were too jumbled.

"Stomach's soft..."

"Get them off me! They're climbing all over me!"

"Christ, maybe it's scorpions, maybe they're still stinging him."

She jerked the underpants off the boy, ran her hands up and down his limbs. "Can't find anything..."

"Get them off! They're everywhere!" Kevin, blind as he was, saw something. "They're coming for me!" His hips thrashed, furiously.

"Maybe he's hallucinating."

"Did your brother swallow pills? Christ, he's pumping faster and faster!"

She knew reservation poverty and she knew drunks and junkies. A stimulant like cocaine? That'd cause the heart to race, yes, definitely, but it'd work on the whole flight system. If this was cocaine, then the boy should be drenched in sweat. And he wasn't. His skin felt strangely dry. Did the boys get hold of the stash of beer in the mesh net, did they swill it fast? Didn't make sense. Beer, alcohol, these were depressants, the heart rate should slow, the pupils constrict, but his eyes were so oddly expanded.

Boyd shook Kent hard by his shoulders.

"What's your brother on? You brought drugs with you, didn't you?"

"No!" The boy looked scared.

He knew something, Lilli could sense it.

"Delusional? Angel dust, PCP?"

"Doesn't make sense, wouldn't get a heart racing like this."

"Did he swallow pills?"

"Christ, he's just pumping faster and faster!"

"What were you two doing? What happened?"

"Nothing, he just went crazy. I just tried to chase him down."

"Christ, I think the boy's gonna seize."

How much time did they have? The boy's eyes no longer looked human. His back arched.

"I can't see!" Kevin screamed.

"Take his legs."

There wasn't time for argument. Lilli let go of his thrashing legs and ran headlong to the campfire, to the bucket, and emptied the water on the fire. The fire hissed back at her. She couldn't risk waiting. She plunged her hands into the coals still steaming from the drenching and scooped up bits of charcoal, grinding them between her palms. She ran back to the boy and shoved her fingers deep into his mouth.

"Hey! What the hell?"

The boy gagged, but she forced the handful of charcoal to the back of his tongue. She felt his involuntary swallow.

"Christ, you're choking him!"

Maybe she was absurdly wrong. Nothing happened. The boy lay eerily still and then the boy gagged. She clutched his head and raised it toward her and he puked all over her.

"What the...? What's all that green gunk?"

She looked over at the silent brother.

"Datura," she said.

"He ate that plant? Where would he get such a crazy idea?"

She didn't say a word. She just remembered Mitch telling the boys that the flower that bloomed in the dark was hallucinogenic.

"I don't have any field experience with this, Lilli. What's happening?"

Dry as a bone, red as a beet, a racing heart, hallucinatory attack—Datura was all over the reservation. It had a special name to the Navajo: the plant-you-don't-even-talk-about. Much less touch. Much less eat.

"Hey, his heartbeat—it's slowing down. What do you think?"

"Think it's good he didn't eat any more of it than he did," Lilli said. "Datura—it's alkaloid poisoning. Induces an amnesia. He probably won't remember any of this."

"There's blessing to that."

"He'll sleep, sleep long, and wake up complaining that the sun's too bright. His eyes will hurt. He'll need a pair of sunglasses."

Frank let out a deep exhale. "All right. Show's over."

She moved back to give Frank space to monitor Kevin's vitals. For the first time Lilli let herself see the circle of people around them, all eyes on the boy. She knew they must have been shouting, but she could only remember hearing Frank's voice.

Lee now rested his hand on her shoulder. "Thank you."

She looked up at his face. The man pretended to be pleased. He was the master of making the gesture. At a deeper level she could see he was furious with her, hated that she had seen something he didn't want anyone to see.

Lilli stared at the underside of her tent roof, too worried to even try to sleep. What would happen in the morning, how would Lee treat her, tomorrow? She asked herself the bigger question: Would Lee now abort the trip? And then she answered herself. You mean, put the boy's welfare above his own? She knew the answer. Lee had stopped doing that a long time ago.

Besides, the last thing Lee would want to provoke was bad publicity, to show he was incompetent, couldn't even handle his own son in isolation. And no matter how much he put a gag on it, the story could leak and make for bad press. No, Lee would stay the plan.

She closed her eyes.

One ego can destroy a family.

But something about the way Lee gathered his family around the exhausted boy made her wonder. Maybe being here in the wilderness, alone, was Lee's attempt to give his family one extended private moment, to better cement them before they became the First Family in the full glare of the public's headlights. Maybe that was what this interlude on the river was about, at least as a minor chord. Maybe he thought their being here together could help this family that was not a happy one.

The night air chilled her. She wrapped the sleeping bag around her legs and tried to drown her thoughts in the sounds of the river that never slept. She kept returning to the image of Datura. Her people called it *Ch'óhojilyééh*. The One That Makes Madness.

Datura-reality was a full blown hallucination, more like going to the dark side. The Moonflower, some called it. Blooms at night, hides at day. Wrapped itself tight in the light to hoard its perfume, unwrapped in the darkness to lure its moth. A seduction of petals glowing white in the night, letting loose their sweet perfume.

She'd seen it used only by a rare Singer, only when it was necessary to ask for Datura's help. Blessing the sacred plant first with pollen, giving it a bead of turquoise in return, taking only a little root, never the seeds.

She was pretty sure the boy hadn't eaten enough of the plant. Hopefully, only his eyes would ache in the light. Certainly tomorrow would tell. She twisted from her back to her side, knowing that sleep was still far away.

What should she do about Jerome, about what was left of tonight? Because, by tomorrow morning, they'd be surrounded by people again.

The last thing she remembered before the boy's scream was standing up, and seeing the swastika drawn in the sand at Jerome's feet. Eons before Hitler, the Navajo had the swastika, although never that word. Hitler's swastika and the Navajo swastika, this was a convergence, two things that came to resemble one another although the resemblance was false.

The fragment of a song came to her. She let it repeat and multiply inside her head. Jerome had erased the image dug in the sand, hadn't he, after she stood up? He must have known by the look on her face, just before the scream, that she'd seen. A new image filled her mind, of a Singer's fingers slowly letting colored sand grains fall to the swept floor of a hogan.

But then another image intruded and she saw the Singer first burying a small bowl in the sand floor of the hogan and filling it with water and then sprinkling it full of golden pollen and carefully laying over the floating pollen a layer of fine black charcoal, and you could no longer see the water, but it was there, in the center. And then the Singer, slowly creating the drypainting, maybe ten feet in diameter, working on his knees for hours until the drypainting was ready for The Dreamer.

Why was she thinking of The Dreamer?

The specific drypainting, what the *bilagáana* called the sandpainting, was formed first by the Singer creating the image of two enormous spruce logs laying across one another at right angles, the way a cross is drawn. And then the sharp bend at the outer tips of each of the crossed limbs was created, the Singer's fingers forming with colored sand two *yé'ii* for each log, two Holy People. One male, she thought, one female. The entire image of the whirling logs and their attendant *yé'ii* rotating sunwise in the water, that's what she saw in her mind. The Navajo likeness of a swastika.

The contaminated symbol of the Nazis was left-pointing, its shape similar to the Tibetan swastika of continuous motion. But to the Navajo the shape was not "swastika," but Whirling Logs.

Was that Jerome's intention? Did he intend to show her another image tonight, beyond the Upside-Down Girl? Lilli twisted in her sleeping bag, uncomfortably confined.

With complete bare honesty, what really was she doing here, in the bottom of the Grand Canyon, alone in a tent? She'd made up her mind to refuse Lee. She shouldn't even be here. But then Bitsoi—and then Ahboah—had given her reasons. With complete bare honesty—come on, that wasn't why she was here, was it? She'd seen the opportunity as a slick solution to her raw need to have Jerome to herself. Because something in his eyes—maybe it was just the deep sadness she saw, the guilt a survivor carries for not being there, for being in the air, when his wife and child died. But she so sensed it was something else. Something not with a Los Angeles core.

Somehow he'd made her "it"—she was supposed to

figure it out, something with a Navajo core. She suddenly felt the presence of someone in the dark, just outside her tent.

She tensed.

Lilli heard the zipper teeth pulling apart. She reached for her flashlight but couldn't find it fast enough. The person slipped inside.

"Let's get out of here, away from camp. I need to talk to you."

"Jerome?" Was he really going to talk with her about something that mattered?

She slid out of her sleeping bag and found her shoes, and followed him out the way he'd come in, zipping the tent behind her. He led her away from the other tents where all was now quiet and still. He led her toward the river. No one would be able to hear them over the river's restless run.

"What is it, Jerome?"

"I've gone and done something stupid." He wasn't taking any chances on being overheard. He whispered in her ear, "Real stupid."

Lilli had no idea where his mind was. She waited in the dark for his next whisper.

"I may have amplified—well, the suggestion."

"What suggestion?" She wished she could see his face, watch his eyes as he found more words.

"Mitch, you know, he's the one put it in the kid's mind. I was just teasing the kid after that."

The kid? "Who? Kevin?"

"Naw, it's Kent. Kid bugs me. You've seen how that kid can't keep his eyes off the Swamper. Like he's lovesick, the way he drools."

"What did you go and say to him?"

"Opened my big mouth, told him what a Navajo might do."

"What a Navajo might do? About what?"

"I was just having fun."

"What did you tell him?"

"How Datura can get a girl to go crazy after you."

"*Ajil'ee*?" Living with Datura was simple: you left it completely alone.

What was the matter with Jerome? Why this cruel impulse?

"You put that—that boy—up to Frenzy Witchcraft?"

"I didn't mean for something to happen. I was just teasing him."

What did Jerome go and tell the boy? That Datura made women tear their clothes off, run around crazy with lust?

But only a Navajo witch would try to misuse Datura, make a woman its victim. She tried to remember, harder, deeper. In Frenzy Witchcraft the woman is given something to drink, maybe something to eat, laced full of the Datura. She goes crazy from the poison, runs away into the night, far from the protection of family. Gets so hot, so confused, she'll take her clothes off and run around witlessly, making a spectacle.

Some Navajo said Datura was used to make her lustful but others said, no, it was used to humiliate, for revenge, to humiliate a woman who refused the sexual demands of a witch.

"Guess Kent..." Jerome let out air. "Guess Kent decided to test me, see if I was telling the truth, way he fed it first to his unsuspecting brother."

A test run, before he tried it on the Swamper?

What did it matter now what she said to Jerome? Tomorrow would surely bring an abrupt end to any further participation in this journey, as soon as Kent pointed the finger.

Lilli wondered what exactly would happen to her and

Jerome now, how their removal would be handled. Would the two of them be quarantined from the rest of the group, made to sit alone, in forced silence, until a helicopter could be brought in to convey them up to the rim, in disgrace?

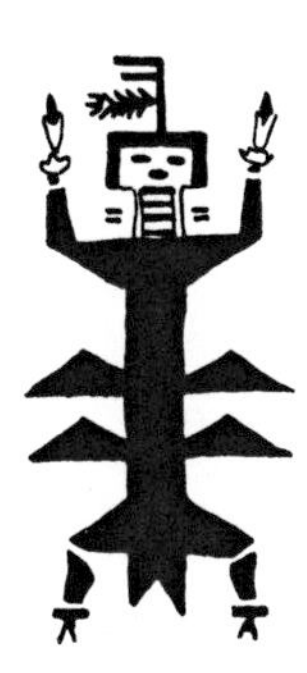

Day Three. Lilli grabbed a handful of sand to rub between her hands. Over-caffeinated on too little sleep, she felt jumpy and slow at the same time. Everyone, so far, was pretending to be normal, except the normally electrified Kent. She'd never seen the boy so subdued. Maybe it was the calm before the storm, maybe he was still waiting to drop his bombshell on Jerome.

No, if he was going to snitch, he would have tattled right away, deflected at least some of the blame onto Jerome, where it conclusively belonged.

But from her furtive reading of the behavior of everyone around her, Kent must be keeping his cards close to his chest because at least so far, no one pointed to Jerome's complicity. Although last night was clearly in all their eyes, especially Lee's—the way his so completely avoided hers.

His wife was less distant. No words except a muffled, "Thank you again, don't know what we would have..." and, in Lee's absence, she'd given Lilli a surprisingly tight hug.

"Let's do it, people." Mitch jumped up on the raft in catcher position and settled his cap. "You know the drill. Make a human chain."

Lilli, too, tried to act normal, to follow Lee's lead. They were putting the incident behind them, at least in words. At least so far.

In the last two days, unloading gear from the raft to make camp and then, in the morning, dismantling camp and repacking the raft had been fun, a game of camp-catch. But today was clearly different. There was no quick patter among any of them.

She found herself glancing between Kent and his brother Kevin, who was sitting out the drill behind a pair of sunglasses. Always interesting to watch a culture handle its children. Navajos believe in letting a child find his true nature. Her people would say of Kent: "He has a Bad Wind."

Bad Winds can come into any family.

Still, Kent was preternaturally calm, certainly not taunting his brother for running around in his underpants last night and then having even those pulled off him in the frantic search for whatever he felt attack him in his delusional paranoia. And so far this morning no one, including Kent, mentioned the sunglasses and Kevin's pseudo-Hollywood look. They all pretended amnesia.

She took her place in line and focused up-chain to where Suzanne stood, ready to start the pitch. The blue rubberized drysacks stood nearly as tall as Suzanne, each folded in a rolled closure to make the sack watertight. Lilli moved a little closer in toward the gear.

She should feel relieved that Jerome hadn't been found

out. Except she couldn't help the suspicion that Kent now had something on Jerome, something he could use at will. Still, there'd been no call for a rescue helicopter to drop into the canyon and lift the undesirable Navajos out.

"Ready?" Suzanne faked the first toss.

In a human chain like this, each of them was responsible for judging the distance between the person to their right and to their left to be no greater than they could catch or lob. Lilli wiggled her feet a little deeper into the sand.

"So now you're all really ready?"

"Hit it," Mitch said.

Suzanne chucked the first drysack to Dougan, down-line from her in the chain of waiting hands. Dougan picked up the rhythm and tossed the bag to Lee. Lilli looked toward Lee, to anticipate his throw. The drysack left Lee's hands. She missed and the drysack thudded at her feet. She wasn't ready for what the day would bring, was she?

Once loaded, Mitch pushed off from shore and the farther down-river they traveled, the more they all seemed to relax. The past was physically behind them. Mitch even managed a small joke about President Harding.

"So, I'll bite, Mitch, but how come I'm the only one who's so nosy?" Dougan said.

"Why was it named President Harding Rapid?" Mitch said. "Government survey team camped at the rapid the day of Harding's funeral. Folks in Washington said Old Harding could finally get some rest, you know, after all those years keeping his wife and mistress apart."

Her mind wandered. She never appreciated how water of this size sings. And with the added acoustics of so much confinement the entrenched river really sang. Peaceful, just as Mitch promised, no rapids for a few miles, and the sun's heat on the top of her head lulled her into closing her eyes. She shifted her weight, trying to catch herself, jerking her head back into alignment. She must have fallen asleep for a moment.

She stroked her sun-warmed hair, smoothing it. Last night hadn't brought much sleep. Maybe that was all it was. But she didn't think so. She didn't feel right. She felt a cramp in her stomach. The river took a gooseneck, executing what seemed like a U-turn in the river's course.

Hansbrough Peak forced the bend. The peak's name, Mitch explained, memorializing not where Hansbrough drowned but where his headless body finally found shore.

"Next piece of river coming up is through the Bright Angel," Mitch said.

Lilli straightened her spine and stretched out her neck muscles. "What's a bright angel to do with it?"

"Who understands how Powell's mind worked? Man named a river that came into the Colorado, up north of here, the Dirty Devil. Guess this is the antidote. The Bright Angel. Anyway it's Bright Angel Shale, all the way down now to the Hopi salt deposits."

Meaning, she realized, to the confluence of the Little Colorado with the Grand Colorado. Maybe Kent had spoken up, maybe a helicopter was enroute to airlift her and her tainted friend Jerome up and out of the canyon, up and out of the lives of the Lees. Maybe that's where they were headed, to the confluence of the Little Colorado corridor, to meet the helicopter. Maybe everyone was just pretending to be normal.

After lunch, Dougan sat down unceremoniously next to Lilli on the narrow ledge and tried to catch his breath. His face was flushed and his breathing heavy. She looked down at least five hundred feet below her dangling legs to the raft holding its own against the river. From up here, the river ran silver.

"Jeez, imagine having to make this climb. Those people had to be lizards." Dougan fumbled with trying to open his water bottle and took a long swig.

"You may be on to something—lizard toes." She'd beat Dougan up to the Anasazi Granaries by ten or fifteen minutes but was still trying to relax her own quivering leg muscles.

"Hard to believe people could make a living, but what did Mitch say? There's more than a thousand ancient sites in the canyon?" Dougan let out a low whistle. "This one looks like a primitive bank vault."

"Close to the mark." A food cache.

She touched the edge between two tightly laid rock slabs. In this impossible site, the Anasazi had built a camouflaged vault of rock for their hard-earned wealth of corn and the masonry perfectly mimicked the natural talus of the cliff below, hiding the wealth except for the granary's too-perfect vertical pitch. But what really gave the site away were the granary's four eyes—its four windows—like what might be afforded four prisoners.

"All this effort. Hard to figure. And then they just walked away?"

She hesitated, wondering if she should try to explain to a man like Dougan how these ancestral sites remain stopping places even in the modern world, that people still came on foot.

"So this strange word, this 'Anasazi,' it's a Navajo word, right?"

"It's a word of ours that's been co-opted." And corrupted, she thought.

"Mitch said it means Enemy Ancestor."

"Linguistically, no, that's wrong. A truer translation to our ears would be something like 'Non-Navajos-who-once-lived-among-us, Now-very-old, Now-scattered-about'."

"And half-lizard. You'd better add that."

"Absolutely," she said.

"Think I'll start down," Dougan said. "You coming?"

"Go ahead." She wanted a little more time alone.

As she watched Dougan descend, the twins' voices carried up to her.

"Quit throwing rocks down on me!"

She recognized the higher-pitched voice as Kevin's.

"Not throwing at you—queer!"

That, of course, would be Kent.

"Don't call me that!"

"Hermaphro..."

As she watched the boys find footing she thought of how the twins of First Woman and First Man were *nádleeh*, two true hermaphrodites. The Male and the Female were not yet separated and the first twins were in-between. But the true *nádleeh*, she thought, unlike the names Kent liked to direct at his brother, never served men sexually. The One Who Is Both Ways is *ádin*, dead: without sexual desire.

She smiled, remembering when the Jesuit priests first came to St. Michael's in Window Rock, how her people interpreted the obvious. They saw these men living without women, without children, dressed as Jesuits did in their long black robes, like a woman's skirt. Many Navajo assumed they knew exactly what was under those skirts.

There was a distinction the Navajo made, though, between real *nádleeh*—born both male and female—and the transvestite who pretended to be a woman. In the old days, it was a great honor to be *nádleeh*. That was then, this was now. Homosexuals used to be safe on the reservation. Recently though there'd been a killing of a gay Navajo teenager, just off the reservation, a killing the city newspapers called a crime of entertainment.

The sound of a rock sliding from above made her look

up. Who could possibly be above the granaries? Jerome and his camera gear slid in beside her, with no evidence of heavy breathing as he hung his booted legs off the ledge.

"Quite a view of the river, almost aerial," Jerome said. "Hey, Mitch asked me who this Barboncito was?"

"Why would he ask you that?"

Every Navajo child was taught about Barboncito, *Hástiin Díghá*, the Man With Whiskers.

"Mitch told me this big butte, that one opposite us here, it's named after Barboncito."

Did Jerome remember how Barboncito had been captured and sent to the concentration camp at Bosque Redondo, and how he somehow escaped and could have so easily run free, but didn't? How he'd turned around instead and come back?

And how he'd spoken for them all, refusing the generals and the guns, insisting that the Navajos, hungry and soul-weary after four years of imprisonment, could not obey and go to Oklahoma, not even if there was water and grass. They had to go home to their own land, to their *Dinétah*, to whatever remained of it after the scorched earth raids of the army. Yes, Barboncito had said, they understood there'd be little left, no peach trees standing, no livestock alive, just the desert and their burned hogans. Yet Barboncito had said he was speaking for them all, even the unborn. He'd chosen home.

Jerome was trying to find his way home, that's what she wanted to believe, and in an elemental way she knew *she* was his home.

"Do you still remember Barboncito's words?" she asked.

"Sounds like you do."

"Barboncito told the men in Washington—he said when the Navajo were first created, four mountains and four rivers were pointed out to be our *Dinétah*, our homeland, and it was given to us by Changing Woman."

"I remember how your uncle used to finish that story," Jerome said.

"Go on, then, finish it." She smiled at him.

"The Army told our people they would be given one or two sheep, to restart their life from nothing. And Barboncito said, a flock of that size, it could die from loneliness."

She placed her hand over his, resting on the ledge. "Those weren't swastika, were they?"

"What do you think?"

She'd lain awake last night for a long time thinking about it. "I think they were Whirling Logs." She'd seen the floor of a hogan, a patient, a ceremony.

"Why would I be drawing Whirling Logs?" He stood up, turned his back on her, and started down the trail, easily overtaking Dougan.

Lilli had no answer.

Late afternoon shadows across the raft. Lilli felt a little nauseous and made her way out of the shade to the sunnier side. Bad timing. She'd arrived in the middle of a joke. Like any Navajo she loved puns, a creative act of hitching words together. But too many *bilagáana* jokes carried a brunt and this one seemed to be about stupid women.

"First marriage," Dougan said. "Hemingway's wife, in Paris, gets a call. Someone's interested in publishing his work. So without even telling him, she packs up a whole suitcase full of a novel, twenty short stories, thirty poems—all unpublished—and gets on a train to join him in Switzerland. Only somewhere between Paris and Switzerland she visits the ladies' room and leaves the bag. When she comes back, the suitcase is gone."

"They've never been published? All that Hemingway—just gone?"

"Poof. True story."

"Beats blaming the dog," Lee said.

"Yeah, put a leash on that woman."

Lee laughed. She didn't. Nothing like giving yourself away by the jokes you resent.

"Attention, folks." Mitch stood at the stern of the raft, all focus. "Kwagunt Rapid. Can you sense it coming?"

Lilli spun around to face forward. Beneath her, the river flowed like spun glass, the deception before the siege. Even though facing forward shot up the fear factor, she liked it better, seeing chaos develop dead ahead rather than imagining it from its roar.

"Get ready, a potential Two-Hander," Mitch said. "Big hole in the middle."

Lilli felt the raft accelerate. The water went frothy with foam. She tightened her grip. She heard herself yelp. One moment she was warm, the next her lap was full of shockingly frigid water and she'd lost her breath.

Lee whooped, "All right, Almighty! Bring it on!"

"Nothing more that exciting for a while," Mitch said. "We're in Blue Moon Graben."

"Graben? Sounds German," Lee said.

"Graben, it's a geologic 'oops'," Mitch said. "Two faults got restless, shifted, and a big old chunk of earth dropped down."

"Dad, what's a blue moon?" Kent shouted out.

"Two full moons in one month, son. Second moon's the Blue Moon."

"Naw, *Blue Moon*'s a song, made famous by Elvis," Mitch said. "*Blue Moon, you saw me standing alone, without a love of my own.*" Mitch howled at the cloudless sky. "Or maybe you boys prefer Fogerty? *I se-ee the ba-ad mo-on rising. I se-ee trouble on the way."*

The Swamper joined in. *Hope yo-ou are quite pre-pared to die. Lo-oks li-ke we're in for na-sty wea-ther...* Shoot. How does it end?"

Lilli surprised herself. She let loose. *"One eye is taken for an eye."*

"Give it some twang, woman. *One e-ye is ta-ken for an e-ye."*

The Secret Service agent seemed to be in charge. Boyd's black pistol lay on a flat slab of rock, its barrel facing the river. Somewhere upriver a night heron called, a solitary hunter taking advantage of the fading light of dusk.

Lilli looked around her at the four faces, Lee, Dougan, Frank and Boyd, and wondered why she'd been sent for. Stranger yet, why it was Boyd who made the summons.

With his left hand, Boyd gripped the gun along its axis to steady it and then, with his free hand, slid out the magazine.

"We have a problem, want to bring you up to speed."

By that time of night, Boyd and Frank were usually invisible.

"Received a heads-up, from up above." Boyd grasped the gun's handle and gave a sharp pull on the top of the gun. With a push on a lever with his thumb and a pull back and then a slide forward, the whole top assembly slid off the frame.

"On the satellite phone. Two men, dead, double homicide. Best guess, maybe thirty hours ago. Happened on the Navajo reservation," Boyd said.

She didn't understand why she was being told any of this.

"Their truck was found."

Their truck. So the identity of the two men was known, and obviously the contents of their truck. She watched Boyd's face, and the practiced movements of his hands as he handled the parts of his gun. Lilli realized she'd tensed her shoulders. She forced her breathing to slow, to flow, smoothly.

Boyd used his thumb and finger to carefully remove a spring. He set it down on a cloth.

"Let me tell you some more about the two bodies, how they presented. Okay, Lilli?"

"Sure."

"Killing was from a bullet. No waste, close-range, single shot per victim." Boyd inserted a rod and brush from the rear end of the barrel.

"Killer took his time after that, did a little cutting. Removed the bottoms of the underside of each of twenty toes."

Boyd had been watching her face while he spoke to her, but now he picked up a cloth and poured a small pool of lubricant on the cloth and wiped the barrel, both the inside and the outside.

"Hopi Indian toes, all twenty."

"You know who these two men are. Isn't that what I understood?" Lee said.

"I want to hear Lilli out first. So, Lilli, there some animosity between the Navajo and the Hopi?"

Was he a step ahead of her? Was he already suggesting that the killer was Navajo?

"Animosity? Between some people, yes—sometimes."

She'd been thinking about the Hopi a few hours ago when, from the river, Lee had twisted around, curious at what they all saw.

"Hey, what's that white stuff—there—oozing down the cliffs?" Lee had been curious. "Looks like major bird poop."

"It's leach," Mitch said.

"Blood suckers?"

"L-e-a-c-h. Salt dissolved in ground water, seeps out here. Whole stalactites of salt back in those caverns."

"Way cool, Dad, let's get a souvenir," Kent said.

"Sure, son. Let's explore."

"No can do. No sir, not a possibility," Mitch said. "Salt is strictly off-limits."

"Surely not to us?"

"Off-limits unless you're Hopi. This particular salt's sacred to them."

"Kind of a tribulation to get to. Why here?"

Why, Lilli wondered, was Jesus born in Bethlehem?

"Help me out, Lilli. I need a technical word," Mitch said. "We're closing in on their...what would you call it? Their belly button?"

Close enough, she thought. "Their *Sipapu*."

"Dad, let's stop and get out."

"Off-limits, didn't I just say that?" Mitch turned toward her. "Lilli, tell these fans some more about this place."

She'd tried. "From an earlier world," she'd started, slowly. "Their *Sipapu* is the Hopi's place of emergence," she said. "And when a Hopi dies they go back, through the same opening." As if with death you re-enter your mother and spend eternity in her womb.

The womb after death. Different than the thinking of the Navajo. Life was about living to the Navajo, following the Beauty Way, living in beauty. Come death, it was over.

Not like the Mormons either, she thought, who expected to meet their husbands and wives in perpetual heaven. Or the Christians who seemed to be waiting for the big reward after death, as if the Creation was not gift enough. Or the suicide terrorists, promised in death the earthly pleasures of seventeen virgins.

"Hey, Mitch," Lee said. "Come on, what harm to our stopping?"

"Yeah, Dad, let's stop."

"Nope." Mitch was obviously enjoying saying no to Lee.

"Tell you what, though, I will slow us down and you can look upstream when we cross the confluence of the Little Colorado with the big Colorado. Tell you, the thing's pretty cool. Kind of looks alive."

"Aha! Now, Mitch? How would you know that if it's so off-limits?"

"Yeah, well, I've taken a small peek." Mitch had delivered by slowing the raft down and giving them a good look upstream, but of course the *Sipapu* was too far in to be seen.

"It's this crazy-looking dome," Mitch'd said. "Thing is spring-fed, still enlarging from the calcium bubbling up. Shaped just like a woman's breast."

Lilli had never hiked down. The Hopi were a protected people; they could travel from their homes up on Black Mesa, cross through the Navajo reservation that surrounded them, and enter their special corridor of the Little Colorado canyon, to make their way to salt and to their *Sipapu*.

"Even a waterfall back up there, higher than Niagara," Mitch had told them.

"No way. I would have heard of it." Lee's tone of voice had suggested there was something un-American about such a claim.

"True fact. Formed when a lava tongue cooled and turned black. Called Grand Falls of the Little Colorado. Usually dry, but come a monsoon and it's a freefall waterfall higher than Niagara."

"Hey, I think I see some graffiti." Lee'd pointed to the Navajo side of the river. "Red and black marks. Look, they're all over that cliff."

"Hopi make those, isn't that right, Lilli?"

"They do, they mark that their Clan has made another visit."

"You mean people walk down here, all the way from the Hopi reservation?"

"All the way," she'd said. For more than a thousand years, she'd thought, often a young man entering a final rite of passage, maybe accompanied by an old man, come to take back the ceremonial salt.

"Tell me more about this animosity."

Boyd brought her back to the present as he passed his cleaned gun from one hand to the other.

"An old reservation boundary issue," she said. "Historically old. One that's forced the relocation of some families, both Navajo and Hopi. Clinton ordered a final fix."

"Identification won't explain the mutilation. We can use toeprints these days, true enough," Boyd said. "But this cutting, this removing the flesh under the toes—it couldn't have been about obscuring an I.D. since the hands were intact."

Of course not. The police had the truck and the driver's licenses. And the faces, she thought.

"So, what's your read on cutting like that? Sound like local stuff to you?"

She understood now why she was the focus of Boyd's attention. "You mean, was this a ritual removal of flesh?"

"Navajo? Hopi? Either way, mean something to you?"

The Winds left whorls at the top of the head, you could see the swirls in a scalp if you looked under the hair. And at the tips of the fingers. And under the toes. A Navajo witch would want flesh like that, to make corpse poison. She looked around her at the faces of Boyd and Frank, and Lee and Dougan. Was she really going to start talking to these men about Navajo witches?

Traditional Navajos had no trouble talking about witches to one another, maybe even making a joke. She remembered her uncle seeing a neighbor out hitching a ride to Nakaibito, and he stopped to pick the neighbor up. But he'd asked a question first, "Hey, why don't you just fly over? How come you need a ride?" In Navajo, the implication that the neighbor could "fly" was clear. But what would these men think?

"It could have ritual meaning," she said. She certainly didn't need to see the mutilated feet.

"Not something gang-related? Punks?" Boyd asked.

"No." She found Boyd's eyes. "The cutting would seem to be...more meaningful."

"Premeditated, you're saying? Ritualistic?"

No, the killing could have been hot-headed, alcohol-stimulated, she thought. But in the aftermath of the killing, if not in premeditation, the idea must have come to remove those specific pieces of skin.

"All I can attest to," she said, "is that the act itself, that...well, it has a ritual allusion." A clear traditional connotation, a subtext.

"Good, agrees with what the boys up top are saying." Boyd said. "And that's what I needed to hear, an authentication."

Boyd started to reassemble the pistol.

"Opinion on the rim is this has nothing to do with Lee. It's behind us. Happened a distance away. Local trouble."

"But I don't want this homicide released to the media, not in any way that ties in Lee," Dougan said. "You make sure you relay that up to the rim."

"Understood," Boyd said. "You agree with this decision, Lilli? All make sense to you?"

She looked into Boyd's unsmiling eyes. In some ways, as bad as Dougan, she wanted their journey through the canyon to proceed. Was she impartial enough to give counsel? She found herself nodding her head in agreement. On the reservation, ninety-nine percent of violent crimes were related to alcohol. No reason to imagine the killer was interested in Lee.

Bik bok bik bok. Twick twick twick. Duane flipped over onto his stomach and opened his eyes. He'd heard something like a soft scuttle of fingernails. He'd probably never be able to prove the packrat was in the rock shelter with him, probably staring at him right now from some safe hidey-hole. Damn curious desert thing. Smart, too. Hell, the thing wouldn't give itself away, not easily. But maybe it could be suckered out.

In a minute. Duane needed to quiet his mind better. He stretched out his spine along the floor of the rock hollow, extending his vertebrae, and closed his eyes. Trouble was closing his eyes, sometimes made his mind worse, just transformed the inside of his head to one big private movie screen. He saw himself on the screen, all ready and waiting for the raft to come into view. Enough. He opened his eyes and sat up.

Had to think like the packrat, yeah. Had to be something irresistible. The thing wasn't going to show itself, not readily, it was all eyes and nervous energy and secretive as hell. But just like people who trusted too easily, the packrat was a sucker. He'd lure him out. Something shiny, that's what he needed.

Duane felt in among the things he carried until his fingers closed around a box of ammunition. Really, sometimes hurting people was too easy. You just had to smile a lot, keep a conversation up in the air and upbeat and all that, and people would trust you way too much. Like they're expecting people who do bad things to have bad breath and bad manners and be born ugly. Somehow people don't want to believe you could be born almost pretty for a skinny boy and know how to smile, and then when you had them alone, had talked them into coming with you. Really, it was too easy.

Duane's fingers opened the box. He slid the smooth bullet away from him, out in the open. Perfect. The packrat was a born sucker for shiny.

Mama used to say to him how he wasn't fooling her none, hiding his stuff under his bed, "like some lousy packrat," she'd say. Only nothing stayed under his bed during one of her rages. Funny how something can be so important to a boy and then it just disappears. Steelies, he called them. He had a whole collection, all sizes, round as marbles only heavy as polished steel and pure shiny. One of Mama's boyfriends pilfered them, couple at a time from where he worked nights in a mill. Used to bring them out of the mill hidden in his lunch box.

Mama said they was nothing but ball bearings, common as a bugbear. But as a kid when he couldn't sleep, he used to sit up in bed at night, flip the light on, and watch himself multiplied in the steelies' gleam. You could see your whole face in every one of them, tiny. A whole horde of Duanes in the curved reflections.

He'd kept those steelies under his bed in a flat tin box with a welded lid. Wonder where they went to? Maybe when he got home, he'd ask Mama. Maybe she was keeping them for him. Keeping them until he settled down more, that's what she'd say.

Duane stretched his hand out and rubbed his fingers over the edge of the packrat's mound. Something in the cactus it ate made its piss sticky, more like a paste than a pure stream of pee. "Amberat," that was the word. Like amber only hardened piss, that's what. The rat was a collector, peed over what it loved. This curious creature with its big feet and long tail, making a mound out of stuff that caught its fancy, preserving tidbits forever with piss thick as molasses.

Made Duane think of Jurassic Park and those movie scientists finding a fossil mosquito preserved in amber, looking deeper inside the nearly transparent mosquito and finding a drop of dinosaur blood. Which started his mind up.

Why not make a contribution of himself, here and now? It'd be like placing something real personal in a time capsule for the future. He decided on skin and tore off a hangnail with his teeth. Then he thought about how hair was personal and pulled out three long strands. But he still needed something shiny, to make the attraction. Duane pulled out his knife and cut loose the metal button from the fly of his pants and stuffed the skin and hair strands carefully inside the thread hole of the button.

He could feel how he was under the scrutiny of two furtive black eyes. He slid the button out away from him. Then he lay back down, feeling like maybe he could sleep, his hips relaxing along the rock floor. As he put his final weight down, he felt the plastic protector in his back pocket.

Just like a packrat, wasn't he, with his prize possession, his photo? He let his mind race forward to Mama, to that part of the plan where it was all over and he got himself out of the canyon and went home, and she smiled at him.

What was she going to say to him? His mind started to go over yet again the words he'd memorized, the ones immortalized in raised bronze lettering at Lee's Ferry. The words proclaimed to all who stopped that this Lee she hated was a "Frontiersman, a Trail Blazer, a Man of Great Faith." How did the words go? "Of Sound Judgment and Indomitable Courage." Yeah. Well, Mama would like the way he'd planned to rewrite the proclamation. The new lettering would let the world know how Lee was a "Coward and a Sneak and a Liar and a Man of Great Betrayal."

And then he thought of the babies.

Hamblin's wife was the one who'd received the bloody babies in the middle of the night. The woman had kept a journal, but what do you know? She never even wrote a word of the massacre superintended by Lee. Bloody wounded children were brought to her out of nowhere. Seventeen orphans? She might have wondered how they became orphans so sudden, so close to her home. She might have noticed how they were shrieking and wet with their own mamas' blood.

Duane lay on his back in the heavy silence with his eyes tightly closed. There were so many ways he'd imagined killing Lee. He saw himself in the canyon, perfectly in position. Over and over in his mind, he replayed the image of the river bringing Lee closer and closer to him, as if on special order. Less than forty-eight hours now, before their paths intersected.

The site he'd chosen was perfect, a complete Zone of Silence. Because at this site there were two bottlenecks. Lee wouldn't be able to reach the outside world, and a helicopter couldn't get in—least not quickly enough.

Sure, he wanted the river quiet before breaking into a long stretch of tricky rapid. But there were lots of those kinds of set-up and delivery—just read the topo maps. What made the spot he'd chosen the perfect killing site was the way the river ran tight and long against an unforgiving southeast bank with a big wall of rock. In that Zone of Silence, not even Lee's guardians could communicate with the outside world.

And even if somehow a satellite call got off, rescue would take too much time. To land deep down in the canyon, a helicopter team needed a flat space, maybe no bigger than a living room. The rounded top of a bluff would be fine, no trees, no rock, no rotor problems. But the Zone of Silence had none of these options. Still, for a rescue of Lee, Duane knew the order would come to risk it.

Except *blam! blam! blam!* He imagined the burst. Always aim for the head. Before the helicopter ever felt air, Lee would already be dead.

Duane closed his eyes. He loved to create the details in his mind. The sun lit the surface of the river, as if a thin film of oil was on fire. Upriver the tongue of moving water was deceptively smooth, quietly sucking, pulling on the water coming toward him. He liked the way the river then bent, hiding the rapid until it was too late to change course. He expected the boatman to be as good as they came, the best. He imagined the boatman standing in the stern, taking the river's pulse.

Duane felt his brain speeding up. The rapid was waiting. Up above, he lay in wait, ready. Just a matter of staying alert.

In his mind's eye, he lay on his stomach, looking down at the stretch of river as if examining an empty stage. Like Oswald in Dallas above Kennedy's motorcade, he'd be unnoticed, up high, shooting down at the moving target.

The spot to first pull the trigger was just before the rapids where the flow was still steady as a moving train. He'd put the sight to his eye. *Blam!*

Maybe he'd kill the boatman first. How would the boat behave once the boatman was gone? Momentum would carry the raft into the rapids roaring with noise, with everyone hypnotically looking ahead and no one noticing the boatman was gone. The river would take charge, spinning the boat down the chute of the wave train into the boils, then into the hole, then slam it full of an exploding wave.

He liked that, removing the boatman first. But then Duane thought of Mama and reassessed his target order. He might fail if he got too greedy. No, it had to be Lee first. That way, no matter what happened next, Mama was happy. Lee first, then the boatman, then all the others.

His fingers clenched. He felt achingly ready. When it was all over and the hiding time was over, he'd finally go home. This time he'd have something important enough to hold her notice.

Home, what a strange sounding word. He tried to remember the details of the last time he'd seen Mama. Of course, he hadn't known it would be the very last time. If he'd known that he'd have paid better attention. He tried hard to remember the particulars of the last time, what exactly she'd said to him, but tonight, like all the other nights, he couldn't come up with the words.

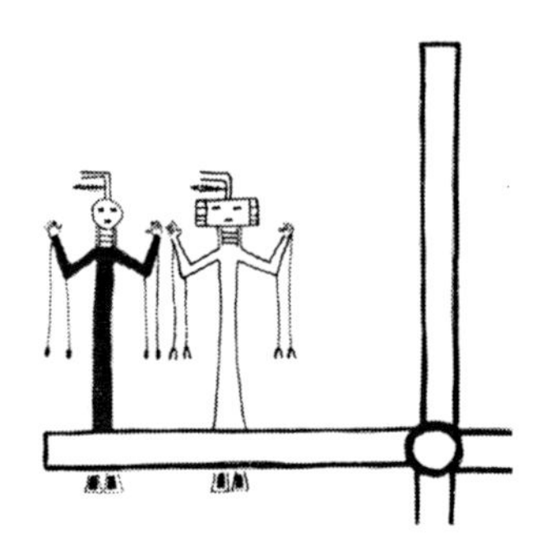

They were camped like squatters among the dead. Lilli pulled her hair off her face, hot with reflected fire. In her undivided opinion, this was surely the worst campsite Mitch could possibly have chosen. The tents rose up in nylon domes among the rock walls of a flattened Anasazi ruin where the river took a hairpin, slowed down and spread out. Unkar Delta. Behind Mitch, on the hill, a ruin like a watchtower peered at them. All around her she read the signs of the dead, even the circular remains of their kivas, the deep subterranean cavities where once they descended on ladders into the earth, to hold their secret rituals.

Mitch laid his last piece of coyote willow across the fire.

Lilli stood to return her empty plate to the soak pan, careful where she put her feet. Potsherds littered the campsite, reflecting back in the firelight their colors of red and gray and black. The Anasazi abandoned their homes along the river. Jerome's family abandoned the reservation for Los Angeles. She wondered if sleeping so close to ruins had any effect on a Navajo like Jerome who'd already slept so many nights among the traffic and sirens of L.A. Sure, she was as modern as Jerome, but even so, she knew better than to lay her head down among the dead.

"Where are the boys, dear?" Lee took his place in the fire circle of camp stools, next to his wife.

She looked around her, puzzled. "Weren't they just here?"

"Better call them back. Mitch is waiting on us."

"They've probably gone to their tent. They need their privacy, too."

"Kent! Kevin! Come on out and join us." Lee's voice carried well into the still night air.

"About to lose our firelight." Mitch balanced the book, open across his knees.

Lilli recognized their own nightly ritual about to begin.

From the shadows, Kevin appeared and dropped down on the sand next to his mother's bare feet. She stroked the back of his head. Kent, just as quietly, dropped down beside the Swamper.

"Glad you've chosen to join us, boys," Mitch said. "These are Powell's words, written as he made camp quite close to where we sleep tonight. We, too, are through with Marble Canyon. Tomorrow we move on."

> *We are now ready to start on our way down the Great Unknown. Our boats, tied to a common stake, chafe each other as they are tossed by the fretful river... We have but a month's rations remaining. The flour has been resifted through the mosquito-net sieve; the spoiled bacon has been dried and the worst*

> *of it boiled; the few pounds of dried apples have been spread in the sun and reshrunken to their normal bulk. The sugar has all melted and gone on its way down the river... We are... but pigmies, running up and down the sands or lost among the boulders. We have an unknown distance yet to run, an unknown river to explore. What falls there are, we know not; what rocks beset the channel, we know not; what walls rise over the river, we know not.*

In that earlier world maybe Powell was invisible, but they had Lee and lots of invisible eyes must be on him. Satellite eyes, GPS tracking nets, Secret Service communications. Lilli watched Mitch close his journal for the night.

"Brave man, this one-armed Powell, don't you think, sons?" Lee said. "But Mitch, you know the Unknown. Give us a teaser—what will tomorrow bring?"

"Tomorrow? Hmm. How shall I put it?" Mitch began the process of quenching the fire his style, slowly trickling water around the edges, spiraling toward its center.

"You think you've got your river legs, do you? Think you've experienced some pretty hot rapids?"

"Yeah."

"Not really, see, we've just been warming up."

"For something big?"

"Enormous. Tomorrow a rapid rated the maximum magnitude of 10."

Lee turned toward the Swamper. "Hey, Suzanne, how'd you put that riddle about boatmen?"

"You mean how can you tell when a river runner's lying?"

"That's the one."

The Swamper smiled at Mitch. "That'd be whenever his lips are moving."

That night, Lilli hoped Jerome could relax and be open and vulnerable to her. Through the surface of his skin, that's how she wanted to comfort him, as a woman could comfort a man.

"May I?" She placed both her hands on top of his head.

"Yes."

Facing him in the darkness, she let her hands slide to the knot holding his hair at the back of his neck. She worked it until she felt the knot loosen and then pulled her fingers gently through the long strands making it into a curtain over his shoulders.

"Turn around."

Jerome rotated his back toward her and she rose up on her knees. He smelled of fire smoke. The pure blackness of the canyon had allowed her mind to settle into other senses. Sounds were enormously magnified. And touch. That part of her brain fed during the day by her eyes lay quiet, and her skin seemed more alive.

She separated his hair into three shanks and wrapped each shaft around a finger, tight enough to control. She twisted the sections of hair over and under each other and when she was nearly out of hair she lifted it all into the figure-eight twist, the *tsiiyéél*, and retied the knot.

She wanted him to talk, about why he'd come home and how long he thought he'd stay. And maybe if they talked enough, he'd convince her she had nothing to fear.

She started softly from behind him to sing. *Ált'áága'sá béé níyáago gá-á* – when I become old, *T'óógá shích'íí náánáádlóóh'ó* – you'll be smiling at me.

"Jóó ashílá," he sang back. The two of them, traveling together, that was *Jóó ashílá*.

She hoped so. But the image of the man laying dead in the Hoodoos rarely left her alone for long.

Jerome turned around to face her. "You know what that son of a bitch went and did?"

"Who?" So Jerome was in a very different mood.

"Dougan, tonight, all in my face."

"What?"

"Bastard asked to see my film. I took it out of the camera bag and he confiscated it, every roll I've exposed. Said it's for insurance, precautionary, he'll give it back after he sees the prints."

"Oh, no."

Dougan probably wanted to make sure there were no images of a half-naked boy with black pupils the size of dimes.

"Man says, 'Lee's family is not a circus.' Like he thinks I'm interested in photographing Lee?"

"I know you're not photographing Lee, you're not photographing people at all, are you?" Would Jerome do something stupid now, in retaliation?

"I'll talk to him, in the morning." She needed to try to soften his anger. "Tell me what you've put on film."

"So far? Found a rock ledge where a Budweiser Ceremony had taken place."

"I'm serious."

"Never know for sure. What do I hope is on the film? Ravens, hunched under their black robes like judges out for a cigar break, cliff swallows surprised into orgasmic explosions of flight."

She smiled in the dark. "What else?" He was becoming more like himself.

"Water slowed down until the water is all of one piece. Oh, and lots of velvet ants."

"Dressed in their ballet skirts?"

The wasps, called ants, were fun to watch, sporting their colored ruffs.

"Exactly. Crossing the sandbar in fluffy ruffles."

She heard his sigh.

"I love being here, Lilli, with you and with the light. Most amazing light, lets the subject glow as if lit like wax from within. Oh, and I think I captured a naked Suzanne taking a shower under a waterfall."

"You didn't!"

"Maybe Dougan hopes I did."

Her fingers tingled from the cold night air and she slid them under her shirt, up against her warm belly.

"Enough of this. Come on, woman, we have work to do."

"Now?"

"Yes, now. There's no better time."

"You're serious." She stood up and followed him.

Once Jerome set up his equipment, nothing, he emphasized, could be disturbed. She was not to move around, not to make any vibration. The tripod was imperative.

"That Anasazi watchtower above us will make for a perfect foreground. Our focus is set on infinity, lens opened to the max, and now we hold still for a good hour of exposure."

"Why so long?"

"Stars move slowly," he said.

"Didn't know they moved at all."

"Figure of speech."

"So the earth moves?"

"Under your feet. But that's not what the image will capture."

"Because? I'm not following you."

"I've centered the aperture on Fire Star."

Fire Star, the one the *bilagáana* called the North Star, lying between the two constellations above them, the male

One Who Revolves About the Fire and the female One Who Revolves About the Fire, the two of them facing each other in the sky.

"If all goes according to plan, the film should capture concentric circles of light, each the moving trail of a star. Like star runners on a wheel. You know, in L.A., I could never even show my..." He stopped himself. "Can't even see the Milky Way in L.A," he finished.

Was he going to say "wife?" Could never even show my wife?

"Did you know, Lilli, that ninety percent of the earth's people can't see the Milky Way on account of so much light pollution."

"Quite a show tonight, though, isn't it?" she said. Above them, the solid black of canyon rock rose in a jagged fin against a phosphorescent-punctured black sky.

"Shit! It's ruined!"

What had she done?

"Damn it! Cigarette light."

"Where?"

"Over there."

She saw it. Someone else was still up.

"Wait here."

She waited alone in the dark. In the distance a second flare of light appeared. As if Jerome had bummed a cigarette and now they were both smoking.

She listened to the river grinding and reshaping its bed. Of course, the Secret Service agents moved around in the dark without flashlights. Probably saw plenty with special night optics. She'd have to remember that she and Jerome were not as invisible in the dark as they thought.

Hours later, with Jerome asleep beside her, Lilli lay awake and felt the cramp tighten again. With its steady cadence, Jerome's breathing comforted her. She tried to match his rhythm. In and out, she breathed, in and out. The cold shaft of moonlight held the river in its beam, the moon's disk not yet visible, only its probe as it frisked the black cliffs.

Lilli rolled her weight off her spine and bent her knees up under her chin. The pain was dull and low, centered in her lower back. She moaned out loud, afraid she'd wake Jerome lying beside her. She felt a wetness between her legs. She shifted onto her knees and pushed herself up.

She felt such a strong urge, a pressure. Buckling the life jacket as she got to her feet, she walked barefoot to the edge of the water. She found a smooth flat sandbar wetted by the river. She squatted down to ease the ache. The rhythm of the night river flowing soothed her.

She took control of her breathing, forced the breaths to go deeper to quiet the pain. She didn't want to think about what was happening. The pain grew stronger. She shifted out of the squat onto her knees. Unmistakably, she felt something move within her, like a letting go. She felt the softness of a warm clot pass, lightly lifting the lips between her legs. She watched the clotted mass, black in the moonlight, slide down the wetted slope toward the silver river.

No name.

The separation came easy. Not like the One Who Never Uttered A Sound, the baby she'd held in its burial blanket until Jake took it away from her. Poor Jake, he didn't even know she was carrying this child. She'd failed him again.

No First Laugh.

She wondered if she would have the courage—no, the weakness—to tell him. What would telling help? She'd always remember tonight, waking up among the ruins of the Anasazi, from a sleep next to Jerome. She knew, too, she would see, over and over again for as long as she lived, the One Who Left Her in the moonlight becoming one with the river.

Because a mother carries all her children, always. The alive ones, and the ones who died, and the ones who were never born.

Lilli wrapped herself in her arms and rocked on the balls of her feet, letting the tears come. She imagined a tiny pair of arms and legs, a tiny belly of its own, all without a lifejacket, floating on ahead of her, into the unknown.

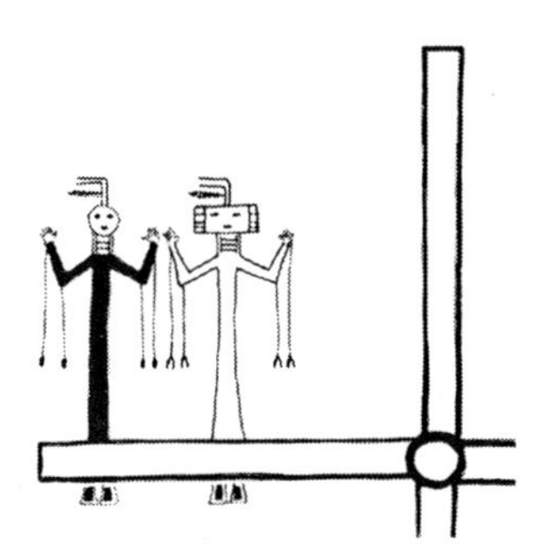

Day Four. The raft slipped along water dappled with reflected light. Lilli couldn't watch the moving water without seeing beneath it The One Who Left Her, and she couldn't stop watching the water, either. From the mug in her hands, she took a sip of cold coffee and felt the dull burn as she swallowed. She'd slept these past three nights next to Jerome, listening to his breathing, wondering what it would have been like, what kind of love between a man and a woman they might have experienced if his family hadn't cast off the reservation for L.A.

The rock surrounding them was soft, the cliffs receding like drapery folds, and the familiar tightness of the canyon had temporarily disappeared. She felt a reprieve at seeing more of the sky. Yet she'd become accustomed to narrowness, to knowing their future only one canyon bend at a time, and the unfamiliar openness placed an odd overload on the senses, like the disorientation a prisoner must feel coming out of a closed space.

In the litany of Mitch's geology, they'd cut through the Kaibab, Toroweap, Coconino, Hermit, Supai, Redwall, Muav, Bright Angel, and Tapeats, into the Dox, a physical survivor of the Earth the way it had been more than a billion years ago. They rode a river, Mitch said, that flowed backward in time, all the while traveling forward in space. He warned them, too, that this unexpected openness would soon be over and the cliffs would shut in with a vengeance.

Mitch pulled the raft hard to re-center their run. Red cliffs suddenly surrounded them and any sense of openness was completely gone.

"How's about we 'Powell' the next big rapid?" Mitch flapped the apparent stub of his arm like a wounded bird.

"What's he doing, Dad?"

"Powell ran the river one-armed." Mitch grinned. "But he was no dummy. He lined his boats."

"What do you mean, 'lined his boats'?"

"Portaged, on line. Wherever Powell could skirt a rapids, he did."

"He walked?"

"He walked. Only where we're headed, he didn't have that option."

"How come?"

"You'll see."

Vertical cliffs came out of nowhere. The river was trapped and angry.

"Hance Rapid," Mitch shouted. "Big bad stuff, drops a full three stories."

What was Mitch doing, aiming the raft left? The river ahead narrowed to an incision into solid rock. For a split second Lilli felt suspended in air and then the raft dove down the chute and she was in another world where not even a scream could be heard. She was inside water, careening through it, no way to know if they were diving deeper down under. Except her stomach screamed that she was riding up at a perilous angle and then she felt herself falling backward until she slammed forward into the next enormous curl and water pounded down on top of her.

She felt the raft heave against the curler and Lee let out a war whoop. They'd been spit out like a watermelon seed.

"Wow!" Jerome's grin went nearly ear to ear.

Of course the perfect 10 of a rapid, Crystal—an order of magnitude more difficult—waited for them, somewhere out of sight, somewhere just ahead.

"Let's take a short breather." Mitch tied up to the bones of a bare tree burned to charcoal, a lightning-struck tree that stood out against the silver water like a black raven drying its feathers.

"Time to dry out, warm up. Suzanne has snacks."

Lilli twisted her hair to wring out the water and stepped onto land.

"How did you like Hance?" Mitch asked.

"Like that it's over," she answered. She didn't mean to be so abrupt. "Is it nice to go back up, Mitch, you know, out of the canyon once in a while? You must live winter on the rim?"

"If I had the choice?" Mitch took a long time settling his answer in place. "I do live winter on the rim, try to but I'm not very adept, especially with women." Mitch was avoiding eye contact with her. "Signals are too many, they criss-cross. And I don't decode so well.

"My women—well, the girlfriends, you know, and then there was a wife, and now there's an ex with my daughter..." Mitch looked up at the rim.

"In season, between the runs, I visit a little and that's when it's best, when they just get glimpses of me, share a little flesh. Then I'm gone. But in the off-season, guess my faults loom large. Not really made for life up there, not anymore. Maybe never was."

Mitch turned his back to her and made busy with straightening out the line.

"If a politician wanted my opinion—and neither Lee nor Dougan do—I'd say blow the dams apart."

"What?"

"Hey? Don't look so surprised, Lilli."

"But don't these dams benefit you river runners?"

"Decapitate, castrate, relieve her of her chaos—all good for the tourists and, hey, I'm nothing but a tourist jockey."

"That's not what I meant."

"Shame it's the truth. Figure Powell's turned over in his grave so often the man's dizzy."

Powell, the river-runner, she wondered, or Powell, the Washington bureaucrat?

"People destroy what they pretend to love," Mitch said. "Powell had a vision for the development of the West, he saw the limits, the man really did, but he was persecuted for it. Public killed the messenger, forced him out, the hero left D.C. a defeated man.

"Oops, heads up." Mitch tipped his head in the direction behind her. "Lee's on his way over."

"Found me a new audience," Lee said. "Dougan told me this joke. Ready?"

"Go for it." Mitch raised his eyebrows.

"You know the 9/11 terrorists, ones that slammed into the Twin Towers? And they got a promise of seventeen virgins apiece, in heaven?"

"Ye-ah," Mitch said, drawing the word out as he

looked at Lilli.

"So Dougan's wife says to him, 'Then what's heaven for a woman?' He says to her, 'Obviously, it's serving men.'"

Neither Mitch nor Lilli reacted. Lee was unfazed.

"So, Mitch, how far to this next big rapid?"

"You'll hear it, long before you see it. Sockdolager."

"What'd you say?"

"Sockdolager Rapid."

"What's a Sockdolager? Another Indian word?"

"Hardly. It's the cue used by Booth to fire the shot that killed President Lincoln."

"You're kidding. Why that word?"

"Lincoln, you remember, was watching a stage play."

"Right, something popular, playing in the theater in D.C."

"And Booth, an actor, was watching Lincoln, biding his time, waiting for the line that always brought out the biggest laugh from the audience."

"To camouflage the shot?"

"You're a thinking man, Mr. Lee. Exactly. Yes, knowing the script, Booth waited until the actor on stage said the line with 'Sockdolager.' It got the laugh, and he pulled the trigger."

"But I've never heard of the word. What does it mean?"

"Great word for the next set of rapids. Any linguists among us?"

Lilli, like any good convert, knew more than the true believers. "In English..." She waited to see if Lee had the answer. "'Sockdolager' means an exceptionally big blow."

"Whomping big blow," Mitch said. "A knockout punch."

"So that's what's ahead of us? Sweet Jesus, we barely survived Hance!"

And Lincoln survived the assassin for only a few hours.

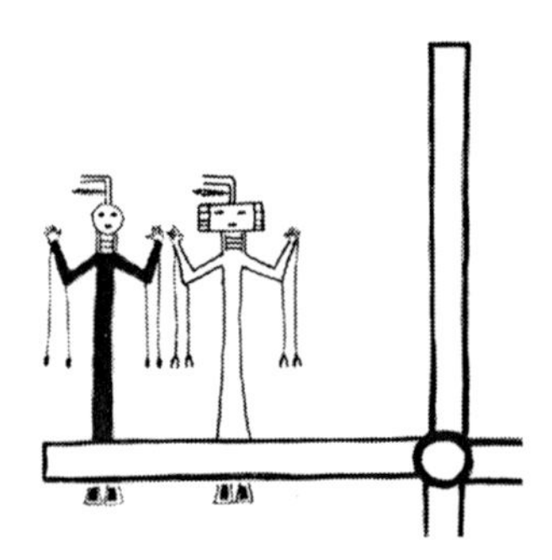

"Welcome to the world of Vishnu Schist," Mitch said.

Lilli felt abnormally alert. The walls of rock that engulfed them were so black and smooth they glowed as if lit radioactively from within. The river had carried them down a hole, it seemed, into an abyss. If she were some fan of dark fantasy, she thought, this would be a perfect setting: no visible exit, blacker than night, a place where by the time anyone heard a call for help it would be too late.

The abyss seemed evil. Lilli found herself remembering how in the Third World the People accused First Man of being evil. He didn't deny it. He said instead, "I am filled with evil, but there is a time to use evil and another time to withhold it."

"Sure we didn't come out onto another planet?" Lee held a hand on Kevin's shoulder. "Hey, Mitch, how old is this rock?"

"Two billion years, give or take," Mitch answered.

"Long before Adam and Eve, right, Dad?"

"That's right, son."

"We're in the jaws of Upper Granite Gorge. Spooky, isn't it?" Mitch pivoted the raft in the narrow chute. "Can you feel the speed? River's in a big-time hurry, really squeezed in."

Narrowed to nearly a ribbon, and like a house of mirrors the angle of the black walls tilted, amplifying the sensation that the river was running downhill faster and faster.

Lilli felt queasy. No shore, no strand line, not even a slope, not one human feet could ever scale to escape.

"Where's the river?" she said. "I mean, where's all the water?" Their world had condensed to two elements, black water and even blacker rock.

"Gone deep, gone swift," Mitch said. "Old Bernoulli principle: squeeze shut the opening, you force fast the flow."

The Inner Gorge felt to her both evil and sensual at the same time.

The rock curved in arcuate hollows as if it were scooped. Solid hard rock, she knew, yet her mind sensed an ability to move, a musculature, lurking just beneath the skin. The sense of blackness was overwhelming. She felt as if she had unwittingly left behind the present and descended back through earlier worlds, into the darkness of the First World where *Tééhooltsódii*, the One Who Grabs Things in the Water, expelled the first adulterers.

She could sense Powell's slow panic. "So what's it called again, this rock?"

"Schist."

"Come again?"

"It's a rock been buried so deep it had a phase change, metamorphism they call it."

And the rock was getting even stranger, starting to

flame. "What's the crimson stuff?" she asked.

"Petrified fire," Mitch said. "No, I'm serious, it was molten once. Like lava. In the Inner Gorge the Vishnu Schist is shot through with intrusions of Zoroaster Granite."

"Vishnu? Now Zoroaster? Aren't we smack in the middle of America?"

Lee joined Lilli and Mitch at the stern. "Who in the world thought up these names?"

"And piled it on. We have Vishnu Schist, Vishnu Rapid, Vishnu Temple."

"I don't get it," Kevin said. "What's a Vishnu?"

"*Who's* Vishnu—he's the four-armed god of the Hindus."

"And Zoroaster?"

"Name of an ancient religion of Iran and Persia," Mitch said. "Or we could help Americanize things here, right, Lilli, and say Zoroaster comes from the Wizard of Oz. O period Z period, right?" Mitch liked to goose Lee.

She decided to go along. "Yes, capital O period, capital Z period—they were the wizard's initials."

"What are you talking about?" Lee said.

"Oscar Zoroaster," she said.

"You two are in cahoots, you're making this up."

"No, Scout's honor, 'twas the Wizard of O. Z." Mitch adjusted their course. He seemed to be running just the surface layer of the river.

Lilli scented the river's breath and wondered what lay beneath.

"Still, why would someone apply such odd names to this uniquely American landscape?" Lee said.

A funny question for Lee to ask, she thought, going over in her mind some of the names the Mormons applied to their promised land north of the Navajo reservation, names like Zion and Jericho. And Kolob, the name they put on the canyon where Lee of Lee's Ferry had lived. Wasn't Kolob the Mormon star that sits nearest their god's home?

"My opinion? This place was plain too impressive for words," Mitch said. "And then Dutton, well, he was a little crazy for mythical images."

"Dutton who?"

"Clarence Dutton, half-geologist, half-poet, with an in to Powell. Man did a ton of naming."

"You're telling me this Dutton named the features of our Grand Canyon after other people's gods?"

"Vishnu, the Hindu Preserver. Brahma, the Hindu Creator. Shiva, the Hindu Destroyer. All Hindu gods, and we have their Temples right here, as our peaks and mesas."

Maybe Lee, once elected, could change this distasteful bit of American history more to his liking.

"This Dutton, though, the man was broad in his branding. He named us a Tower of Babel, and Krishna's Shrine."

"What happened to our Bible?"

"Not to worry. Dutton labeled a splendid piece of canyon Solomon's Temple. And we have Sheba, the temptress, remember her? Tested Solomon's wisdom, shall we say?"

"You've been holding out on us, Mitch. Where are all these places?"

"Everywhere around us. We've passed in front of Apollo, and to the north there's Juno. Dutton honored the Egyptians with Cheops Pyramid, and the Towers of Ra and Set, the one who murdered Osiris. And he gave Osiris his own Temple, too."

"Good grief!"

"Sure. Honored the Chinese with Confucius and Mencius Temples. And the old Germanic gods. Wotan sits on Wotan's Throne. But there are some place names a little closer to home. Holy Grail Temple. King Arthur Castle, Guinevere Castle. Excalibur."

The Kennedy presidential metaphor, thought Lilli.

"And one very obvious omission. Don't you think, Lilli? I mean, what's your read?"

She probably should keep her mouth shut. She knew what Mitch was thinking. One glaring omission of place names: Dutton attached none of their names, not of the people who lived here. Why? Because he was ignorant or because he was stubborn. Did it matter? He refused to acknowledge that the Navajo, as well as the Hopi and the Havasupai, had their own religions and these religions were as old if not older than any on earth.

"Dutton lathered the landscape of the canyon with honorific images..." She hesitated. "With one glaring exception."

"Apparently the New Testament," Lee said.

She changed her mind about saying more. Even if she tried to explain the omission, she knew what Lee would think. He'd imagine she was telling him about something long gone extinct, not a part of the modern world. Lee had every ounce as much hubris as any Powell or Dutton. But she had directions to a cave given to her by *Hosteen* Ahboah and they were getting close. She held her tongue.

"How much farther?" Lee asked.

"Think there's an odometer on this raft?" Mitch said.

Lilli didn't buy Mitch's answer. Mitch could read the river as confidently as a map. The man just liked to surprise.

It was all approach now to Crystal and the river ran cunningly smooth. The approach was silky, a siren's call.

"On a rating scale that goes from 1 to 10..." she said. "Crystal is really rated a 10-plus?"

"Off the scale, a predator. Keeps her holes hidden," Mitch replied. "Until it's too late."

You keep away from predators. She knew better than to drive around curves on the wrong side of the road. She knew better than to ignore lightning. Yet here she was, moving toward Crystal.

"What exactly is it about Crystal?" Lee asked.

"Hmm, well, the tongue, it's sleek," Mitch said. "Deceptive, way too fast. Then there's a rebound wave. And the initial drop is huge, a hydraulic jump, and that powers the water like a diabolical funnel into an unbelievable hole we need to avoid."

"How did it get so bad? I mean how did it get that way?"

"Largest flash-flood in the canyon in more than a thousand years, that's how. Worse, happened just before the dam went online, so this mountain of a rockpile's going nowhere now, just stuck in the river's craw, and that makes her boiling mad."

So far, the river still ran calm. A bird's song magnified in the constricted gorge. Lilli closed her eyes to better hear the repeat. If ever a birdsong were to be fashioned of something tactile, it should be this one, the canyon wren's song of perfectly descending half-tones, and the material should be polished silver.

Funny how the memory found things you'd lost. She suddenly remembered Jerome and her, trying as kids to out-jockey one another, leaping into a bush to snatch a snagged feather. Her People believed that if you found a feather that hadn't yet touched the ground it could be used in sacred ceremonies, to heal.

She found herself watching the side of Jerome's face, tracking, she imagined, so many images with eyes that must function nearly as camera lenses. He must be beside himself wanting to get off the moving raft and set up his tripod to photograph such a black and molten landscape.

"Come on, Mitch, seriously. Where was our explorer Powell?" Lee said. "Didn't he get first crack at all this naming?"

"And we owe the man," Mitch said. "His mind came up with the appellation of 'Grand Canyon' and I am forever grateful. Could have lost out to other suggestions on the table."

"Like what?"

"My personal favorite of doomed suggestions? The Really Big Canyon."

"Say, boys," Lee said. "Want you to appreciate what it was like to be the first man to run this Inner Gorge. Mitch, we got time for a little Powell?"

"Hey, why not?"

Lee unzipped Powell's journal from its water-tight shroud. He opened the book and inserted his fingers to hold it open and started to read:

> *Down in these grand, gloomy depths we glide, ever listening, for the mad waters keep up their roar; ever watching, ever peering ahead, for the narrow canyon is winding and the river is closed in so that we can see but a few hundred yards, and what there may be below we know not; so we listen.*

"How about a little dueling Powells?" Mitch held up his own well-worn copy.

"Go ahead." Lee closed his.

"No one, including Powell—you understand—no one knew if anyone would come out alive. Here's what Powell had to say about the ultimate mutiny, what was happening the morning after—you know, between those who decided to stick with Powell and take their chances on the river, and those, like Howland, who were giving up."

"The last..." Mitch pitched his voice deeper a notch:

> *The last thing before leaving, I write a letter to my wife and give it to Howland. Sumner gives him his watch, directing that it be sent to his sister should he not be heard from again. The records of the expedition have been kept in duplicate. One set of these is given to Howland; and now we are ready. For the last time they entreat us not to go on, and tell us that it is madness.*

As she surveyed the ten of them in the raft with Mitch, Lilli thought about how Powell began his dream to run the Great Unknown with ten men but ended with only six. There was irony in the outcome. The mutineers had decided to crawl out of the canyon and were never heard from again. No one ever found their bodies. She suddenly felt as if she should have left a letter behind. Something in case she didn't come back home.

"So what happened to the deserters?"

"Powell never called them deserters," Mitch said. "Never heard from them, either."

"They just disappeared?"

"Guess they figured staying with Powell meant sure death and trying to hike out was better odds. Never seen again, though, that's what happened. Never found the extra copy of the journal either, or the letter, or the watch."

"Or the bodies?"

"Makes you wonder, doesn't it?" Mitch returned his copy of Powell's journal to its protected place.

"Second expedition, Powell was less fond of rolling the

dice. Forged himself a friendship with the Mormons, especially with Hamblin whose ranch sat at Mountain Meadows."

"Mountain Meadows? Dad, isn't that where someone in our family used to live?"

"You're right, son. And we're real proud of him. John D. Lee who ran Lee's Ferry."

The reservation was peppered with Mormon names, Lilli thought. Hamblin Ridge itself ran along the highway north out of Tuba City. But proud? Hamblin once farmed up there with its natural spring, then sold the place to Lee. Thought Lee would be safer hiding out there after the Mountain Meadows Massacre.

"Hey, a little something for the politicians," Mitch said.

"Uh, oh, he looks gleeful." Lee smiled himself.

"Right after Crystal, if we make it, we'll scoot past Nixon Rock, middling rapid smack in the middle of the river."

"Nixon? Here? Not much of a wilderness man, that one. Why would anyone go and name a rapid after Nixon?"

Rapid what, Lilli thought. His rise to power? Or his fall from grace?

"Must celebrate his nickname," Mitch said. "Tricky Dick."

The raft rounded another bend. Still nothing of Crystal. Maybe it was the anxious anticipation that made them so chatty with each other.

"OK, Lilli. I want a valid story," Lee said. "Is Mitch putting me on about World War II?"

"What story's that?"

"Mitch?"

"I told him earlier how the Japanese set loose these vengeance balloons. Don't know what else to call them," Mitch said. "Huge paper contraptions more than thirty feet in diameter, hydrogen filled, each loaded with a personnel fragmentation bomb."

"Keep it coming, Mitch," Lee said.

"Sure. Intelligence, see, needed to know if these nasty balloons were being launched off Jap submarines or if they were coming off our own concentration camps? And intelligence favored the concentration camps cause how the hell could a paper balloon make it across the Pacific?"

"That's what the man says, Lilli. Now you look me in the eye. Did our U.S. government really put a Japanese concentration camp on the Navajo reservation?"

"Yes—at Leupp, near Bird Springs," she said. "Why?"

"Hah, figured me for a liar," Mitch said.

"But how is it this is a World War II story I haven't heard before?"

"Your problem, not mine," Mitch said. "But there really were some nearly three hundred confirmed landings of these balloon contraptions on American soil. And here's where the Military Geology Unit came into play."

"Oh, come on, you're really fabricating now."

"No, just listen. See, fossils—tiny little things, unique—in the balloon's sand ballast proved to our intelligence they were being launched all the way from Japan—and not from concentration camps, like on the Navajo reservation."

"He is, how shall I say, prevaricating, Lilli, isn't he?"

"Hmm, probably not." She wiped her mouth with the back of her hand. Anything to keep from thinking about Crystal and how they were closing the gap.

"All right," she said. "Let's see if either of you know this parachute story."

"Go for it."

"There were indigenous people in Borneo suffering from malaria. 'In its wisdom,' as lawyers are trained to say, the World Health Organization sprayed the area with DDT, causing all the cats to die. Rats began to flourish, and rat-carried diseases, so World Health decided to parachute in replacement cats."

"Seriously?"

"Would you believe fourteen thousand cats, with parachutes?"

" 'In its wisdom'—yes, exactly the predicament with the Colorado River," Mitch said. "How do you fix something you broke, without making things even worse?"

"What's broken with the Colorado River?" Lee asked.

Mitch looked at Lilli and shrugged his shoulders. All right, she'd take a stab at it.

"Mitch would like to let his river go wild again. But it's hard to unscramble eggs."

"Eggs? What are you saying?"

"It's a natives vs. invaders problem. You keep the dams in, you favor the invaders," she said. "And if you don't take the dams out soon, you're going to lose all the natives."

"She ran warm," Mitch said. "River surged when the rains came, flowed furious, then settled back down. Favored the lives of the humpback and bonytail, the razorback and cottonwood.

"Dam is inserted, the water's all pulled from the bottom, like at Lake Powell. What was once warm is now a frigid thing, and what was once muddy is now clear."

"And the invaders fit the new?" Lee said.

"Like a glove."

"I'm not anti-ecology," Lee said. "But I'll always put human need way above the needs of other species."

What about the needs of other humans, like the Navajo, Lilli thought. Trying to hold on in the desert without enough water? She felt an odd increase in their velocity.

"How soon before Crystal?"

The Swamper swung her bare legs over to straddle the

raft's inflated cell. She looked like one of the rodeo boys, easing her crotch down gently on the back of an unsuspecting bull.

"Soon. But you'll hear it coming, way before you ever see it."

"Is Suzanne crazy?"

"No, just spirited. Doesn't matter much where you sit. Crystal is going to feel at first like an elevator ride."

"And then?"

"Like the elevator cable broke."

Duane dropped his load, slid to the ground, and unlaced his boot. He was so stupid. He'd gone and underestimated the damage to his feet from the extra weight. He pulled his foot out and peeled off the thicker sock, then the inner liner. Definitely a bruise, right under the fleshy pad of his big toe and it wasn't going to disappear. Damn it, that last trail got so narrow, more like tightrope walking. He'd have to tough it out. Nothing he couldn't ignore if he put his mind to it.

He closed his eyes. He'd give his foot an extra fifteen, twenty minutes to air out. Just a matter of time, wasn't that the plan? The river was doing its work, bringing the targets closer and closer as if on special command. But he had to keep pace, and now this.

A bluebottle fly buzzed past his shoulder and he opened his eyes to watch it land on his vacant boot. He conjured up an image of a girl he hadn't thought about in a long time, a little thing with lots of spite. Couldn't have stood sixty inches high but even buck-naked she liked that no one could see all of her, not at the same time.

"Can too, if I make you spin around fast enough," he used to say.

She'd spin around fast and laugh at him. "See? Told you. You never seen the bottoms of my feet."

Duane rolled over to his side and flexed the bare toe above the bruise. Even in solitary confinement, you had your mind to yourself. You went over things, again and again, maybe editing things out, editing things in, changing what you wanted to remember.

And then you had yourself to play with. He spent hours, days, weeks in isolation doing private stuff to keep fit, knowing the camera was always on. So what? Guards called him "Clown," "Circus Boy," but it was none of their goddamn business. It was his own religion, the religion of doing something when they all wanted you to do nothing except drive yourself crazier.

He'd close his eyes because the lights were always on, and he'd listen to nothing but the smallest of his motor moves twitching to hold him in balance. He'd add difficulty, finding balance even when he swung most of his body weight way out to one side or way out in front of him. He'd gotten so he could balance barefoot not just on one foot, but on any part of the bottom of a foot, on a swatch of foot skin that got narrower and narrower until he felt like his feet had become knives and he was balancing on just the edges of those blades.

Duane started to put his sock back on but changed his mind. Maybe he could lighten up the load. He emptied his backpack of all the things he carried, to see if there was something he could do without, and got sidetracked staring at the photo.

Just the two of them, Mama so young, him so little. Look at the way he rested against her leg so easily.

Killing Lee, killing the ones that surrounded Lee, none of that bothered him. It was the risk of going straight back to prison and never seeing Mama. That bothered him. Simplest thing would have been to take the sure bet. Get his release, get his bearings, get cleaned up, go find Mama. But he wanted to show her how he'd been listening all the time she raised him, show her how he'd never forgot.

Nope, didn't see much of anything in the pack he wouldn't need to get the job done, then buy him some hiding time. He'd just have to cinch the belt tighter around his hips so the weight didn't shift, and try favoring the bruise. He began reloading the pack.

You know, Duane, when you go home don't you go showing her any reproach on your face, don't you go showing her your big dumb expectations, because there's no way she saved all your stuff.

Nothing she'd ever experienced, not even the nearly hundred miles of river, had prepared Lilli for what she now heard. Crystal, the pluperfect ten, the more than perfect ten. The ten plus. Straight ahead of her the river turned white. She looked over at Mitch. This is why he came. The boatman's eyes were on fire. He wanted Crystal.

For one brief moment, Lilli's mind locked on the pure present.

If you didn't think, if you removed all awareness of consequences, the image itself was a dazzling study in silver and white, all curves and spray and shimmer, the frozen image of a bridled river in complete fury. She felt the river draw her toward Crystal with collusion. And then the fixed image unlocked and took on motion and brought with it sound. The noise that had somehow been held outside her consciousness filled her head. She felt oddly detached, hyper-alert as if one eye had left her body and hovered above Crystal, watching all she couldn't clearly see.

And then as if the real Crystal had been lurking underwater—waiting, hiding—a glistening wall of water exploded in a wave curling toward them, lifting them. They were on its shoulders. They started to climb the wave train the way a carnival car ratchets up the roller coaster.

Her head fell back. She was pointed toward the sky. The raft hung for a raw moment at the top of the standing wave, then started a headlong dive into the maw. She saw the depth of the drop below. They rocketed nose-down toward a hole big enough to swallow them. The river exploded all around her. She was mostly under water, no, now hammered up again in a lurch. The raft moved faster than anyone could ever execute a decision. And then in full clarity they shot out of the rapid and the predator stayed behind.

"Wow! What a ride!" Jerome put his arms around her and pulled her in close. "You're shivering, woman. Hey, it's over."

Everyone seemed to be whooping and waving wet arms over their heads.

Mitch looked exultant. "You're all now Honorary Members of the ABC Club," he shouted.

"How's that?"

"Alive Below Crystal!"

Lilli approached Lee. How impossibly awkward was this going to be? She kept her voice low.

"Two women are probably enough, don't you think? Suzanne and your wife?"

"She'd like your company, Lilli."

"I'd rather sit this one out." Especially the skinny dipping, she thought.

"And I want you to spend some time with her. Suzanne's almost a kid."

Point-blank, Lilli wanted to refuse, but wasn't that part of the deal, that she provide female company to his wife?

She tightened her boot laces and joined Brianna. Already they'd traveled together more than a hundred river miles since Lee's Ferry but the intimacy of friendship required more, an act of disclosure, something that passed for true between them. Maybe this private excursion would open them both up a little. Certainly it would be the first time she'd be exclusively with women since the trip began.

"Come on, ladies." Suzanne twirled her brimmed baseball cap on the tip of her finger. "Mitch promises to keep track of the rest of them."

Suzanne took the lead and the river soon disappeared as they hiked single-file, mostly in silence, until they took a bend in the wall-rock. Suzanne first, then Brianna, then Lilli entered an oasis between draperies of fern.

"Oh, my!" Water fell in rope lengths to a plunge pool. "What is this exquisite place?" Brianna asked.

Suzanne stood surveying the plunge pool and then turned back around to face her. "Elves Chasm. Not making this up, ladies."

"My husband and the boys are really missing out."

"For good reason." The Swamper stripped her baseball cap off her head and her sandals off her feet.

Lilli bent down to unlace her boots. She heard a shriek and looked up. The Swamper stood starkly naked under the falling water with her arms raised above her head.

"Come on in, you two, and do the waggle dance! No one here but us girls!" Suzanne turned her back to them and shook her bare fanny.

Lee's wife lifted her T-shirt over her head and slid out of her shorts and bolted toward the water in her panties and bra until she seemed to disappear behind the water falling in silver lengths of chain. Brianna's head emerged, splitting the water open like a pair of curtains.

"Oh, this feels so good!"

Neither of them understood a thing about Navajo modesty, did they? Traditionally, Navajos never even took off their clothes at night. You needed complete privacy to do something like change your clothes. But Lilli needed to join in, to play at being "one of the girls." The best she could do though was remove her socks. Barefooted, she joined them under the curtain of water and felt her clothes plaster to her skin.

Within the falling cascade, she couldn't see either of them clearly. Mimicking Suzanne, she lifted her arms palms-up over her head and intersected the strangely warm, strangely soft water.

Lilli then held perfectly still, concentrating on the sensation as a blind experience until she couldn't stand not knowing and opened her eyes to look straight up and the world was no longer in color but gleaming. The rush of water over her head made it impossible to hear.

When she finally stepped out into the quiet pool, Suzanne lay sprawled naked on her back on a broad rock with only the brim of her hat pulled down.

Asdzáá nadleehé, Lilli thought, remembering how Changing Woman lay in the warm sunlight with her legs apart and how the Sun lusted after her, and how she conceived her first child, Born for Sun, the Twin who became Monster Slayer, and then how Watermist lusted after her and entered her and she conceived her other twin, Born for Water.

Lilli stepped out of the pool on the opposite side from Suzanne. She felt a tingling sensation as her wet clothes began to steam.

Brianna joined her. "Lilli? Your clothes, they're completely soaked!"

With her wet hair flat against her head, the woman looked like an older sister to her sons. She had one of those triangular faces, a Nancy Reagan face, where the eyes take up more space than they should.

"I'll dry out quickly."

"Yes, you're right, the sun feels delicious. Suzanne asked if we'd let her catch a cat nap." Lee's wife checked the time. Even on the river, the Lees and their entourage wore waterproof watches.

"Shall we settle over here, to not disturb her?" She'd selected two flat rocks a distance away and lay down on her stomach.

Lilli looked at the Swamper who seemed fast asleep, her belly breathing soft and even. She must look ridiculously overdressed.

"This is nice," Brianna said. "We finally get a real chance to talk. I still want to thank you, for helping out with the boys."

What should she say? "They're active, aren't they?"

"The campaign's been rough on them. This is their final interlude. Free, together, boys being boys, before they're in the fishbowl looking out."

Unless Lee was defeated, but that didn't seem likely.

"I'm really glad you're enjoying the trip," Lilli said.

"Oh, absolutely." Lee's wife nestled her head in her arms. "So, tell me more about Jerome. You've known him a long time?"

What should she say? She needed to forge a better bond with this woman of influence. But she feared she'd make it worse.

"Further back than I can even remember."

On the river she'd come to realize that if time had taken her on a different journey, one where Jerome and his family never left the reservation, she would have become a very different adult. She would have fallen in love with Jerome, the easy way a woman falls in love with a man. But she wouldn't have become the person she was now. Something about her losing Jerome sent her on another journey. She wanted to protect her people better, lose fewer of them to the outside world, patrol the boundary that kept the dominant culture at bay.

"Did you two used to date?"

"No, oh, no—we were just kids together."

Would this woman understand? Because it was a child's love, a love of a girl for a boy, she had discounted it, didn't think it would come to play in her adult life. Well, she'd been wrong.

"Sorry about the other night and Dougan's heavy-handedness. Seems like Jerome has trouble with authority."

"So it's that obvious, their battle of nerves?"

"A bit like one of my sons."

They lay together, silent in the sun.

"I overheard Jerome say something funny to you about Dougan, about his ears," Brianna said.

"His ears? Oh, right. Jerome said the man's so narrow minded he could applaud with his ears."

Lee's wife had a sweet laugh.

"My husband wasn't always surrounded by people like Dougan, you know. He wasn't always so..." She lifted her chin to look directly at Lilli. "In that language of yours, what do you call politicians?"

"*Na'adlo*," Lilli said, realizing this was one word she would not translate. It meant too simply the-one-who-deceives. What should she say instead? She decided instead to tell Brianna about the frogs.

"Important people, like your husband? We have a special way in Navajo of explaining the effect they have on other people." Lilli rested her weight on her elbows. "Notice how when he clears his throat..."

"In that special deep way?"

"Yes, and we all go quiet, like frogs. In Navajo we

would say *ch'al baa tóó 'íílne'*. Literally, 'I threw at the frogs in the water and made them hush.' Frogs, *ch'al,* are wary."

"So you use that phrase to describe a person?"

"Someone like your husband, yes, who can merely clear his throat and command center stage."

"Hmm, I like the image. But my husband was different when we first married. Not so sure of himself. Not so scary to frogs."

Lilli used her finger to push through the soft grains of sand. She could smell the dry heat rising from the small piles with their play of colors that when pushed too far became unstable and let go in falling sheets, miniature pyramids shedding their skin.

"Say that word again for me. Your mouth and breath, I don't know. I love the way your language sounds."

"*Ch'al*?"

"How do you spell it?"

"Weirdly. When we write out a Navajo word, we try to make it look like what you English speakers hear."

"Queer for you, I would think."

"Especially since we make sounds your ears don't pick up. Here, let me write *ch'al* in the sand."

"Now what's that slash, like a railroad crossing?"

"Cracked 'l'. Try it. Put your tongue against the back of your top teeth. Use pressure, like putting a 't' and 'l' together at the same time. Then push out your wind."

"Cha-tl?"

"Good, but you ignored the apostrophe. That's our glottal stop."

"Oh, dear."

"Sorry. Some linguist in English decided on 'glottal'. Means you stop your air in the back of your throat. One syllable interrupted by a quick change in the flow of air. *Ch'al.*"

Like when the hermaphrodite, Klah, went east with the wealthy philanthropist Mary Wheelwright and they had to sleep in her car because no motel would rent out a room to a "nigger" – the skin of a Navajo being so much darker than a *bilagáana*. But recently his name, when printed, had morphed from Klah to *Tl'aii*. All in the English trial-and-error of getting the pronunciation closer for their ears, which is hopeless since it's not in the spelling but in the mouth and the tongue and the wind.

"Enough about my frog-startling husband. How about we mothers? In Navajo, how do you say Mother?"

"We say *'amá'* to include our birth mother – and anything that gives life, sustains life: the earth, our sheep, our corn. Life-giving. It's all *amá*." Not metaphorically either. But this mother of twin boys might have trouble understanding that literal a definition.

"Have you any children?"

"No, none." Not for lack of desire. But motherhood was a topic she definitely did not want to discuss. She was afraid of what she would do when she saw Jake. Would she tell him how she lost their second child to the river? How she'd made a choice and risked something of theirs he didn't even know they had? Or would she keep it her secret? And then there was her own mother's mother. Walk in beauty to old age, that was the goal. Alzheimer's was an interesting by-pass, her *amá sání* dissolving slowly the way an old adobe house melts back into the ground.

But it wasn't Navajo to answer questions with only a "yes" or a "no." Answering was more like weaving; it involved thinking and thinking meant no talking but that didn't mean the answer was finished yet.

Funny. *Bilagáana* seemed relieved when people were talking all at once. Navajo had a different take, that when silence was operating, that's when things were happening. You just had to wait.

"Ama. I like the sound." Lee's wife lay still with her eyes closed. "A comforting word."

Then she slid her shirt down over her head. "You probably know, my husband and I, we're Mormon."

"Yes." The Church of Latter-day Saints was well known on the reservation. Their original goal had been to divvy up the reservation. Latter-day Saints—and Baptists, Catholics, Jehovah's Witnesses—they all came to take their divine share. In some ways, the Mormon way of life with its capitalism and success ethic was most at odds with the Navajo traditional way of life.

"What church do you attend?"

Church? What kind of blinkers did this woman wear?

"Well, I'm Navajo."

"But you must have churches? I'd love to see one of yours."

They didn't have churches. "No, a hogan serves instead." What else should she say? For a traditional Navajo there was no need for a church since there's no distinction in the mind between life and religion.

"Just a regular house then?"

"Once it's made ready, yes. A hogan makes do."

Dawn was the most sacred time of day. Healing ceremonies ended at dawn, when everyone stood outside the hogan and threw pollen at the whitening horizon.

Christians talked about heaven, and hell, and sin, and Satan—more words without translation. And the Christian seemed to be biding his time on earth waiting for the everlasting reward. The Jewish religion, as best she could tell, seemed more about nation states, a kind of political religion in which the side winning expanded its territory.

But her religion was not about trying to go to heaven, or to avoid hell, but to help someone who'd asked for help to walk in beauty. Family, kin, friends, came to a healing ceremony, dropping whatever needed to be done in their lives, to be present with the Singer and the One-Sung-Over, moving that person toward harmony with what is. An epistemological shift as cure, the experts would say, a shift in the way of thinking. Always trying to walk in beauty.

At the ceremony, you carried corn pollen in the right hand, maybe an arrowhead in the left hand, like carrying the Bible in the right hand, a pistol in the left. You didn't turn the other cheek—that was not Navajo practice. Their way was to walk in beauty, and be ready to shield, to protect.

"A little out of the ordinary. But certainly practical, having no churches," Brianna said.

Her tone of voice was flat. Lilli should have kept her mouth shut. She'd probably just made things worse between herself and Lee's influential wife.

"Don't mean to pry, but alcohol on the reservation? Still a big problem?"

Practicing Mormons didn't touch alcohol, did they?

"Yes, quite a problem." It would make sense to a Navajo but probably not to this woman how in the Creation Story when the sexes separated, the women had unnatural sex and bore *naayéé*, literally, the things that get in life's way. Figuratively they bore monsters, and alcoholism was one formidable monster, along with poverty, sickness, crazy sexual jealousy, all *naayéé*.

"Someone actually told me you Navajo believed in witches," Brianna whispered.

Lilli wasn't going to volunteer any more. Certainly not tell her, *We are all witches. We hold the potential, in each of us.*

The Swamper suddenly sat up in the sun. "Hey, thanks for letting me nap." She stood up and stepped a foot at a time into her tiny flowered underpants, then searched around until she found her bra, a sheer thing the lavender color of broomrape.

Already their fourth night on the river. The world up above was waiting and what, really, Lilli asked herself, did she know? She'd been trying to read the real Jerome, trying to let her heart open up to him again. But he wasn't the boy she used to know. She loved the boy. She wasn't sure she knew the man.

The man, uncertain how far in the dark Frank and Boyd roamed, had led her a distance from the tent camp until he granted they were out of range, that Boyd and Frank would stay tethered at some far shorter radius to Lee.

The coyote sounded close but in darkness a coyote always sounds close. One of her favorite visual memories was of a coyote standing in the soft light of dusk with his tail held out full and horizontal to the ground, but she was never completely sure if she saw its perfect stillness or dreamed it. In earlier worlds, Coyote had color names. The Child of Darkness, Child of Dawn, Child of Sky Blue, Child of Twilight, because he was so good at visual tricks.

She lay with Jerome on top of their sleeping bags. The world of the canyon compressed the night sky. She felt his fingers reach out for her and she took his hand. It was too dark to see his face. She had to read him without being able to watch his eyes.

"Did you know I was a lawyer, Jerome?"

"What?"

She felt him stiffen.

She was trying hard to remember his face, and his eyes,

when he'd come to find her in Window Rock.

"Did someone tell you I was a lawyer?"

"I heard."

Before she went too fast and let words ruin it, she needed to think.

"Is that why...is that why you came to find me?"

Had it nothing to do with how much they once meant to each other?

He didn't answer her. The man was far more mute than the boy she remembered.

"Why me? There are a lot of lawyers in L.A." She needed to narrow her questions, force him out.

"I didn't need one in L.A."

Something had been nagging at her all day. When he had come to her, that first time in Window Rock, how had he known she drove an old Dodge? He'd said to her that his plane took unleaded gas, just like "your sorry Dodge," hadn't he?

Don't be so jumpy, she kept telling herself. It has nothing to do with mutilated coyotes on the hood of her car. Someone probably pointed out the Dodge when he started asking around to see if she'd come in to work.

How else was he different from when he was a boy? He was troubled. His eyes gave that away. He was a risk-taker, impulsive. She'd seen plenty of evidence for that. But he was like that as a kid, too. That hadn't changed. She remembered what he'd said the other night. "It's up to you. *Nila*." He'd used the Navajo word.

"Why me, Jerome?"

"Why you?" The pause was long. "So you can judge me."

Rain started to fall. The rain was soft. Lilli didn't move. Neither did he.

When she'd first seen his photographs, she thought she was seeing something very close up. The detail had a microscopic feel. The shadings were so perfect in their gradations, the edges so sharp, but then her mind did a phase-shift and she realized she was seeing something from far off, that the effect was not microscopic but telescopic. He'd looked down with eyes from the sky.

"Are you in trouble, Jerome?"

"Words are your thing, Lilli. Images are mine."

He was just stubborn enough to not help her. But what was he trying to tell her? Speak from your heart, Jerome. Come on. What do you want from me?

"You decide," he said. "That will be good enough for me."

He'd laid out the rules of their engagement. He dealt in perceptions. Well, didn't lawyers, too?

"But what if I can't?"

He didn't answer.

The man was stubborn. She'd try one more time.

"Do we have enough time, for me to solve this?"

He let out a muffled laugh. "Well, I hadn't figured on you being so slow."

"What will I judge, Jerome?" Judge him as a lawyer? As a Navajo? As someone she still wanted to love?

"If I..." He was whispering. "If I did the right thing."

By day, the world of the river and its canyon was so visually sensual, light-filled, an experience she'd never had: the vertical world. By night, though, the world of the canyon was compressed to sounds and scents, and touch. She held onto Jerome's hand.

"What if you did the wrong thing?" she finally said.

"*Nila*. Then it's up to you. But I want to hear it from your lips."

She felt a soft pressure against her left temple and knew, even in the rain, it was his lips he'd pressed there, and now the talking was over.

Day Five.

Mitch kept his voice private between them, out of range of Lee and Dougan. "Just what I figured, Lilli. You don't even know where you're going, do you?"

Of course not. Not in a literal way. The cave's secret was its protection.

"I understand, Mitch. You have a schedule to keep."

No description of the cave existed anywhere in writing, only in the minds of a few living Singers, but she had Ahboah's directions and the memory-song he promised worked like a map.

"Then you change your plans to suit me, hear. You take both Frank and Boyd with you so that when you're good and lost with Lee, they can call for help."

She'd always known she'd have to trust the closed

mouths of Frank and Boyd. But at least she'd won a small concession from Lee. Frank and Boyd and their communications gear and whatever armament they carried would come with them as far as the entrance to the cave. But only she and Lee were going in.

"So you get lost, you give up. Nothing heroic, hear?"

"Nothing heroic, Mitch."

The official word was that she and Lee were leaving the others for a few hours to talk privately. Even Dougan seemed unsuspicious. And the afternoon light was good.

Now if she could find it.

Ahboah had to know the risk. Arizona and California's favorite site for a new dam, and the site Lee favored, lay ahead of them at River Mile Marker 238. Simulation computer runs of that dam online backed the river up over a hundred miles of canyon, all the way to where the raft now waited for their return. Lilli had followed beltway politics long enough to know that if the cave came into play in arguments about a new hydroelectric and water storage scheme, its whereabouts would not remain secret for long.

Maybe not a secret with Lee either, after today. Maybe Lee was a man of his word, maybe he was not. Only time would tell.

The route to the cave twisted upon itself so tightly she couldn't see very far ahead of her feet. The size of cobbles in their path, like bleached pumpkin heads, said something about the behavior of storms. Beautifully hidden. This was it, the final ascent.

She understood that for Lee, the lawyer-turned-politician, this was a discovery trip. He wanted to see the cave with his own eyes to assess how much weight the Navajo Nation might be able to throw around in the arena of public opinion. After all, the vacant dam site behind them in Marble

Canyon was stopped by an advertising campaign when the Sierra Club had asked the public, "Would you flood the Sistine Chapel?"

Good thing Lee was agile. Good thing, too, she'd had years of experience chasing after stray sheep on slickrock. Ahboah warned her the final leg would require a chimney climb.

"Lean in."

She'd probably just insulted Lee's athletic ability.

"Place looks tight," Lee said.

"I'll go first."

"You're part mountain goat, aren't you?"

Lilli put a foot on one side of the cleft, then the other foot on the other side, and started up, letting the width of the chimney work to her advantage, a human wedge pushing out against the rock walls. And then, there it was, the entrance, just like Ahboah had said. All in blackness.

She waited for Lee. This was no alcove in the rock cliff, nothing like what the Anasazi used for shelter. This looked like a slash, a linear mouth low to the ground, a dark opening more like something an animal might use. She heard something. For a moment she felt as if she'd already slipped inside. Her legs stiffened.

Ahboah had brought her this far. She opened the bundle he'd given her. Now what? Lee was going to judge her the fool. But she loosened the strings on the leather pouch.

"Here. Take a pinch and rub this powder over your face." She held the bag out for Lee.

"What in the world? What is that stuff?"

"Mirage stone. For invisibility."

"Protection? Think I've got Frank and Boyd and the twenty-first century here for that. Not to worry."

Frank and Boyd had taken their positions on either side

of the mouth of the cave. She turned her back to the three men and rubbed the powder over her cheeks and forehead and chin, then closed her eyes and felt the soft powder stick to her eyelids. She opened her eyes and turned back to face them. She hoped Lee wouldn't state the obvious. She was still visible.

"So, now? Are you ready?" Lee asked.

"Not quite."

What if she took Lee inside and this cave turned out to be nothing more than smoke stains and the ashes from an old fire? Or maybe the place had been vandalized.

She slid her hands into the bundle and withdrew two objects, each shaped from a chunk of mirage stone, with mouths of turquoise. She needed to give them voice. She tried to forget Lee and Frank and Boyd.

She started with a soft call that could barely be heard, and then she let wind into her throat and called out louder and louder, each of four times, until she spit out *"Pah!"* She breathed the Bear, all darkness except for its eyes, into being and followed the Bear in.

She wished she could leave Lee outside, with Frank and Boyd, but that would never fly, not with this man. She ducked down and entered the inner cave. The light from his high-powered beam followed her in, until it filled the silent chamber.

What had she expected? Not this. Certainly not this. Lilli had a sense that Lee was saying something to her but she couldn't hear him clearly. Slowly, she turned in full circle. The air held the coldness that dark carries. She was caught off guard. Why had she been so wrong?

Lilli closed her eyes to travel back inside her mind. She had such a sorry imagination. She'd expected the cave to contain a kind of abbreviated set of cheat notes.

All coming down the river, she'd let herself assume

what she would have done if she'd been one of the few remaining Singers, desperate with fear, weak with agony at all that had already been lost, hiding herself from the army and its guns and its Executive Order from Washington, D.C. to round up every living Navajo and put them into captivity. To relocate them within prison fences hundreds of miles to the east with no intent to ever return them.

She imagined herself one of them, hiding deeper and deeper in the canyon, then finding this imperceptible opening to a large protected cave. They wouldn't know the future. They were afraid no Navajo would survive the Executive Order. But if any did physically survive, what would they most need to remain Navajo?

She pictured those few, hiding in the canyon, frantic that the healing ceremonies, carried only in memory, would vanish. Yet that was exactly what she did not see on the walls of the cave.

She wasn't as Navajo as she thought, was she? She'd pictured the few escapees trying to transcribe from their minds as many of the sandpaintings from their ceremonies as could fit inside the cave. But that was precisely what was not here.

She turned again in a complete circle.

The cave held much more ancient information.

She wanted to reach out and touch the silent images, let her fingers trace their edges. She'd left time and entered into a much earlier world.

"A little commentary?" Lee's voice echoed inside the cave.

She felt as if she was present as the Holy People, the *Haashch'ééh dine'é*, figured out what life would mean. Because the walls of the cave held the primary Navajo secret of the center.

"Some interpretation?"

It would have been easier to talk with Lee if she'd been right. This was going to be very hard to explain. But she couldn't run away from the effort.

The Navajo had a unique way of thinking. How could she possibly connect with Lee?

In *bilagáana* science the most elegant of the truths was the one formulated by Einstein, that energy is matter, and matter energy. But how do you take a universe like that and give it human dimension, human imperative? The Navajo long ago came up with *Sa'a Nagháí Biké Hózhó*. This, on the walls of the cave, was their answer.

"What does all this mean? Any ideas?" Lee strafed his beam of light back and forth across the images.

It meant so many things. That all is motion, all is dualistic. Nothing in the universe is whole. Everything exists in unbalanced halves. Everything must come together in twinned pairs. She could try to say it, but Lee couldn't really hear her, could he?

She felt uneasy.

Yet, like Einstein's cosmic machine, the Navajo's central secret was simple. She saw the image, over and over again, in a hundred variations: *Sa'a Nagháí Biké Hózhó*.

"Wholeness," she said. "Twins, really." Their universe was first thought out and then sung into existence.

"They don't look like twins."

She could feel the rising impatience in his voice.

And in the First World, sexual desire was created. First Woman worked on it, called it *áníť'í*, and made it important for the male and the female to pass the desire back and forth between them. And every time the Navajo emerged into a new world, they brought with them sexual desire.

There was *Begochiddy*. And *Eshkay-nah-ashi*, the Two-Who-Go-Together. Only the oldest singers, like Ahboah, were trusted with the deep meaning of *Sa'a Naghái Biké Hózhó*. But even in the darkness illuminated by artificial light, she saw the yellow line that went from one mouth to the other. Turquoise Boy and Corn Girl. Talking God and Calling God. Monster Slayer and Born-For-Water.

Pairs—what she would call *Alkéé naa'aashii*—were all over the walls, and in each, one was male and one was female. These were not the Ones the children heard about. These were not those stories. If she'd allowed Jerome to come with her, he wouldn't have recognized what she saw.

The advertising gurus of the *bilagáana* world used sexual desire to sell soft drinks and cars. But with sexual desire came the responsibility for carrying on Life. So inside each birth would be found again the *áníťí* of sexual desire, and the ability to give birth. Except sexual desire had its twin, its *alkéé naa'aashii* of adultery, betrayal, incest, even murder.

"Do these images have names?"

"Not exactly," she lied. The cave's dry air settled on her tongue with a taste like white shell.

The present always finds us, and we must choose. She busied herself with planting the two mirage stones. It is life itself that is holy, which makes the act of sex a sacred act. We have the capacity to pass life on: we are Creators. We are, in a sense, all gods.

Life is brief, she thought, tenuous, but it has a point. We are here to create life, and to teach it, and to die old in beauty. "Beauty" did not mean you walked to old age with no illness, or you walked to old age with cosmetically enhanced qualities of the young. It was not about physical attributes. It was about a quality of character.

Even good and evil are twinned *Alkéé naa'aashii*. Good is the other side of evil. Evil is the other side of good. The words were *hózhó* and *hóchxó*. If she were to say them out loud to Lee, his English ear would miss the difference, think she'd said the same thing. You needed a Navajo tongue to even say the words right.

"Kind of quiet in there."

She recognized Boyd's voice from outside, distorted by the hollowness of the cave.

"Everything all right?"

Time was short, they couldn't stay here long.

"We're fine," Lee answered back.

She was stalling. Why, in the beginning, would the Holy People have created such a world? Because this act of combining with another is the best way they could think of to make sure that the line of life continued, yes, but that it changed, too, that the new ones born might think differently, because difference is good. So each new generation is different from the generation it replaces. We are never copies of one another. And because difference is good, you do not want authority, you do not want hierarchy.

Even their Holy People did not command. And so the Navajo had no priests of special authority, only Singers who healed, no elected presidents or henchmen, not until Washington D.C. insisted.

Lee shuffled his feet behind her.

The man thought differently. He nurtured his ego, fed it continually. He was trained to think that way.

In Lee's *bilagáana* world, the Self reigned supreme. An error in logic, she thought. In her People's world, there was no pure 'self' that was whole. The universe worked by pairing opposites.

"Glad I got to see this, Lilli. Let me give you credit. Some ambitious art here. Cave art," Lee said.

No, this was decidedly not "art." These images *are* language. All things have their male side, all things have their female side. The maleness is *bika'*, violent, its evil side, but protective, its good side. Female is *ba'áád*, gentle, its good side, but weak, its bad side. Within each of us, there is both. And without both, there is no balance, no completeness.

"I've seen enough, though. How about you?"

She felt the growing intolerance in his voice. She owed it to Ahboah to try. The central dilemma, how do you protect something and keep it secret? Ahboah had seen the dilemma with Lee. If Ahboah kept the cave secret, he realized it might drown. She decided to confront Lee and waiting wouldn't help.

"This is... This is our religion."

Politics drove Lee. He might pretend to be a friend to her culture. He might pretend to be saving "art." But this cave's existence spelled trouble for him.

"Religion? You call this a religion?"

What would he call it? Primitive symbols of an unenlightened people? It wasn't about going to church. Breathing, thinking, speaking, acting, it all mattered. Their "heaven" was internal. You could find it. *Walk in beauty*. There were no Ten Commandments. There was no hell, there was no punishment. Only "it's up to you."

"Yes," she said. "This is our answer."

She would fight its being drowned all the way to the Supreme Court.

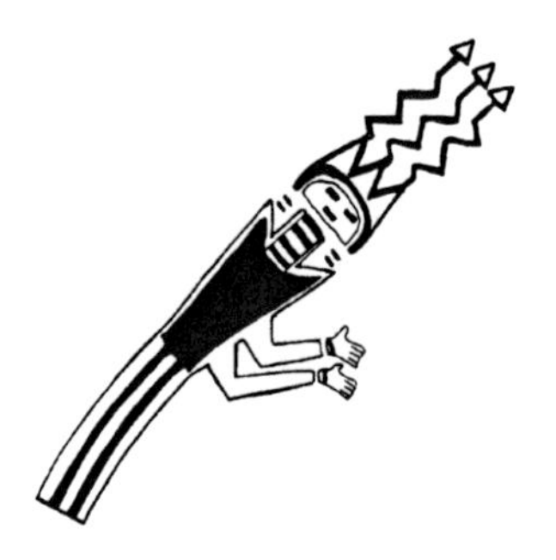

She was taking to these smaller rapids, starting to enjoy the ride. Lilli sat lazily sandwiched between Mitch and Jerome, all six of their legs stretched out in parallel.

"So that was Helicopter Eddy?"

"Not the name of some helicopter pilot. 'Eddy,' as in whirlpool," Mitch said. "Spins a back-eddy with the speed of a helicopter's rotors, but we avoided it."

Beautifully, she thought. She ran her fingers through her hair, a make-shift combing, lifting the warm strands closest to her head up, then letting her loose hair fall around her shoulders. But, almost immediately, she felt vulnerable, the way their water world collapsed to a lair. The sky was suddenly inconsequential.

"What's happened?"

"Welcome to the absolute narrowest stretch of the river.

Granite Narrows," Mitch said. "A long chute coming."

Lilli didn't like it. There was no way out, was there? No way off the river. There was absolutely no landing place, no shoreline. But in its own elemental way, it was beautifully serene, a simplicity of polished rock and the music of moving water. She breathed deep, on purpose. Somehow the constriction acted to concentrate the faint odors coming off the canyon's upstream corridors, the scent of mesquite and seep willow and catclaw.

She tipped her head back to better follow the ribbon of sky so far above them. The light in the canyon seemed to be getting dimmer. The polished cliffs, so close together, reflected less of sky than of each other which turned the water black.

"Little physics quiz, Lilli. If the river gets squeezed to its tightest here, what happens?"

She'd already felt the answer. "Goes faster."

"Correct. And anything else?"

The water had to go somewhere.

"Must be deepest here, too."

"That it is. Fast and deep."

She tried to relax, not think about how the river was deepest here. Maybe that was the secret: resistance only made things worse.

Duane felt his brain speed up. Easy now, nothing to do but breathe and wait. The gorge was narrow and straight with no bends to block his view. And he was achingly ready. But what did Mama used to say? How every plan of his starts to fall apart nearly as soon as it hatches. Not this time.

The target was on its way. He could see the raft upstream, coming toward him. In his mind, the question was always the same: Who first? He liked the idea of so many choices.

He wanted Lee, first. But even itching to take Lee he'd better go slow, take the boatman first. He didn't want the boatman to go tricky on him. Besides, he had plenty of time. If he kept a cool head he could do it all.

Just don't get jittery and don't get greedy. Worst-case scenarios played in his mind. He pictured one of the Secret Service agents getting off a satellite call for help, the transponder on the raft pinpointing its exact location, the rescue helicopters lifting off. But that was where planning came in.

So take your time.

He'd picked the helicopters a nice tough spot to access. He could have opted for the site with the longest overland haul, the worst spot on the river for helicopter rescue, which would have put him downstream in the Jewels. Because all along that whole stretch from Tuna to Bass there were no spots large enough to put the helicopter down, not when it needed a safety zone for circling of seventy-five feet.

No, he'd opted for Granite Narrows because it favored the shooter. True enough, a helicopter could land easy below the Narrows, land river left down at Deer Creek, that'd be the safest bet. The rescue team could run overland upriver, or rappel down over the Narrows. He knew that. That was the trade-off.

But what he liked about the Narrows was how it ran cruel, a chute with no shore, the water met the rock and that was that. He had himself the longest, narrowest, straightest shooting gallery. Ducks in a row. I mean, what was the biggest problem for the shooter? That the targets go out of sight before he finishes up the plan.

Plus, either site, time enough was on his side. Even with special cargo like Lee. He'd figured the stats. Even if the rescue team kept the copter all packed, humming on the tarmac ready to go, it'd still take at least twenty minutes of flight time. Realistically, he probably had twice that much time.

He lifted his head up, carefully. In the distance he could make out the orange PFDs they were each wearing. In the Kennedy motorcade in Dallas, the footage he remembered best was how Jackie Kennedy, in her pink suit, had climbed up on the open car and tried to gather together bits of her husband's skull.

All night, trouble falling asleep, he'd imagined how the .50 caliber rounds were going to add their high-pitched whistle to the deep-throated roar of the river. But them on the raft, they wouldn't hear it. They wouldn't appreciate what was going on, not soon enough.

He wanted to make sure the news stories on TV used the word "massacre." Yeah, he had it all figured out, who he would explode first, who second. A kind of reverse order of the Mountain Meadows Massacre, where they made the women and children come out first to meet their deceiving killers.

Mama'd always had hopes.

You breathe, Duane, that's all, in and out, keep it regular. You align the optics, you relax, then you squeeze.

He tightened his finger against the trigger. As simple as shooting the ear off a distant Hereford.

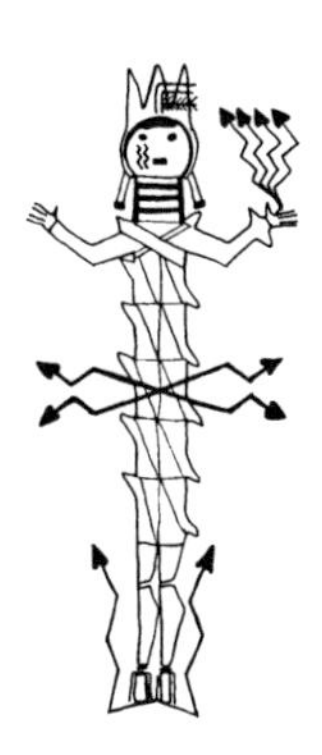

"So, Lilli, you figured out yet why the river's so tight here?" Mitch stood at the stern.

She sat comfortably on the inflated air chamber, warmed by the sun.

"No, tell me more."

"Bright Angel Shale failed right here. A big bedrock landslide choked the river. The fault block dropped down..."

What was going on with Mitch, had he gone goofy? His arms came up and his back curved as if the raft were a diving board and he gracefully entered the river, leaving them all behind.

"Hey!" She turned toward the others. Lee sat opposite her and in her field of view lurched forward as if an invisible force struck him in the gut, and then his head exploded.

She heard screams. Nothing made sense.

But then the blood made sense.

"Shooter!" Boyd lunged toward Lee and Frank toward Brianna. Too late. Brianna's face disappeared. Boyd sat up suddenly, then creased, stick-like as if his spine had snapped.

She heard Frank shouting into the phone.

"Shooter!" He slammed his weight against the two boys. "Go for cover! In the water! Hang on to the side!"

Like a dream sequence where one thing happens after another for no apparent reason, Lilli felt something push her hard, and her world go dark, and then she felt the cold and knew she was moving underwater.

Some force acted on her oddly and she bobbed to the surface and swallowed a gulp of air. She was in the chute of fast-moving water held buoyant by her life jacket. What did Frank mean, take cover? Wouldn't the orange PFDs look like bull's-eyes against the black water, showing the shooter exactly where each target lay?

She was hyperventilating from the intense cold. Why was she so alone?

The empty raft floated ahead of her, too far downstream to reach. But then it swerved and listed and she watched as its chambers burst open and its weight took it down. The shooter must have opened it with one long strafing.

She couldn't stand the thought of helping the shooter by wearing her life jacket.

She wanted to unbuckle it and let it drift away from her, a decoy.

Where was Jerome?

Suddenly she understood what she saw toward the river's center. A human raft. She shouted. Frank, Suzanne, the two of them making a ring, holding on to each other. And then the bullets must have found them because their heads snapped back and they each let go.

She felt light-headed and numb. Pretty soon she'd lose whatever judgment she had left. Either she found the river's edge and eddied out of the river's rush or her body went through its final game of survival, shutting down her extremities, trying to preserve temperature in her core, in her brain, until that was impossible.

She wasn't breathing right. She was so close to the canyon wall. She was afraid to look up. Maybe the shooter couldn't make her out from where he lay positioned. She tried to remember how to swim.

She felt something grab around her. She felt dreamy and uncoordinated and felt the Water Monster. No, it was a human arm. And then it was Jerome. His chest pressed against her. His leg beneath the water clawed out for her and then he crushed her, hard, between himself and the cliff rock.

Everything was moving so fast. She couldn't hold on. An orange jacket swept toward her. It supported Dougan's head. But she couldn't reach out for him. If she didn't cling to Jerome she'd be swept back into the river. But she couldn't let Dougan sweep out into view of the shooter. She grabbed for him. Jerome seemed to be kicking out. She grabbed again for Dougan.

"No, Lilli! No!" She was sure that was Jerome shouting at her.

His eyes wild in his head, Dougan clutched at her arm until he had hold of her life jacket and then he clambered up on her like she was the shore and he was finally beached. She couldn't support his weight. She started to go under. She felt Jerome's grip loosen. And then it was black as Dougan's full weight pushed her under and she felt the river take her again.

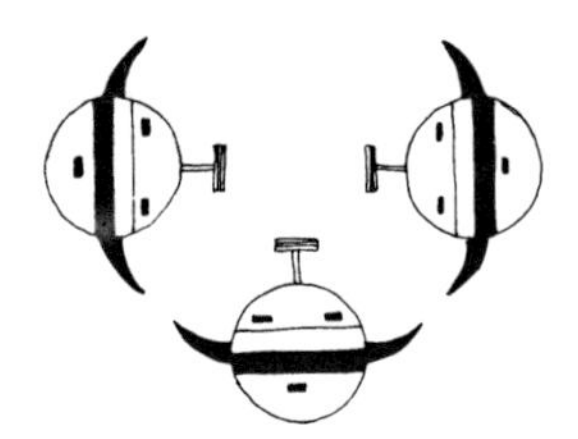

The rotor pilot of the McDonnell MD 901, acting as Incident Commander, fumbled with his communication helmet.

"This is NP 368. Come in. We've got a potential MCI. Repeat: Mass Casualty Incident. All units in the air, respond."

"This is Ranger 1 responding, we're up."

"What's on-board?"

"DPS short-haul team. What's the situation?"

"Don't know yet. No communication since the emergency call for help."

"This is Angel 1, enroute. Closing in behind you."

OK, so they had a mother ship.

"This is Long Ranger, Classic 206, we're up."

Good, another SAR. Already there were four Search and Rescue teams in the air.

"This is Ranger 1. Request clarification. Distress signal came out of Granite Narrows?"

"Roger that."

"Where's our Landing Zone?"

"Hope they've eddied out cause there's no good LZ."

"This is Long Ranger. Anywhere to come in on a one-skid or a toe-in?"

"Negative on the Narrows. We're about to do a fly-over." The Incident Commander executed a low reconnaissance of the canyon below him, waiting for his Spotter to give detail.

"Come on, give me something."

"Nothing yet, not human."

"I'm dropping in deeper. Keep an eye on our rotor clearance."

The Incident Commander reduced the collective and applied right pedal pressure.

"Hey, there's a PFD with nobody home."

"Come on, where's the raft? Where's everybody?"

The Incident Commander went over the statistics in his head. Average distance traveled by a dead body wearing a PFD was fifty miles per day. But the average lied, because the most likely distance traveled by a body wearing a float jacket was a lot shorter. And without the float the body went underwater. Corpses without flotation had a tendency to suffer entrapment.

"Damn, we got a Charlie Foxtrot!" The Spotter's voice quickened. "A real Cluster Fuck."

"How many do you spot?"

"Code 901. I see a whole lot of dead people. All with PFDs."

The Incident Commander raised the collective lever to increase pitch of the rotor's blades.

"This is NP 368. Long Ranger, take reconnaissance, give me short-haul site evaluation. Ranger 1, get ready to transport."

"Wait, I see two more!"

"Come on, Spotter, where?"

"They look alive! What the hell?"

"Where are they?"

"Lost 'em."

"Did they go under?"

"Just disappeared. Looked like two kids. No, they're in all that debris."

"Where's the raft?"

"This is Long Ranger. Recon is negative: no short-haul site available in the Narrows."

"Roger, Long Ranger. Can you insert rescuers from Deer Creek?"

"Negative on rescue, EMT only. We can assist with scene work, run air ambulance."

"Affirmative. Set down with Angel 1. We're going to need lots of transport."

The Incident Commander applied the cyclic forward and felt his airspeed increase. So he had four rescue teams in the air but no good site to anchor them, and these two floaters—if they were alive—had been in the river too long. Now what? His team was authorized to rescue but not required to die trying.

Swift water rescue was all about getting ropes across the water, or getting personnel in the water to intercept. This was neither, this was presenting as air pursuit rescue, and he knew his mandate: his team did not chase people in the water. Not from the sky.

He had one cardinal rule: takeoffs of NP 368 are optional but safe return is mandatory. If the helicopter crashes, they all die.

"Let's get the rescue teams in kayaks, downstream, to intercept. We can launch from land at Deer Creek." And eat up valuable time, he thought.

"Ranger 1, responding. We think we can short-haul."

"Negative. Too risky."

Short-haul was all about inserting and extracting personnel on the end of a rope dangling beneath the belly of the chopper from a site too lousy to land. They trained for short-haul from land, even from exposed boulders in the middle of a rapid, but not from moving water. They called the rescuer they sent out on the flying rope beneath the copter their Dummy on the Rope.

"This is Ranger 1. We want to try."

"To pluck out of moving water?"

"Affirmative."

That was the trouble with Ranger 1. Their mindset was plain different.

"How big's your sky hook?" HEC, they called it, Human External Cargo. It sounded like a real bad idea in Granite Narrows.

"With the Dummy on, we can lift one at a time."

Or die trying.

But he knew Ranger 1. "Don't use the Bauman bag to rescue. In moving water, it'll act like a sea anchor." And pull both the rescuer and the victim down.

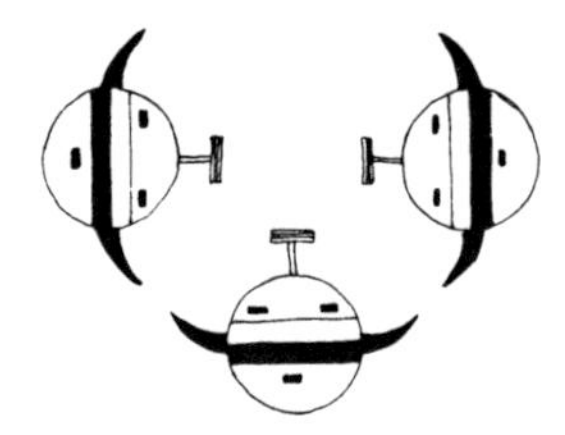

Lilli could barely think. She felt the cold creep into her brain. Noise was suddenly everywhere, or maybe all the noise was inside her head. She needed to stay awake but she could feel the coldness moving toward her heart. She felt so numb. She was shutting down. She was going to drown.

No, Lilli tried to twist her head, she was being shot at, or had the shooting stopped? Where was Jerome? She'd let Dougan pull her away from him. She couldn't see Jerome anymore, she couldn't see anyone. She was all alone in the water, so close to the cliff. But she couldn't will herself to kick, to claw at the water. The river had her, she was moving with the river. Maybe she was dreaming. She saw something coming toward her out of the air.

A white bird with a shiny belly marked in numbers hovered above her. There was something white climbing down a rope toward her.

Helmet Head, screaming at her.

She could see a face inside the helmet, all contorted. His mouth was moving. He grabbed at her. Too late, she tried to say.

She felt herself lift up out of the river. She was flying.

Someone was cutting off her clothes. She couldn't stop shaking.

"You're hypothermic, ma'am. You're safe, you're in a helicopter."

Her head felt like cotton. She tried to talk but nothing seemed to move.

"How are her vitals? Watch for signs of shock."

"Let's stabilize her. Need to hurry, she's not going to be in the Golden Hour much longer."

"Keep her airway open."

"Hand me the non-breather mask."

"Initiate two large bores, I want IVs with warm saline. Watch for seizure."

"Let me get chemical heat to her groin, to her armpits."

"Careful not to throw her in V-fib."

"Spotter says we're missing one."

"We're full."

"We'll come back."

"There isn't time."

"There never is."

The hall was long and well-lit compared to the darkened rooms whose doors stood open to the night shift. Noiselessly, the man walked toward a room numbered 223 and went in.

Lilli sensed him leaning over her. The room was too dark for her to see very well. He didn't smell like Jerome. Where was Jerome? He's dead, isn't he?

Her mind locked. She couldn't make it go forward. She started instead to follow her thoughts backward, to a fragment, an image—Lee's head exploding. Her mind revolted.

The man seemed to be trying to talk to her. What was he saying? His mouth was moving. Why couldn't she hear him? Now he was touching her. She felt him take her hand. It seemed like his voice was coming from so far away. Her mind mutinied and locked again.

"Ms. Chischilly, can you understand me? They're going to keep you overnight. You'll be monitored, that's all, OK? Just a precaution."

She tried to sit up. "Where am I?"

"Excellent. Ms. Chischilly, you're sounding a lot more alive. A little amnesia is perfectly normal. You don't remember me, do you? I was your Dummy on the Rope."

He started to rest his hip against hers and then seemed to change his mind. He released her hand. She watched him pull a chair close to her bed.

"Hypothermia can masquerade as death, but we have a saying: 'No one's declared dead until they are both warm and dead.' And you were so cold. Eighty-six degrees, if you like numbers."

Hanging in the air?

"Rope?" Her throat burned. "You?"

"The helicopter, yes, ma'am. Your body didn't give up on you, tried to protect your core—the heart, the brain. You were dazed, had what we call 'the umbles' for a while."

"What?" She struggled to focus.

"You mumbled, you fumbled—a person's body temp drops to ninety degrees, the body tries to slip into a state of hibernation, make like a bear. Body temp drops lower, we call it the metabolic icebox. You may look dead, but it ain't necessarily so."

He held up something to her face.

"Hey, the guys wanted me to give you a souvenir, it's us, the helicopter and the crew."

She squinted at what looked like a white helicopter with a blue tail, brand new shiny, and five men standing in front of it, each holding a white helmet.

"We were on standby, you know, for Lee. Rigged sideways and backwards for every possible type of rescue.

Decreased our response time, that's for sure."

The man's head was bald, out of the helmet. She cleared her throat to see if she could really talk.

"The other ones?" She wasn't managing to say much. She wanted to know if they'd found Jerome's body, but she couldn't will herself to ask.

"Trauma took them. We were too late to do any good."

Her face collapsed. She couldn't help herself.

"Don't worry, this overnight stay, it's just a precaution. You'll be yourself by morning."

No. She didn't think she'd ever be herself again.

She lay with her weight against the inclined hospital bed. Her sense of sound quickened. Something noisy was moving down the hall. She willed her toes and fingers to move. They obeyed. She scanned the contents of the room. Her eyes read a brand name on a machine and found the wall clock. She placed the palms of her hands against her cheeks. She felt warm enough.

"How are you doing?"

She turned toward the door and the familiar voice. "I'm being released to our own medical team." Dougan and a retinue entered the room. "On board the airplane."

"Sir, the plane's waiting."

"At 8 a.m. tomorrow morning, Eastern time, we'll go live with the news. But we had to have time, you understand, had to keep the lid on, institute a news blackout."

So no one knew, not yet. And the shooter, where was he?

"Apparently there's talk of putting me in the vice presidential slot, and moving the VP candidate up to take Lee's place on the ballot. We're going to win, Lilli."

"Sir, the plane."

"Makes Lee a hero, for sure," Dougan said. "And heroes are great vote getters."

She wondered if Lee would have sacrificed himself to save his sons. There wasn't enough time. His head had exploded before he'd had any choice.

"We'll have sympathy, empathy, soul support on our side. And you can never shut off the conspiracy spigot. Who's to deny that the opposition didn't set up someone with sniper talent?"

"No..." she tried to say. Lee was the target. But it wasn't a simple surgical strike on Lee, it had to be some other motive, because after Lee, the strafing was relentless.

"Doesn't matter, it gets votes. Tomorrow morning, I suggest you be careful with your answers. Here's how to contact our lawyers."

Someone placed a file folder on her bed.

"Just wanted to thank you, you know, for grabbing me."

"The shooter?" She coughed into her closed hand. "Did they get him?"

"Not yet." He squeezed her shoulder. "Take care of yourself. I've got to get to D.C. We have to take control, there are sure to be conspiracy theories galore."

The aide arrived with the wheelchair which Dougan refused. Another aide closed the room's door and Lilli was alone.

She'd rescued the wrong man.

Jerome was lost somewhere in the river, to a bullet, or to the water in his lungs. She'd taken him with her to give her time to figure out how to save him. Now her final memory of him would be of Dougan pushing her down under his own frantic weight, and Jerome's hand slipping away.

Lilli lay in bed, alone. Jerome was gone. She tried to will herself to sleep. The darkened hospital was so quiet. Her mind started to race instead, imagining tomorrow and the news reporters who would descend on her. And some heavy duty Secret Service agents, or Homeland Security, or the FBI, they'd all have the same questions. *In your own words, tell us.* That's how it would start.

How long had she been asleep?

She'd dreamt of the noise and the panic and then the whirring wings of the white helicopter with its blue tail hovering above her, and a man coming toward her, and then the whirring wings morphed into Whirling Logs and she saw the Upside-Down Girl.

A nurse gestured with a thermometer and she lifted her tongue and felt the probe slide in. In hypothermia, does the brain shut down? Maybe it hadn't fully started up again. Because the last thought she had before seeing the nurse was how she'd had the man in the Hoodoos' murderer with her all along. Jerome. The man's mouth, Bilgehe's mouth, had been stuffed with the genitals of a pair of coyotes, one male, one female. Jerome had taken a healing ceremony and turned it into a murder message.

The nurse removed the thermometer and wrote on her chart.

"You're feeling much better, aren't you? You all are. The two men, the two boys." The nurse hooked the chart to the foot of her bed.

So only four had survived. Dougan, and herself and the two boys? No, the nurse said two men. Five survived?

"What other man?"

"Mr. Dougan, and a Mr. Bah. That's the other man."

Jerome? "Where is he!" Lilli slid her feet to the floor.

"Two doors to your right. Wait a minute. Are you stable? Don't you want some help?"

Lilli stood in his doorway. Jerome's eyes were closed. She walked barefoot over to his bed and lay her head on his chest. He must have been asleep but his eyes opened.

"Shh," she said. "They just told me you were alive."

He found her fingers and held on. "How did you..." He stopped.

What did he need to hear?

"A helicopter, a man on a rope, I was lifted up. And you?"

"I don't really remember. I've been told I came ashore, eddied out."

They lay quiet together in the dim light. They were both wide awake.

"I wasn't listening, Jerome, was I? You gave me the images. I didn't understand what you were trying to say."

But now she understood it was Jerome who came in the middle of the night and draped the two coyotes over the hood of her Dodge. His Upside Down Girl, his Hoodoos. He worked in pictures. She hadn't decoded it. Now she hoped it wasn't too late.

She imagined tomorrow morning, after 8 a.m. Eastern time. Dougan had warned her to be careful with her answers. There would be questions about the final minutes in the canyon, about the shooter, and the shots, and the memories of Mitch, the first to leave the raft, and the order of the strafing.

"Let's get out of here," she said.

"The hospital?"

"Now."

She was Darkness Girl.

Lilli slipped under the red exit sign into the empty stairwell of the hospital, leading Jerome noiselessly down the concrete flight of steps. Her mind was racing even faster than her feet. She tried to wrap her mind around the undeniable image of Jerome with Bilgehe, when he was still alive, and then when he was dead. Jerome had calculated a plan. Willful, purposeful, premeditated murder.

But why had he involved her?

She heard a door opening above them. She willed herself to act natural in the borrowed scrubs, not to turn and gape. Act normal, but hurry, don't get stopped. Look down, keep your face hidden. So far, that was all the plan she had. Get out of the hospital.

Dougan had had no trouble being released. Of course not, with an official jet waiting and a medical team on board.

Lilli peered through the small window of the stairwell door before pushing it open onto the first-floor corridor. Empty, except for two muffled voices carrying on a he-said, she-said conversation from within a lighted room.

The seeing-eye beam of the front door sensed their approach and the door slid sideways. Probably less than four minutes had elapsed since she'd made her decision but already the hospital room seemed far away and from another life. She had a choice to make.

Jerome might already be facing first-degree murder charges.

She led him between parked cars, across the parking lot, moving toward the distant stoplight that spoke of convenience stores and people still moving about at night.

Bilgehe was alive when the coyote parts were stuffed in his mouth. She tried not to see Jerome with Bilgehe, but her mind flooded with images. She saw him strap Bilgehe into the seat that would lift him into the sky. Probably he was already dead. She wondered how close Jerome had come to earth before he'd let the man fall.

What the police would find interesting was a singular fact. The coyotes had ended up on the hood of her Dodge.

Did Jerome understand the law? Maybe already there was direct evidence linking Jerome to the killing. But direct evidence isn't necessary. Circumstantial evidence alone can convict in a *bilagáana* courtroom.

She reached for Jerome's hand.

"I buried the coyotes."

And what was that, besides tampering with evidence? She could be charged with obstructing justice, maybe even hiding a fugitive.

The southwest corner of the Navajo reservation was less than twenty miles away. She had a cousin in Leupp. He had a truck. The store clerk handed her the phone.

Her cousin found them waiting in the shadows near the dumpster behind the convenience store. He couldn't give them the truck, he explained, he needed it tomorrow. He could give them a ride. They slipped inside.

All the way across the black roads, Jerome sat in the rear seat, asleep mostly. The roads were empty and they made good time. The stars were still bright. Dawn wouldn't find them for a couple more hours.

The lies of omission. She and her cousin talked about news that mattered to family and in the long silences she worked on her plan.

In the top-down system of *bilagáana* justice, the judge says, "How do you plead? Guilty or not guilty?" In the Navajo tongue, there was no such simple word as "guilty."

Jerome could have left Bilgehe's body to rot in the Hoodoos. But he deliberately went back up in the air. He took a witness. He took her. Why?

Because she had lawyer credentials? She didn't think that was close to correct. He'd taken her up in the sky to see Bilgehe lying dead, and to wait with him for the police. In Jerome's mind, Lilli needed to be involved, but why?

Suddenly she understood. To decide what fate he deserved, the *bilagáana* answer, or the Navajo answer? It was as he'd said. He needed to hear from her lips. Was he still Navajo in his heart?

She turned around to watch Jerome, sleeping fitfully in the rear seat.

Did he understand that in their tradition The Holy People made the laws. The laws are *beehaz-aanii*. They have existed since the beginning.

In war, killing an enemy is *nicxóní*, meaning ugly and contaminating. But it can take courage to kill an enemy and that courage is beautiful, it is *nizhóní*.

Jerome didn't have anyone to protect anymore, not his wife, nor his child.

She closed her eyes and saw Mitch, standing at the stern of the raft. And Suzanne. And Lee and his wife. And the two loyal bodyguards, Frank and Boyd. They had been eleven. Now they were five. Dougan and the two boys. Her and Jerome.

In a few more hours, there'd be no hiding from the questions and the press. All Lilli would be able to confirm was what? Mitch unexpectedly left the boat. Yes, from the stern. He'd been standing up. Then Lee's head exploded. Then the agents dove to protect someone. Things got murkier, she couldn't see, she remembered next being in the water.

But none of her feeble answers pointed toward the big question. Who was doing the shooting? Lee had almost been president. No, she thought, the answer would turn out to be stranger. The way the shooter went after them when Lee was so obviously dead.

She was sure, though, of one thing. Dougan would keep the spotlight focused on winning the election. That would involve him, and his retinue, and the new candidate, and probably even the funerals.

She needed to finish what Jerome had started. She needed to find Ahboah, tonight. Jerome feared he wasn't Navajo any longer, that L.A. had washed it out of him. But he reacted intuitively as Navajo. He had protected Asan, the Upside-Down Girl, by killing the witch.

She started to imagine a conversation. When she and Jerome got out of the car, after her cousin dropped them off, she'd ask Jerome the question. *The old man, Bilgehe – you saw it, didn't you, from the air, how he made the little girl stand on her head? Photographed it, too, didn't you?*

But she already knew the answer. Standing on her head,

held upside down. He'd probably wrapped her spread legs around him. That was the photograph Jerome never showed her. That was the image he'd captured that led him to compose the image he'd taken her to see of Bilgehe, lying dead in the Hoodoos.

To a traditional Navajo, killing such a witch is defensible. But not under *bilagáana* law, not within their adversarial justice system.

She closed her eyes for a minute. Jerome had known what he was doing. He'd known it would change the child's life. He'd known, too, it was murder and could change his life.

But he was not the only one being tested. She still had a choice to make. Forgiveness and not punishment is the Navajo way of justice. Reintegration of Jerome on the path of beauty is justice, not imprisonment. But a homicide like this would fall outside the Navajo Peacemaker courts.

She directed her cousin to turn north. Some deaths are necessary.

Lilli sat in the stillness of the night outside Ahboah's place, with the sky wide open to the stars, and imagined Dougan touching down at the airport in Washington, D.C. A few more hours of grace before the news exploded. Nothing for her to do now but wait for the old man.

She felt anxious. The slackness of Jerome's head and the odd timbre of his breathing told her he was sleeping, fitfully. Not even a possibility for herself. Instead she rested the weight of her back against a girdled stump, pulled her legs up tight against her chest, and sat wide awake in the cold.

The night sky was changing, losing all but the brightest stars. *So'tsoh* remained, and the constellation that rose up this time of year, *Hastiin Sik'ai'í*, the Man With Legs Ajar. She closed her eyes and remembered the little girl, trying to pass her string figure of the stars between her small fingers.

Lilli needed to grab just a few minutes of sleep. She closed her eyes. This was useless. She couldn't sleep. Her mind seemed to be drifting away from her. She was having trouble thinking of the little girl as The Upside-Down-Girl. Her mind balked at the image.

With her eyes open to the night sky, she thought instead of one of her favorite petroglyphs pecked into the rock on some lonely land near *Dinétah*. She liked to visit, walk in its silence. The rock figure, part incised petroglyph, part painted pictograph, a girl in sandstone, her legs turned sideways so you could see the shape of her calves. Her arms are held out, bent up at the elbows, and her fingers are clearly spread. But what is so beautiful about the girl is that she is wearing a skirt made of stars. Not a constellation. Simply stars. That was how she would think of the little girl. The Girl With Skirt of Stars.

Jerome coughed and lifted his head. "Anything yet?"

"Soon," she said, thinking of Ahboah.

She would represent the little girl. She would be the go-between with Ahboah. She would finish what Jerome had started.

They both heard the sound of the door opening and shutting, and watched silently as Ahboah come out of his house and moved toward the white rind of dawn, to send his prayers to *Ya*, to the universe. Most non-Navajo translated the Navajo greeting *Yá'át'ééh* as "Hello" but it meant instead the announcement of realization, *Yá -'át'ééh*, the whole universe is still in existence.

"I am going," she said to Jerome. "Stay here."

"Don't come?"

"No." Not yet.

She waited until the old man threw pollen up into the

air and it fell toward him in a shimmery arc. She waited until he finished his songs. And then she walked toward him until she was close enough that he could see her face.

"I was waiting for someone this morning," Ahboah said as he reached out for her hand. "Maybe it was you."

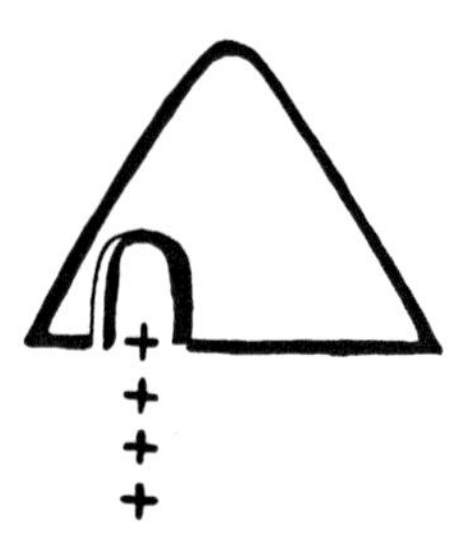

Ahboah turned on no lights. He nodded to a wooden chair near a table and she sat down. He sat in the chair under the small window.

She'd seen so much death.

"Mr. Lee?" He spoke gently.

"He's dead, with the others."

Ahboah with his hooded eyes said nothing for a long while. Then, very quietly, he said, "And the cave?"

"All dead, except for me."

He closed his eyes and she tried to hold her mind still.

"You didn't come in the middle of the night to tell me this."

The Old Singer was right. With her thumb, she stroked the worn edge of his wooden table. She agonized over how to start. He got up and opened a cupboard and found two cups and brought them back to the table. She watched him crush a piece of dried herb that had hung from a hook on the wall. The silver-white light of dawn started to fill in through the window. He took each cup to the metal sink and filled it with water. She slid her thumb through the cup's handle and felt the water's cold.

"You don't want that man—the one outside—in here, with us?"

Lilli looked out the window toward the light and toward Jerome.

"No."

"Quiet, then," Ahboah said. "I will wait. Listen to yourself, and tell me, slowly."

She did not tell him about Jerome and his airplane and his photographs from the sky of the Upside-Down Girl. She told him only about Jerome at the Shoe Game, and the little girl, and then she described slowly the way the little girl stopped moving and let out an odd cry and then she described the epileptic seizure. She didn't have to tell him what people whispered, how she heard people say under their breath, *'Iich'aa,* the Moth Madness.

Ahboah was a slow listener, with small questions, who needed her to remember more detail. She wanted a healing ceremony for the little girl, she would shoulder the expense, but she wasn't sure which ceremony should be done. She understood the uniquely Navajo problem. The little girl's family did not want the shame of the ceremonial for epilepsy because it revisited the cause.

The problem was complex.

'Iich'ahii is the one that goes into fire—the moth, so crazy it flies into fire.

'Iich'ah is the one that falls in a fit, the one that has a seizure, and the cause is incest.

'Iich'ahjí is the ceremony to heal, the one they call Moth Way, except that would disclose the secret of the crime of incest.

And then there was another problem. Maybe no Singers still knew Moth Way. Maybe that ceremonial was extinct. Yet Jerome had remembered right. She did now, too. Some of the ceremonial medicine is made from the genitals of a sibling pair of coyotes.

"Do you know any Singer who can still do the Moth Way?"

"Yes," Ahboah said. "I can do it."

So it was not extinct.

"But..."

She waited.

"But the man, and the little girl—he was not her brother?"

"No," she said.

"A clan brother?"

"No, he was her grandfather."

There was a long silence until Ahboah finally said, "So. Then he was a witch."

Yes, she said to herself. A murdered witch. And she looked out the window to find Jerome still sitting with his back against the stump.

Ahboah seemed to recede, even though his eyes were open and he was looking at her. But she knew he wasn't seeing her. She saw in her own mind Black God, with the stars of *Dilyéhe* over his left eye. And then she saw the little girl's fingers, before she fell toward the fire, her fingers working the string, creating the shape of stars.

"Do I need to know more about this man sitting outside?"

About Jerome? "No," she said.

"I see." Ahboah walked to the open door and watched Jerome for a long time.

"Why was he with you, on the river?"

"For his protection," she said.

"I see."

Ahboah sat down to face her. "An old Navajo, I heard about him and his mouth. Stuffed up with the male and female parts of coyote. *Bilagáana* police came here, asked me questions. What if this, what if that, that's how they liked to talk to me. 'Message writing,' they said to me, trying to get me to tell them something. What if? I kept my mouth shut, didn't say anything about what I was thinking."

Ahboah pointed with his lips toward Jerome.

"So your friend? He had that idea, did he? Go and stuff the mouth?"

She watched Ahboah's face, but she didn't answer him. Not with any words.

"You don't want to talk, even to me. But maybe this will interest you. The police are stupid. They told me this old man with his mouth, he was mean, tangled with people. This mouth, police say, the message of trouble between coyote killers, contest killers. These police have no Navajo imagination."

She should keep completely quiet, say nothing. But she needed to know. "And these police? Do they have ideas about how the body came to be so deep into the Hoodoos?"

"Maybe tire treads will keep them busy."

Ahboah stood up. Lilli stood, too.

"So much death. I will cleanse you first. Then your friend outside. Then it will take time, a healing ceremony for your little girl. But not Moth Madness."

Lilli adjusted the eyeholes in her blue mask to better see the doorway of the hogan, and the eight fires set ablaze, four in a line to her right, four in a line to her left, that marked out a dance floor of dirt for her and the other masked *ye'iis* in the huge dark night. Tonight was the ninth and final night of Asan's healing ceremonial.

Nine days ago, on the first night of the ceremony, Asan's family hogan had been made a temporary sacred space, with Ahboah's blessing, and Lilli had carried fresh dirt inside, and water, to make a clean dirt space tamped and level and ready. Now, on the ninth night, she could hear Ahboah's familiar old voice rising and falling inside, singing the *xatal*. By dawn, Ahboah would be finished passing the Holy People and the Dreamer through the little girl, the one they had called for the last nine days and nights The-One-Sung-Over.

Against her will, the smell of the fire smoke took Lilli to the campfires Mitch had lit every night on the river, in the canyon. She'd shared a special world with Jerome, a world of shimmer, and water music, and a disappearing sky. The Lees—all of the bodies, Suzanne, and Frank, and Boyd—came back for their well-televised funerals, except for Mitch. Like her second child, Mitch was lost to the river.

Of course, Dougan was right. They'd won the election. In late January, Dougan's hand-picked successor to Lee would be inaugurated in Washington, D.C. She had an invitation, but she didn't intend to go. So far, the assassin remained unknown, or dead. Which made her think of the little girl, and the grandfather Jerome had dumped in the Hoodoos. The police had interrogated known contestants in the coyote calling contests, but, as with Lee's killer, there'd been no arrests.

Lilli noticed Jerome watching her. He'd wanted so badly to protect a child, to have protected his child who was gone. He'd protected instead this child, Asan.

She smiled, inside her mask. Earlier today, while there was still natural light, Jerome had asked if he could photograph her, posed.

"Me?"

He insisted. He arranged her hands. She'd thought he wanted to photograph her hands in her lap, but she was wrong. He was clearly studying her face.

"I'm going to say something to you," he said. "Something about when we were children." He held the end of a long cable, a shutter release, in his hand. "Just listen."

"Why?"

"Because I want to squeeze the shutter at the moment you remember."

Ahboah's voice carried out of the hogan. It wouldn't be long now before he and the little girl emerged. Lilli kept her eyes on Jerome. She had pollen that went from her mouth to Jerome's. And she had pollen that went from her mouth to Jake's. She wanted them both, didn't she? Two kinds of love.

Lilli, with her bare arms and bare legs, shivered in the cold. It would be good to start dancing. She would "personate" a *yé'ii*, one of the visiting Holy People. *Im*personate seemed the wrong word, with its hint of pretense, and deception.

The nine-night ceremony of *Tl'éé'j'í*, Toward-The-Night, was unusual for the Navajo. In it, the gods appeared. Talking God and Calling God, and Water Sprinkler and the Fringemouths. On the second day, Talking God, the maternal grandfather of all the *ye'iis*, had appeared in his white mask, and the little girl's mask had been trimmed in spruce. On the fourth day, the women had prepared the ancient foods, a feast of no cedar, and bee weed, and three ears, and the masks had been fed. On the fifth day, the little girl walked, with Talking God, in pollen footprints.

At the Lake of Whirling Waters the Dreamer had his seizure, and was restored by the Fringemouths. On the sixth day, Ahboah prepared the Whirling Logs sandpainting on the floor of the hogan. In their language, the word for sandpainting was *iikááh*, which says nothing about "sand," and nothing about "painting" but means the place where the Holy Ones come and go.

When it was finished and it was time, the little girl sat, just like the Dreamer, on the western arm of the swastika shaped Whirling Logs, rotating sunwise. In the sandpainting, Talking God stands to the east, and Calling God to the west. On each of the four ends of the crossed logs sit two *ye'iis*, one male, and one female, each wearing a blue mask, just like she was wearing tonight.

Then, on the seventh day, Ahboah had made a sandpainting of twelve *ye'iis* dancing—six male, six female, each with yellow legs to show how deep they are dancing in sacred pollen. This was the sandpainting shown to the Dreamer, in the lodge of Talking God and Calling God. But on the eighth day, Ahboah had added something from Coyote Way, and something from Moth Way, something special for the Upside-Down-Girl.

The night went silent. Ahboah had stopped singing. For the past nine days, Ahboah had sung into being a world that recreated the Dreamer's world, and taken the little girl there, into the care of Talking God and Calling God, and tonight, she would emerge from the hogan, just as the Dreamer had emerged, and she would watch the *ye'iis* who had come to dance for her, all night long, until dawn. She would be changed not in body, but in mindbody. The little girl would be returned to Beauty.

It was time to dance.

Lilli looked up at the sky full of stars through the eyes of her mask. She started to sing as she moved between the alleyway of fire, dancing in a line of *ye'iis* behind Talking God. Her arms swept up, then down, her hands carrying wands of spruce. Her feet stomped the ground, and she whirled, singing the old words.

She rose up on the balls of her feet between the downtread. She felt her hair, hanging loose, sway as she stepped. Against the firelight the cold breath of winter rose in a cloud from her mouth.

Ahboah emerged with the One-Sung-Over. Then, together, Ahboah and the little girl moved down along the line of dancing *ye'iis*. As Ahboah passed her, Lilli felt him sprinkle the cornmeal on her right arm. She held still, bending her elbows up in the position of the Girl with Skirt of Stars incised in rock.

When dawn finally came, Ahboah would send the little girl out of the hogan. She would breathe in the air of dawn, four times. She would be holy again, and whole.

With air breathing from her mouth, she ran,
With Happiness behind her, she ran,
With Happiness before her, she ran,
With Darkness becoming Light, she ran.

Lilli searched until she found Jerome. He was so clearly watching her. She loved him still. She knew it and he knew it. The love of a girl for a boy. She hoped it would stay between them, visible, until they could look at one another in old age and say it is the love of an old woman for an old man.

Navajo Terms and Concepts

Achee, also spelled ***'ach'íí'*** The word means intestine in Navajo, and generally refers to a food delicacy made from twisting the intestines of a freshly butchered sheep into a rope-like fashion, and grilling or roasting it on an open fire.

'Ádin The word means that something is non-existent or absent.

'Ajilee This is one of the Navajo healing ceremonials, sometimes referred to as Lustway in that it is done to restore a person to harmony who has previously been abnormally lustful or behaved promiscuously.

Alkéé naa'aashii The term literally means The Two Who Followed One Another. The concept of the Follower Pair relates to the Navajo concept of opposites and complementarity and completeness.

Amá This is the word for mother; *amá sání* is a grandmother. In the Navajo kinship system, *shimá* refers to "my mother," and *shimásani* refers to "my maternal grandmother" or my mother's mother. "My paternal grandmother" or my father's mother is referred to as *shinálí*.

'Ana'í This term refers to someone who is alien or non-Navajo. In one sense, the Navajos refer to themselves as *Diné* and all others as *'Ana'í*. The term may also be used to denote an enemy; this usage would depend on context. The Navajo noun *'Anaasází* comes from the combination of *'a*, meaning someone, plus *naa* meaning non-Navajo, plus *sá* meaning ancient or abandoned, plus *zí* meaning something animate that stands erect.

'Asdzáá Nádleehé This refers to the One Who Changes Repeatedly, or in English a Navajo deity most commonly referred to as Changing Woman. She is connoted as "changing" in the sense that she (like the life cycle of humans, plants, animals, even mountains, lakes, and so on) moves from creation to old age and then, through the creative or generative process, to youth again.

Bilagáana The Navajo language had very few of what linguists call "loan words" or nouns borrowed from other languages, but *bilagáana*—meaning White Man—is a word that is thought to have entered Navajo terminology from the Spanish word "Americano" at a time in history when few Navajos were yet bilingual.

Dóone'é This is the general term for clan. The mother-child relationship is the most important relationship in Navajo culture. One's born-to clan for the Navajo is matrilineal, in that it connects a person to their mother and then to their mother's mother and then to their mother's mother's mother, and so on, back into time. One's born-for clan is similar, except that it first connects a person to their father, but then to their father's mother, and then to their father's mother's mother, and so on. Because of this strong commitment to the mother-child relationship, the oral history of the Navajo includes both the set of clans first created by Changing Woman, as well as the "adoption" of other people encountered during their migration and journeying, including more recently in historical times when groups of Puebloan peoples fled persecution from the Spaniards and the Mexicans. The kinship structure of the Navajo rests then on the concept of mother-who-gives-life and mother-who-sustains-life by giving both emotional and physical sustenance.

Dilyéhé This is the Navajo term for the star constellation frequently referred to as the Pleiades. *Dilyéhé* also appears on the mask of *Haashch'ééhzhiní*, the Holy One referred to as Black God. The twilight appearance of *Dilyéhé* in the fall (end of October) and its disappearance in the spring (end of April) also delineates the period of time during which the nine-night Nightway ceremonial may be performed.

Diné is the term that describes a person whereas *Dine'é* describes the Navajo people as a group. The *Diné Diyinii* refers to the Holy People. *Nihookáá' dine'é* refers to the Earth Surface People.

Dinétah This term has a historical definition that is intended to represent the area of earliest inhabitation of the Navajo in the Southwest, including Largo Canyon, Blanco Canyon, and Gobernador Canyon in northeastern New Mexico. Literally the term means "among the Navajo." It also has a spiritual definition, and is the birthplace and early home of Changing Woman. Political decisions that led to the creation of the Navajo reservation did not include consideration of their sacred landscape, and so the *Dinétah* is not included within the current reservation boundaries.

Dzil Ná'oodilii This is one of the three sacred mountains of the interior of the Navajo homeland. Its ceremonial name is Soft Goods Mountain. The Navajo name for this mountain (Huerfano Mesa, New Mexico) refers to an event in their spiritual past that involved the Mountain-Around-Which-Moving-Was-Done.

Haashch'ééh This is a group of supernatural beings who have specific identities such as *Haashch'ééshzhiní*, translated as Black God, or *Haashch'éélti'í*, translated as Talking God. The term itself more literally means the Speechless Ones, and some of their names refer to the sounds they make, such as *Haashch'éé'ooghaan*, or Growling God.

Hastiin Sik'ai'i This is one of the recognized and named constellations of the Navajo: Man With Legs Ajar. As with landscape, the naming of features of the sky ties into Navajo narratives of their past and creation and journeys, thereby linking mythic events to present-day living. Some have pointed out how this tendency changes the conception of time as a linear vector to a conception of time as omnipresent. Man With Legs Ajar is one of the eight primary Navajo constellations.

Hastiin The noun means man: *Áltsé Hastiin* refers to First Man. In earlier English attempts to write out the sound of this word, the spelling *Hosteen* was commonly used. *Hastiin* may also be used to function as the English "Mr.," or be applied to an elder.

Hataalii The term refers to The One Who Sings. In the Navajo ceremonials, it is the *hataalii* who conducts the ceremony, which may last up to nine days. The overarching purpose of the ceremonial is to "cure'"(in the Navajo sense) a person by restoring them to harmony.

Hooghan This is the Navajo term for a constructed dwelling place, and there are several types, such as the stacked log hogan and the cribbed log hogan and the stone hogan, as well as the vertically walled hogan and more recently the *Tsineheeshjíí bee hooghan* made out of commercial lumber. These are all female *hooghans*, which are round, or hexagonal or octagonal; the more cone-shaped male *hooghan* is called *'alch'i' 'adeez'á*. Within the interior space of a *hooghan*, the doorway faces the direction of dawn. The smokehole is central. Ceremonials are done inside *hooghans* that have been made ready for the event. The college campus of Diné College at Tsaile, Arizona has an architecture and design that follows the overarching theme of the *hooghan*.

Hózhó This term has no simple translation into English, because it refers simultaneously to states of the intellect, of emotion, of morality, of aesthetics, of physical health. The general purpose of Navajo behaviors in song, story, prayer, ceremonial and so on, is to recreate or restore *hózhó*.

'Iich'ah This term literally translates to "falling into the fire," and refers to a person experiencing an epileptic seizure. To understand such a term, one needs to understand the oral stories of the Navajo that attribute such fits to incest, an exceptionally strong taboo among the Navajos. Their word for moth is *'iich'ahii*, which in a literal translation means "the one that goes into the fire." The curing ceremonial is termed Moth Way or *'iich'ahjí*.

'Iikááh This refers to what in English is frequently called a sandpainting, or in the anthropological literature, a drypainting. It is not an artistic work; rather, it is a temporarily constructed surface to attract supernatural aid, and to act as an entrance where good and evil may be exchanged. The patient in a ceremonial, referred to as the one-sung-over, is made to sit on the sandpainting, and via aid by the *hataalii* identifies with the figured beings. In keeping with the Navajo tradition of valuing knowledge over material goods, the sandpainting is obliterated after its use, and is made of substances that are not so rare as to be hoarded.

Kiníí' Na'igai This place name references an archaeological ruin known in Navajo as House with White Stripe Across or House of the Horizontal White, and in English as White House ruin, located in Canyon de Chelly, Arizona. The word "Chelly" is derived from the Spanish mispronunciation of '*tseyi*' which means "in rock" or "canyon" in Navajo. In the Night Way ceremonial, House with White Stripe Across is referred to as the homeplace of the holy ones who taught them how to make the night chant ceremonial medicine.

Na'ni'a hatsoh This is the term for Navajo Bridge (sometimes referred to as Marble Canyon Bridge or Lee's Ferry Bridge) that crosses the Colorado River downstream from Lee's Ferry, at the opening of the Grand Canyon into the fifty-five mile long Marble Canyon. The word refers to a bridging across, and specifically to a slender or narrow spanning.

Tééhooltsódi This is the name of "the one in deep water who grabs things," who resides in rivers and lakes. According to their creation stories, *Tééhooltsódi* caused a flood that forced First Man and First Woman, and many other entities, to flee their Fourth World, leading to emergence into the present or Fifth World.

Tségháhoodzání Literally, "the rock with a hole through it" is now the administrative capital of the Navajo Nation, known as Window Rock, Arizona. The site of this natural and well-known landscape feature was selected by John Collier, the Commissioner of Indian Affairs, to become the future home of the Navajo Center Agency and in the 1930s construction of both government buildings and residences was completed; the Navajo Tribal Council Chamber was constructed in the shape of a stone *hooghan*. The particular sandstone rock with its erosional window had, up until this time, served the Navajos as an important shrine from which to collect water for certain ceremonials.

Tsiiyéél This is the traditional Navajo manner, for both men and women, of wearing their long hair in a twist or hair-knot, frequently tied with white yarn. During the first *kinaaldá* or puberty ceremony, which was held for Changing Woman by the Holy People, her hair was washed with suds made from the root of the yucca (*tsa'ászi*) and then her hair was tied back. To this day, the *kinaaldá* ceremony for Navajo girls that marks their passage into womanhood begins the same way.

Xatal This refers to the special activity of singing or chanting what might be called a "singing ceremonial" by the *Hataałíí*, The One Who Sings (sacred songs), and performs the ceremony. These song ceremonials are many: *Tł'éé'j'í*, The Night Way ceremonial has on its final night up to a series of 252 songs including Songs of the First Dancers, Songs of the Whirling Logs, Songs of the Darkness. The word *sin* is used to refer to a song, and the Navajos are great singers and song composers, frequently singing while engaged in various activities of daily life, and once said to count a person's wealth by the number of songs a person knew.

Yé'ii The term refers to supernatural beings. In sandpaintings, the *yé'ii,* which may be female or male, are depicted with what is called a breath feather on the top of their head. Their maternal grandfather is *Yé'ii bicheii.* The last or ninth night of The Night Way ceremony has an outdoor public dance frequently termed the *Yé'ii Bicheii* that lasts until dawn, in which there are twelve dancers (or teams of dancers), including six *hashch' bika'* (male) and six *hashch' ba'áád* (female), recreating the sense of families of *yé'ii* who came to visit the Dreamer.

Acknowledgments

The quoted document that Duane Fatt carries with him regarding the Mountain Meadows Massacre is not fictional. The document titled *Special Report of the Mountain Meadows Massacre* by J. H. Carleton, Brevet Major U.S.A., Captain 1st Dragoons, was written in 1859, and later published by the Government Printing Office, Washington, D.C. as national government publication No. 605, House Document, United States 57th Congress.

The chapter heading images are elements of Navajo ceremonial sandpaintings, redrawn and reinterpreted from these resources: Bahti, M. 2000. *Navajo Sandpaintings,* Rio Nuevo Publishers, Tucson, Arizona; Crossman, S. and J.P. Barou, 2002. *Hozho: Peintures de guerison des Indiens Navajo, Indigene Editions;* Newcomb, F. J. and G. A. Reichard, 1975. *Sandpaintings of the Navajo Shooting Chant,* Dover Publications, New York; Oakes, M. and J. Campbell, 1991. *Where the Two Came to Their Father,* 3rd edition, Princeton University

Press, Princeton, New Jersey; Reichard, G. A., 1977. *Navajo Medicine Man Sandpaintings*. Dover Publications, New York; Wheelwright, M.C., 1988. *The Myth and Prayers of the Great Star Chant and the Myth of the Coyote Chant,* Navajo Community College Press, Tsaile, Arizona; Wyman, L. C.,1960. *Navajo Sandpainting, The Huckel Collection*, The Taylor Museum, Colorado Springs, Colorado; Wyman, L. C., 1983. *Southwest Indian Drypainting,* School of American Research, University of New Mexico Press, Albuquerque, New Mexico.

Additionally, I would like to thank all the people who helped contribute to this story, including the people who live between their four sacred mountains, and the scholars, and Singers; the boatmen and swampers; the search-and-rescue teams; the historians, lawyers, and medical investigators; the pilots and photographers; the friends from childhood who continue to inspire and the friends and family who have gone with me into this landscape; the geologists who read the rocks; and all the ones who carry forward the human imperative of storytelling.

About the Author

Jennifer Kitchell has a Ph.D. in geology and has been a professor in paleontology at the University of Wisconsin, Madison, and the University of Michigan. She has always enjoyed writing. Novelist Fred Leebron has called her writing "evocative and often lyrical, the setting evoked masterfully in what can only be described as a joy to read." This is her first novel.

Although raised near the Canadian border, she belonged to a Southwestern family on her mother's side, a mother who faithfully took her children "home" every year. Her interest in the Navajo culture runs deep and to her earliest memories. A mother with children of her own, she remembers riding the dirt roads of the Navajo reservation and coming upon a hand-lettered stake with the words *Yé'ii bicheii* written on it to mark a turnoff in the dirt where an extended Navajo family was holding a healing ceremony.

She enjoys river rafting, and in general water, desert, mountain, hiking on slickrock, big skies and starry nights.

Breinigsville, PA USA
01 March 2010
233394BV00005B/25/P